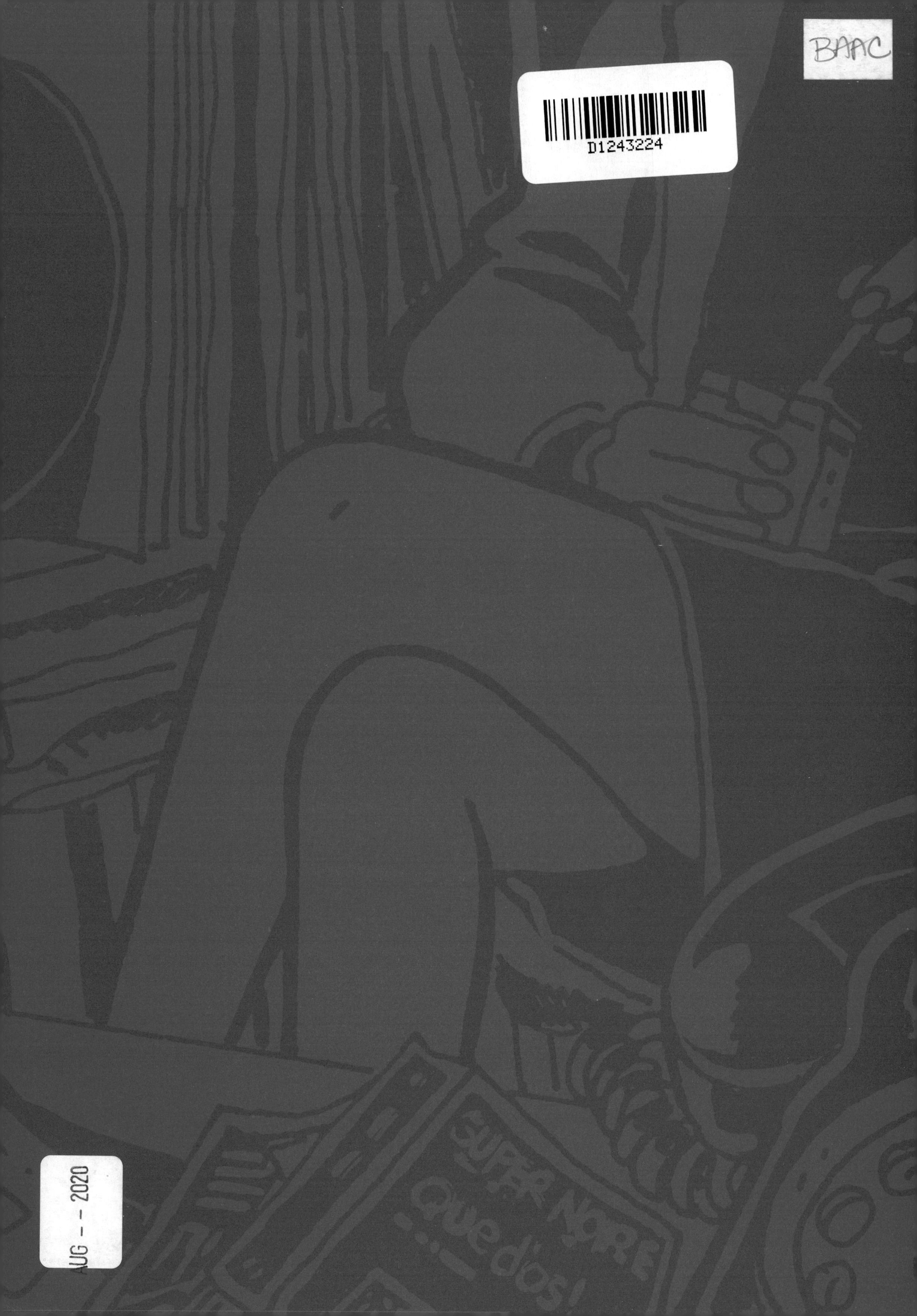

Streets *of* Paris, Streets *of* Murder

THE COMPLETE GRAPHIC NOIR OF
MANCHETTE + TARDI

VOLUME ONE

FANTAGRAPHICS BOOKS

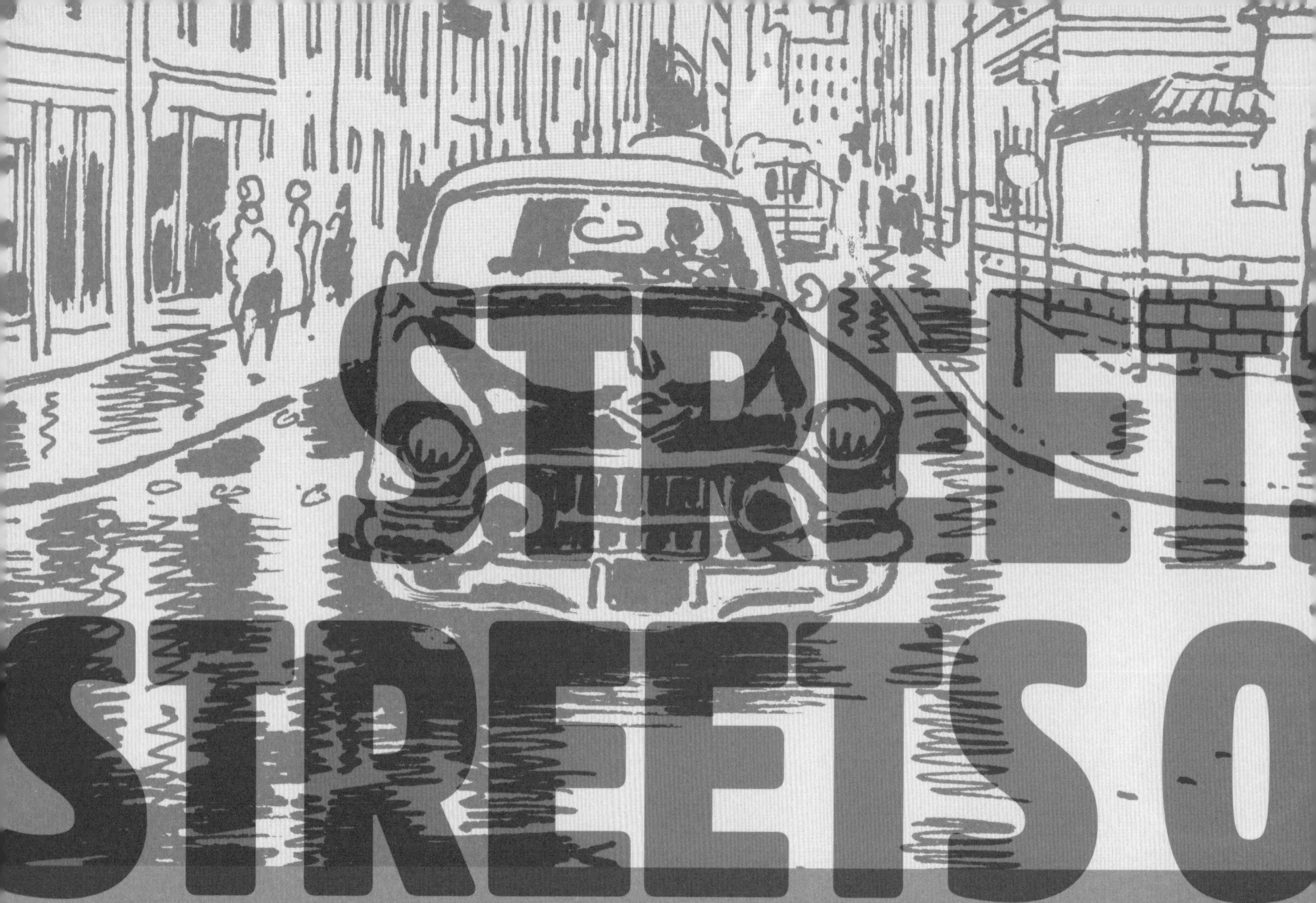
STREETS O

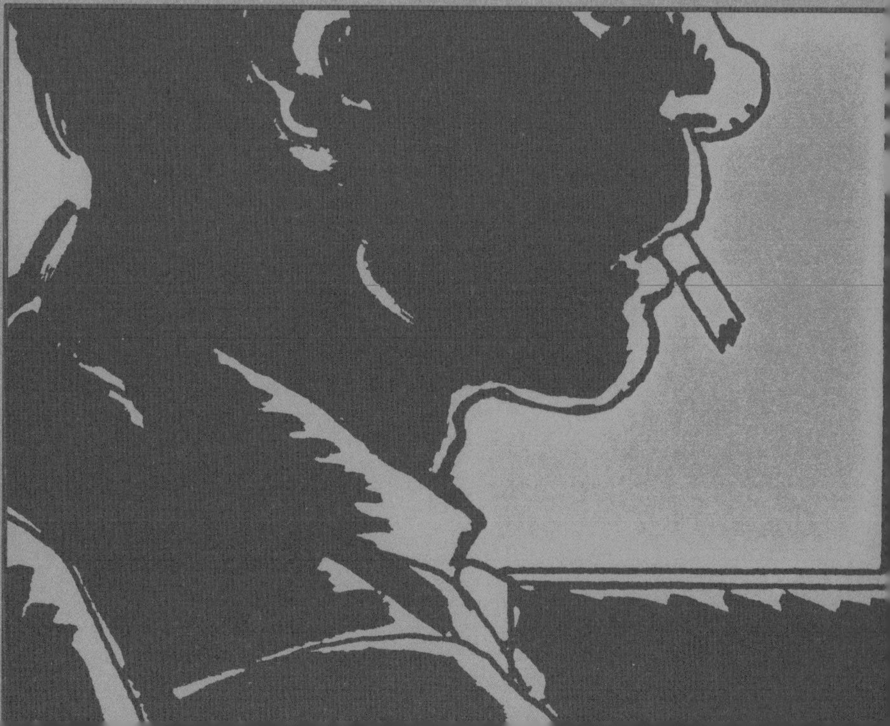

FANTAGRAPHICS BOOKS

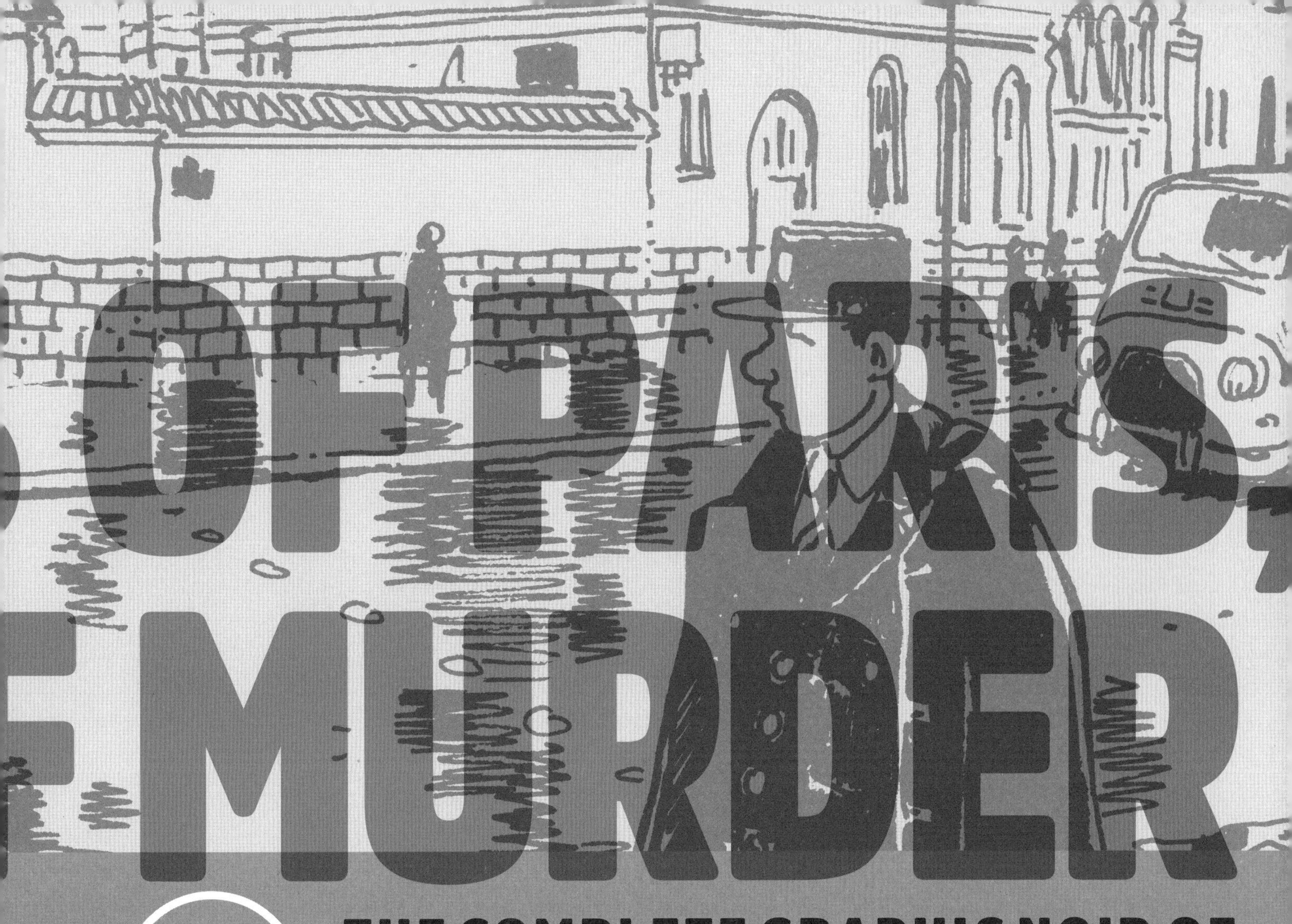
OF PARIS,
MURDER

1 THE COMPLETE GRAPHIC NOIR OF
MANCHETTE + TARDI

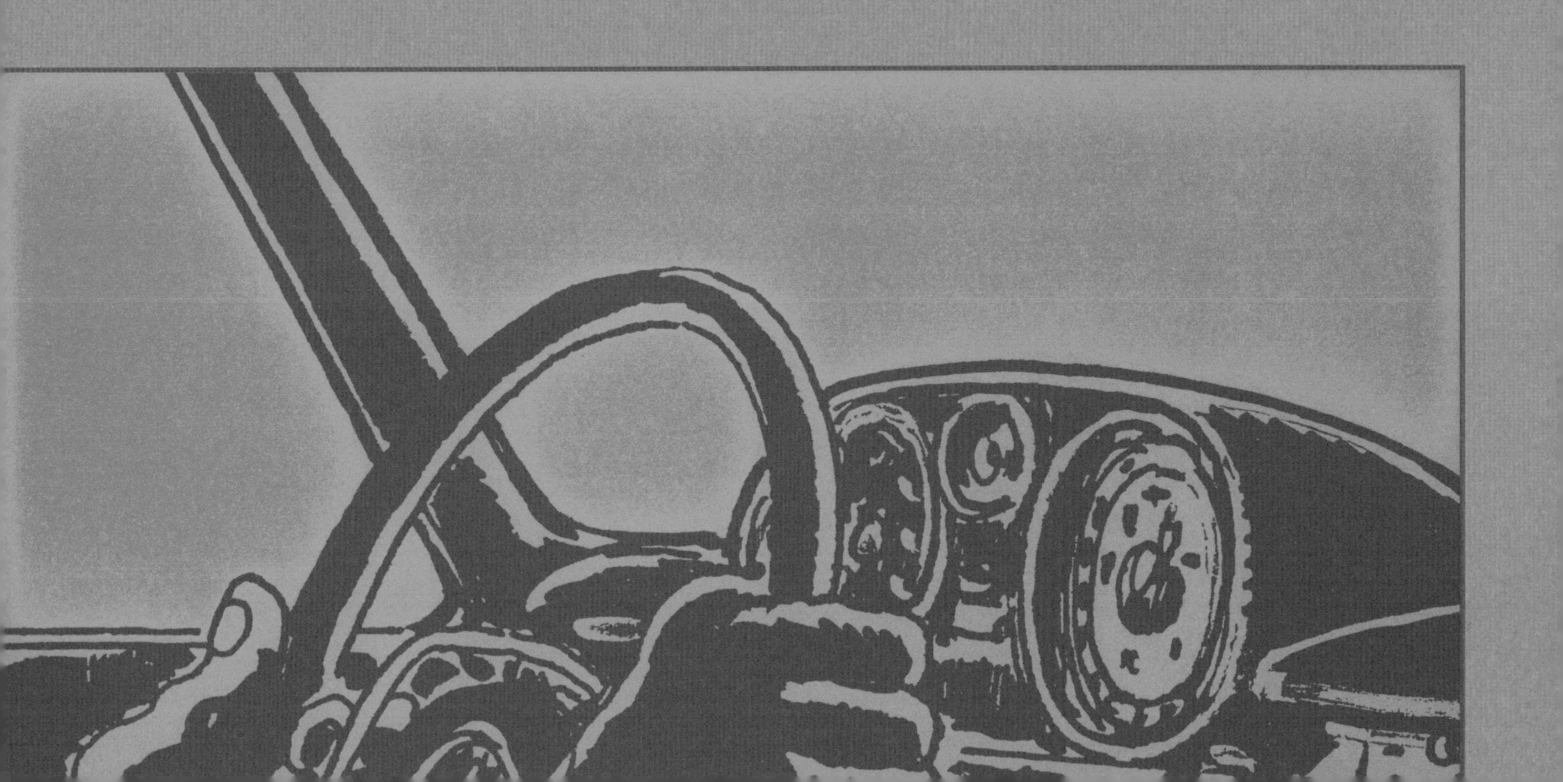

PUBLISHER - Gary Groth
SENIOR EDITOR - J. Michael Catron
ASSOCIATE PUBLISHER - Eric Reynolds
DESIGNER - Chelsea Wirtz
PRODUCTION - Christina Hwang
+ Paul Baresh

Fantagraphics Books
7563 Lake City Way NE
Seattle, WA 98115
WWW.FANTAGRAPHICS.COM • TWITTER: @FANTAGRAPHICS • FACEBOOK.COM/FANTAGRAPHICS

FIRST FANTAGRAPHICS BOOKS EDITION - August 2020
ISBN - 978-1-68396-324-0
LIBRARY OF CONGRESS CONTROL NUMBER - 2019945285
PRINTED IN THE REPUBLIC OF KOREA

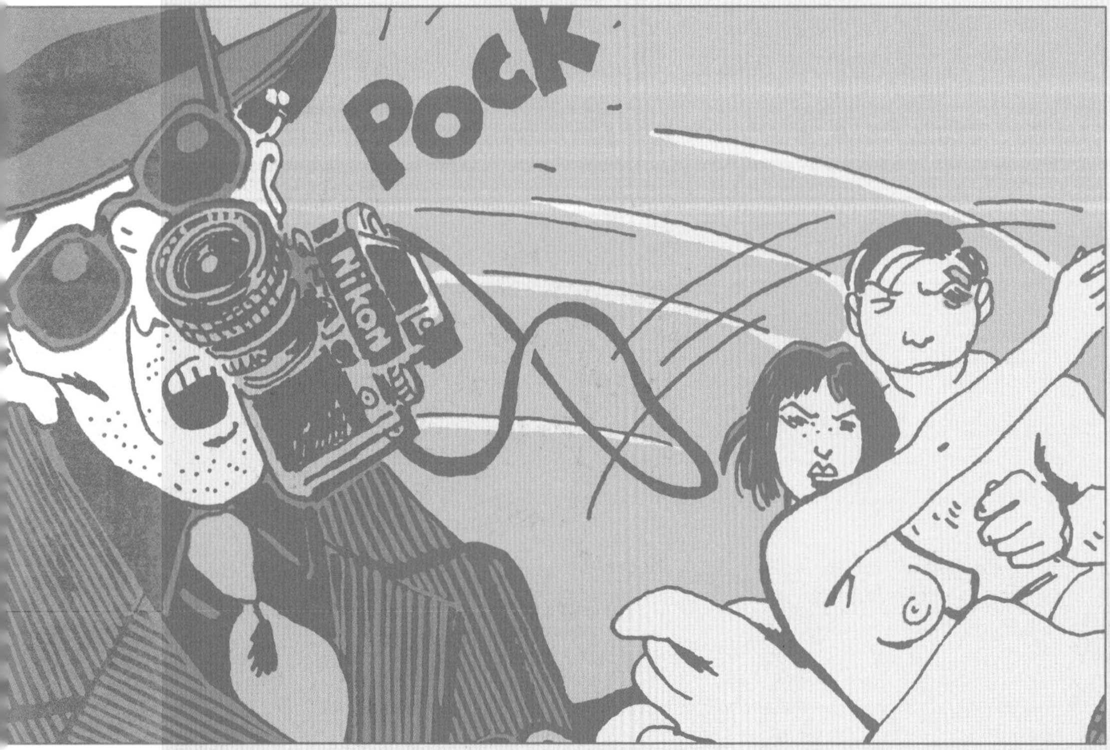
POCK
NIKON

CONTENTS

STORIES BY
Jean-Patrick Manchette

ARTWORK BY
Tardi

PREFACE

In a letter to his friend Pierre Siniac, dated August 26, 1977, Jean-Patrick Manchette mentioned his writing projects and added, "I'm also doing some comics."

"What genre are you doing?" asked Siniac.

"The genre of comic I'm doing?" responded Manchette on September 16. "...For now, I've been approached as a thriller writer, so I'm doing a thriller. There aren't many in French comics." And, he added, he was doing "two comics with Tardi."

His first comic with Jacques Tardi, *Fatale*, was the adaptation of a novel, itself initially a screenplay for Claude Chabrol, and didn't get further than 21 pages. Manchette's novel was published by Gallimard in December 1977 with a cover by Tardi.

The second, *Griffu*, was serialized in *BD, l'hebdo de la BD*, a weekly comics publication, from October 1977 to April 1978 (issues #1 to 27) and released as a book by Éditions du Square in October 1978. *Griffu* would be "a lightning-fast thriller, intentionally an exercise in style (attempting to capture the feel of [Robert] Aldrich's [1955] film *Kiss Me Deadly*) with plenty of punches, cars, gunshots, booze, and sex ... only the good stuff, the raw stuff, as you can see. I love hackneyed scenarios, as you know."

Hackneyed scenarios and archetypical characters — an amateur private detective, an investigative journalist, and a shady politician, all against a background of real-estate fraud — the exercise in style is brilliant.

If Manchette sticks to his principles ("What is a crime novel? What is written in a crime novel? I'm reinventing it like the great American authors, but to reinvent the great American authors, you must do something different than they did ... To refresh a stale style you must use it referentially, honor it while critiquing it, exaggerate it, distort it in every way."[1]), Tardi gives to this "referential" story a verisimilitude that is clearly of his time, his scenery teeming with meticulous details, notably of the urban evolution of 1970s France.

---

[1] *Polar* #12, June 1980

The meeting of these two fans of noir was not, alas, to have an immediate sequel. It took nearly 30 years before Tardi sought out Manchette's work again, this time to adapt a Manchette novel published one year before *Griffu* — *West Coast Blues*. But 30 years later, Manchette's writings could be seen as a manifesto, particularly his defense of the noir novel against what he called "art literature." Regarding the founders of the genre, he wrote, "I believe it's much too narrow-minded — the idea that they chose the noir novel because they had to make a few bucks and went to where the consumers were. That plays into it, sure. But the love of writing comes first ... The authors of noir novels insinuated themselves into the public's tastes, but they weren't whores. They disembarked with their personalities and found the right angle of attack for telling the public things they didn't necessarily want to hear." And he reconnects with Tardi when he states, "There are a few of us, perhaps many, who hold fast to the well-known saying about the noir novel as a witness to its time ... You can read practically nothing else. They are the novels that speak to our time."[2]

West Coast Blues speaks to us, with background music by Gerry Mulligan (American jazz saxophonist, clarinetist, composer, and arranger) and Bob Brookmeyer (American jazz valve trombonist, pianist, arranger, and composer), of a time gone by, of a man's profound malaise that reflects the malaise of the world around him. The world of yesterday is the world of today. The crisis is still there, profoundly. And Gerfaut, drawn by Tardi, continues to have the blues and to spin at night on the Parisian beltways at 145km/h [90 miles per hour], toward inevitable violence.

Tardi found the "realistic and critical" visual equivalent of this society adrift. He keeps the story tight and uses the freeze frame with clinical precision, especially when everything spins out of control. True to the spirit of Manchette, he's careful not to make it "more than just a crime novel." At a time when Manchette attains "literary" status, Tardi takes pride in restoring the radicality to his world. You can just as well say that Tardi invited Manchette into his world.

— FRANÇOIS GUÉRIF

---

[2] *Chroniques*, published by Éditions Rivages

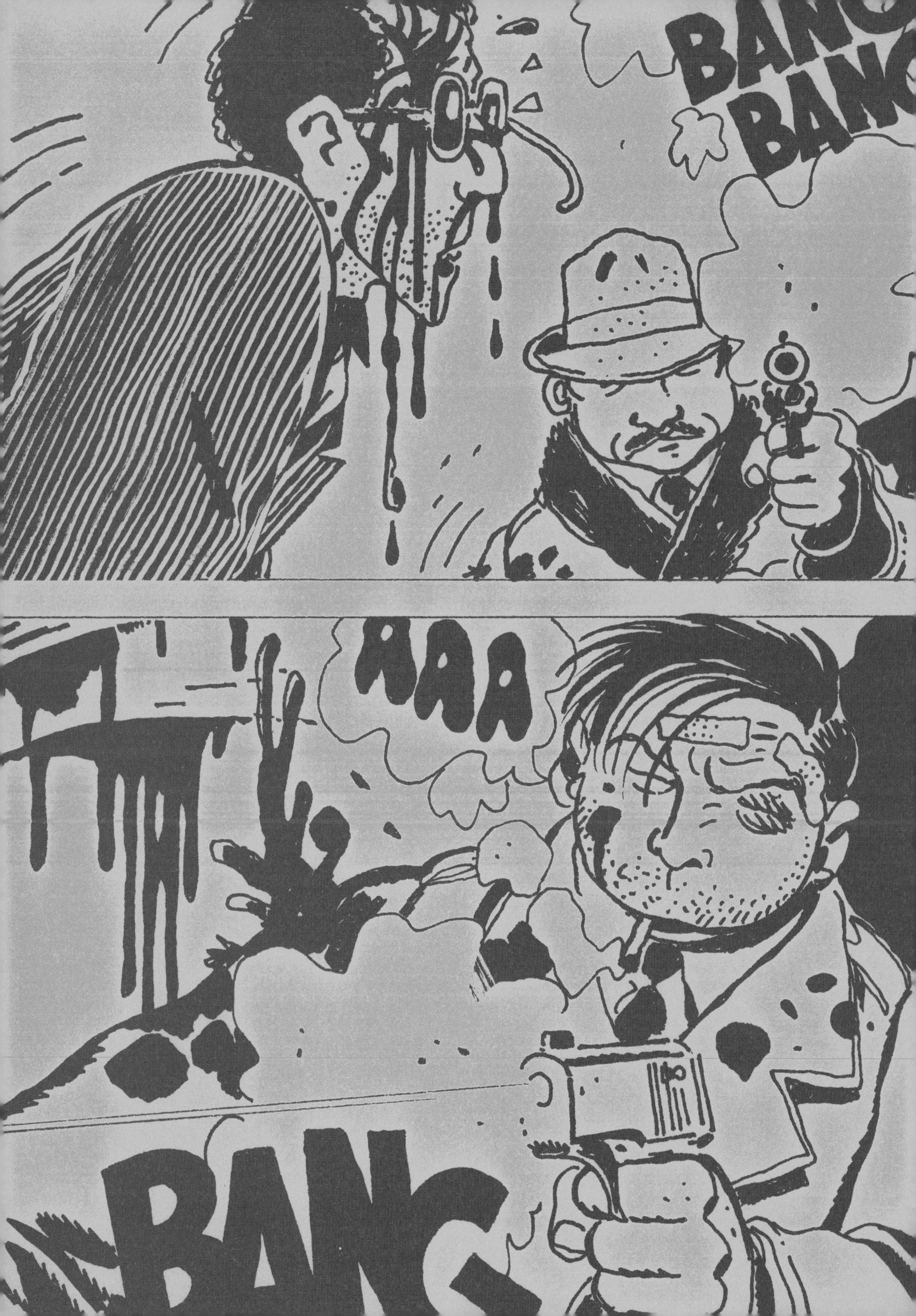
BANG
BANG
AAA
BANG

GRIFFU

Griffu

STORY - Jean-Patrick Manchette
ART - Tardi
TRANSLATION - Frank Wynne

A Conversation

Ring! Ring!

"Hello, Mr. Manchette? Griffu here — Mr. Manchette, why must I always encounter violence everywhere I go? What did I ever do to you?"

"Well, Griffu, first I'll point out that that's a facetious question, because it comes from American comics — *Silver Surfer* and *The Fantastic Four*. Your words are basically the same as in the *Silver Surfer* and *The Fantastic Four*.

"Second, you're the type of character who doesn't belong just to comic books, but also to American noir novels, French modernist noir novels, American film noir, Humphrey Bogart films — all those. You belong to an entire genre — noir — that depicts a world which, from 1920 to now, has been dominated entirely by bastards — bastard cops, bastard politicians, and people who fight like dogs to seize power and to dominate others! It's not much different from what I see on the streets!"

This is Manchette's response to the anguished words of Griffu, who called him from a telephone booth in Pigalle.

In October 1977, *Griffu* was serialized in *BD*, the weekly comics magazine.

We were certain of one thing: in this story, there would only be characters who were rotten, nasty in every way, including the so-called hero, who would meet his end in garbage, like Orson Welles in *Touch of Evil*.

— TARDI

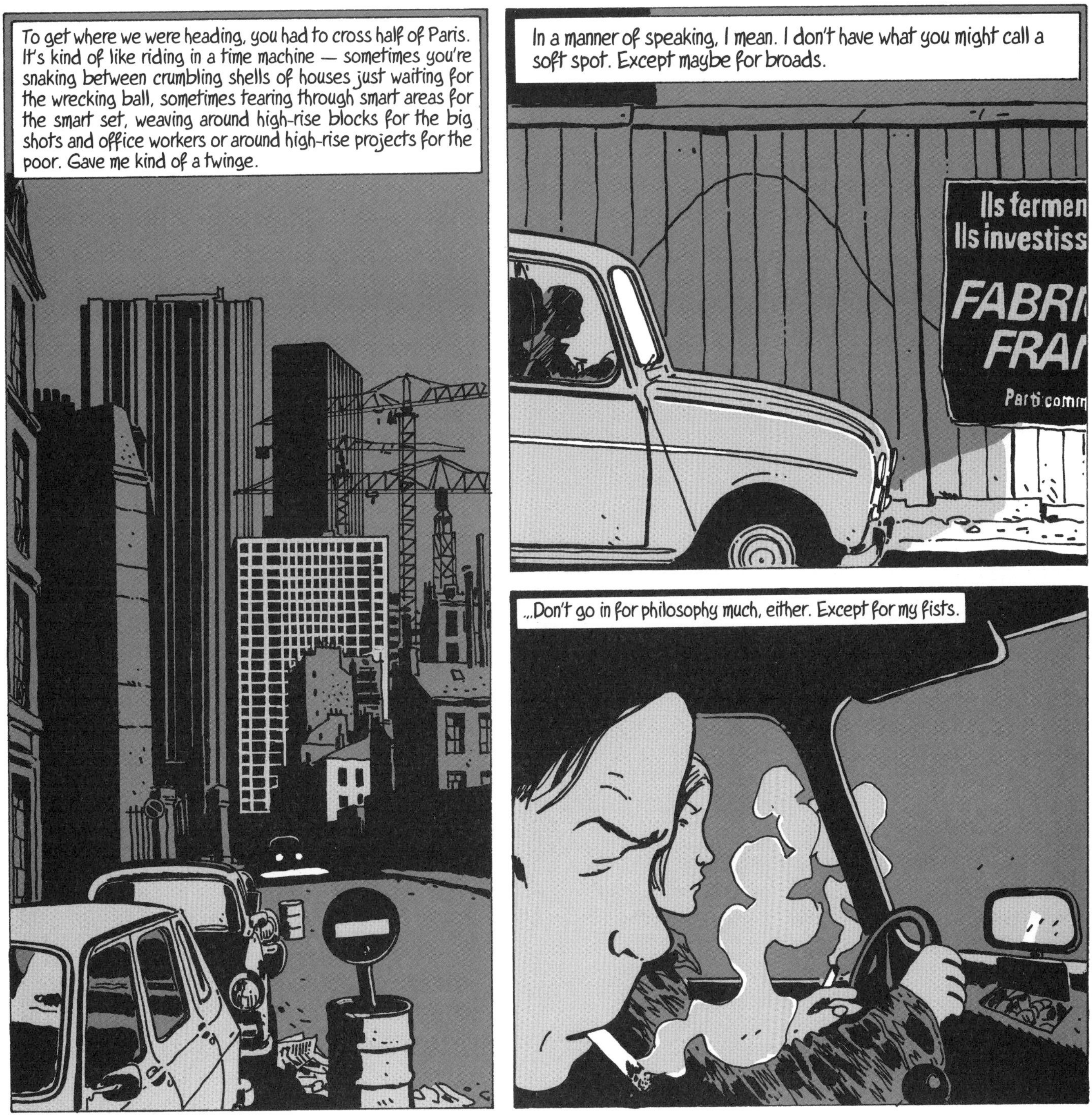
To get where we were heading, you had to cross half of Paris. It's kind of like riding in a time machine — sometimes you're snaking between crumbling shells of houses just waiting for the wrecking ball, sometimes tearing through smart areas for the smart set, weaving around high-rise blocks for the big shots and office workers or around high-rise projects for the poor. Gave me kind of a twinge.
In a manner of speaking, I mean. I don't have what you might call a soft spot. Except maybe for broads.
Ils fermen
Ils investiss
FABRI
FRA
Parti comm
...Don't go in for philosophy much, either. Except for my fists.

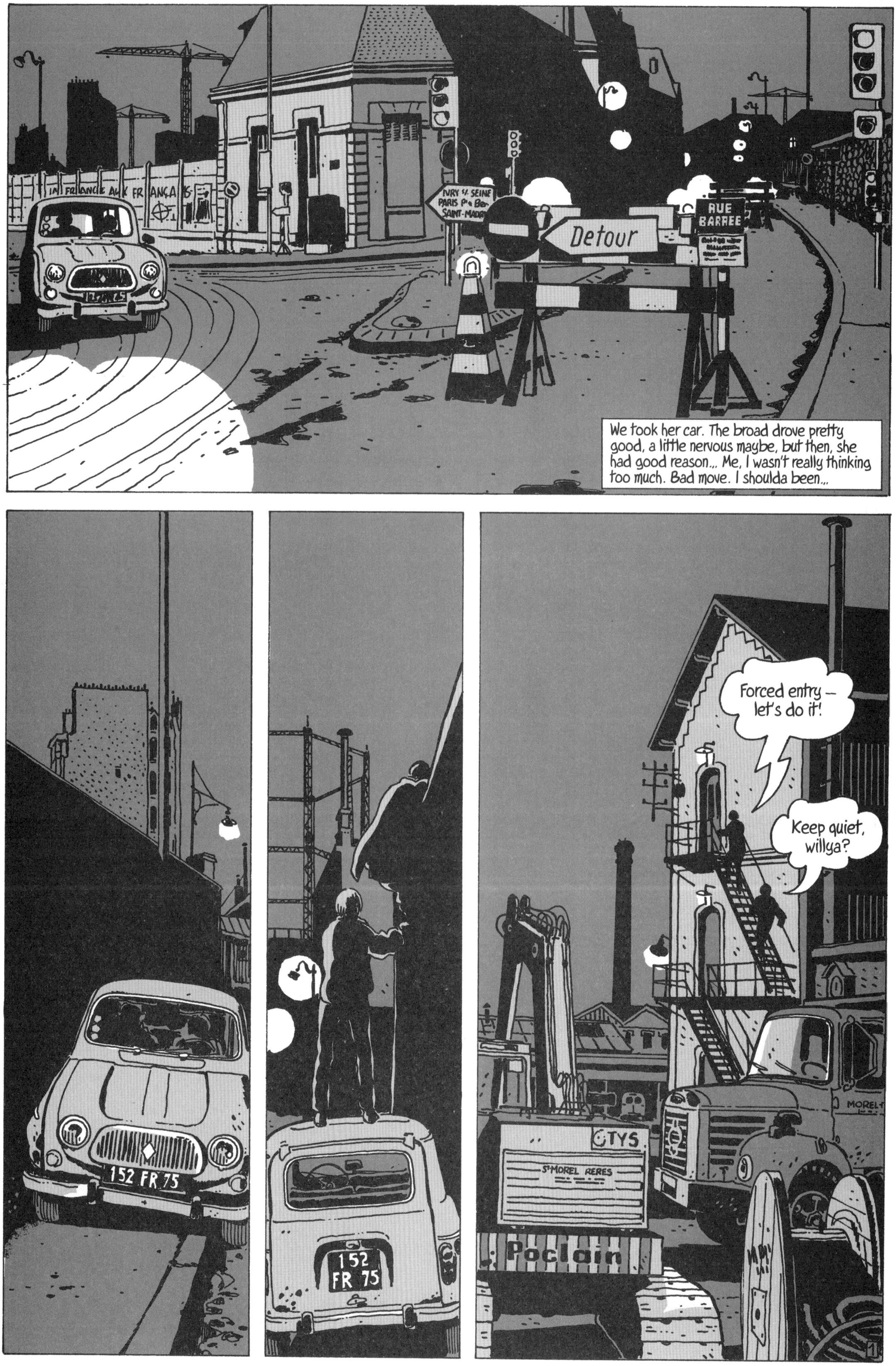
Detour
RUE BARREE
We took her car. The broad drove pretty good, a little nervous maybe, but then, she had good reason... Me, I wasn't really thinking too much. Bad move. I shoulda been...
152 FR 75
152 FR 75
Forced entry – let's do it!
Keep quiet, willya?
Poclain

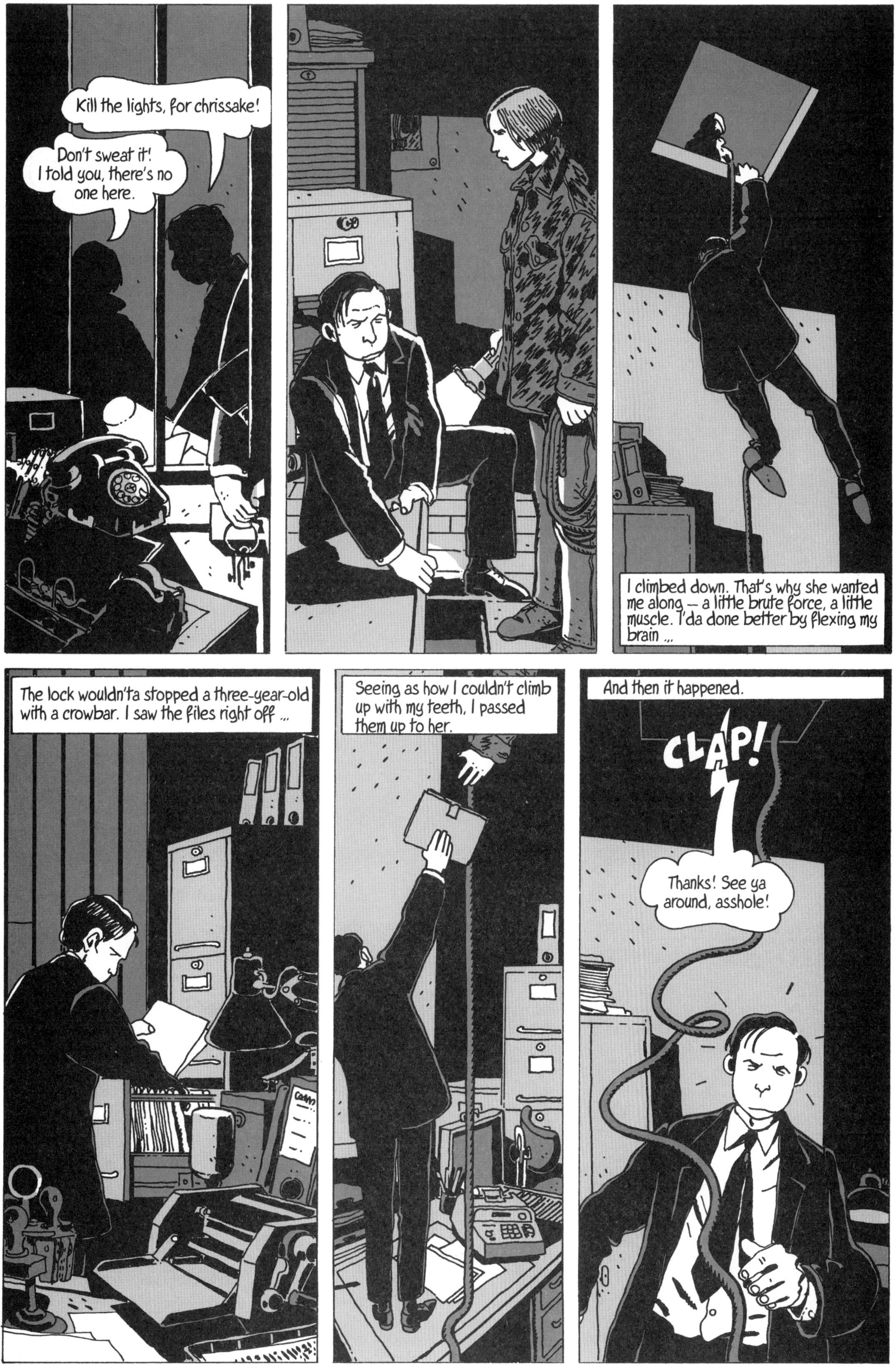
Kill the lights, for chrissake!
Don't sweat it! I told you, there's no one here.
I climbed down. That's why she wanted me along -- a little brute force, a little muscle. I'da done better by flexing my brain ...
The lock wouldn'ta stopped a three-year-old with a crowbar. I saw the files right off ...
Seeing as how I couldn't climb up with my teeth, I passed them up to her.
And then it happened.
CLAP!
Thanks! See ya around, asshole!

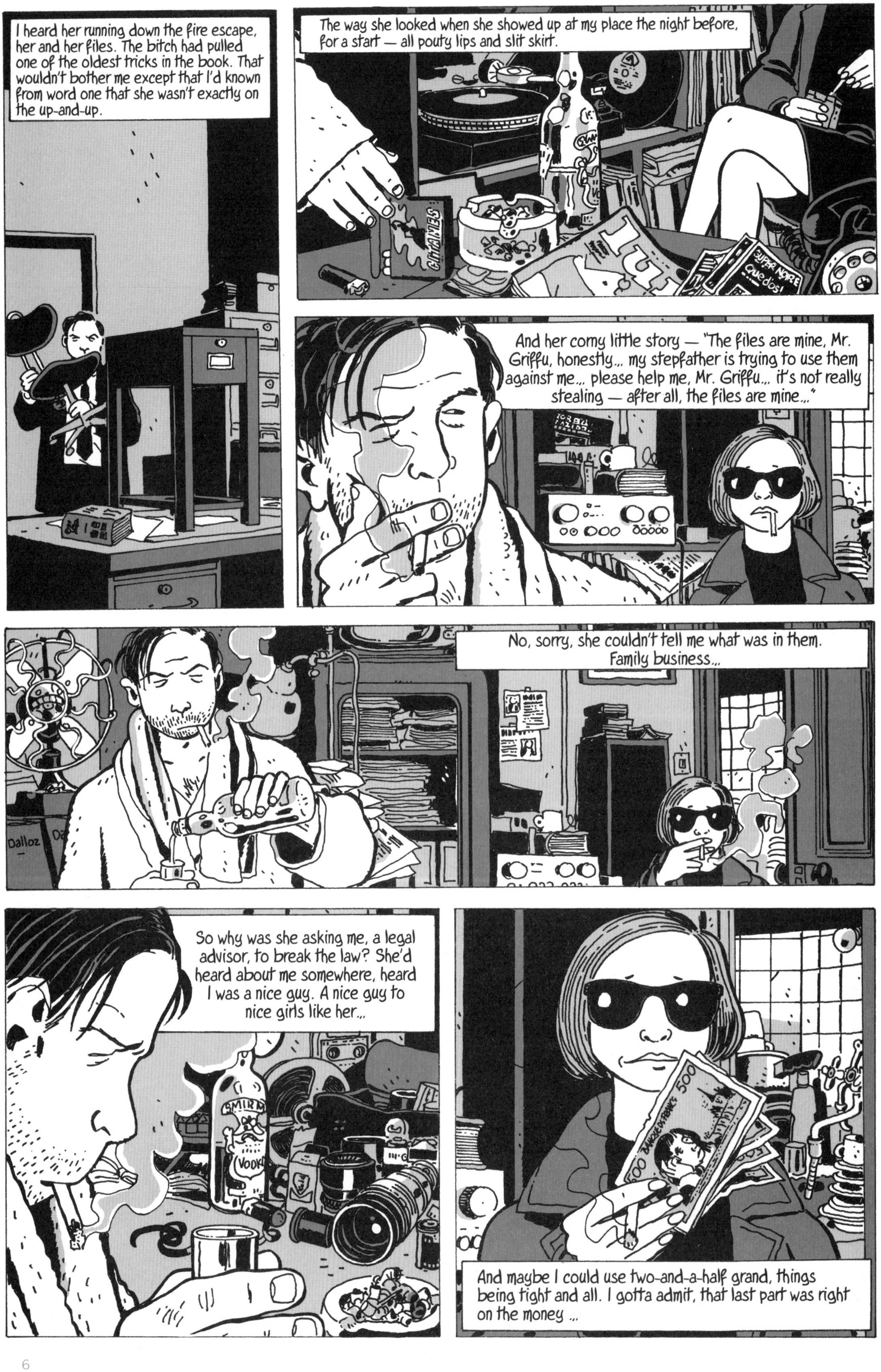
I heard her running down the fire escape, her and her files. The bitch had pulled one of the oldest tricks in the book. That wouldn't bother me except that I'd known from word one that she wasn't exactly on the up-and-up.
The way she looked when she showed up at my place the night before, for a start — all pouty lips and slit skirt.
And her corny little story — "The files are mine, Mr. Griffu, honestly... my stepfather is trying to use them against me... please help me, Mr. Griffu... it's not really stealing — after all, the files are mine..."
No, sorry, she couldn't tell me what was in them. Family business...
So why was she asking me, a legal advisor, to break the law? She'd heard about me somewhere, heard I was a nice guy. A nice guy to nice girls like her...
And maybe I could use two-and-a-half grand, things being tight and all. I gotta admit, that last part was right on the money ...

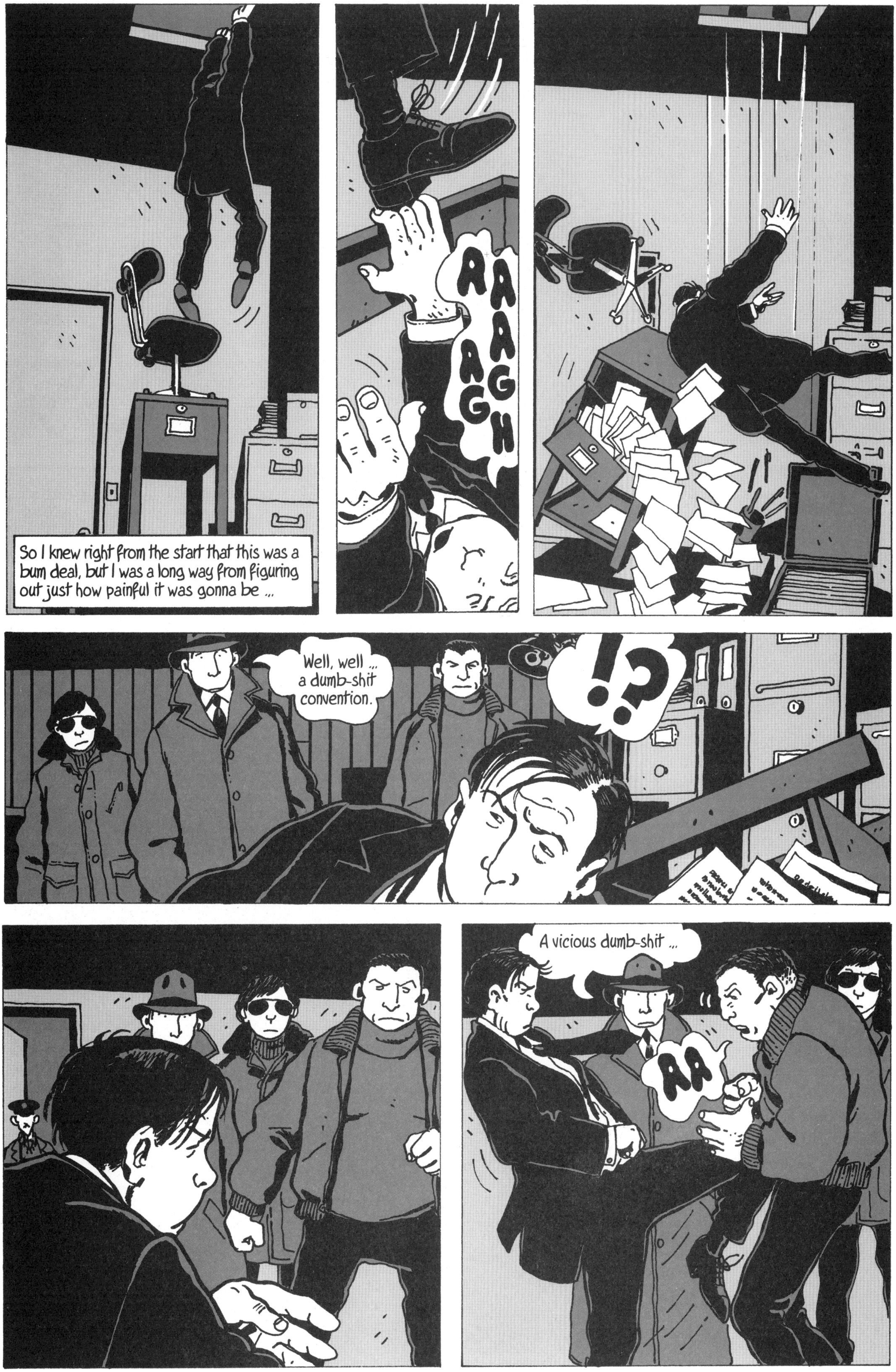

So I knew right from the start that this was a bum deal, but I was a long way from figuring out just how painful it was gonna be ...
RAAAGAGH
Well, well ... a dumb-shit convention.
!?
A vicious dumb-shit ...
AA

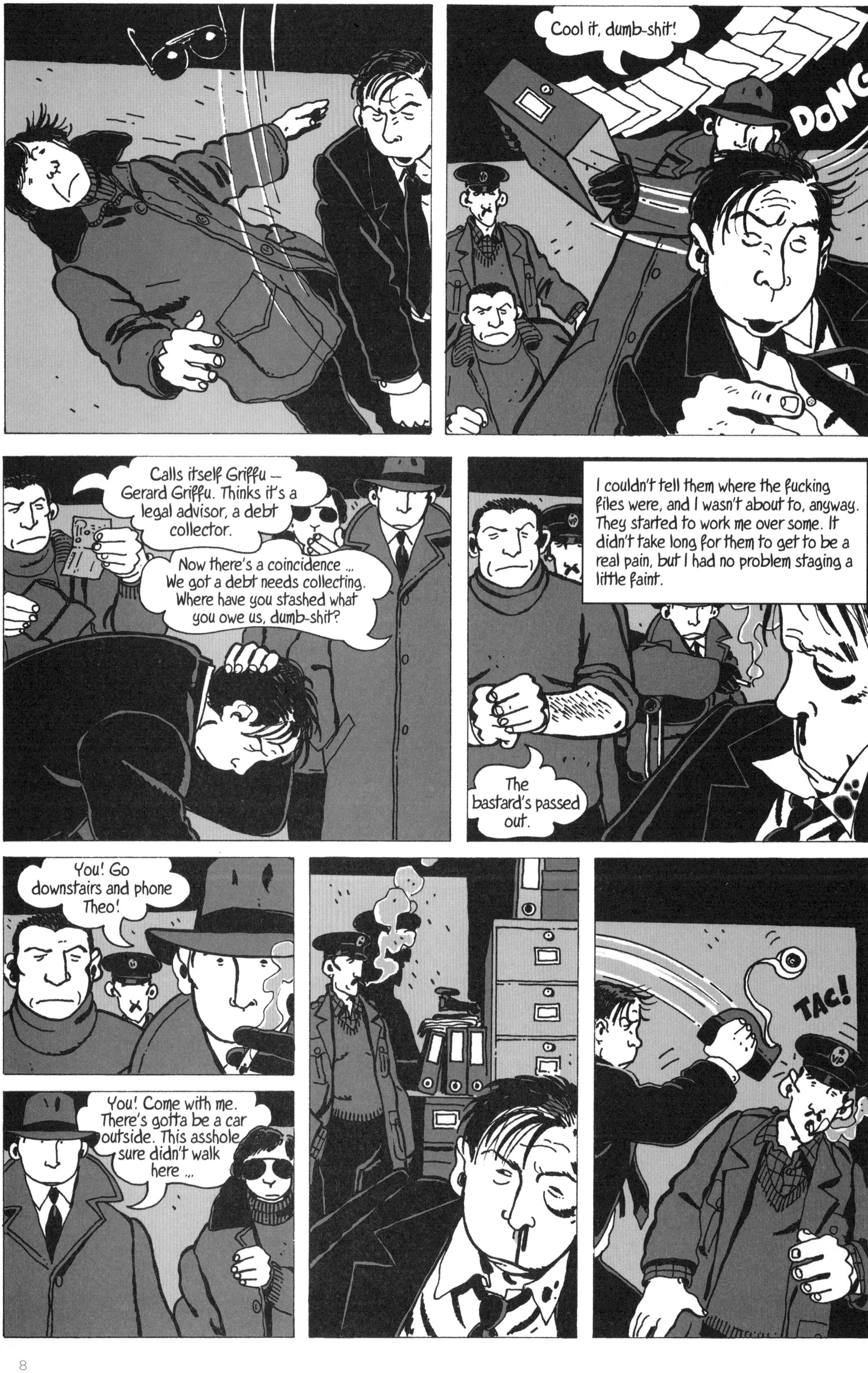
Cool it, dumb-shit!
DONG
Calls itself Griffu -- Gerard Griffu. Thinks it's a legal advisor, a debt collector.
Now there's a coincidence ... We got a debt needs collecting. Where have you stashed what you owe us, dumb-shit?
I couldn't tell them where the fucking files were, and I wasn't about to, anyway. They started to work me over some. It didn't take long for them to get to be a real pain, but I had no problem staging a little faint.
The bastard's passed out.
You! Go downstairs and phone Theo!
You! Come with me. There's gotta be a car outside. This asshole sure didn't walk here ...
TAC!

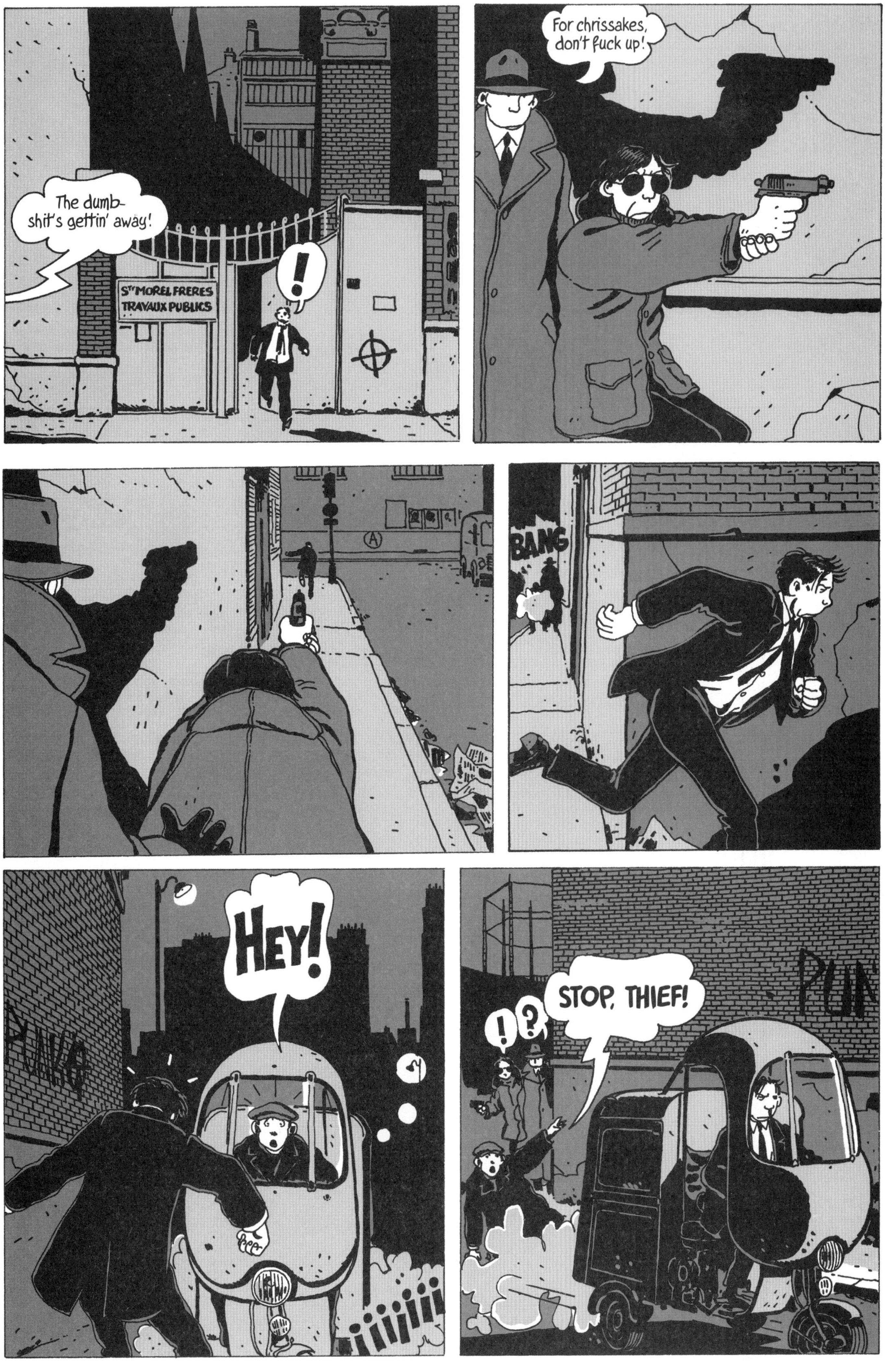

The dumb-shit's gettin' away!
Ste MOREL FRERES
TRAVAUX PUBLICS
!
For chrissakes, don't fuck up!
BANG
HEY!
PUNK
STOP, THIEF!
!
?
PUN

I headed home to clean up my face and do some thinking. None too soon, either.

It's 7:15 and shaping up like a regular Monday morning on the Paris loop ..

Just as well, I always ask my clients for a calling card ...

Of course, the little bitch had probably slipped me a phony address, but it was worth checking out.

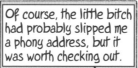

?!

It was the right address, all right, but the wrong broad. For a minute, I thought the gorillas had done this little number in, but she soon proved me wrong ...

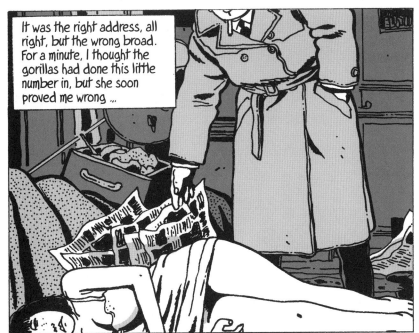

AAAAHH

Calm down, kid.

She calmed down, and I explained. I told her I was looking for someone named Luce Minetta. She said, get in line. From the state of her face and the state of the room, I figured I could believe her.

Coffee?

That'd be nice, thanks.

Those guys lookin' for your girlfriend, they didn't ... uh, show you much respect?

You're a real joker ... but nice ...

You're pretty nice yourself, kid ...

I always say ya gotta know how to be pushy to get ahead, but ya also gotta pay attention to the little things. Once I broke the ice with the kid, I quizzed her pretty good. We were gonna have to move fast to catch up with her friend and those files.

I dunno ... I met Luce at the university cafeteria. She was looking to share an apartment. OK, fine. I think she's trying to get into journalism. She's been working on some big story the last few days.

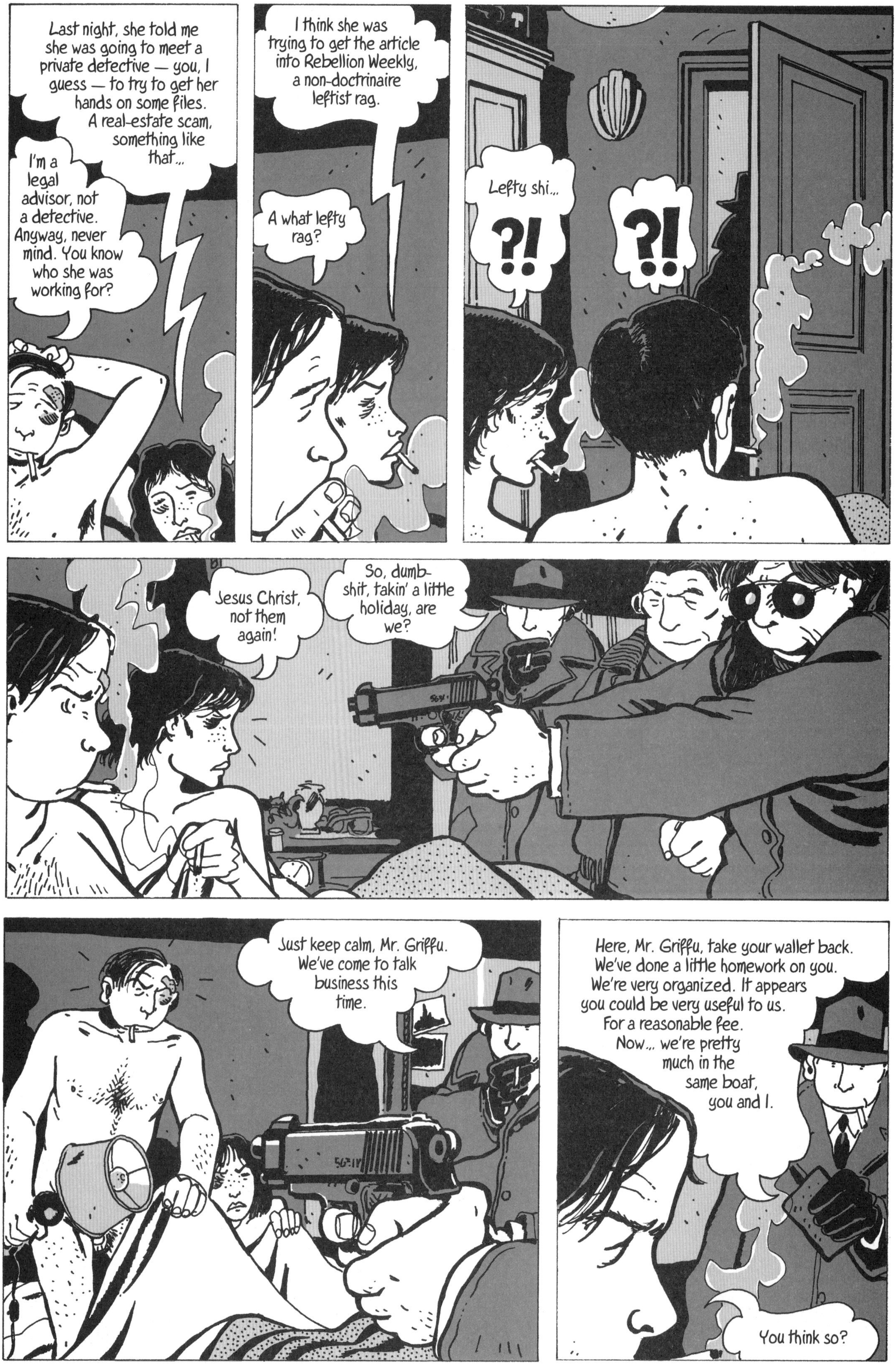

Last night, she told me she was going to meet a private detective — you, I guess — to try to get her hands on some files. A real-estate scam, something like that...
I'm a legal advisor, not a detective. Anyway, never mind. You know who she was working for?
I think she was trying to get the article into Rebellion Weekly, a non-doctrinaire leftist rag.
A what lefty rag?
Lefty shi...
?!
?!
Jesus Christ, not them again!
So, dumb-shit, takin' a little holiday, are we?
Just keep calm, Mr. Griffu. We've come to talk business this time.
Here, Mr. Griffu, take your wallet back. We've done a little homework on you. We're very organized. It appears you could be very useful to us. For a reasonable fee. Now... we're pretty much in the same boat, you and I.
You think so?

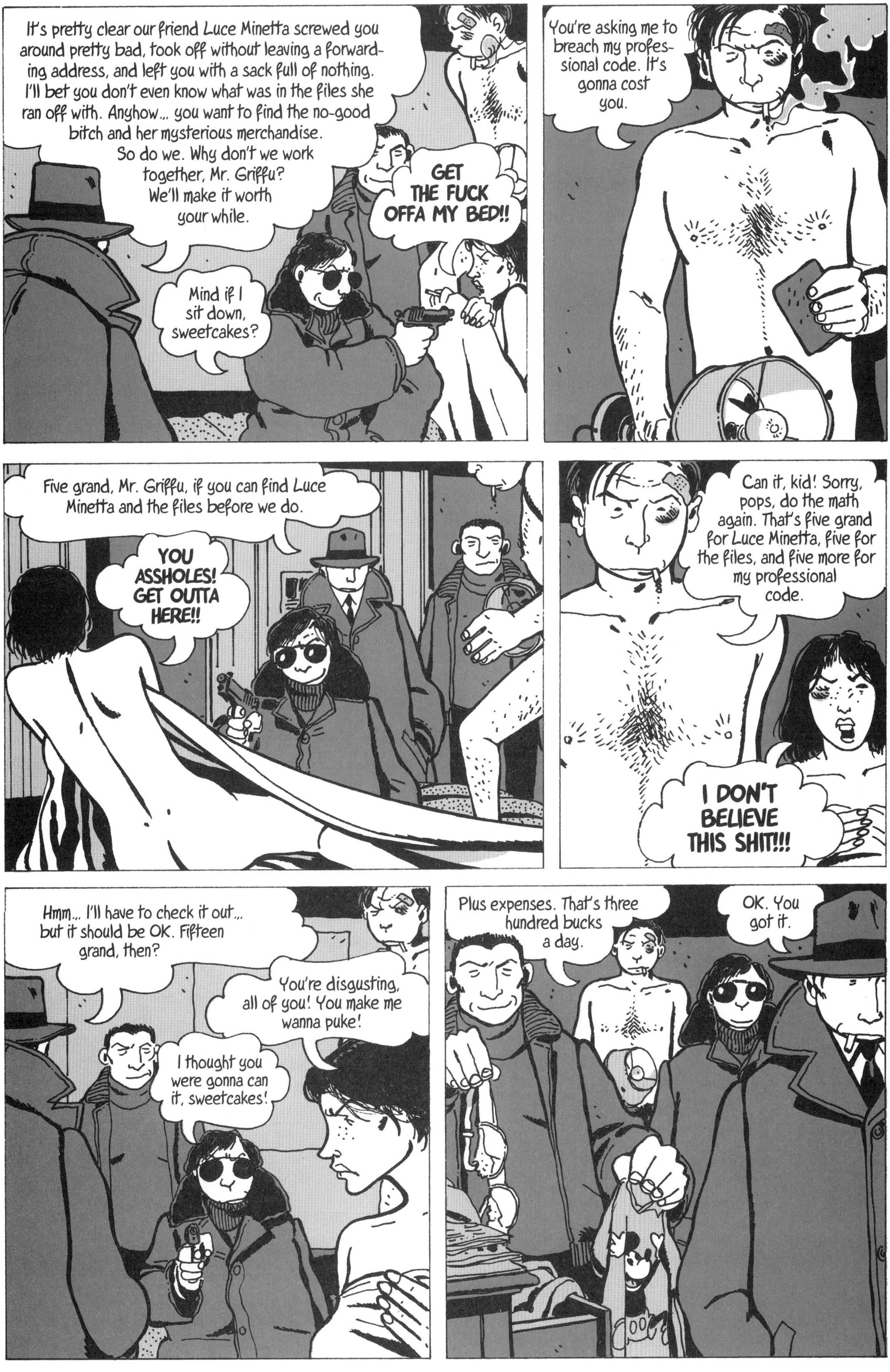
It's pretty clear our friend Luce Minetta screwed you around pretty bad, took off without leaving a forwarding address, and left you with a sack full of nothing. I'll bet you don't even know what was in the files she ran off with. Anyhow... you want to find the no-good bitch and her mysterious merchandise. So do we. Why don't we work together, Mr. Griffu? We'll make it worth your while.
GET THE FUCK OFFA MY BED!!
Mind if I sit down, sweetcakes?
You're asking me to breach my professional code. It's gonna cost you.
Five grand, Mr. Griffu, if you can find Luce Minetta and the files before we do.
YOU ASSHOLES! GET OUTTA HERE!!
Can it, kid! Sorry, pops, do the math again. That's five grand for Luce Minetta, five for the files, and five more for my professional code.
I DON'T BELIEVE THIS SHIT!!!
Hmm... I'll have to check it out... but it should be OK. Fifteen grand, then?
You're disgusting, all of you! You make me wanna puke!
I thought you were gonna can it, sweetcakes!
Plus expenses. That's three hundred bucks a day.
OK. You got it.

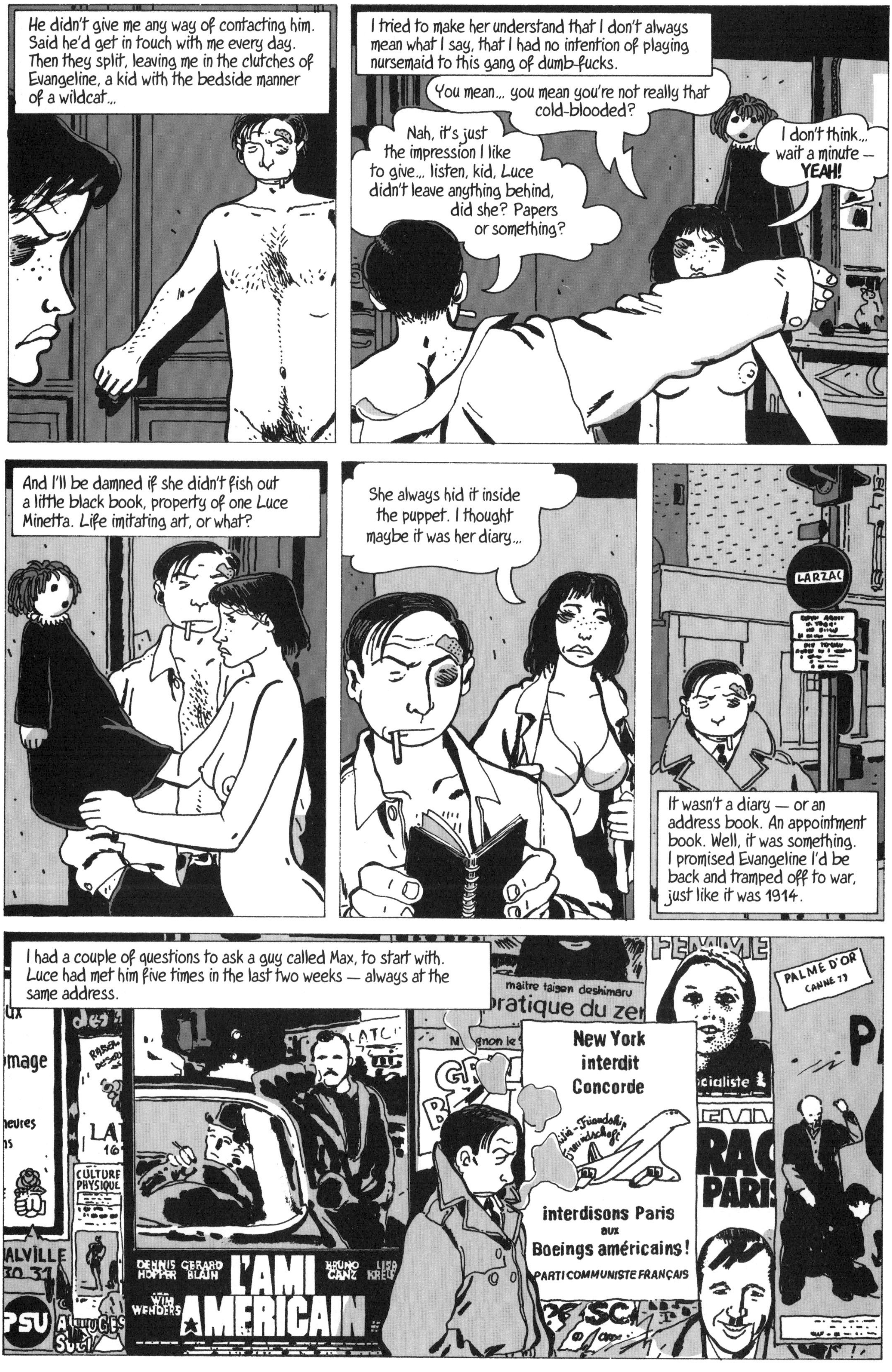
He didn't give me any way of contacting him. Said he'd get in touch with me every day. Then they split, leaving me in the clutches of Evangeline, a kid with the bedside manner of a wildcat...
I tried to make her understand that I don't always mean what I say, that I had no intention of playing nursemaid to this gang of dumb-fucks.
You mean... you mean you're not really that cold-blooded?
Nah, it's just the impression I like to give... listen, kid, Luce didn't leave anything behind, did she? Papers or something?
I don't think... wait a minute — YEAH!
And I'll be damned if she didn't fish out a little black book, property of one Luce Minetta. Life imitating art, or what?
She always hid it inside the puppet. I thought maybe it was her diary...
LARZAC
It wasn't a diary — or an address book. An appointment book. Well, it was something. I promised Evangeline I'd be back and tramped off to war, just like it was 1914.
I had a couple of questions to ask a guy called Max, to start with. Luce had met him five times in the last two weeks — always at the same address.
FEMME
maitre taisen deshimaru
pratique du zen
PALME D'OR
CANNE 77
New York
interdit
Concorde
interdisons Paris
aux
Boeings américains!
PARTI COMMUNISTE FRANÇAIS
CULTURE PHYSIQUE
PSU
DENNIS HOPPER
GERARD BLAIN
BRUNO GANZ
WIM WENDERS
L'AMI AMERICAIN
PARIS

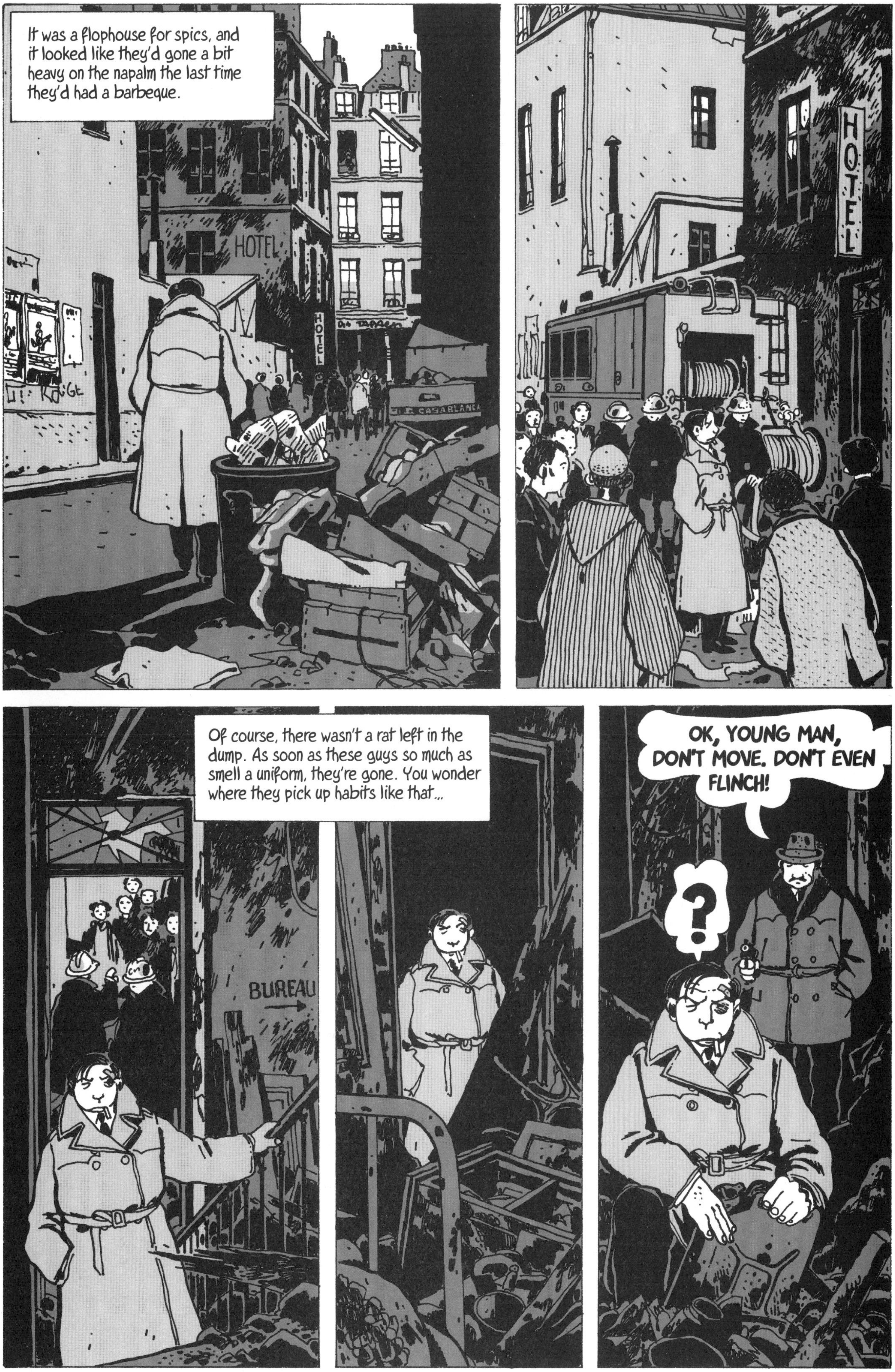
It was a flophouse for spics, and it looked like they'd gone a bit heavy on the napalm the last time they'd had a barbeque.
HOTEL
HOTEL
CASABLANCA
HOTEL
Of course, there wasn't a rat left in the dump. As soon as these guys so much as smell a uniform, they're gone. You wonder where they pick up habits like that...
BUREAU
OK, YOUNG MAN, DON'T MOVE. DON'T EVEN FLINCH!
?

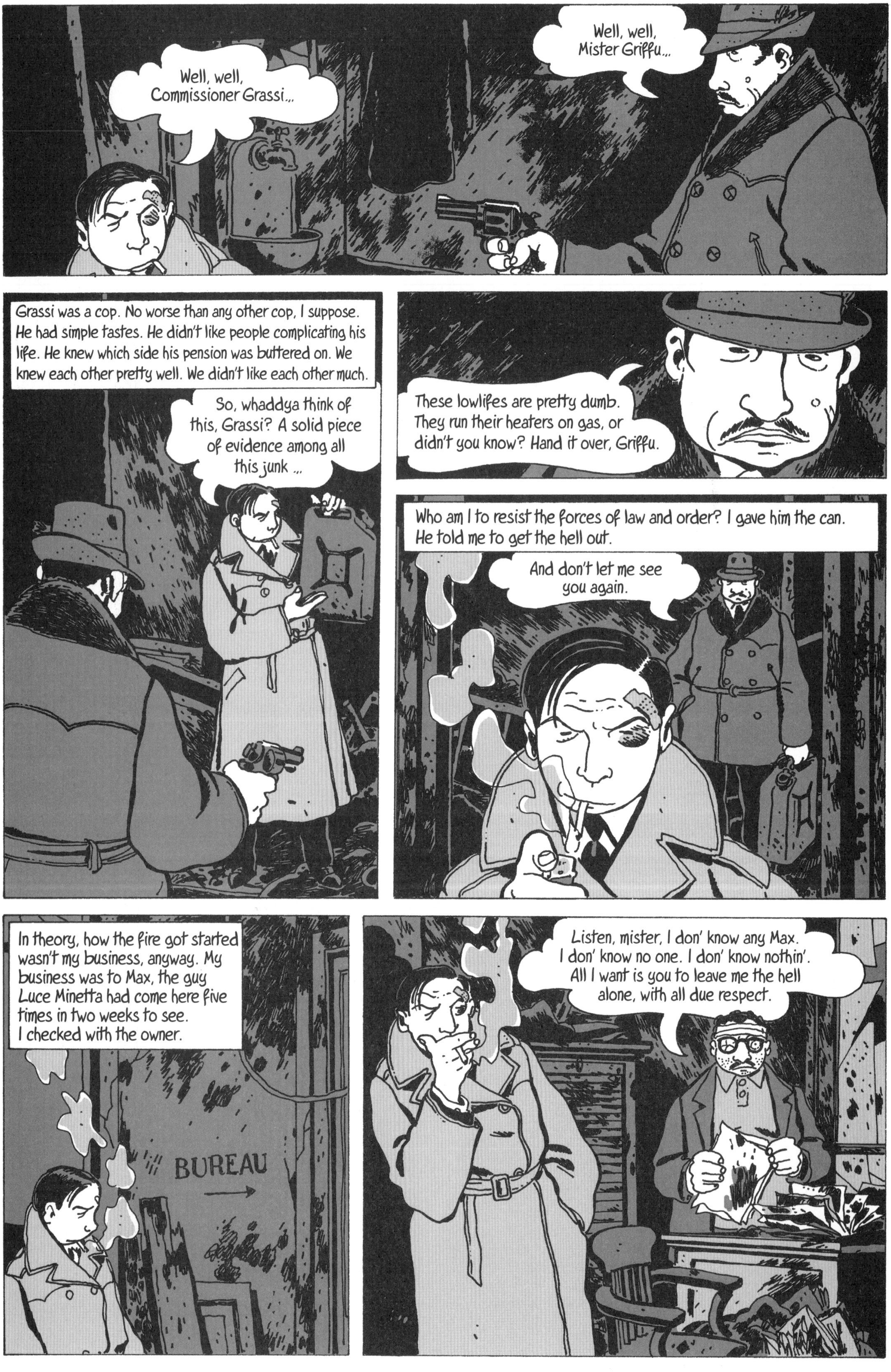

Well, well, Commissioner Grassi...
Well, well, Mister Griffu...
Grassi was a cop. No worse than any other cop, I suppose. He had simple tastes. He didn't like people complicating his life. He knew which side his pension was buttered on. We knew each other pretty well. We didn't like each other much.
So, whaddya think of this, Grassi? A solid piece of evidence among all this junk ...
These lowlifes are pretty dumb. They run their heaters on gas, or didn't you know? Hand it over, Griffu.
Who am I to resist the forces of law and order? I gave him the can. He told me to get the hell out.
And don't let me see you again.
In theory, how the fire got started wasn't my business, anyway. My business was to Max, the guy Luce Minetta had come here five times in two weeks to see. I checked with the owner.
BUREAU
Listen, mister, I don' know any Max. I don' know no one. I don' know nothin'. All I want is you to leave me the hell alone, with all due respect.

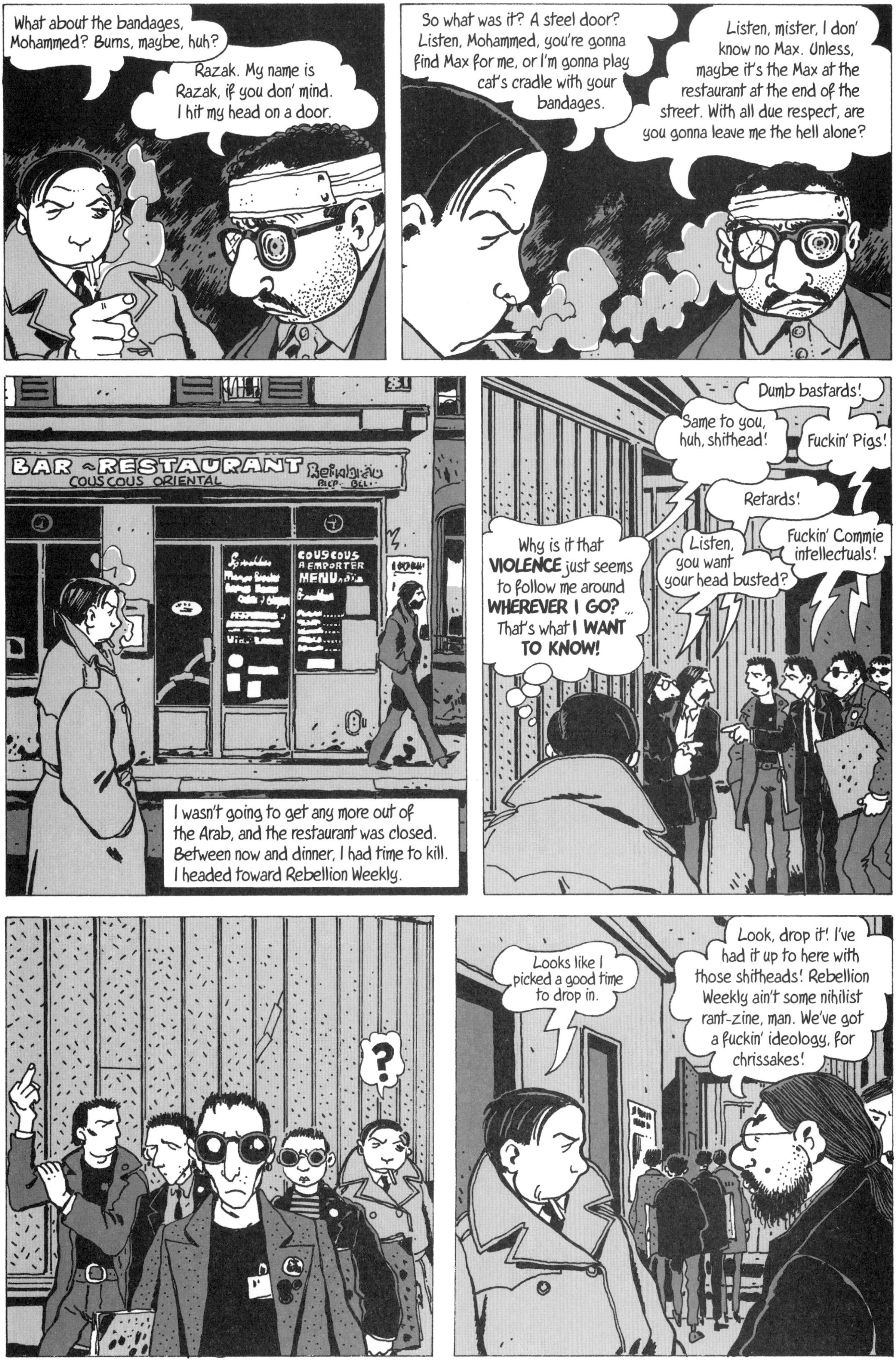

What about the bandages, Mohammed? Burns, maybe, huh?
Razak. My name is Razak, if you don' mind. I hit my head on a door.
So what was it? A steel door? Listen, Mohammed, you're gonna find Max for me, or I'm gonna play cat's cradle with your bandages.
Listen, mister, I don' know no Max. Unless, maybe it's the Max at the restaurant at the end of the street. With all due respect, are you gonna leave me the hell alone?
BAR RESTAURANT
COUSCOUS ORIENTAL
COUSCOUS A EMPORTER
MENU
I wasn't going to get any more out of the Arab, and the restaurant was closed. Between now and dinner, I had time to kill. I headed toward Rebellion Weekly.
Why is it that **VIOLENCE** just seems to follow me around **WHEREVER I GO?** ... That's what **I WANT TO KNOW!**
Same to you, huh, shithead!
Dumb bastards!
Fuckin' Pigs!
Retards!
Listen, you want your head busted?
Fuckin' Commie intellectuals!
?
Looks like I picked a good time to drop in.
Look, drop it! I've had it up to here with those shitheads! Rebellion Weekly ain't some nihilist rant-zine, man. We've got a fuckin' ideology, for chrissakes!

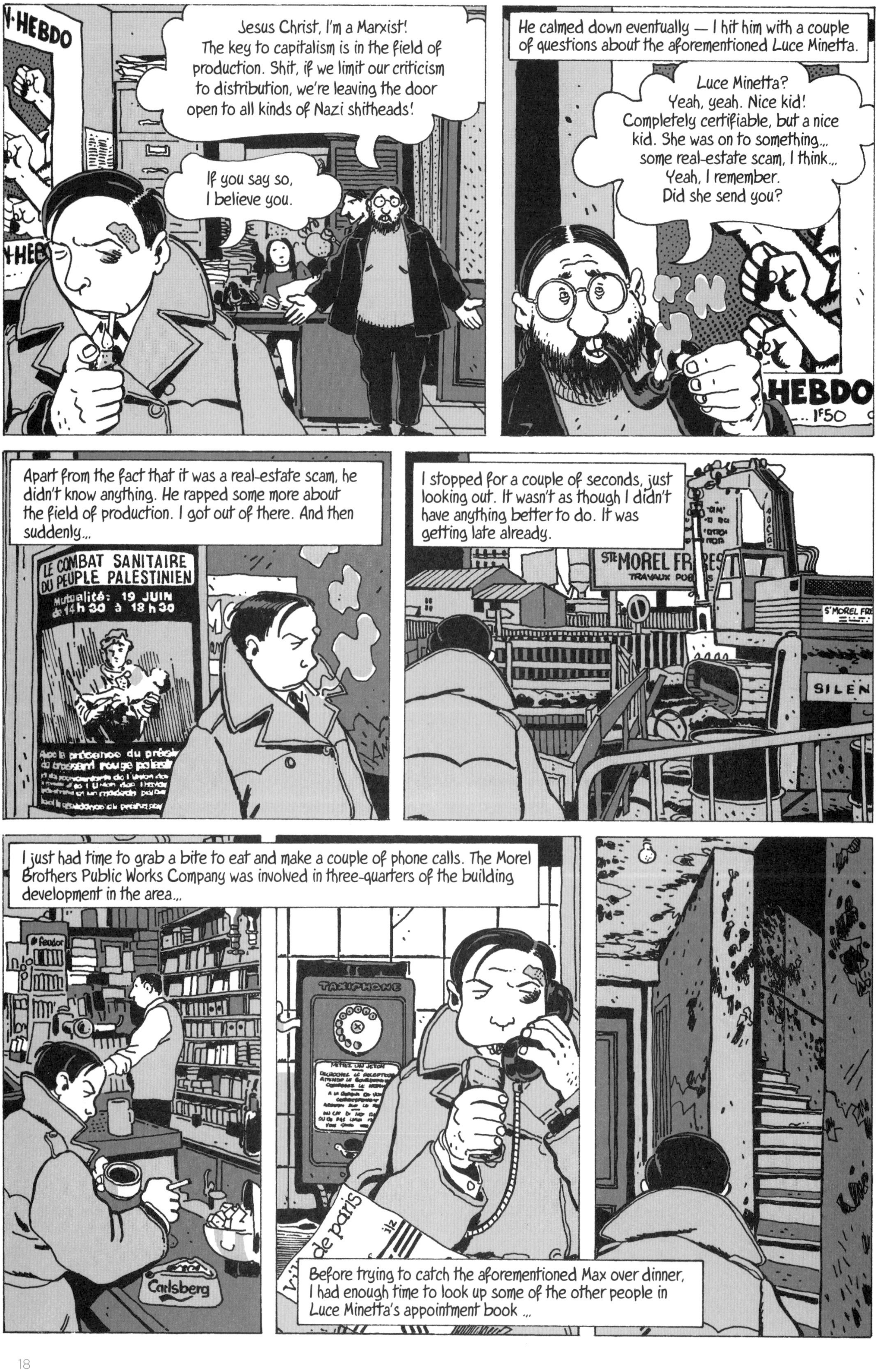

Jesus Christ, I'm a Marxist! The key to capitalism is in the field of production. Shit, if we limit our criticism to distribution, we're leaving the door open to all kinds of Nazi shitheads!
If you say so, I believe you.
HEBDO
He calmed down eventually — I hit him with a couple of questions about the aforementioned Luce Minetta.
Luce Minetta? Yeah, yeah. Nice kid! Completely certifiable, but a nice kid. She was on to something... some real-estate scam, I think... Yeah, I remember. Did she send you?
HEBDO
Apart from the fact that it was a real-estate scam, he didn't know anything. He rapped some more about the field of production. I got out of there. And then suddenly...
LE COMBAT SANITAIRE DU PEUPLE PALESTINIEN
Mutualité: 19 JUIN de 14 h 30 à 18 h 30
I stopped for a couple of seconds, just looking out. It wasn't as though I didn't have anything better to do. It was getting late already.
STE MOREL FRERES
TRAVAUX PUBLICS
SILEN
I just had time to grab a bite to eat and make a couple of phone calls. The Morel Brothers Public Works Company was involved in three-quarters of the building development in the area...
Carlsberg
TAXIPHONE
de paris
Before trying to catch the aforementioned Max over dinner, I had enough time to look up some of the other people in Luce Minetta's appointment book ...

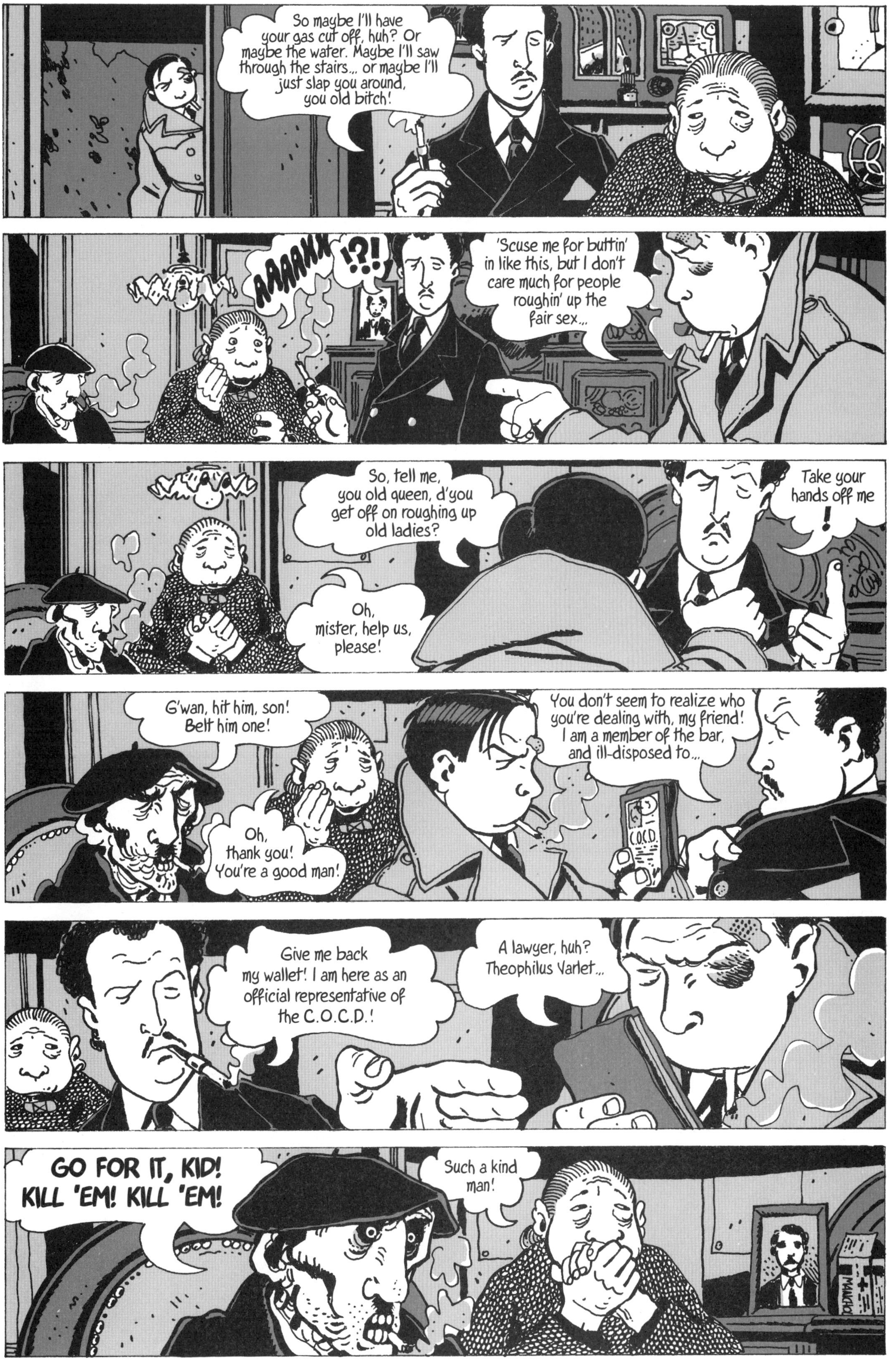
So maybe I'll have your gas cut off, huh? Or maybe the water. Maybe I'll saw through the stairs... or maybe I'll just slap you around, you old bitch!
AAAAHH
!?!
'Scuse me for buttin' in like this, but I don't care much for people roughin' up the fair sex...
So, tell me, you old queen, d'you get off on roughing up old ladies?
Take your hands off me!
Oh, mister, help us, please!
G'wan, hit him, son! Belt him one!
You don't seem to realize who you're dealing with, my friend! I am a member of the bar, and ill-disposed to...
Oh, thank you! You're a good man!
C.O.C.D.
Give me back my wallet! I am here as an official representative of the C.O.C.D.!
A lawyer, huh? Theophilus Varlet...
GO FOR IT, KID! KILL 'EM! KILL 'EM!
Such a kind man!

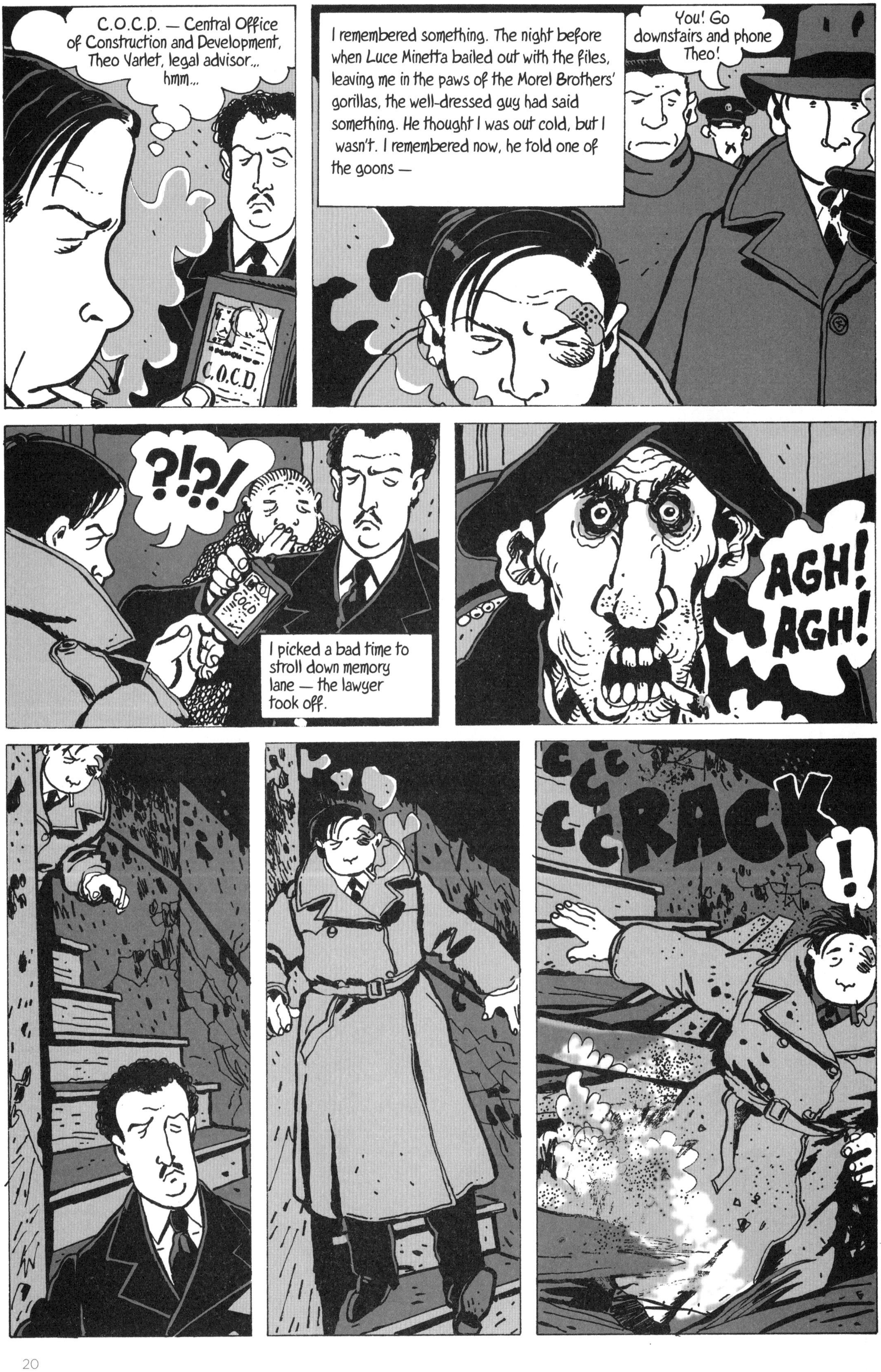
C.O.C.D. — Central Office of Construction and Development, Theo Varlet, legal advisor... hmm...
C.O.C.D.
I remembered something. The night before when Luce Minetta bailed out with the files, leaving me in the paws of the Morel Brothers' gorillas, the well-dressed guy had said something. He thought I was out cold, but I wasn't. I remembered now, he told one of the goons —
You! Go downstairs and phone Theo!
?!?!
COCD
I picked a bad time to stroll down memory lane — the lawyer took off.
AGH! AGH!
CCCCCRACK!

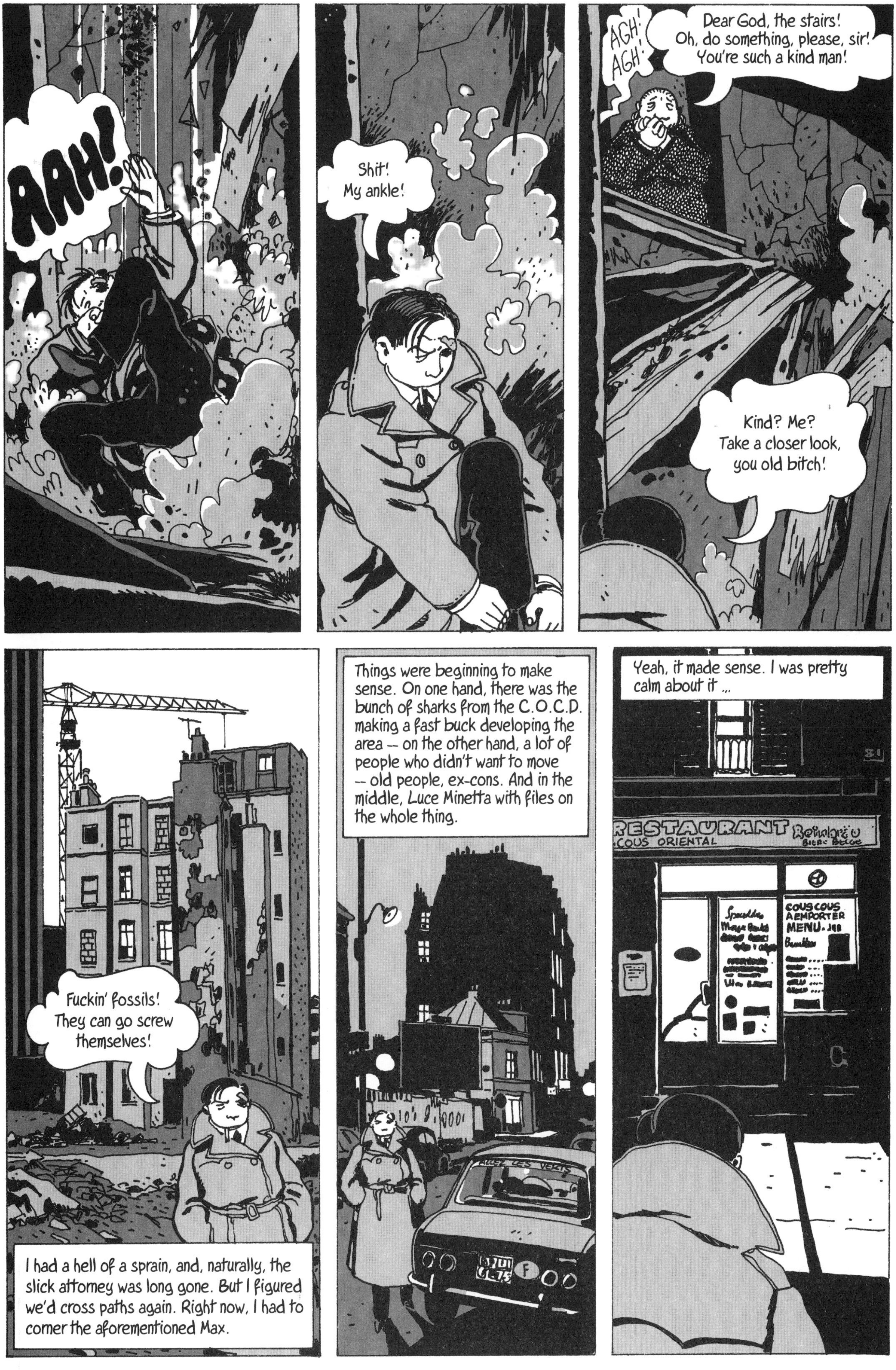
AAH!
Shit! My ankle!
AGH! AGH!
Dear God, the stairs! Oh, do something, please, sir! You're such a kind man!
Kind? Me? Take a closer look, you old bitch!
Fuckin' fossils! They can go screw themselves!
I had a hell of a sprain, and, naturally, the slick attorney was long gone. But I figured we'd cross paths again. Right now, I had to corner the aforementioned Max.
Things were beginning to make sense. On one hand, there was the bunch of sharks from the C.O.C.D. making a fast buck developing the area -- on the other hand, a lot of people who didn't want to move -- old people, ex-cons. And in the middle, Luce Minetta with files on the whole thing.
ALLEZ LES VERTS
Yeah, it made sense. I was pretty calm about it ...
RESTAURANT
COUS ORIENTAL
COUSCOUS A EMPORTER
MENU

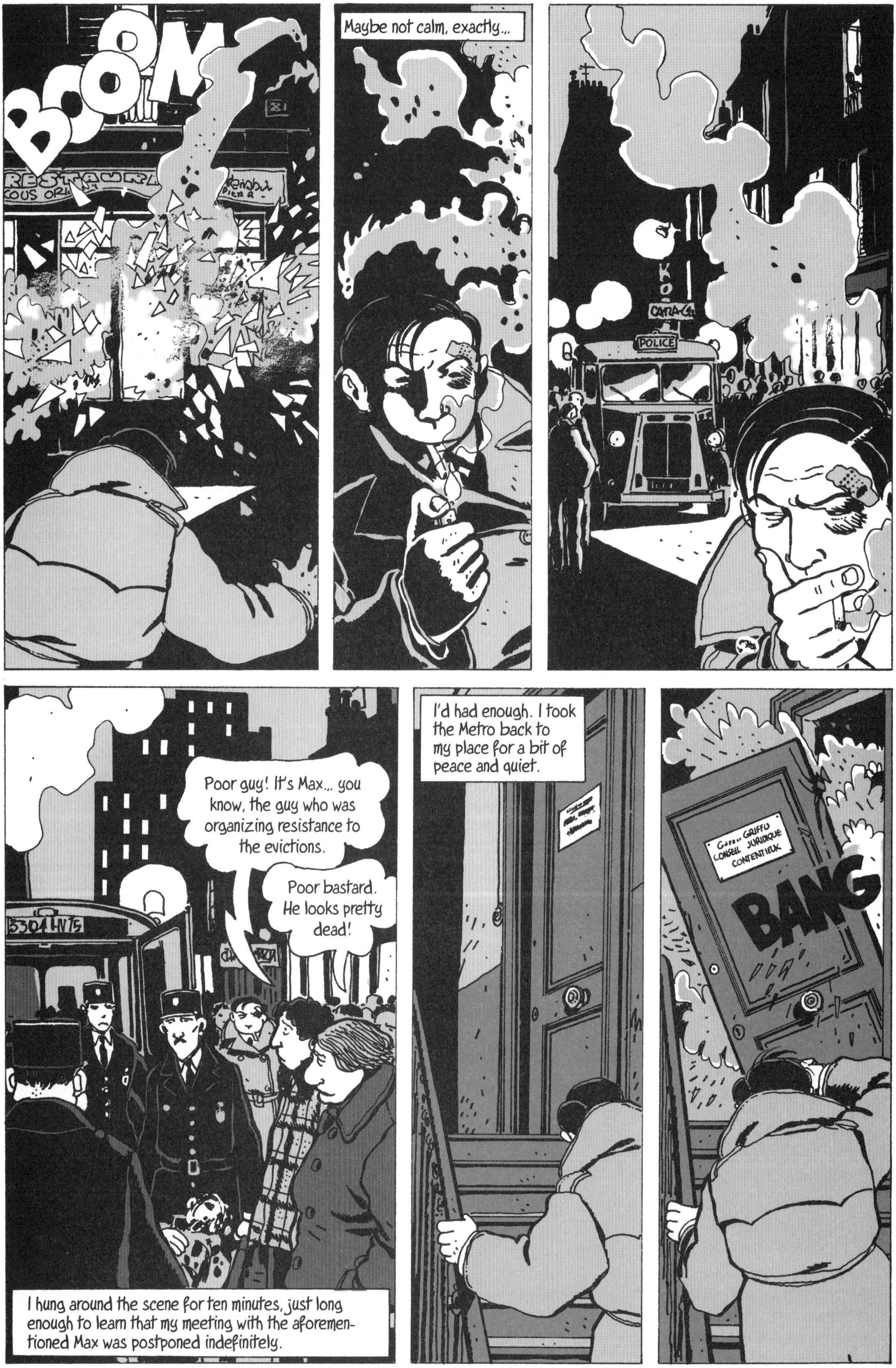
BOOOM
Maybe not calm, exactly...
POLICE
Poor guy! It's Max... you know, the guy who was organizing resistance to the evictions.
Poor bastard. He looks pretty dead!
I hung around the scene for ten minutes, just long enough to learn that my meeting with the aforementioned Max was postponed indefinitely.
I'd had enough. I took the Metro back to my place for a bit of peace and quiet.
CONSEIL JURIDIQUE CONTENTIEUX
BANG

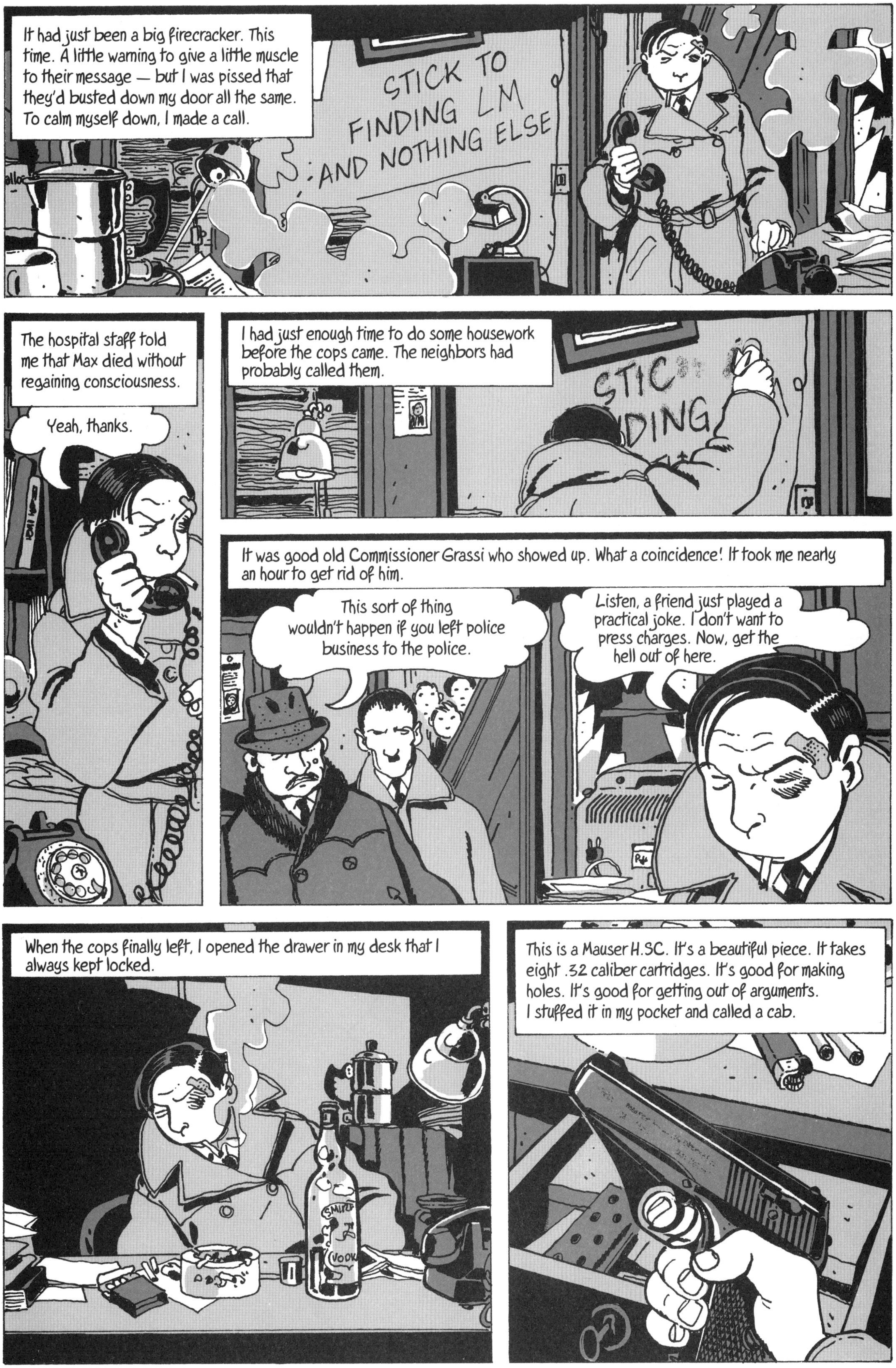
It had just been a big firecracker. This time. A little warning to give a little muscle to their message — but I was pissed that they'd busted down my door all the same. To calm myself down, I made a call.
STICK TO FINDING LM AND NOTHING ELSE
The hospital staff told me that Max died without regaining consciousness.
Yeah, thanks.
I had just enough time to do some housework before the cops came. The neighbors had probably called them.
It was good old Commissioner Grassi who showed up. What a coincidence! It took me nearly an hour to get rid of him.
This sort of thing wouldn't happen if you left police business to the police.
Listen, a friend just played a practical joke. I don't want to press charges. Now, get the hell out of here.
When the cops finally left, I opened the drawer in my desk that I always kept locked.
This is a Mauser H.SC. It's a beautiful piece. It takes eight .32 caliber cartridges. It's good for making holes. It's good for getting out of arguments. I stuffed it in my pocket and called a cab.

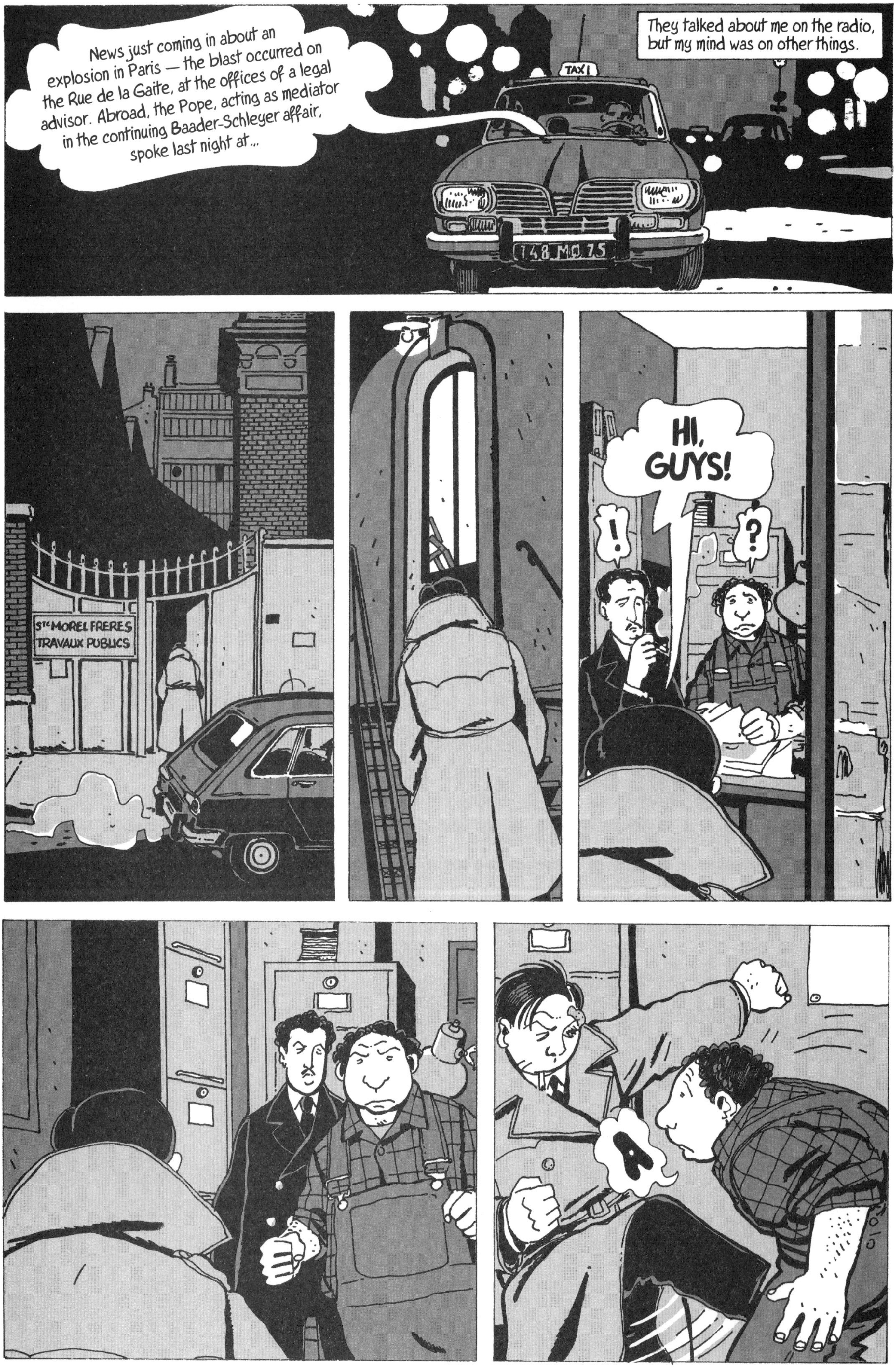

News just coming in about an explosion in Paris — the blast occurred on the Rue de la Gaite, at the offices of a legal advisor. Abroad, the Pope, acting as mediator in the continuing Baader-Schleyer affair, spoke last night at...
They talked about me on the radio, but my mind was on other things.
TAXI
148 MQ 75
STE MOREL FRERES
TRAVAUX PUBLICS
HI, GUYS!
!
?

Okay, shithead, you're going to tell me who your boss is. Tell me who's in charge of the C.O.C.D

Pl-pleas don't hurt I beg y

He gave me the name and address of his boss. Then I really hurt him, just to make sure he was telling the truth. Then I pistol-whipped him — knocked him out cold — and left.

Congressman Archimbault lived in Neuilly, a pretty long haul on the Metro.

DIRECTION
PONT DE NEUILLY

It should have given me time to calm down, to think. But it didn't. See, when I'm pissed, I need to get it out of my system. I leave the thinking to other people.

LA GUERRE SOCIALE

ABOLITION
U TRAVAIL SALARIÉ

By the time I arrived at Archimbault's place, it was midnight. But I'd picked a good time to call.

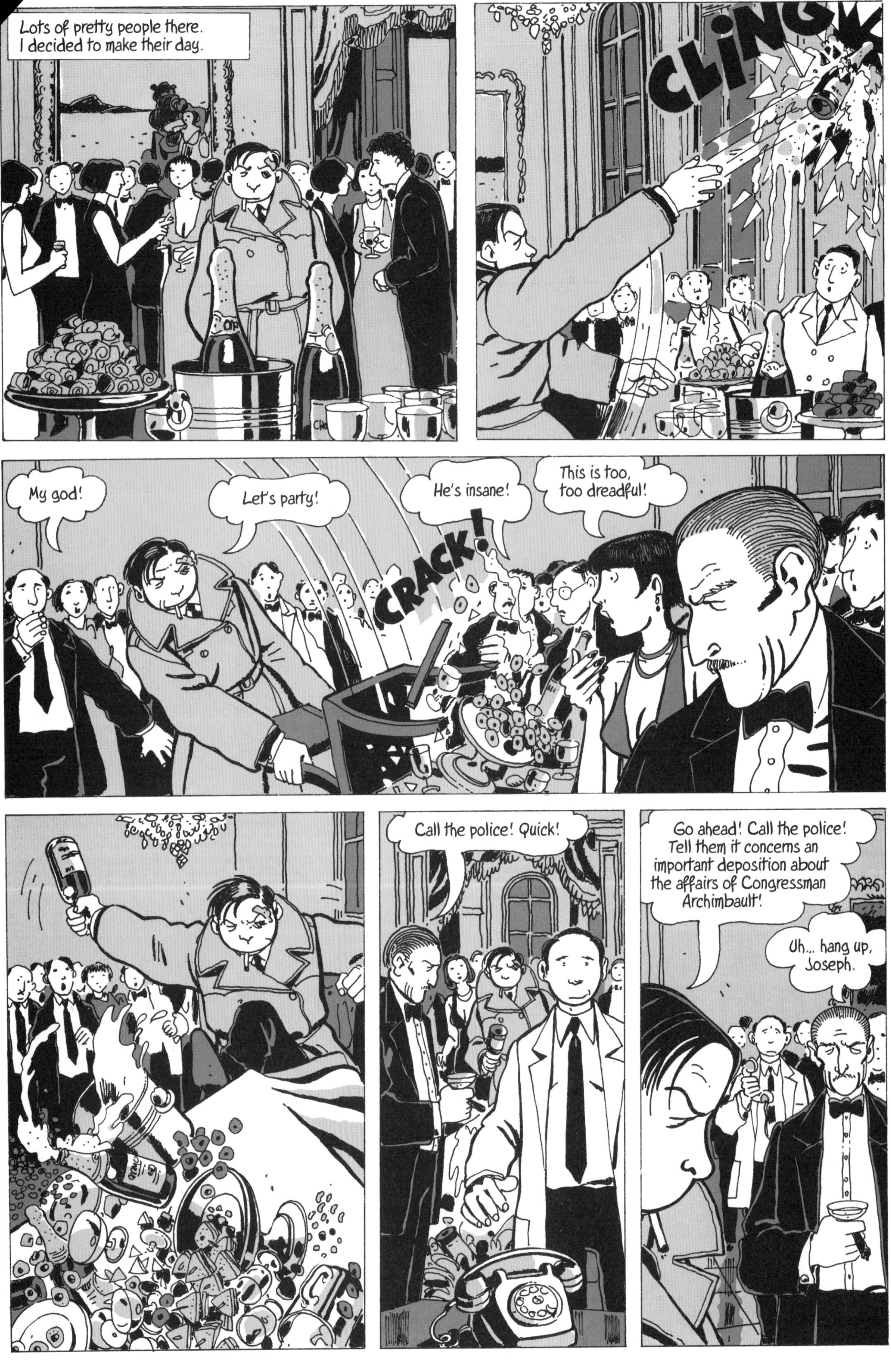
Lots of pretty people there. I decided to make their day.
CLING
My god!
Let's party!
He's insane!
This is too, too dreadful!
CRACK!
Call the police! Quick!
Go ahead! Call the police! Tell them it concerns an important deposition about the affairs of Congressman Archimbault!
Uh... hang up, Joseph.

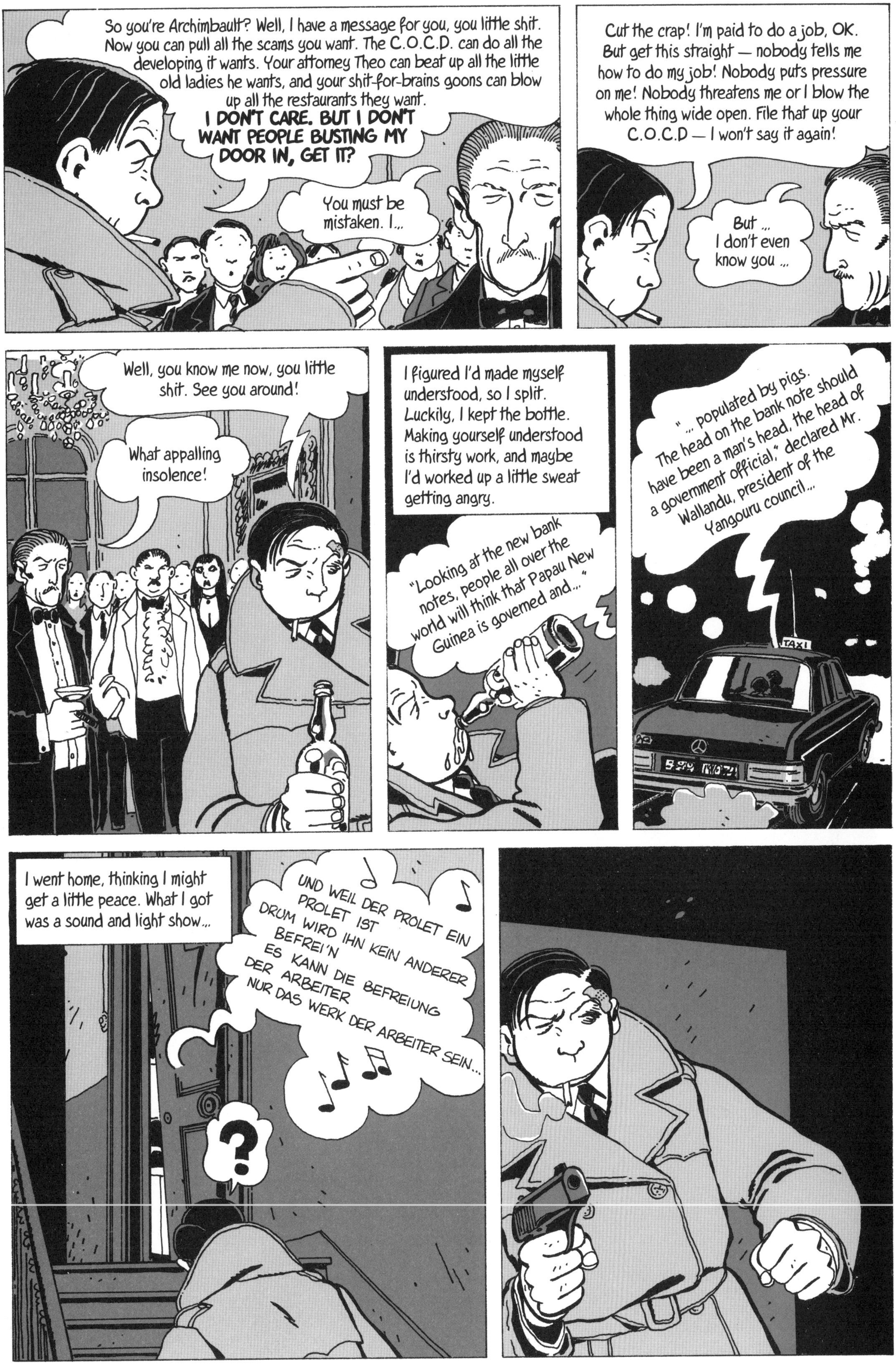

So you're Archimbault? Well, I have a message for you, you little shit. Now you can pull all the scams you want. The C.O.C.D. can do all the developing it wants. Your attorney Theo can beat up all the little old ladies he wants, and your shit-for-brains goons can blow up all the restaurants they want.
I DON'T CARE. BUT I DON'T WANT PEOPLE BUSTING MY DOOR IN, GET IT?
You must be mistaken. I...
Cut the crap! I'm paid to do a job, OK. But get this straight — nobody tells me how to do my job! Nobody puts pressure on me! Nobody threatens me or I blow the whole thing wide open. File that up your C.O.C.D — I won't say it again!
But ... I don't even know you ...
Well, you know me now, you little shit. See you around!
What appalling insolence!
I figured I'd made myself understood, so I split. Luckily, I kept the bottle. Making yourself understood is thirsty work, and maybe I'd worked up a little sweat getting angry.
"Looking at the new bank notes, people all over the world will think that Papau New Guinea is governed and..."
"... populated by pigs. The head on the bank note should have been a man's head, the head of a government official," declared Mr. Wallandu, president of the Yangouru council...
TAXI
I went home, thinking I might get a little peace. What I got was a sound and light show...
UND WEIL DER PROLET EIN PROLET IST
DRUM WIRD IHN KEIN ANDERER BEFREI'N
ES KANN DIE BEFREIUNG DER ARBEITER
NUR DAS WERK DER ARBEITER SEIN...
?

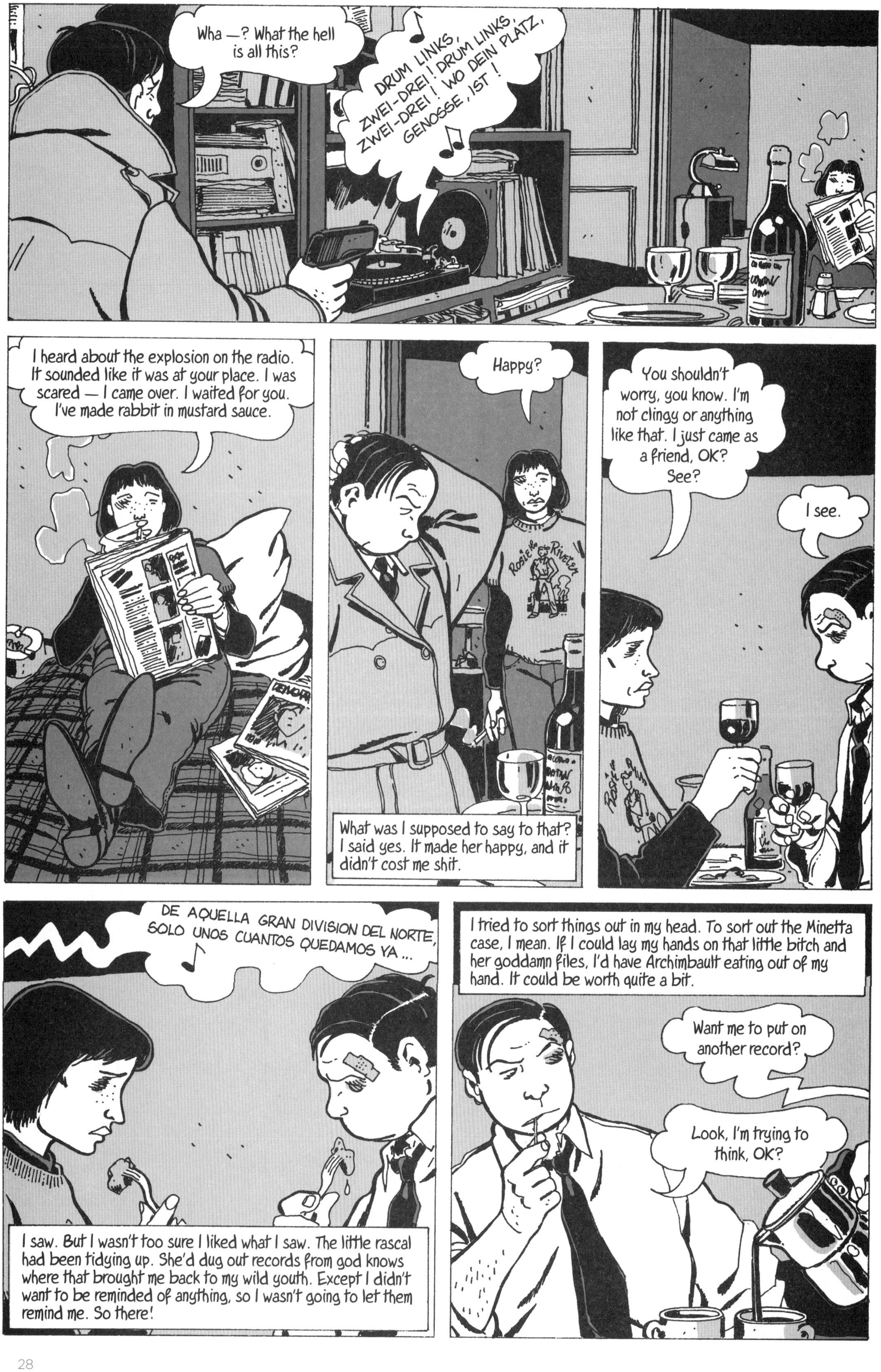
Wha —? What the hell is all this?
DRUM LINKS, ZWEI-DREI! DRUM LINKS, ZWEI-DREI! WO DEIN PLATZ, GENOSSE, IST!
I heard about the explosion on the radio. It sounded like it was at your place. I was scared — I came over. I waited for you. I've made rabbit in mustard sauce.
Happy?
What was I supposed to say to that? I said yes. It made her happy, and it didn't cost me shit.
You shouldn't worry, you know. I'm not clingy or anything like that. I just came as a friend, OK? See?
I see.
DE AQUELLA GRAN DIVISION DEL NORTE, SOLO UNOS CUANTOS QUEDAMOS YA...
I saw. But I wasn't too sure I liked what I saw. The little rascal had been tidying up. She'd dug out records from god knows where that brought me back to my wild youth. Except I didn't want to be reminded of anything, so I wasn't going to let them remind me. So there!
I tried to sort things out in my head. To sort out the Minetta case, I mean. If I could lay my hands on that little bitch and her goddamn files, I'd have Archimbault eating out of my hand. It could be worth quite a bit.
Want me to put on another record?
Look, I'm trying to think, OK?

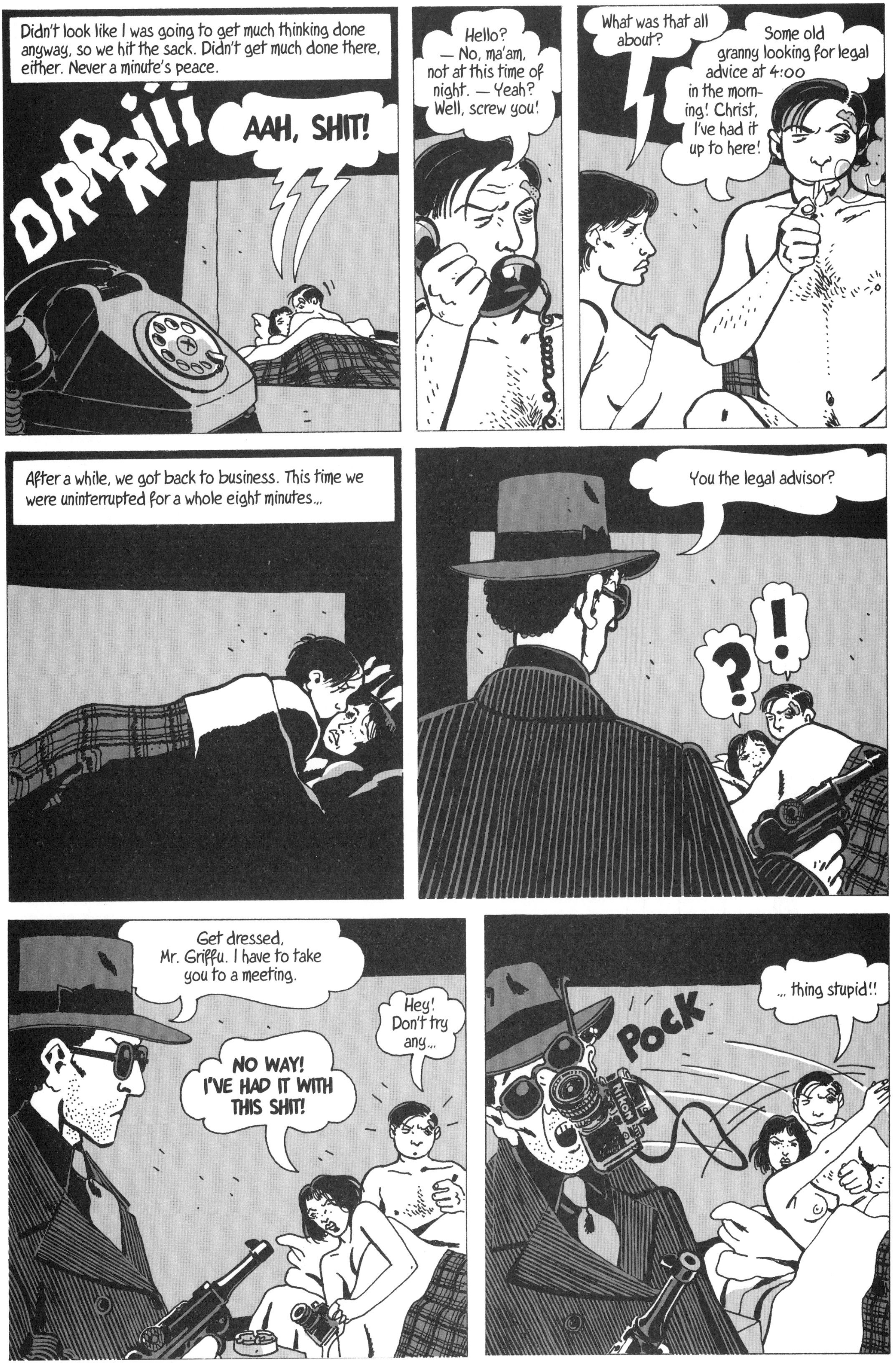
Didn't look like I was going to get much thinking done anyway, so we hit the sack. Didn't get much done there, either. Never a minute's peace.
DRRRiii
AAH, SHIT!
Hello? — No, ma'am, not at this time of night. — Yeah? Well, screw you!
What was that all about?
Some old granny looking for legal advice at 4:00 in the morning! Christ, I've had it up to here!
After a while, we got back to business. This time we were uninterrupted for a whole eight minutes...
You the legal advisor?
?
!
Get dressed, Mr. Griffu. I have to take you to a meeting.
NO WAY! I'VE HAD IT WITH THIS SHIT!
Hey! Don't try any...
POCK
NIKON
... thing stupid!!

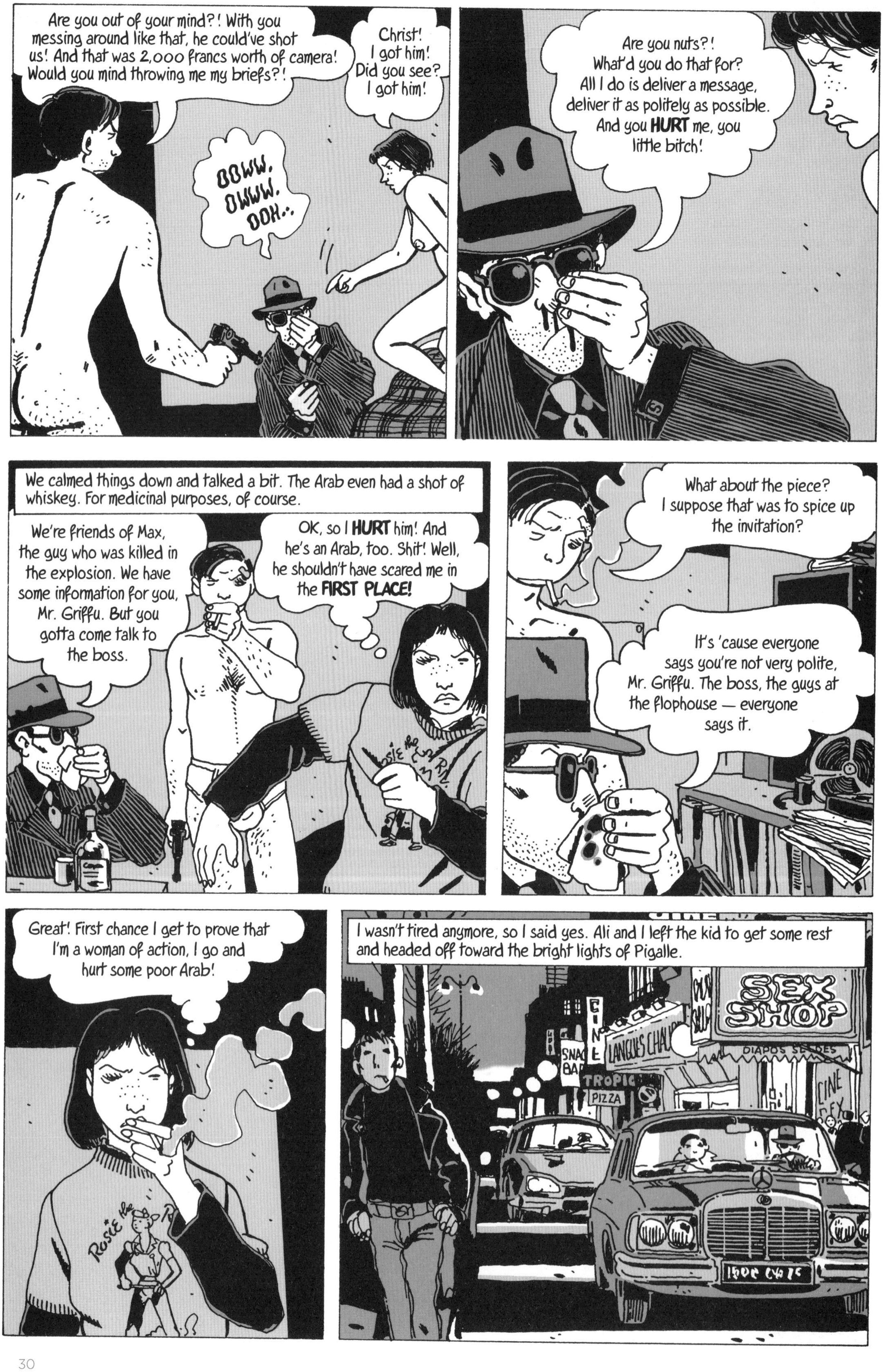

Are you out of your mind?! With you messing around like that, he could've shot us! And that was 2,000 francs worth of camera! Would you mind throwing me my briefs?!
Christ! I got him! Did you see? I got him!
OOWW, OWWW. OOH..
Are you nuts?! What'd you do that for? All I do is deliver a message, deliver it as politely as possible. And you **HURT** me, you little bitch!
We calmed things down and talked a bit. The Arab even had a shot of whiskey. For medicinal purposes, of course.
We're friends of Max, the guy who was killed in the explosion. We have some information for you, Mr. Griffu. But you gotta come talk to the boss.
OK, so I **HURT** him! And he's an Arab, too. Shit! Well, he shouldn't have scared me in the **FIRST PLACE!**
What about the piece? I suppose that was to spice up the invitation?
It's 'cause everyone says you're not very polite, Mr. Griffu. The boss, the guys at the flophouse — everyone says it.
Great! First chance I get to prove that I'm a woman of action, I go and hurt some poor Arab!
I wasn't tired anymore, so I said yes. Ali and I left the kid to get some rest and headed off toward the bright lights of Pigalle.
SEX SHOP
TROPIC
PIZZA

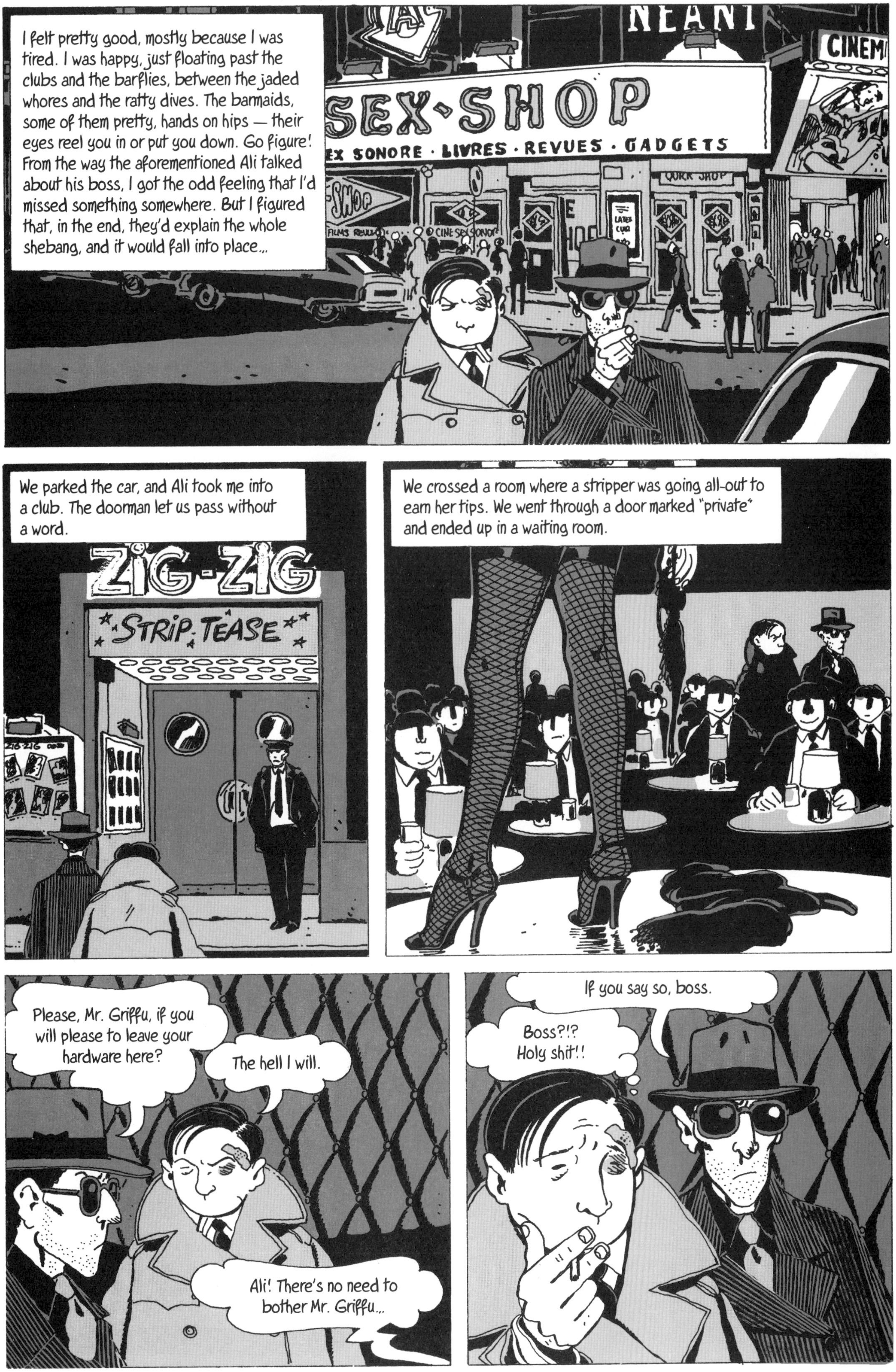
NEANT
CINEM
SEX-SHOP
EX SONORE · LIVRES · REVUES · GADGETS
I felt pretty good, mostly because I was tired. I was happy, just floating past the clubs and the barflies, between the jaded whores and the ratty dives. The barmaids, some of them pretty, hands on hips — their eyes reel you in or put you down. Go figure! From the way the aforementioned Ali talked about his boss, I got the odd feeling that I'd missed something somewhere. But I figured that, in the end, they'd explain the whole shebang, and it would fall into place...
We parked the car, and Ali took me into a club. The doorman let us pass without a word.
ZIG-ZIG
STRIP-TEASE
We crossed a room where a stripper was going all-out to earn her tips. We went through a door marked "private" and ended up in a waiting room.
Please, Mr. Griffu, if you will please to leave your hardware here?
The hell I will.
Ali! There's no need to bother Mr. Griffu...
If you say so, boss.
Boss?!?
Holy shit!!

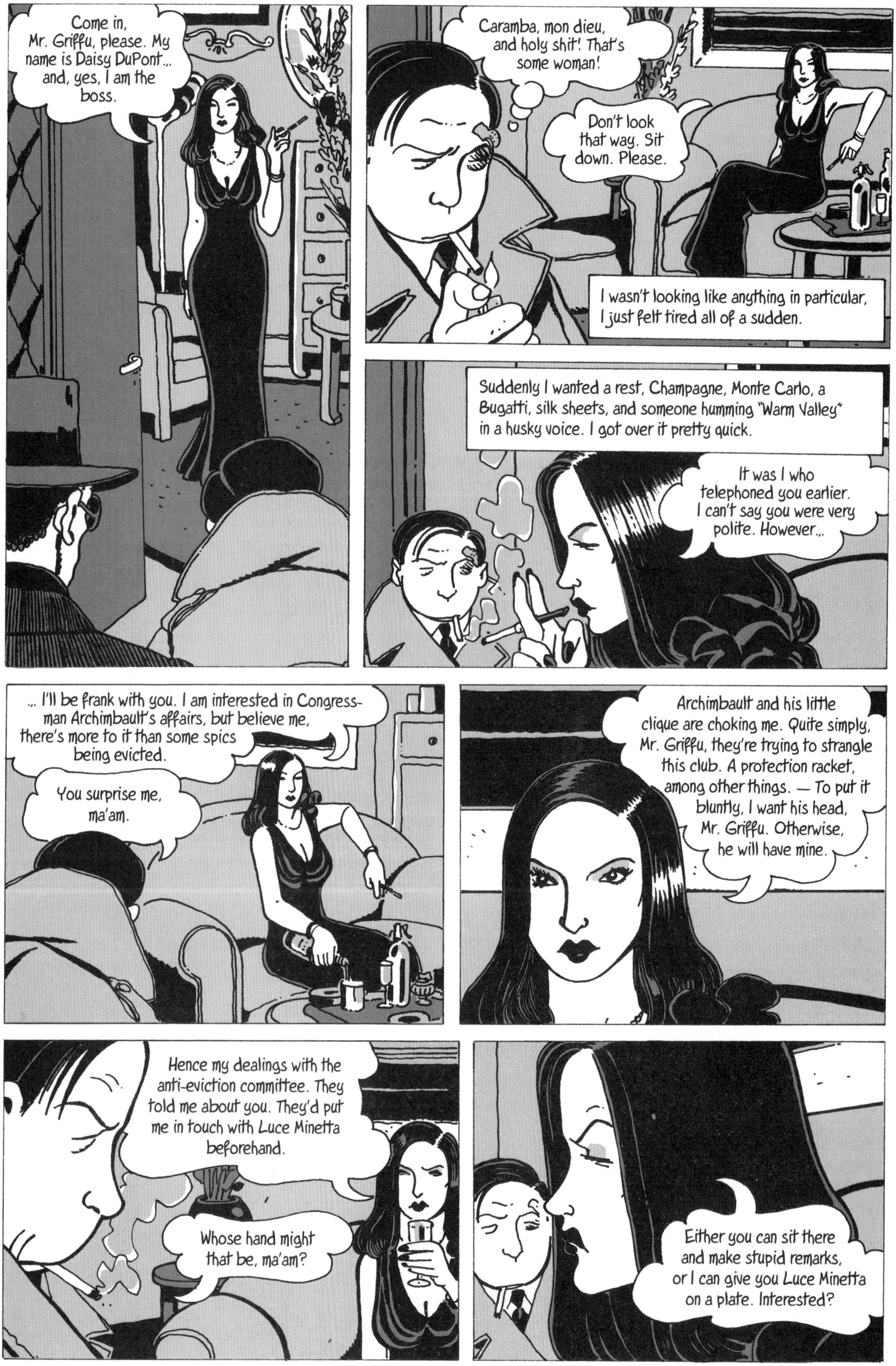
Come in, Mr. Griffu, please. My name is Daisy DuPont… and, yes, I am the boss.
Caramba, mon dieu, and holy shit! That's some woman!
Don't look that way. Sit down. Please.
I wasn't looking like anything in particular, I just felt tired all of a sudden.
Suddenly I wanted a rest, Champagne, Monte Carlo, a Bugatti, silk sheets, and someone humming "Warm Valley" in a husky voice. I got over it pretty quick.
It was I who telephoned you earlier. I can't say you were very polite. However…
… I'll be frank with you. I am interested in Congressman Archimbault's affairs, but believe me, there's more to it than some spics being evicted.
You surprise me, ma'am.
Archimbault and his little clique are choking me. Quite simply, Mr. Griffu, they're trying to strangle this club. A protection racket, among other things. — To put it bluntly, I want his head, Mr. Griffu. Otherwise, he will have mine.
Hence my dealings with the anti-eviction committee. They told me about you. They'd put me in touch with Luce Minetta beforehand.
Whose hand might that be, ma'am?
Either you can sit there and make stupid remarks, or I can give you Luce Minetta on a plate. Interested?

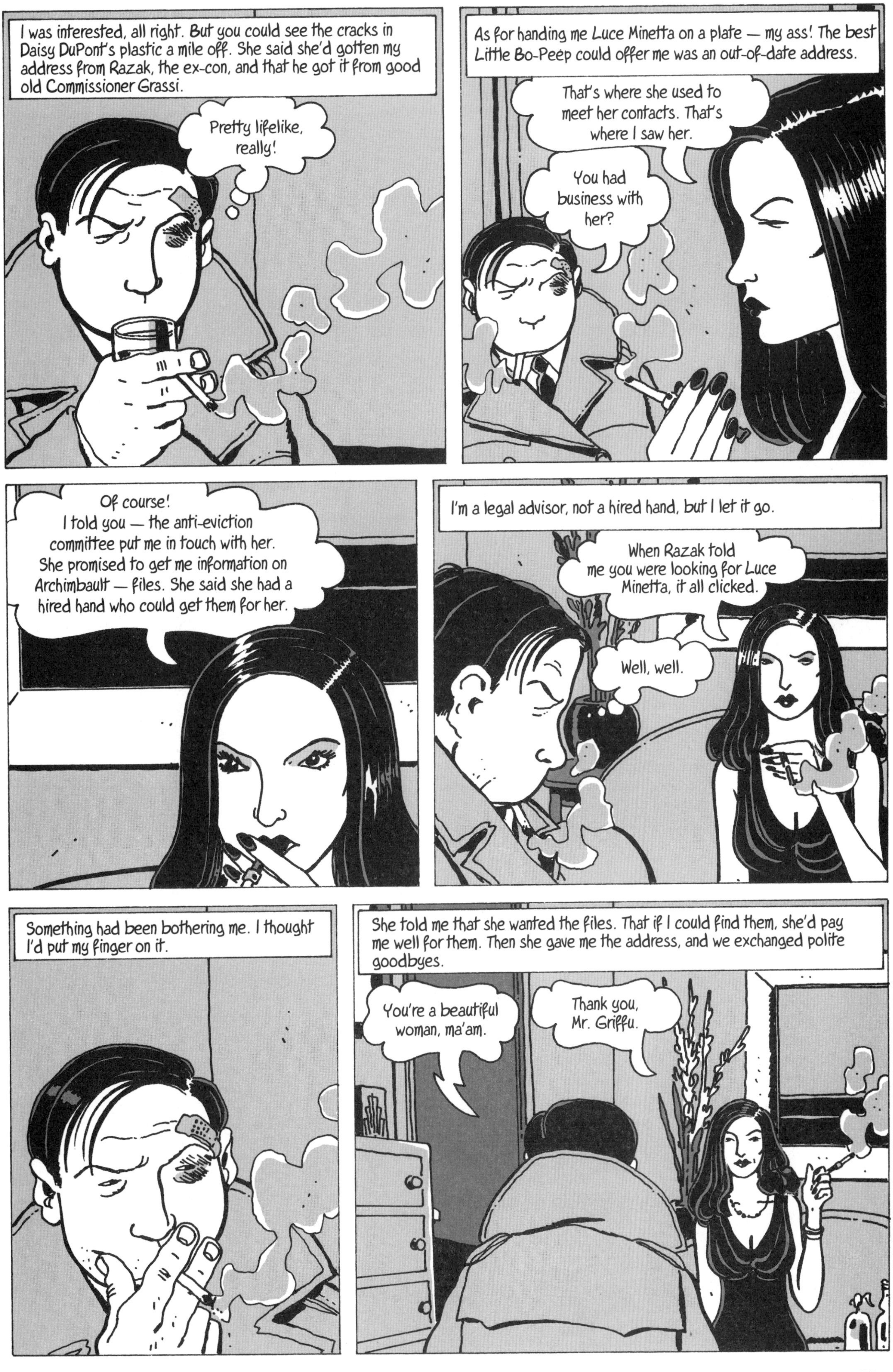
I was interested, all right. But you could see the cracks in Daisy DuPont's plastic a mile off. She said she'd gotten my address from Razak, the ex-con, and that he got it from good old Commissioner Grassi.
Pretty lifelike, really!
As for handing me Luce Minetta on a plate — my ass! The best Little Bo-Peep could offer me was an out-of-date address.
That's where she used to meet her contacts. That's where I saw her.
You had business with her?
Of course! I told you — the anti-eviction committee put me in touch with her. She promised to get me information on Archimbault — files. She said she had a hired hand who could get them for her.
I'm a legal advisor, not a hired hand, but I let it go.
When Razak told me you were looking for Luce Minetta, it all clicked.
Well, well.
Something had been bothering me. I thought I'd put my finger on it.
She told me that she wanted the files. That if I could find them, she'd pay me well for them. Then she gave me the address, and we exchanged polite goodbyes.
You're a beautiful woman, ma'am.
Thank you, Mr. Griffu.

Then I left.

It was nearly 6:00 a.m. I might as well check out the address she'd given me right away. It was way out in the sticks. I took a cab.

I was sweating, and I felt cold. It was Tuesday morning. I hadn't slept since Sunday. I felt tired.

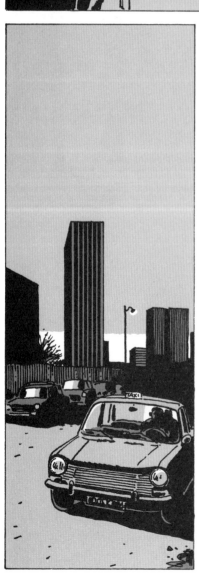

Wait for me.

BANG

?!?

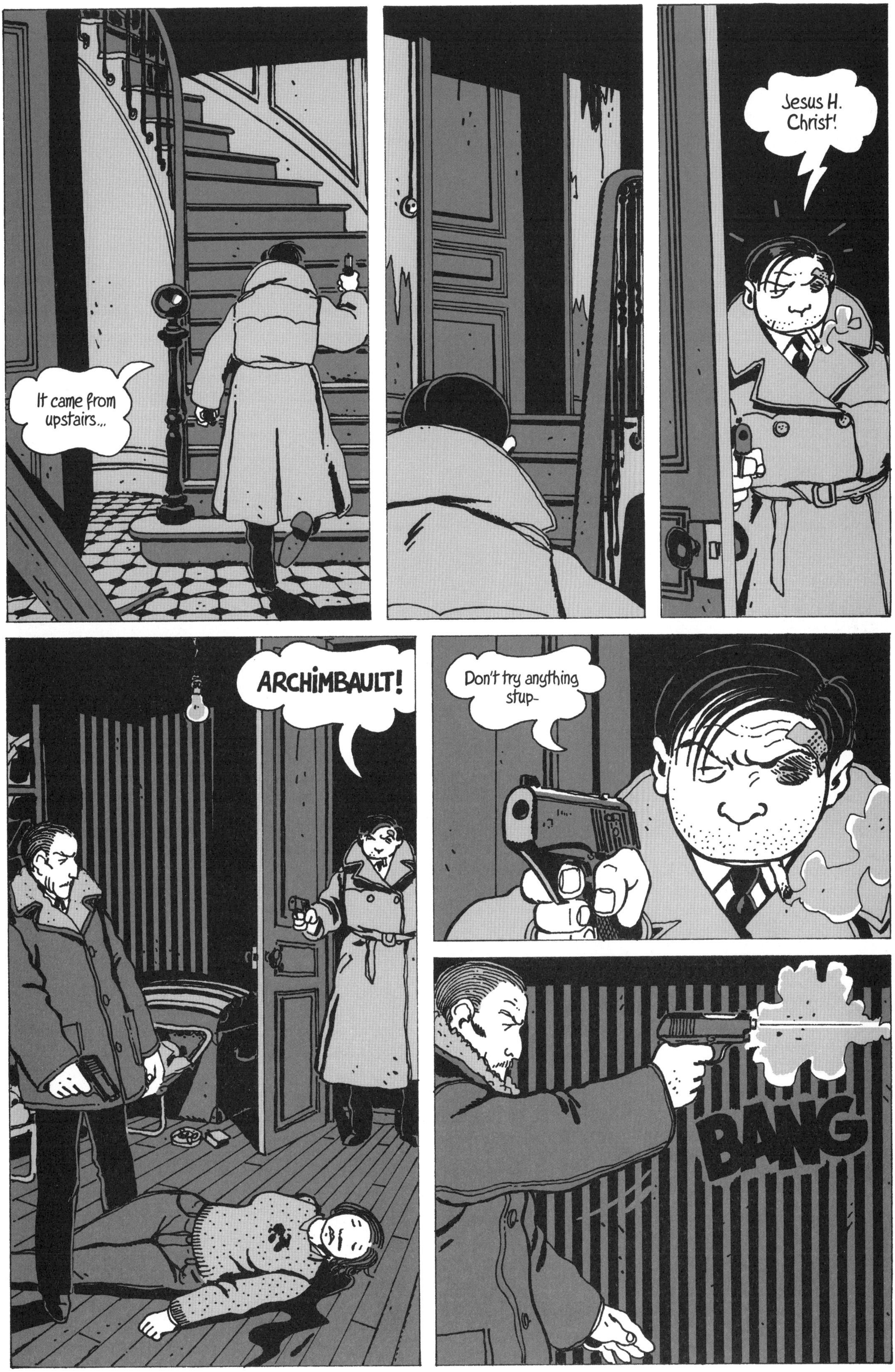

It came from upstairs...
Jesus H. Christ!
ARCHIMBAULT!
Don't try anything stup-
BANG

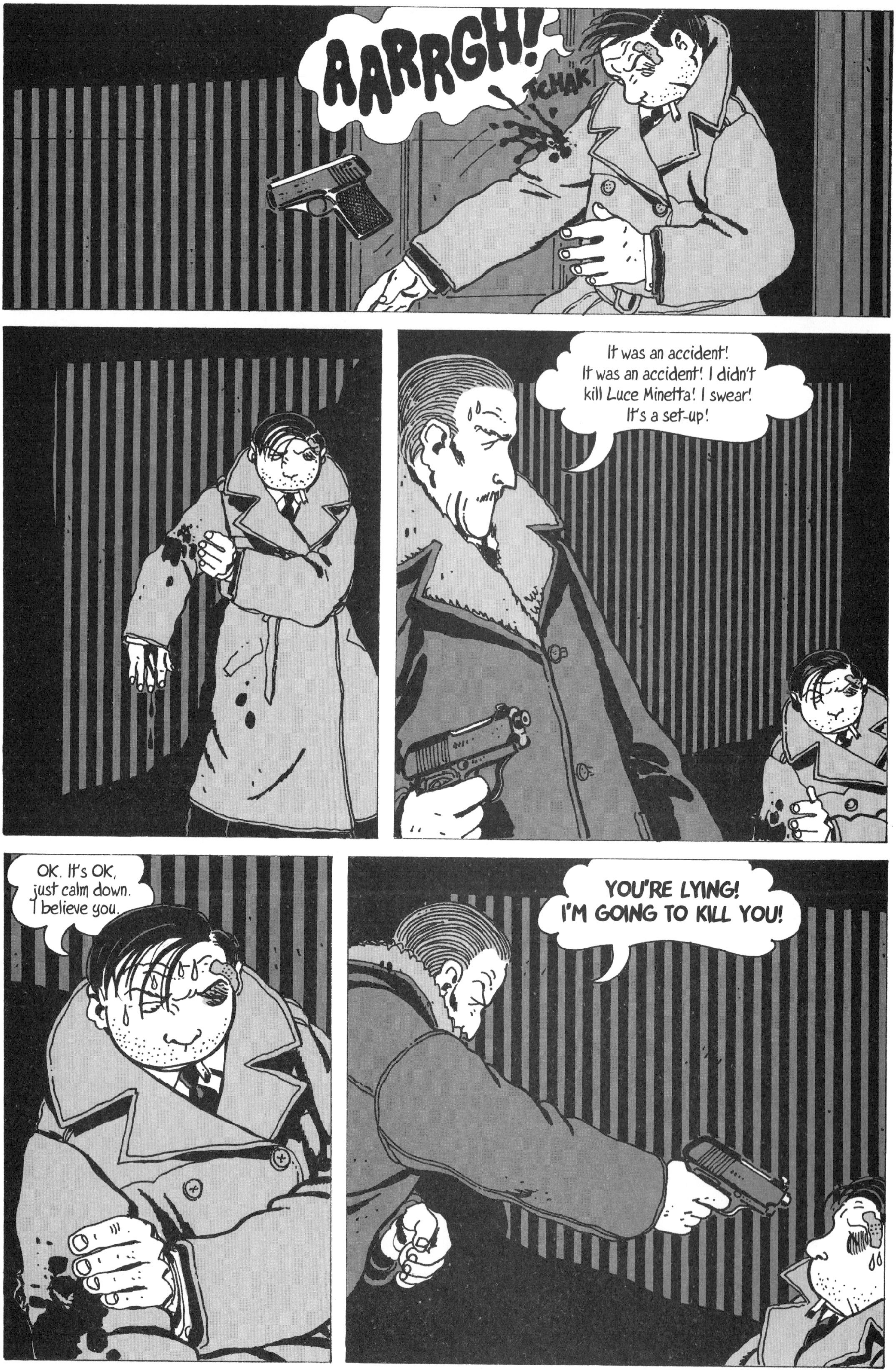
AARRGH!
TCHAK
It was an accident! It was an accident! I didn't kill Luce Minetta! I swear! It's a set-up!
OK. It's OK, just calm down. I believe you.
YOU'RE LYING! I'M GOING TO KILL YOU!

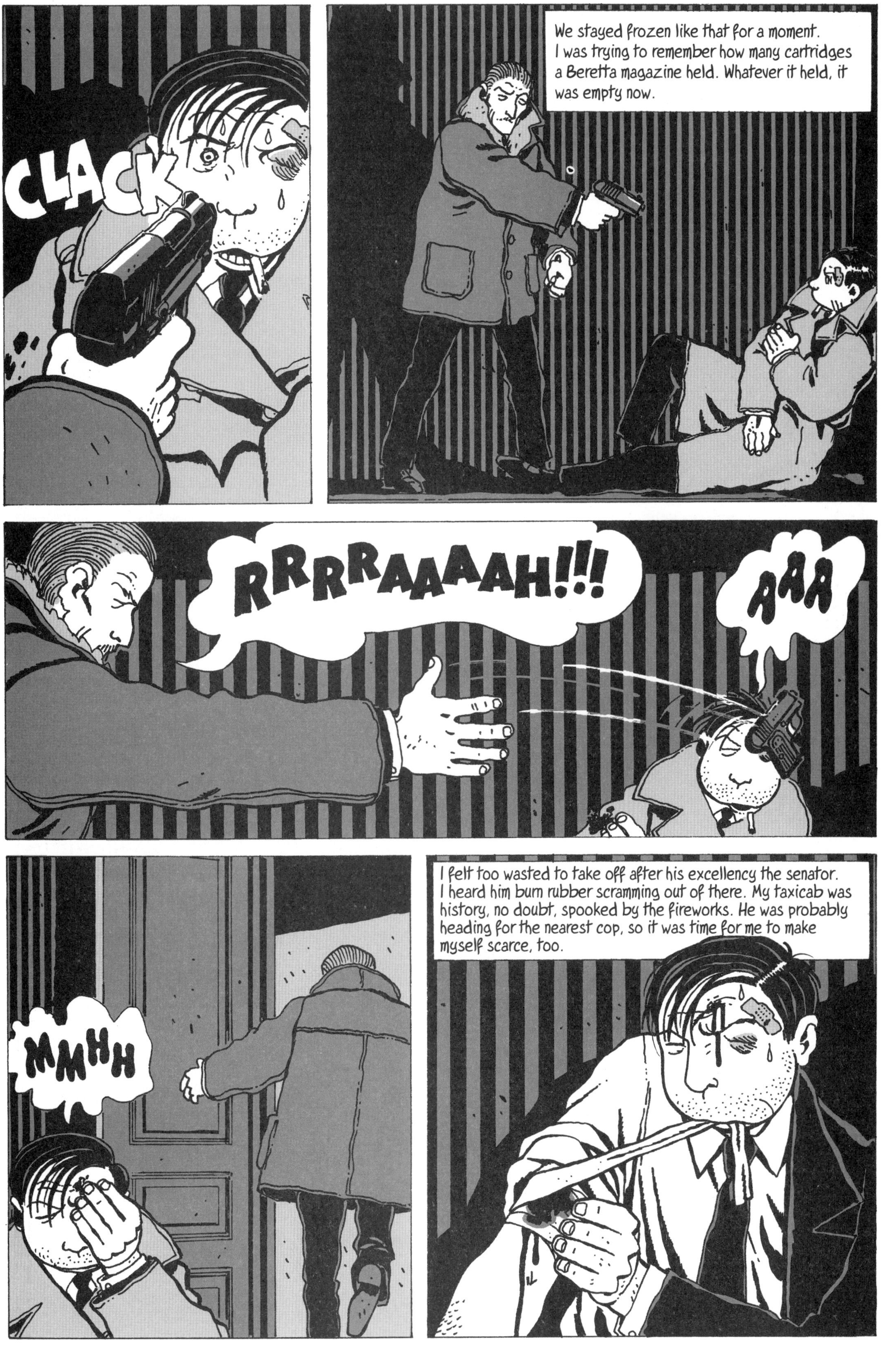
CLACK
We stayed frozen like that for a moment. I was trying to remember how many cartridges a Beretta magazine held. Whatever it held, it was empty now.
RRRRAAAAH!!!
AAA
MMHH
I felt too wasted to take off after his excellency the senator. I heard him burn rubber scramming out of there. My taxicab was history, no doubt, spooked by the fireworks. He was probably heading for the nearest cop, so it was time for me to make myself scarce, too.

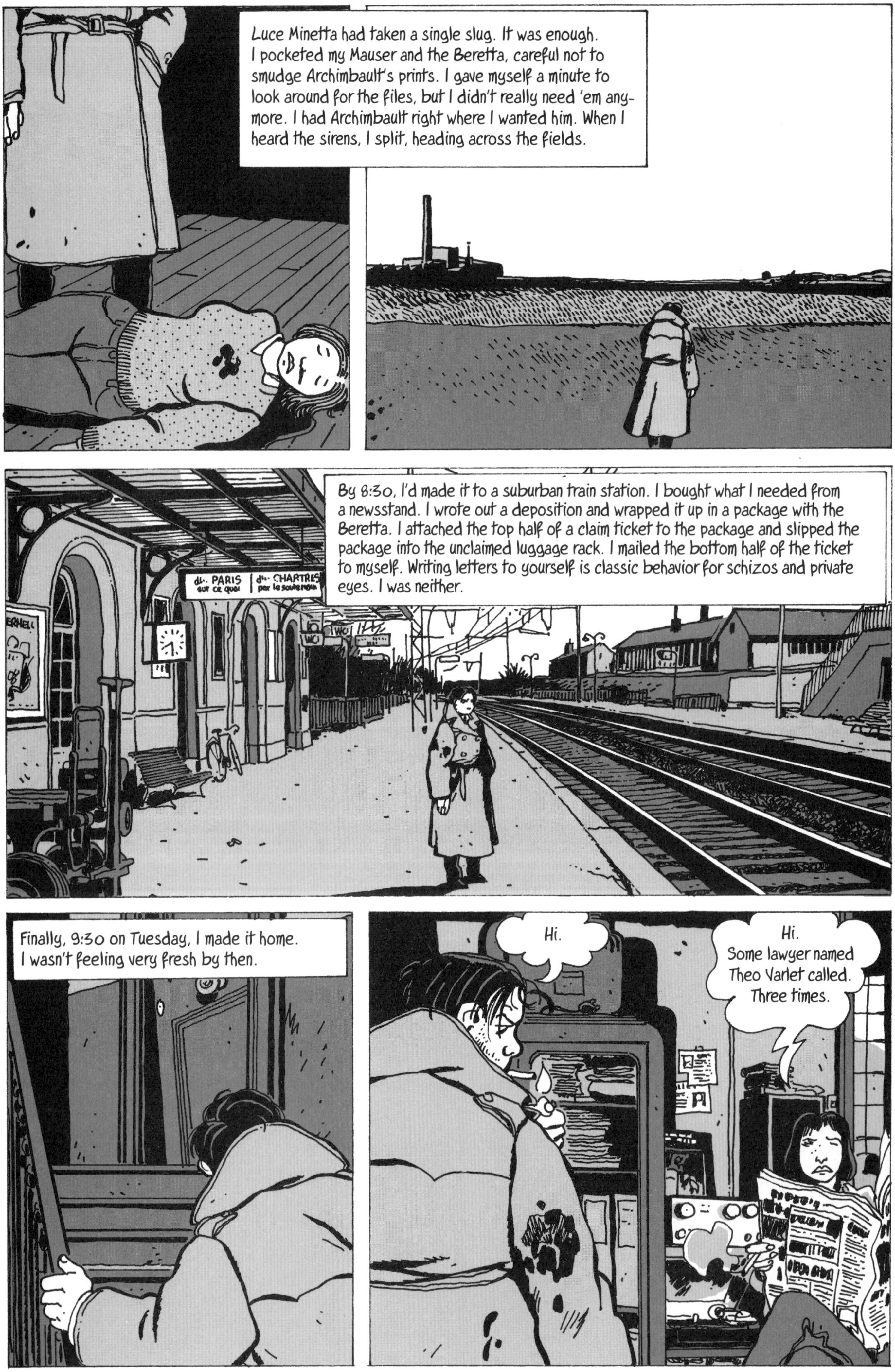
Luce Minetta had taken a single slug. It was enough. I pocketed my Mauser and the Beretta, careful not to smudge Archimbault's prints. I gave myself a minute to look around for the files, but I didn't really need 'em anymore. I had Archimbault right where I wanted him. When I heard the sirens, I split, heading across the fields.
By 8:30, I'd made it to a suburban train station. I bought what I needed from a newsstand. I wrote out a deposition and wrapped it up in a package with the Beretta. I attached the top half of a claim ticket to the package and slipped the package into the unclaimed luggage rack. I mailed the bottom half of the ticket to myself. Writing letters to yourself is classic behavior for schizos and private eyes. I was neither.
PARIS
CHARTRES
WC
Finally, 9:30 on Tuesday, I made it home. I wasn't feeling very fresh by then.
Hi.
Hi. Some lawyer named Theo Varlet called. Three times.

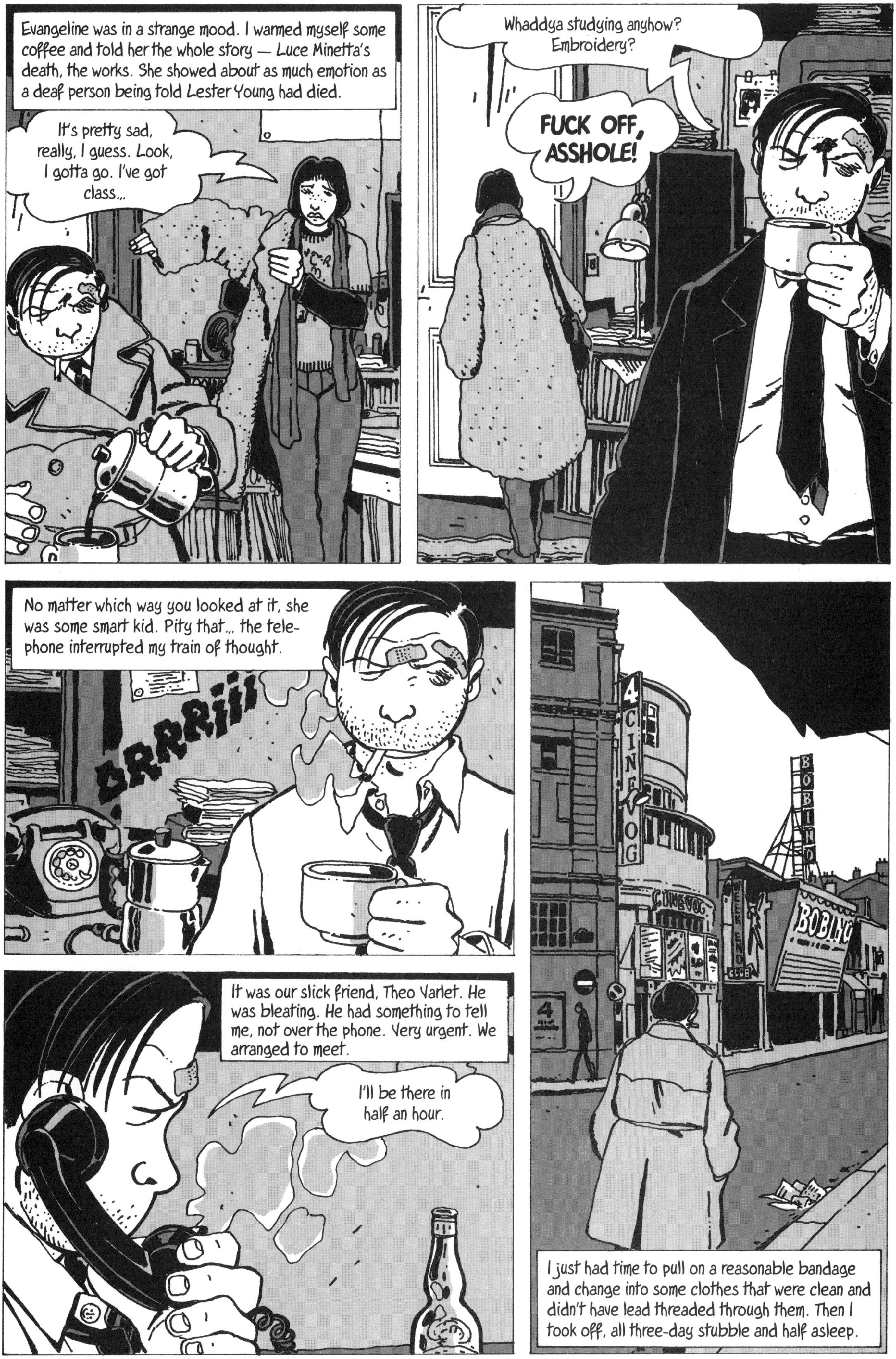
Evangeline was in a strange mood. I warmed myself some coffee and told her the whole story — Luce Minetta's death, the works. She showed about as much emotion as a deaf person being told Lester Young had died.
It's pretty sad, really, I guess. Look, I gotta go. I've got class...
Whaddya studying anyhow? Embroidery?
FUCK OFF, ASSHOLE!
No matter which way you looked at it, she was some smart kid. Pity that... the telephone interrupted my train of thought.
DRRRIII
It was our slick friend, Theo Varlet. He was bleating. He had something to tell me, not over the phone. Very urgent. We arranged to meet.
I'll be there in half an hour.
CINE VOG
BOBINO
CINEVOG
WEEK END CLUB
I just had time to pull on a reasonable bandage and change into some clothes that were clean and didn't have lead threaded through them. Then I took off, all three-day stubble and half asleep.

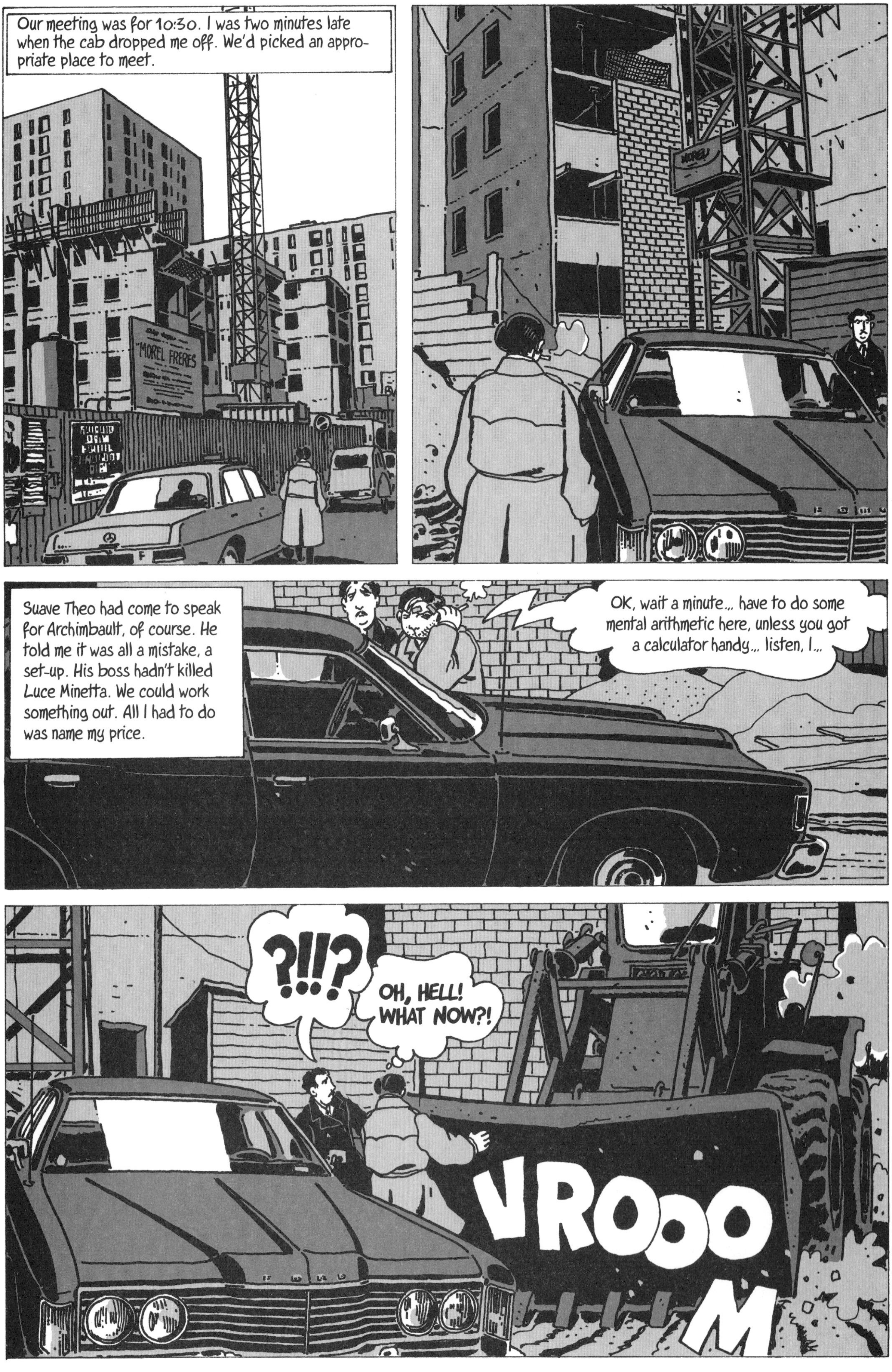
Our meeting was for 10:30. I was two minutes late when the cab dropped me off. We'd picked an appropriate place to meet.
MOREL FRERES
Suave Theo had come to speak for Archimbault, of course. He told me it was all a mistake, a set-up. His boss hadn't killed Luce Minetta. We could work something out. All I had to do was name my price.
OK, wait a minute... have to do some mental arithmetic here, unless you got a calculator handy... listen, I...
?!!?
OH, HELL! WHAT NOW?!
VROOOM

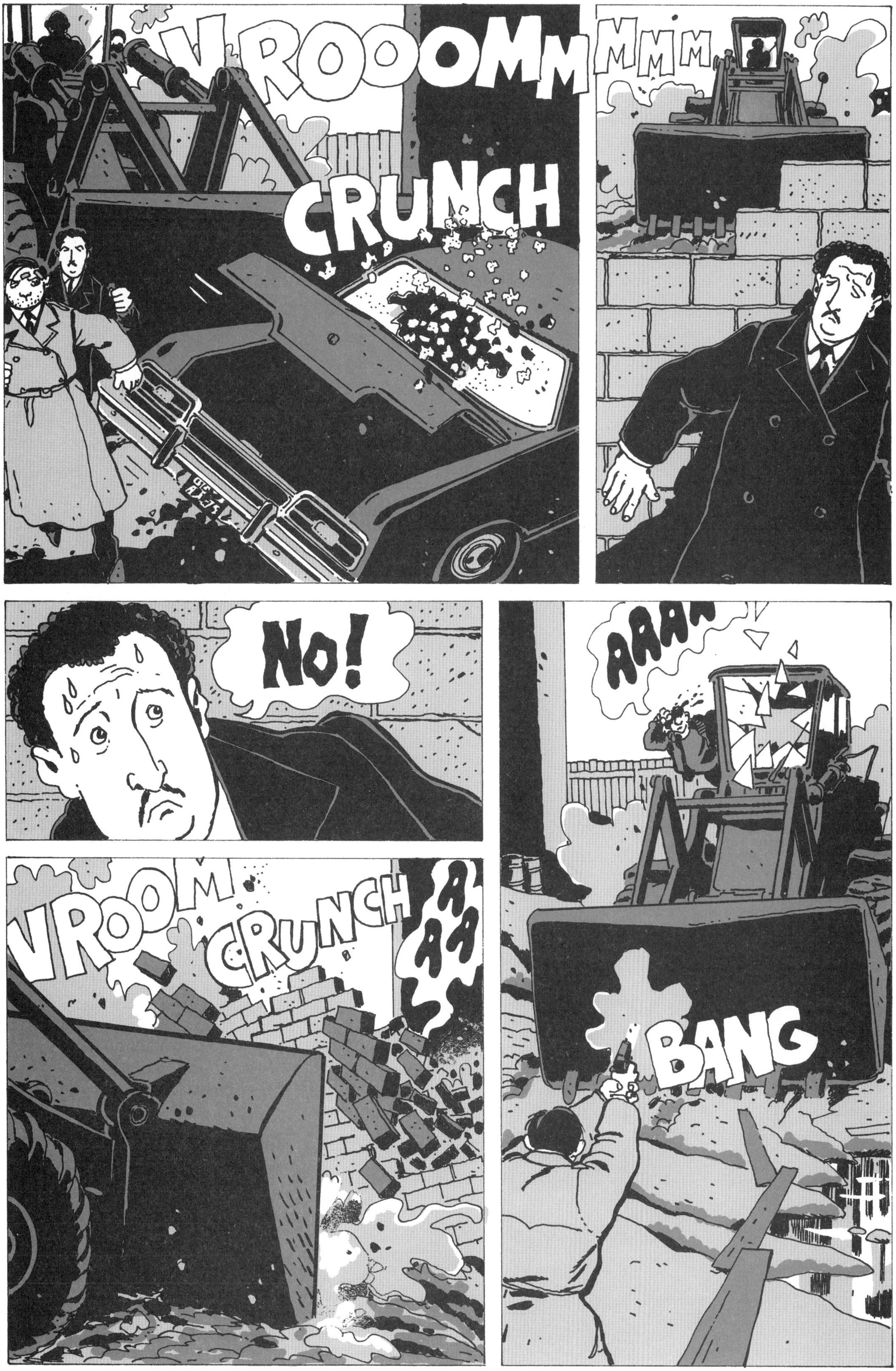
VROOOMMMMM
CRUNCH
NO!
AAAA
VROOM
CRUNCH
AAAA
BANG

I checked out the stiff. It was one of the heavies I'd had a chat with at the Morel Brothers' place that first night. My slug had destroyed half the frontal lobe and pretty much all the back brain, so he wasn't really in a position to answer the couple of questions I'd prepared. Then people started coming out of nowhere to see what the noise was. I got out of there, fast. I had a call to make to a member of congress...

It can be a real hassle getting in touch with your congressman sometimes. But I can be a real stubborn guy.

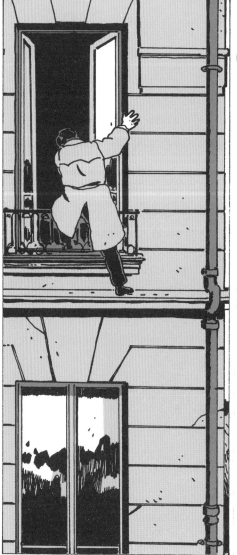

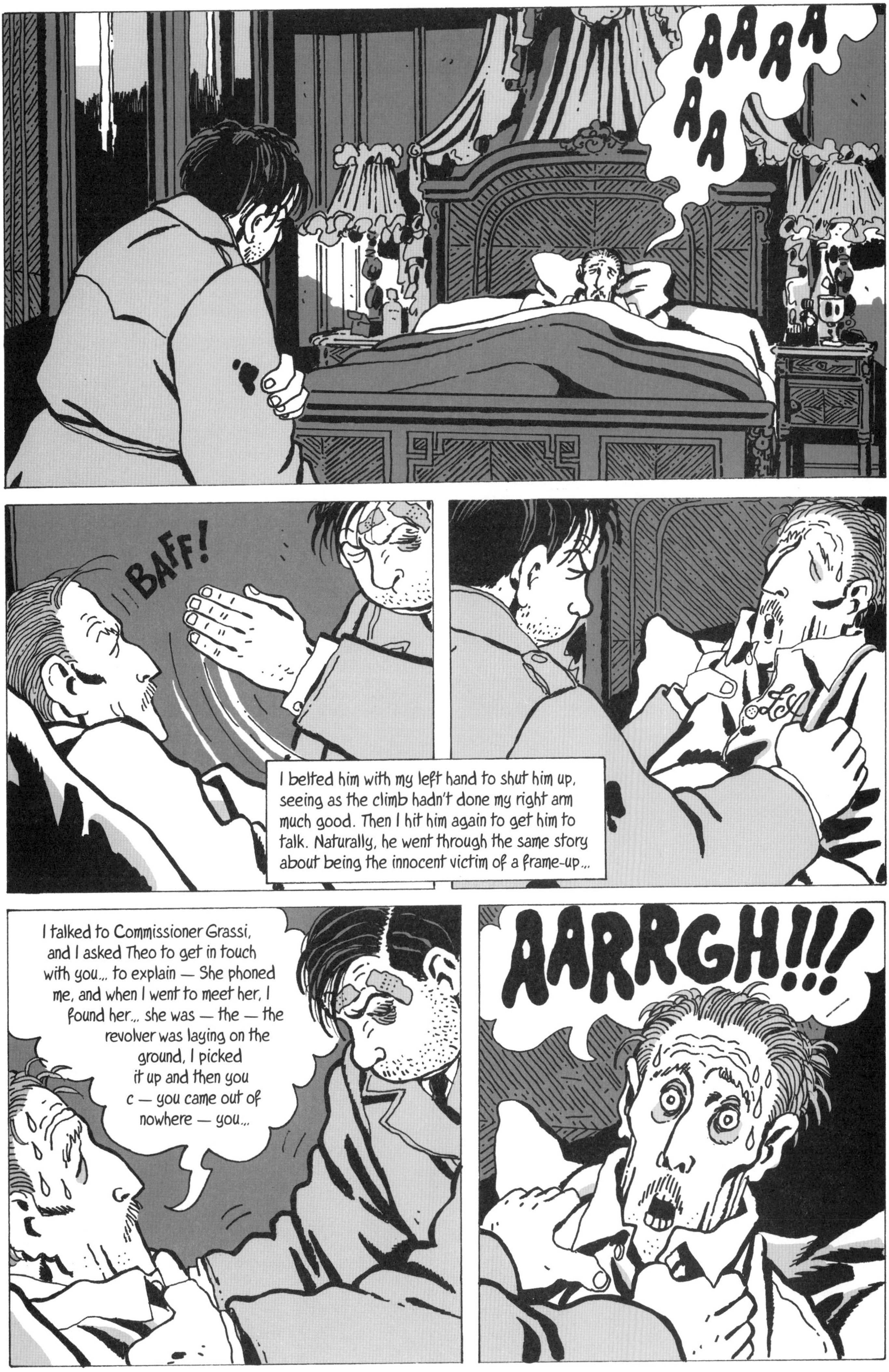
AAAAAA
BAFF!
I belted him with my left hand to shut him up, seeing as the climb hadn't done my right arm much good. Then I hit him again to get him to talk. Naturally, he went through the same story about being the innocent victim of a frame-up...
I talked to Commissioner Grassi, and I asked Theo to get in touch with you... to explain — She phoned me, and when I went to meet her, I found her... she was — the — the revolver was laying on the ground, I picked it up and then you c — you came out of nowhere — you...
AARRGH!!!

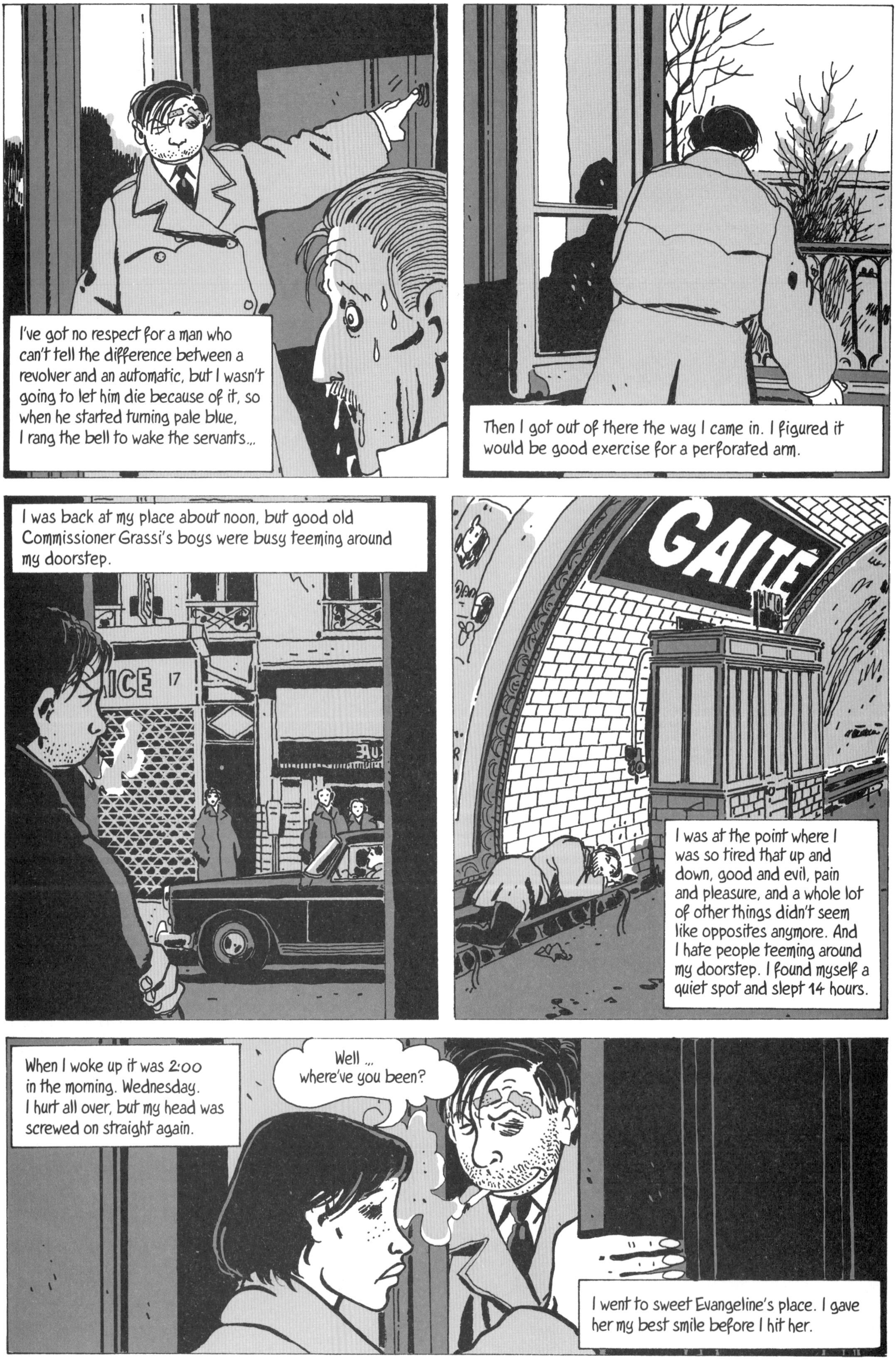
I've got no respect for a man who can't tell the difference between a revolver and an automatic, but I wasn't going to let him die because of it, so when he started turning pale blue, I rang the bell to wake the servants...
Then I got out of there the way I came in. I figured it would be good exercise for a perforated arm.
I was back at my place about noon, but good old Commissioner Grassi's boys were busy teeming around my doorstep.
GAITÉ
I was at the point where I was so tired that up and down, good and evil, pain and pleasure, and a whole lot of other things didn't seem like opposites anymore. And I hate people teeming around my doorstep. I found myself a quiet spot and slept 14 hours.
When I woke up it was 2:00 in the morning. Wednesday. I hurt all over, but my head was screwed on straight again.
Well ... where've you been?
I went to sweet Evangeline's place. I gave her my best smile before I hit her.

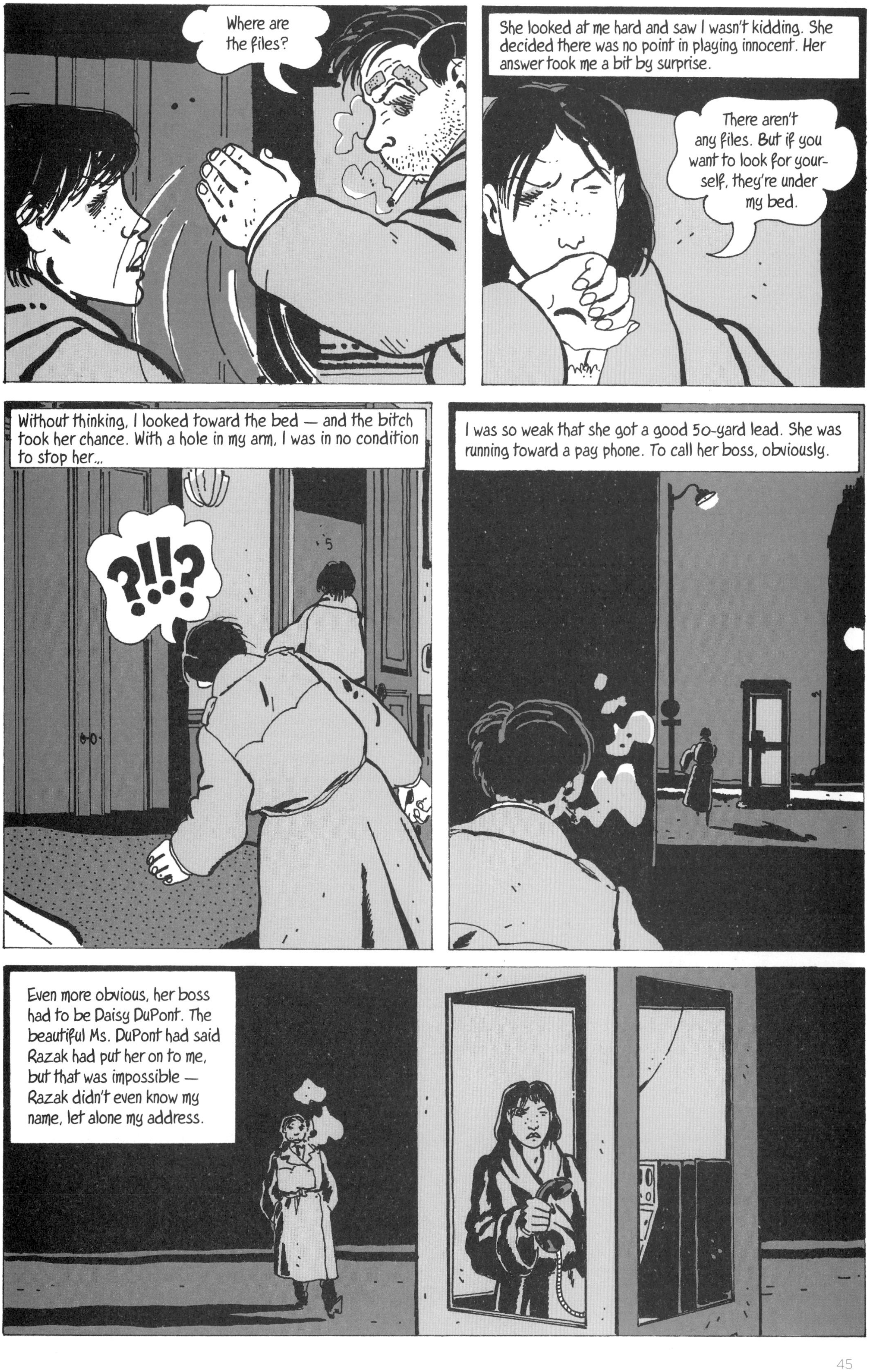
Where are the files?
She looked at me hard and saw I wasn't kidding. She decided there was no point in playing innocent. Her answer took me a bit by surprise.
There aren't any files. But if you want to look for yourself, they're under my bed.
Without thinking, I looked toward the bed — and the bitch took her chance. With a hole in my arm, I was in no condition to stop her...
?!!?
5
I was so weak that she got a good 50-yard lead. She was running toward a pay phone. To call her boss, obviously.
Even more obvious, her boss had to be Daisy DuPont. The beautiful Ms. DuPont had said Razak had put her on to me, but that was impossible — Razak didn't even know my name, let alone my address.

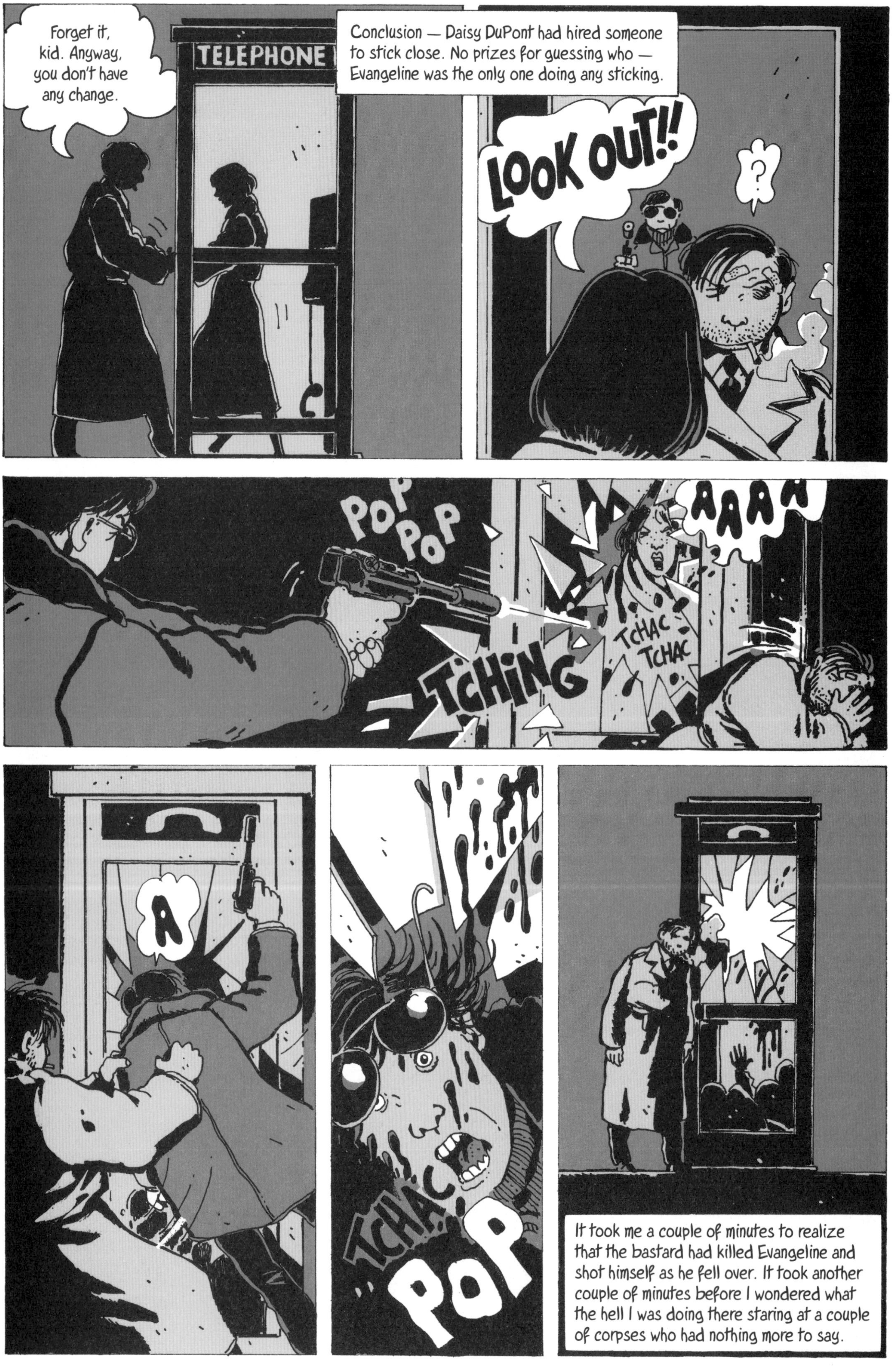
Forget it, kid. Anyway, you don't have any change.
TELEPHONE
Conclusion — Daisy DuPont had hired someone to stick close. No prizes for guessing who — Evangeline was the only one doing any sticking.
LOOK OUT!!
?
POP POP POP
AAAA
TCHAC TCHAC
TCHING
A
TCHAC
POP
It took me a couple of minutes to realize that the bastard had killed Evangeline and shot himself as he fell over. It took another couple of minutes before I wondered what the hell I was doing there staring at a couple of corpses who had nothing more to say.

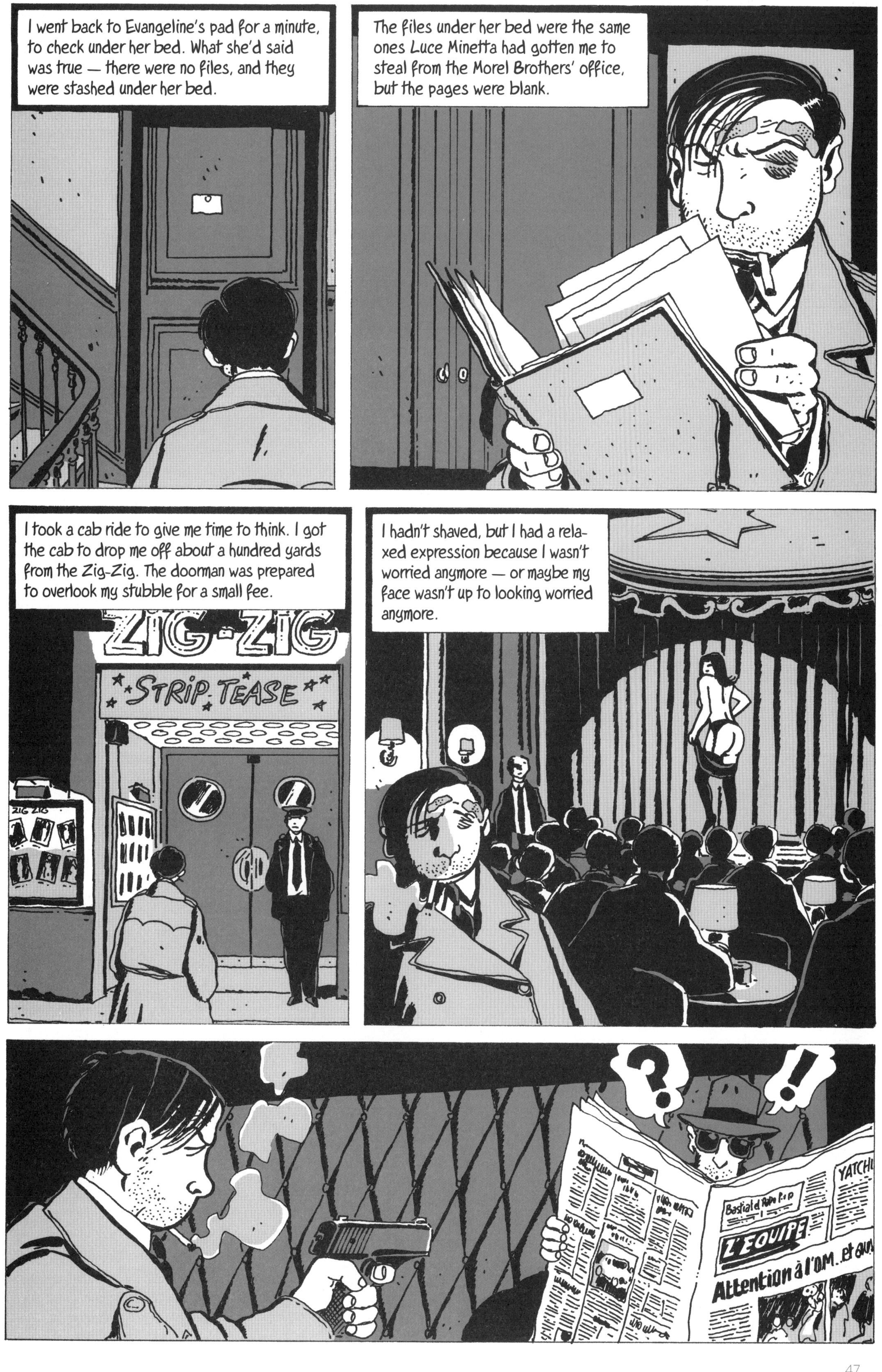
I went back to Evangeline's pad for a minute, to check under her bed. What she'd said was true — there were no files, and they were stashed under her bed.
The files under her bed were the same ones Luce Minetta had gotten me to steal from the Morel Brothers' office, but the pages were blank.
I took a cab ride to give me time to think. I got the cab to drop me off about a hundred yards from the Zig-Zig. The doorman was prepared to overlook my stubble for a small fee.
ZIG-ZIG
STRIP-TEASE
I hadn't shaved, but I had a relaxed expression because I wasn't worried anymore — or maybe my face wasn't up to looking worried anymore.
?
!
L'EQUIPE
YATCHI

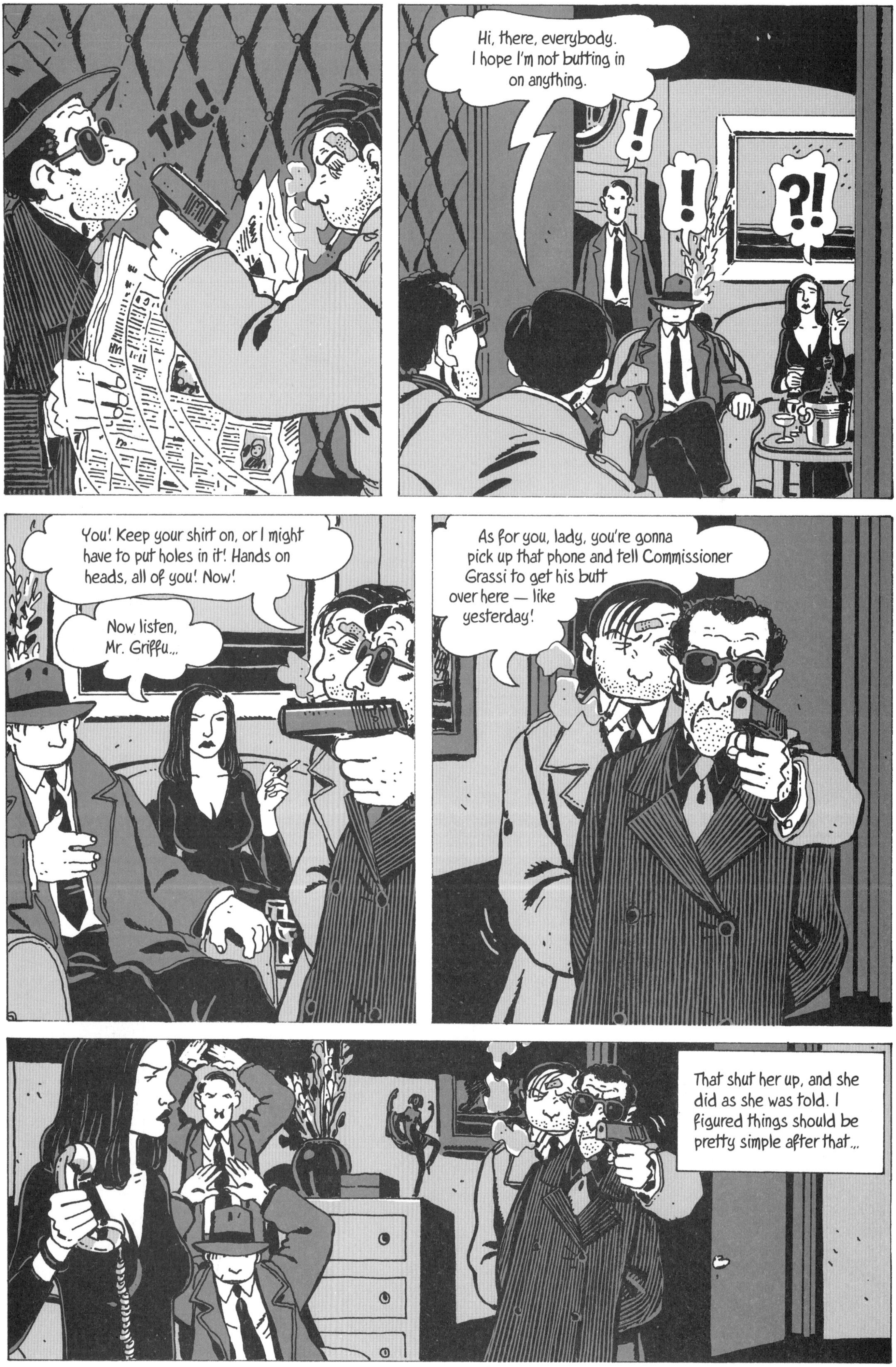
TAC!
Hi, there, everybody. I hope I'm not butting in on anything.
!
!
?!
You! Keep your shirt on, or I might have to put holes in it! Hands on heads, all of you! Now!
Now listen, Mr. Griffu...
As for you, lady, you're gonna pick up that phone and tell Commissioner Grassi to get his butt over here — like yesterday!
That shut her up, and she did as she was told. I figured things should be pretty simple after that...

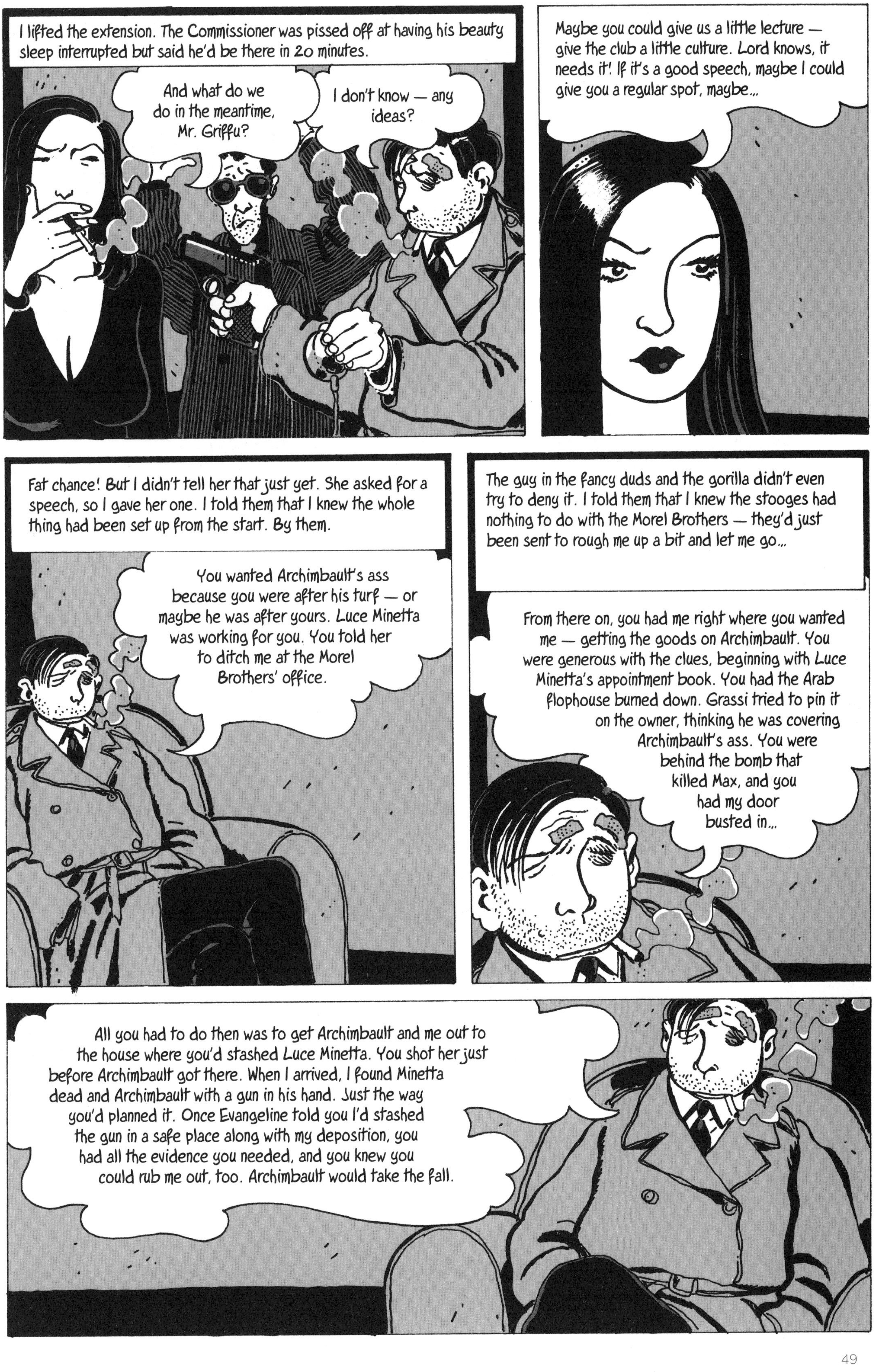
I lifted the extension. The Commissioner was pissed off at having his beauty sleep interrupted but said he'd be there in 20 minutes.
And what do we do in the meantime, Mr. Griffu?
I don't know — any ideas?
Maybe you could give us a little lecture — give the club a little culture. Lord knows, it needs it! If it's a good speech, maybe I could give you a regular spot, maybe...
Fat chance! But I didn't tell her that just yet. She asked for a speech, so I gave her one. I told them that I knew the whole thing had been set up from the start. By them.
You wanted Archimbault's ass because you were after his turf — or maybe he was after yours. Luce Minetta was working for you. You told her to ditch me at the Morel Brothers' office.
The guy in the fancy duds and the gorilla didn't even try to deny it. I told them that I knew the stooges had nothing to do with the Morel Brothers — they'd just been sent to rough me up a bit and let me go...
From there on, you had me right where you wanted me — getting the goods on Archimbault. You were generous with the clues, beginning with Luce Minetta's appointment book. You had the Arab flophouse burned down. Grassi tried to pin it on the owner, thinking he was covering Archimbault's ass. You were behind the bomb that killed Max, and you had my door busted in...
All you had to do then was to get Archimbault and me out to the house where you'd stashed Luce Minetta. You shot her just before Archimbault got there. When I arrived, I found Minetta dead and Archimbault with a gun in his hand. Just the way you'd planned it. Once Evangeline told you I'd stashed the gun in a safe place along with my deposition, you had all the evidence you needed, and you knew you could rub me out, too. Archimbault would take the fall.

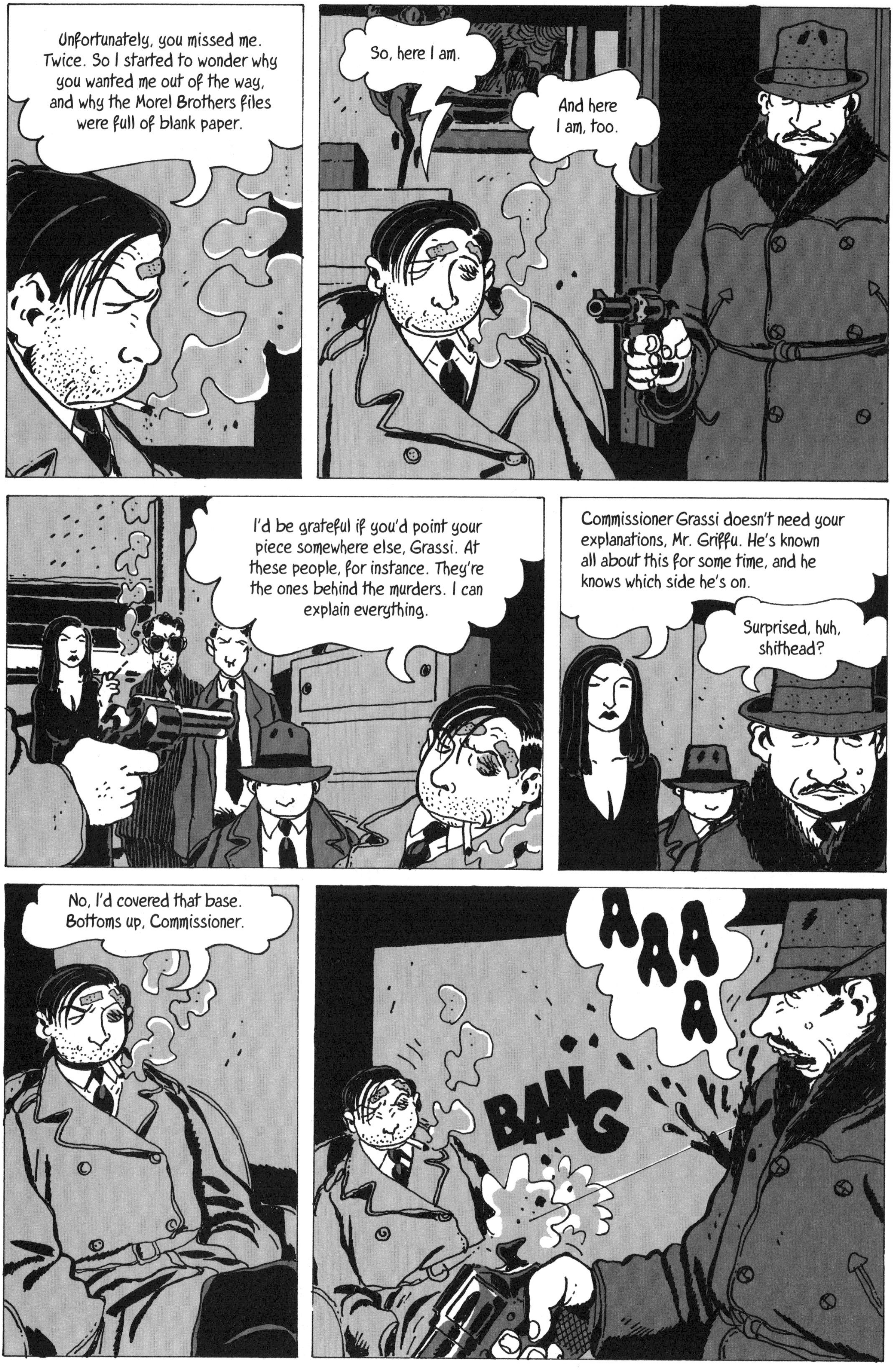

Unfortunately, you missed me. Twice. So I started to wonder why you wanted me out of the way, and why the Morel Brothers files were full of blank paper.
So, here I am.
And here I am, too.
I'd be grateful if you'd point your piece somewhere else, Grassi. At these people, for instance. They're the ones behind the murders. I can explain everything.
Commissioner Grassi doesn't need your explanations, Mr. Griffu. He's known all about this for some time, and he knows which side he's on.
Surprised, huh, shithead?
No, I'd covered that base. Bottoms up, Commissioner.
AAAA
BANG

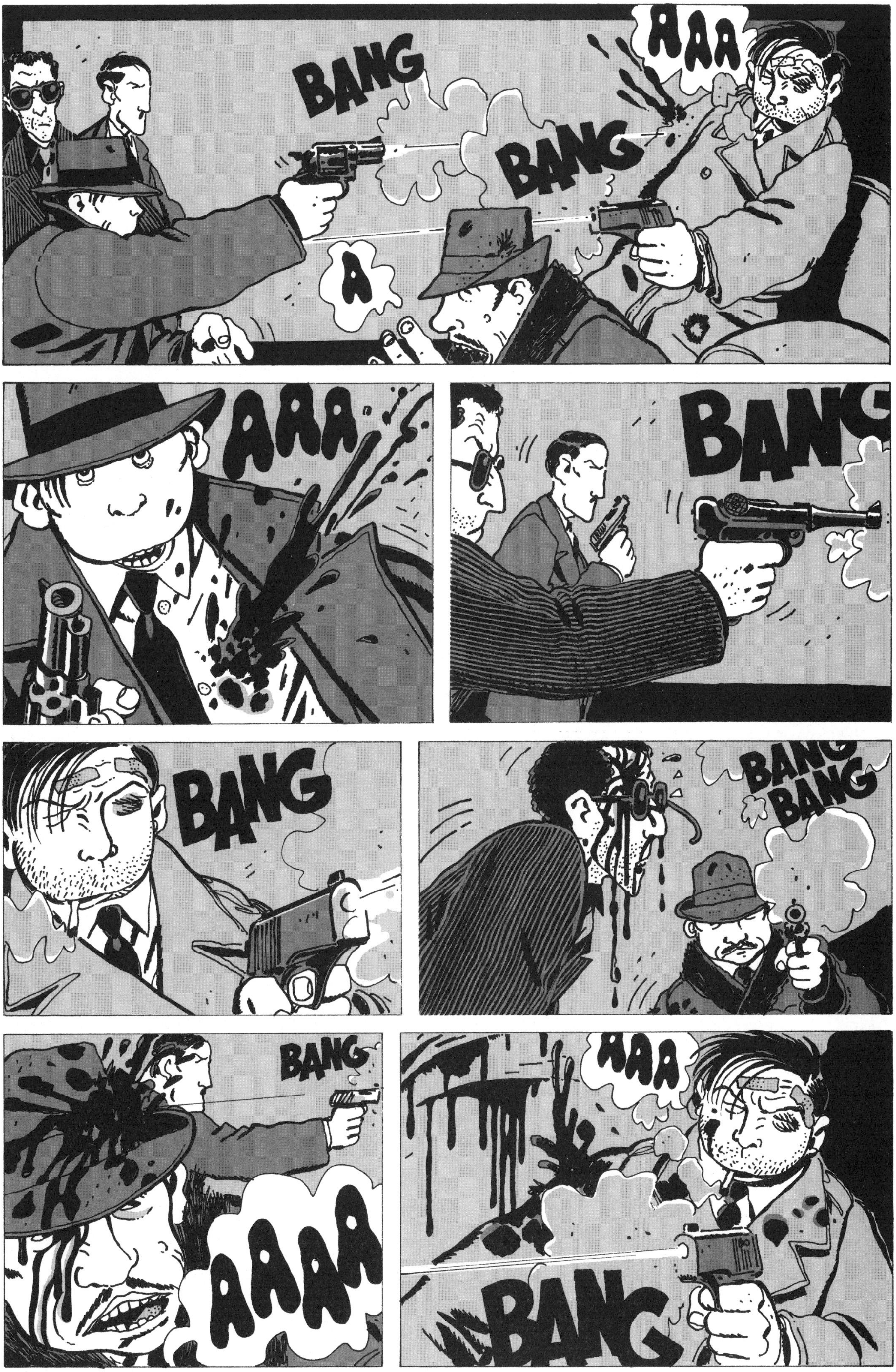
BANG
AAA
BANG
A
AAA
BANG
BANG
BANG
BANG
BANG
AAAA
AAA
BANG

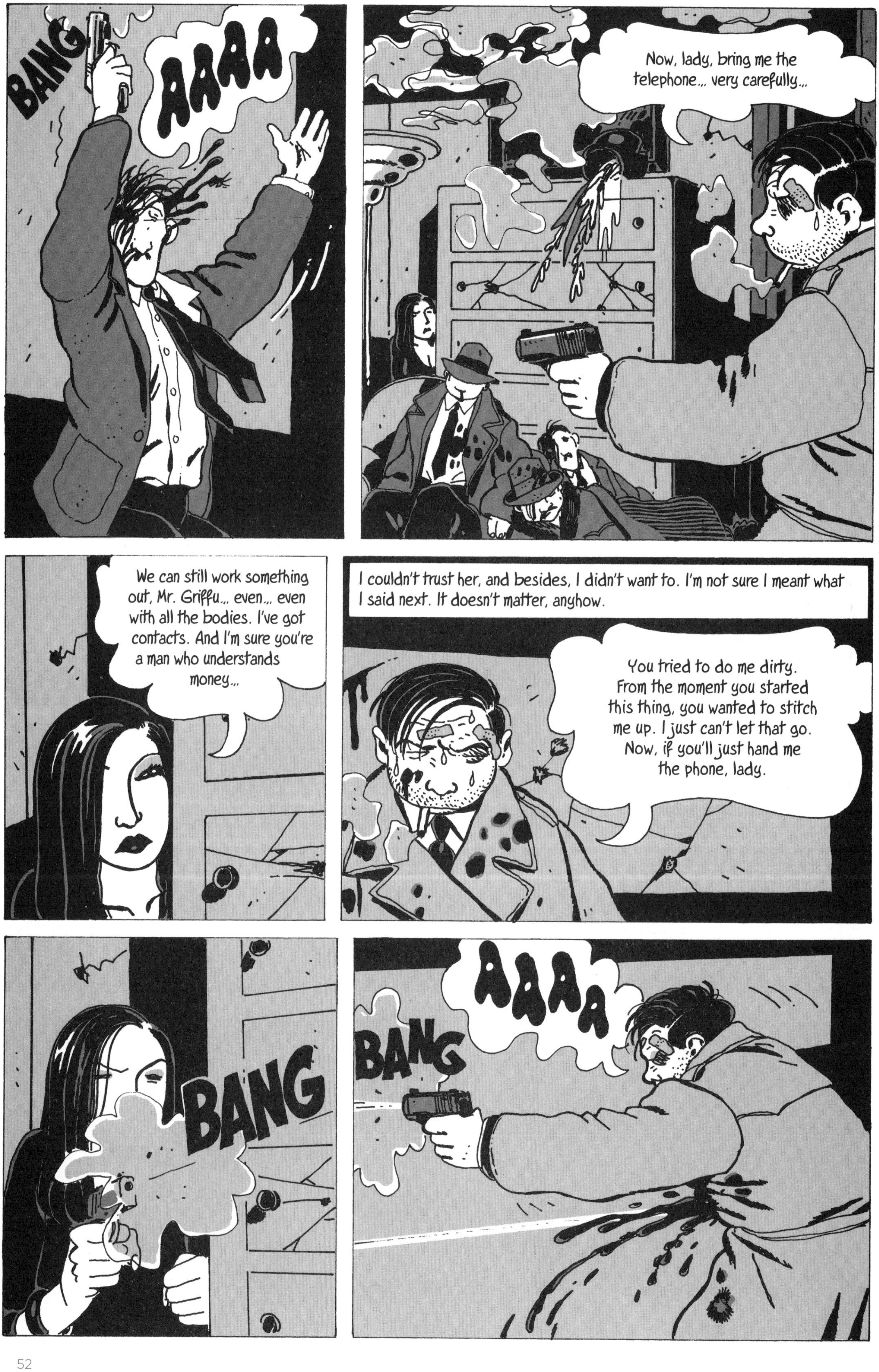
BANG
AAAA
Now, lady, bring me the telephone... very carefully...
We can still work something out, Mr. Griffu... even... even with all the bodies. I've got contacts. And I'm sure you're a man who understands money...
I couldn't trust her, and besides, I didn't want to. I'm not sure I meant what I said next. It doesn't matter, anyhow.
You tried to do me dirty. From the moment you started this thing, you wanted to stitch me up. I just can't let that go. Now, if you'll just hand me the phone, lady.
BANG
AAAA
BANG

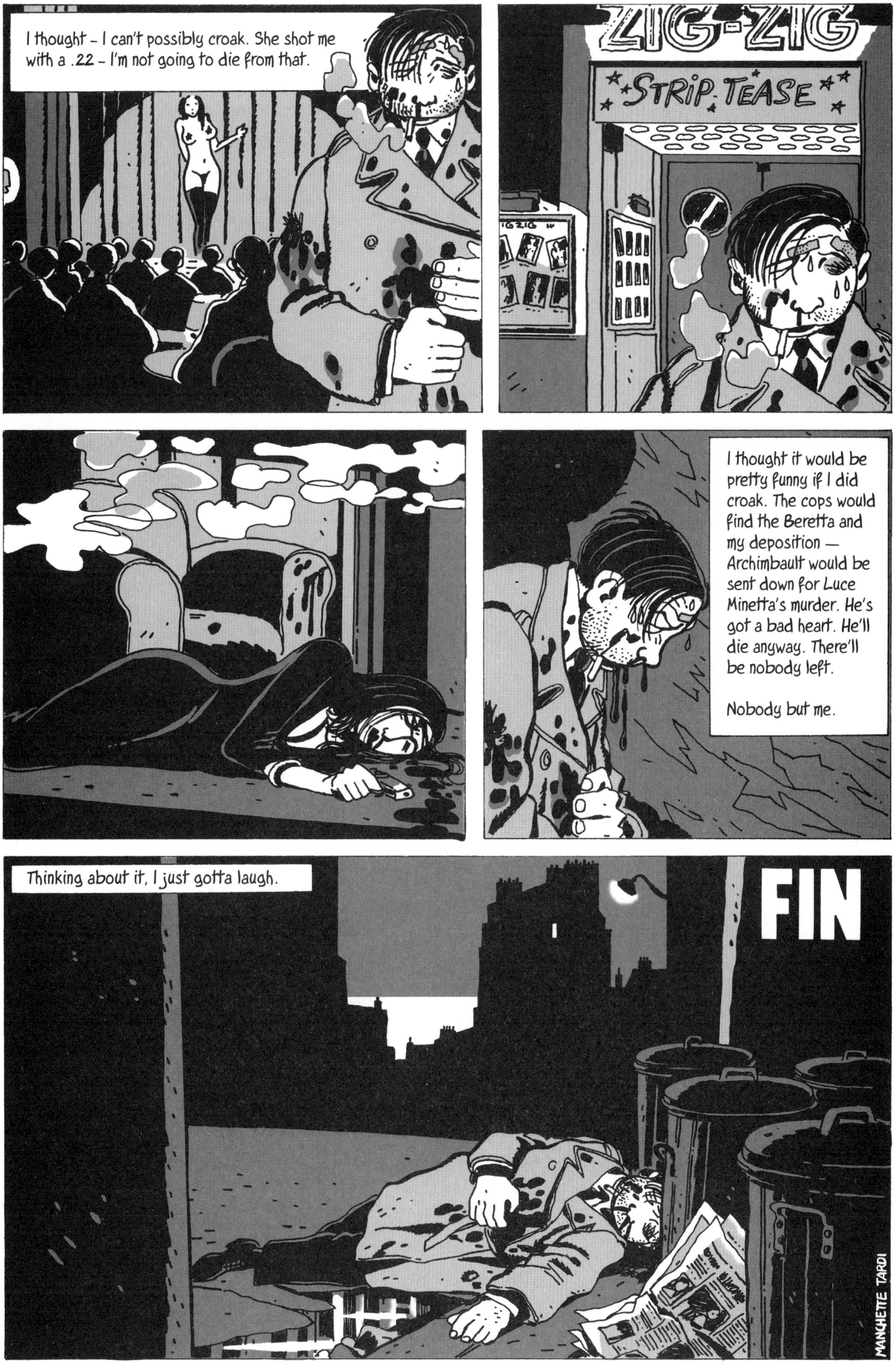

I thought - I can't possibly croak. She shot me with a .22 - I'm not going to die from that.
ZIG-ZIG
STRIP-TEASE
I thought it would be pretty funny if I did croak. The cops would find the Beretta and my deposition — Archimbault would be sent down for Luce Minetta's murder. He's got a bad heart. He'll die anyway. There'll be nobody left.
Nobody but me.
Thinking about it, I just gotta laugh.
FIN
MANCHETTE TARDI

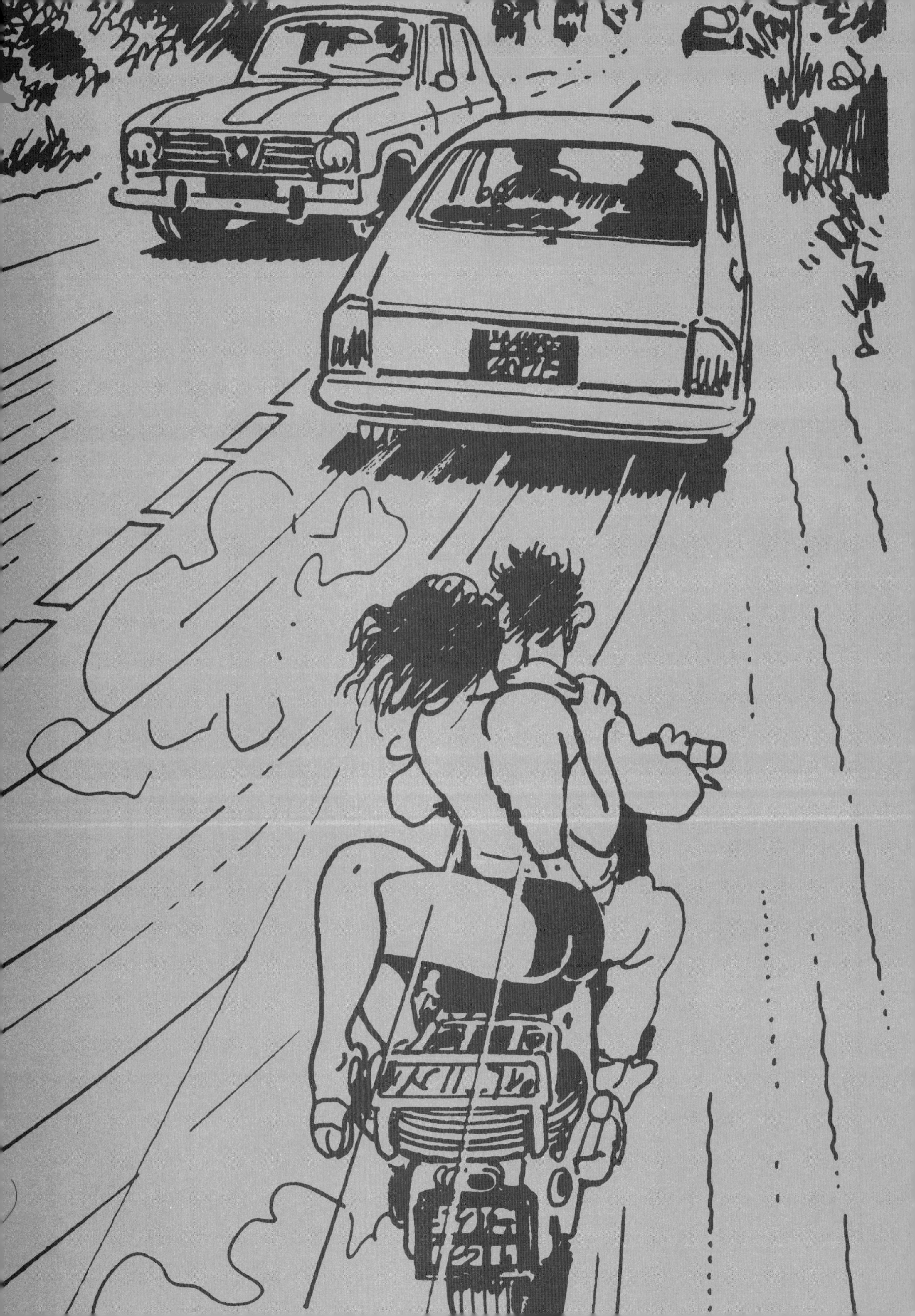

WEST
COAST
BLUES

West Coast Blues
STORY – Jean-Patrick Manchette
ART – Tardi
TRANSLATION – Kim Thompson

Circling

West Coast Blues is a flashback:

It begins and ends on the beltway — the protagonist circling his city in a car.

It's symbolic of his life, spinning in circles...

This sums him up nicely: "To understand why George zooms along the beltway with diminished reflexes while listening to that particular music, you must look closely at George's position within the Marxist system of production."

George Gerfaut feels perturbed because he leads a useless life as a middle manager. Doubtless there are innumerable sociological studies on the matter, but the central point of *West Coast Blues* is to explore that theme through an enjoyable novel that reads like a crime novel without being one and yet nevertheless flirts with the genre.

That is Manchette's power: to update the problems of an era without boring people — the problems, which, in my opinion, are always also current.

– TARDI

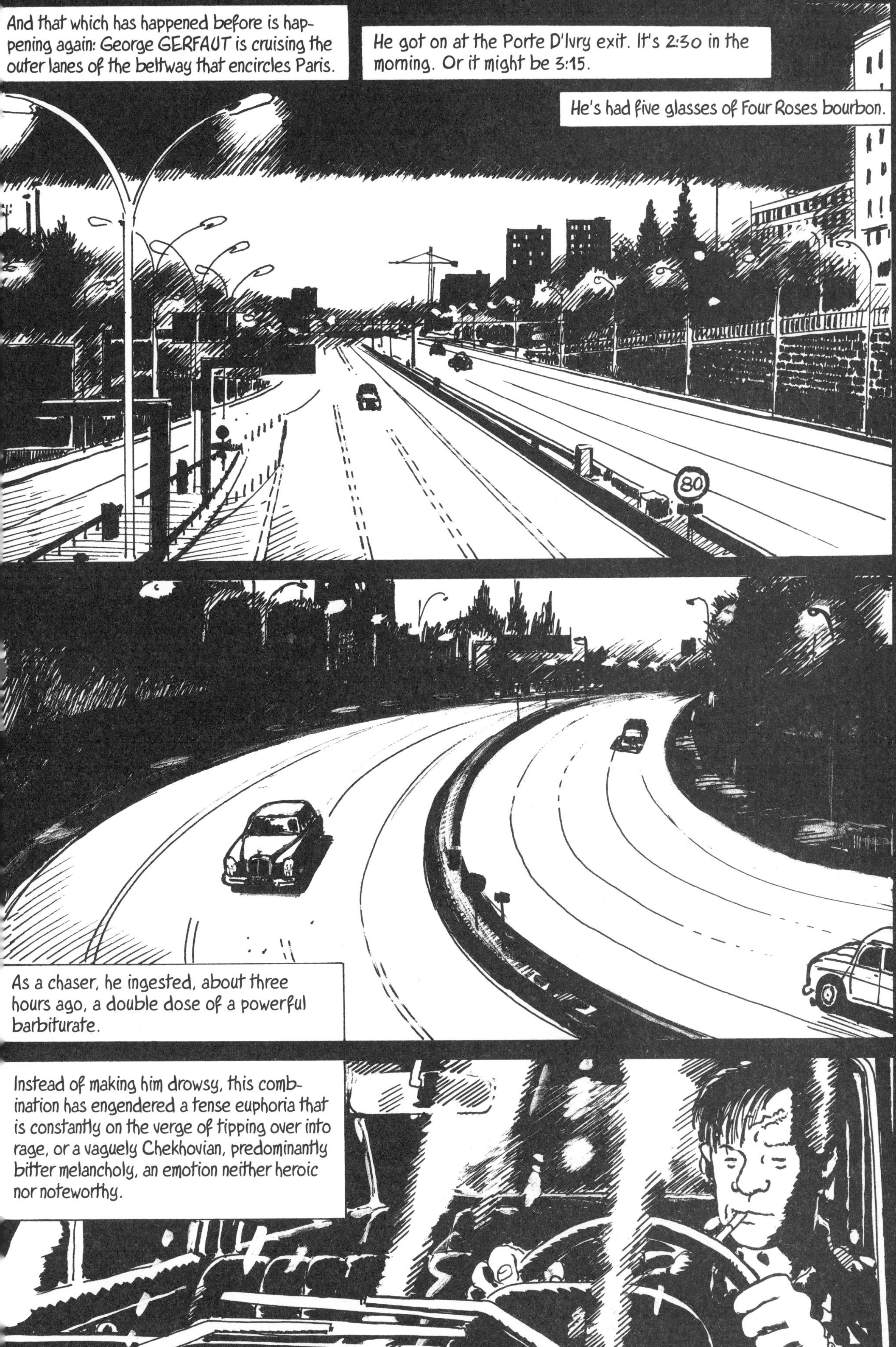

And that which has happened before is happening again: George GERFAUT is cruising the outer lanes of the beltway that encircles Paris.
He got on at the Porte D'Ivry exit. It's 2:30 in the morning. Or it might be 3:15.
He's had five glasses of Four Roses bourbon.
80
As a chaser, he ingested, about three hours ago, a double dose of a powerful barbiturate.
Instead of making him drowsy, this combination has engendered a tense euphoria that is constantly on the verge of tipping over into rage, or a vaguely Chekhovian, predominantly bitter melancholy, an emotion neither heroic nor noteworthy.
George GERFAUT is driving 90 m.p.h.

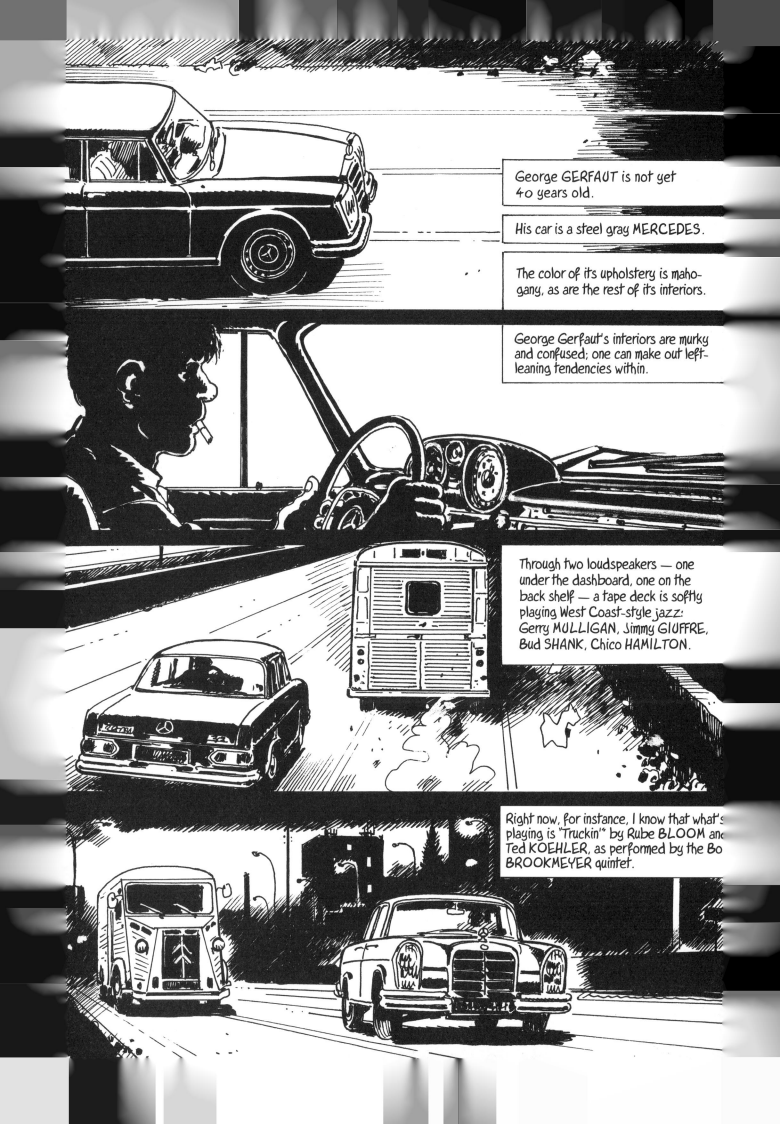

George GERFAUT is not yet 40 years old.

His car is a steel gray MERCEDES.

The color of its upholstery is mahogany, as are the rest of its interiors.

George Gerfaut's interiors are murky and confused; one can make out left-leaning tendencies within.

Through two loudspeakers — one under the dashboard, one on the back shelf — a tape deck is softly playing West Coast-style jazz: Gerry MULLIGAN, Jimmy GIUFFRE, Bud SHANK, Chico HAMILTON.

Right now, for instance, I know that what's playing is "Truckin'" by Rube BLOOM and Ted KOEHLER, as performed by the Bo[b] BROOKMEYER quintet.

George GERFAUT is an executive salesman.

His job is to sell, to individuals and to corporations, all over France and Europe, the pricey electrical components manufactured by his company, a subsidiary of the I.T.T. Group; he knows how they work because he is an engineer.

The reason George is speeding along the beltway in this manner, with compromised reflexes and while listening to that particular music, is mainly to be found in George's status within the means of production.

The fact that George has killed at least two men during the last year has nothing to do with it.

That which is happening now has happened before.

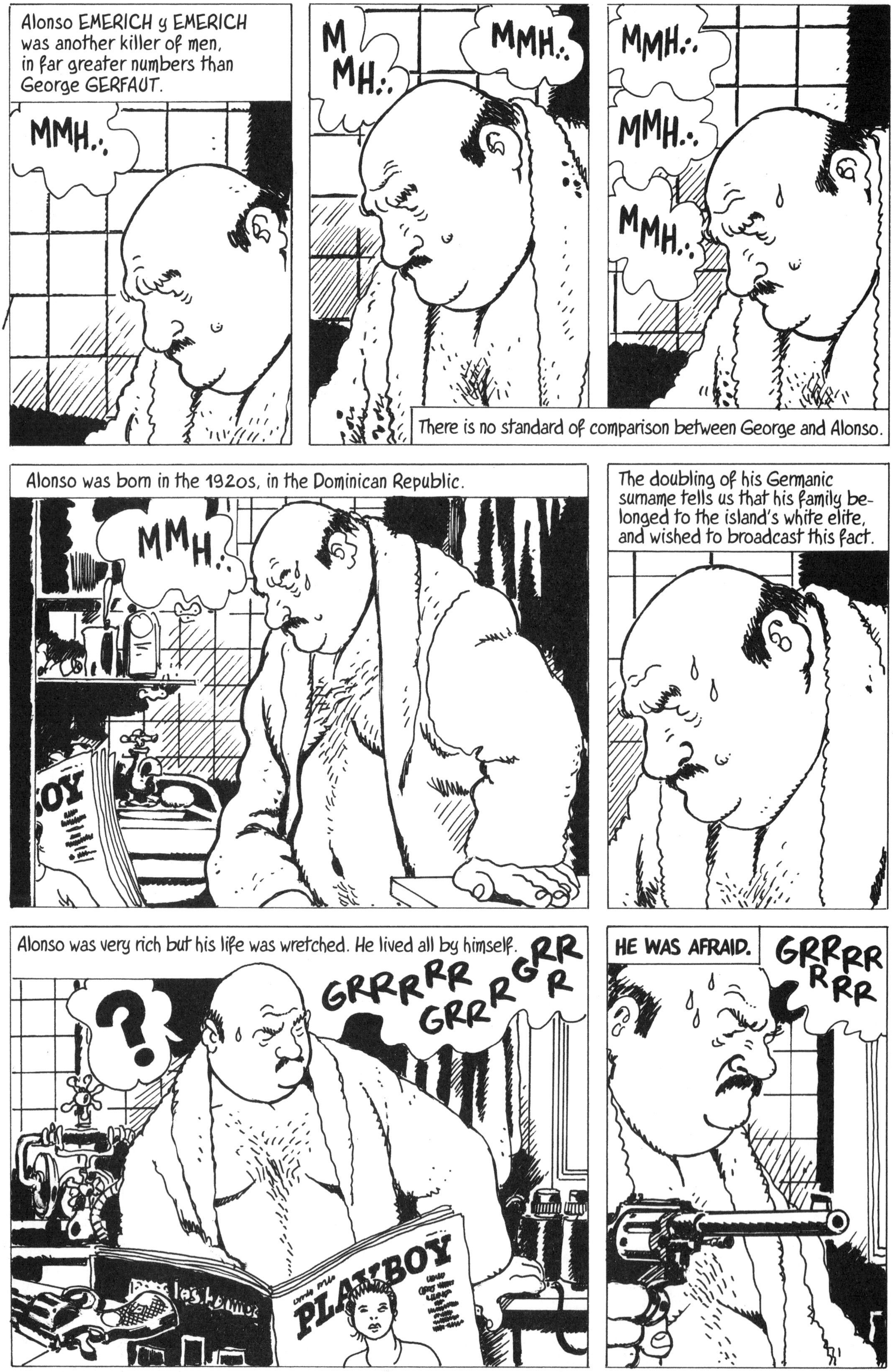
Alonso EMERICH y EMERICH was another killer of men, in far greater numbers than George GERFAUT.
MMH.:.
M MH.:.
MMH.:.
MMH.:.
MMH.:.
MMH.:.
There is no standard of comparison between George and Alonso.
Alonso was born in the 1920s, in the Dominican Republic.
MMH.:.
The doubling of his Germanic surname tells us that his family belonged to the island's white elite, and wished to broadcast this fact.
Alonso was very rich but his life was wretched. He lived all by himself.
?
GRRRRR GRRRGRR R
PLAYBOY
HE WAS AFRAID.
GRRRR RRR

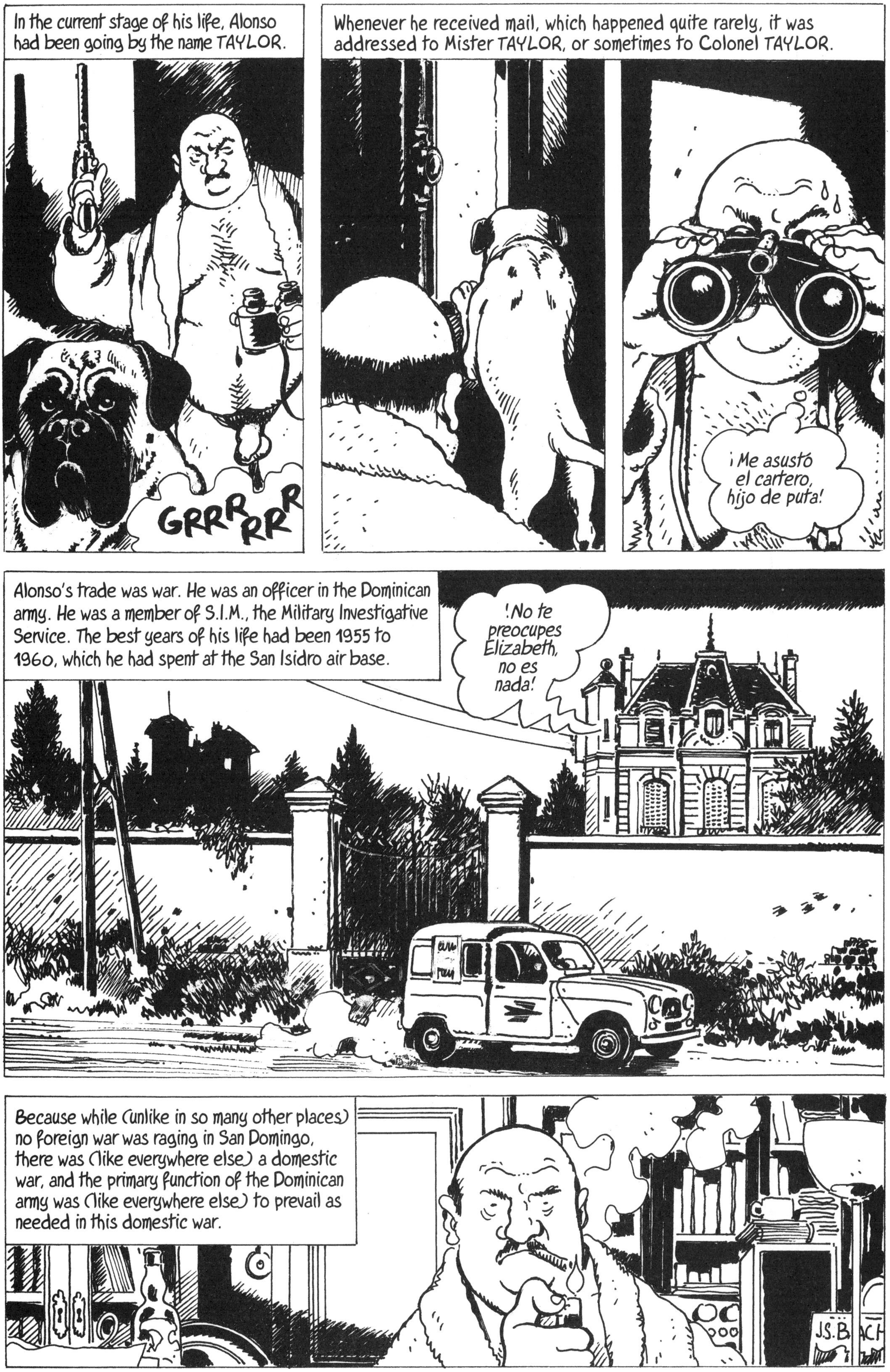

In the current stage of his life, Alonso had been going by the name TAYLOR.
GRRRRRR
Whenever he received mail, which happened quite rarely, it was addressed to Mister TAYLOR, or sometimes to Colonel TAYLOR.
¡Me asustó el cartero, hijo de puta!
Alonso's trade was war. He was an officer in the Dominican army. He was a member of S.I.M., the Military Investigative Service. The best years of his life had been 1955 to 1960, which he had spent at the San Isidro air base.
!No te preocupes Elizabeth, no es nada!
Because while (unlike in so many other places) no foreign war was raging in San Domingo, there was (like everywhere else) a domestic war, and the primary function of the Dominican army was (like everywhere else) to prevail as needed in this domestic war.

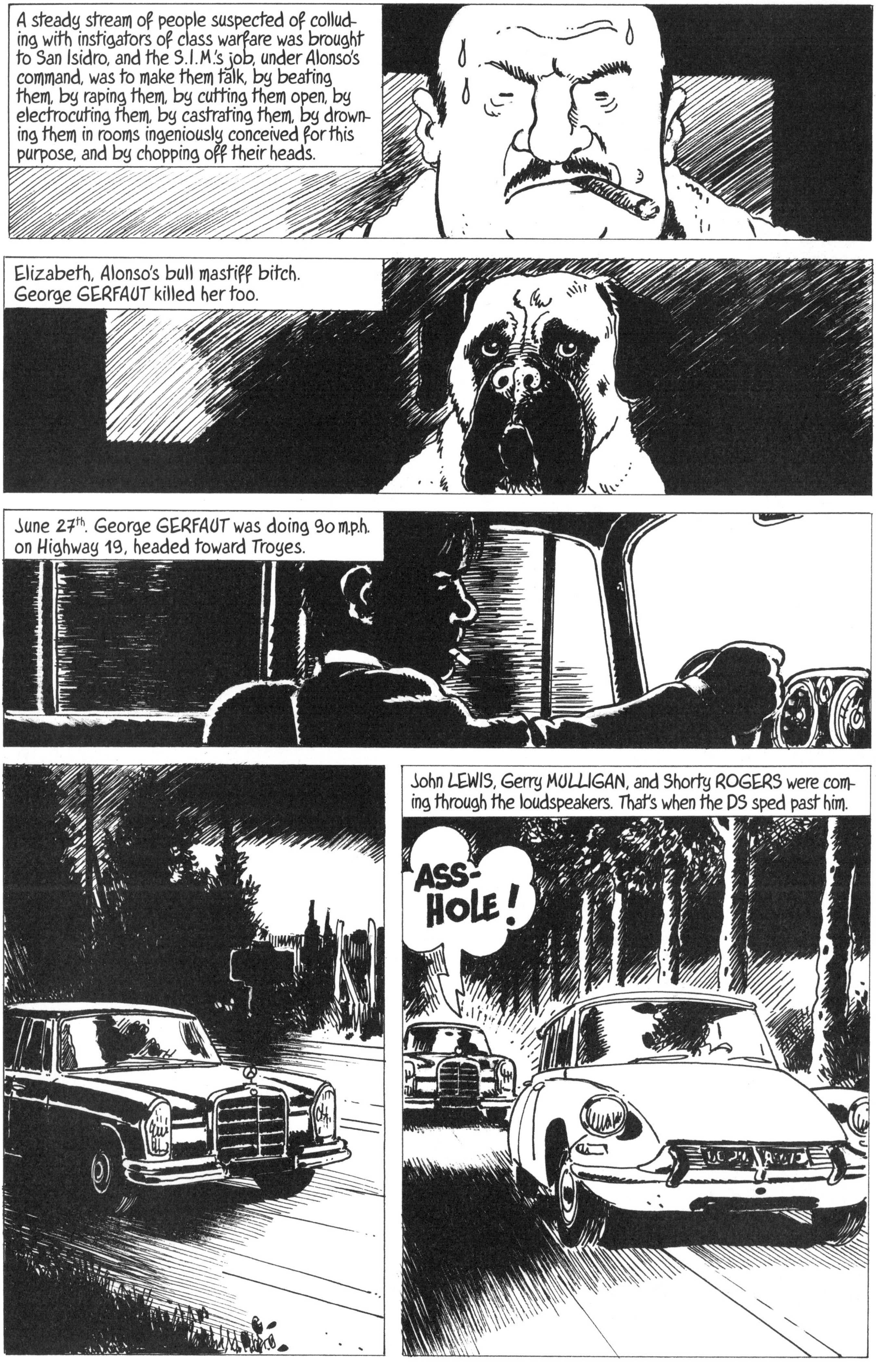
A steady stream of people suspected of colluding with instigators of class warfare was brought to San Isidro, and the S.I.M.'s job, under Alonso's command, was to make them talk, by beating them, by raping them, by cutting them open, by electrocuting them, by castrating them, by drowning them in rooms ingeniously conceived for this purpose, and by chopping off their heads.
Elizabeth, Alonso's bull mastiff bitch. George GERFAUT killed her too.
June 27th. George GERFAUT was doing 90 m.p.h. on Highway 19, headed toward Troyes.
John LEWIS, Gerry MULLIGAN, and Shorty ROGERS were coming through the loudspeakers. That's when the DS sped past him.
ASS-HOLE!

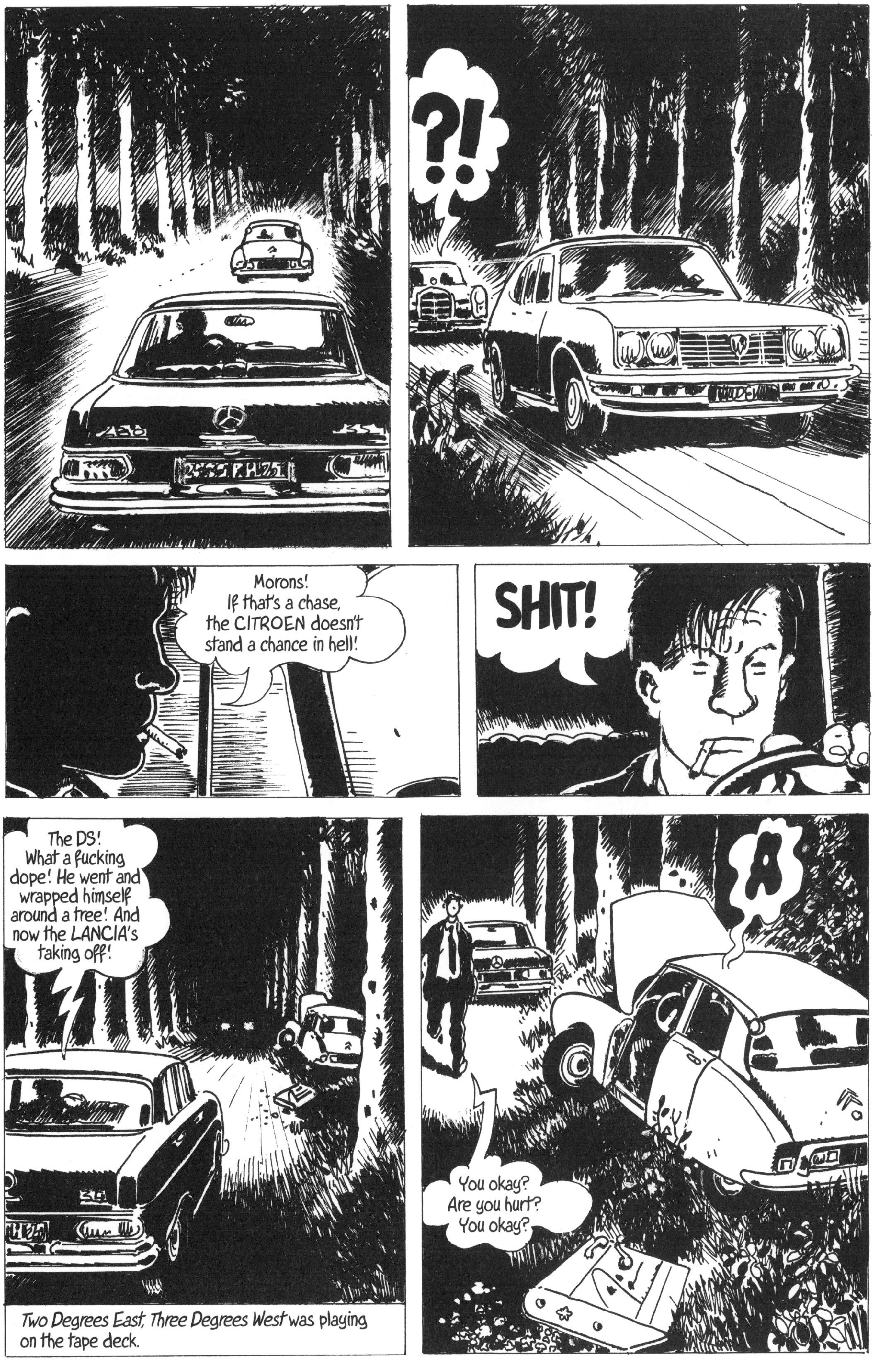
?!
Morons! If that's a chase, the CITROEN doesn't stand a chance in hell!
SHIT!
The DS! What a fucking dope! He went and wrapped himself around a tree! And now the LANCIA's taking off!
Two Degrees East, Three Degrees West was playing on the tape deck.
A
You okay? Are you hurt? You okay?

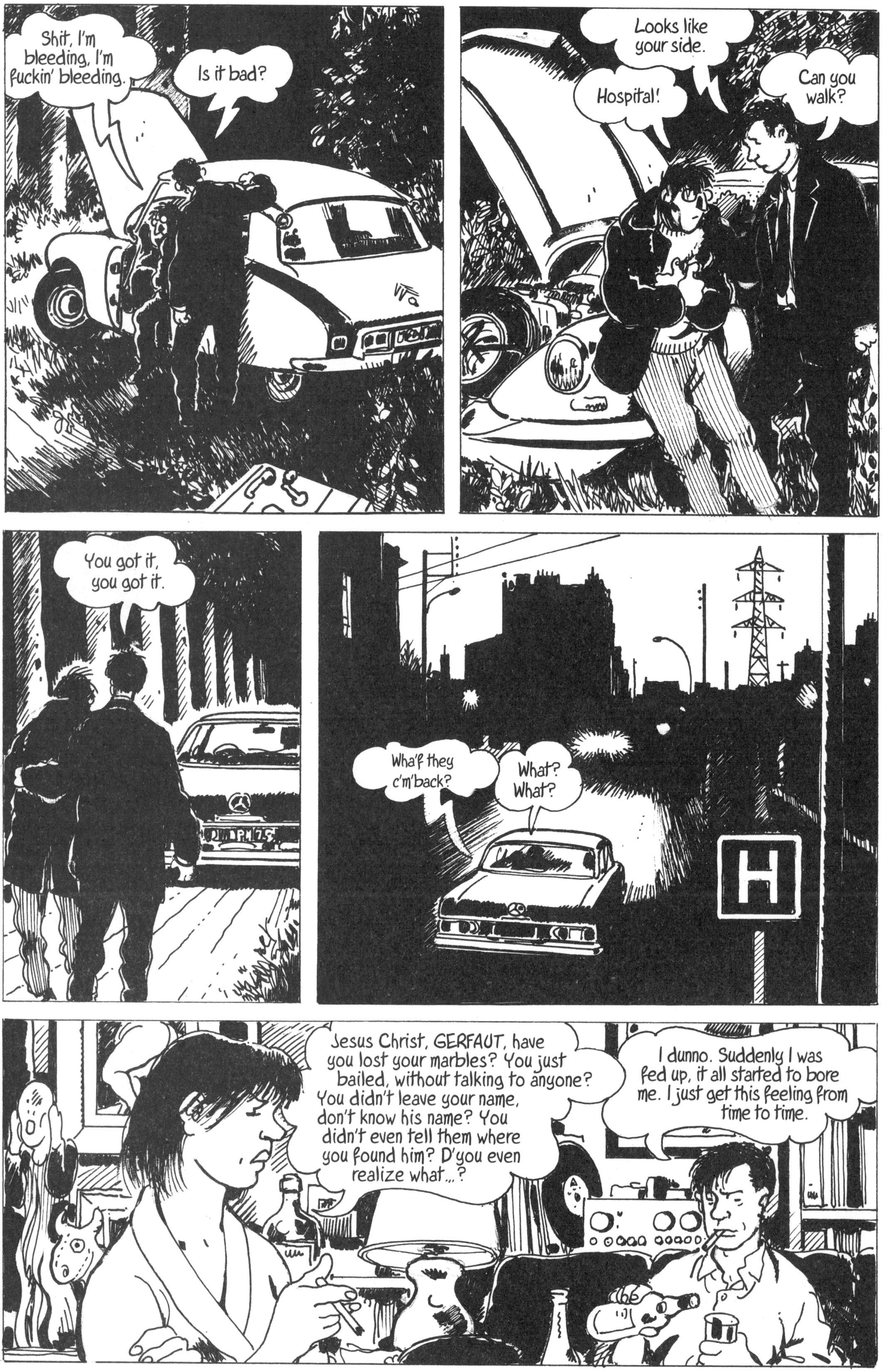
Shit, I'm bleeding, I'm fuckin' bleeding.
Is it bad?
Looks like your side.
Hospital!
Can you walk?
You got it, you got it.
Wha'f they c'm'back?
What? What?
Jesus Christ, GERFAUT, have you lost your marbles? You just bailed, without talking to anyone? You didn't leave your name, don't know his name? You didn't even tell them where you found him? D'you even realize what...?
I dunno. Suddenly I was fed up, it all started to bore me. I just get this feeling from time to time.

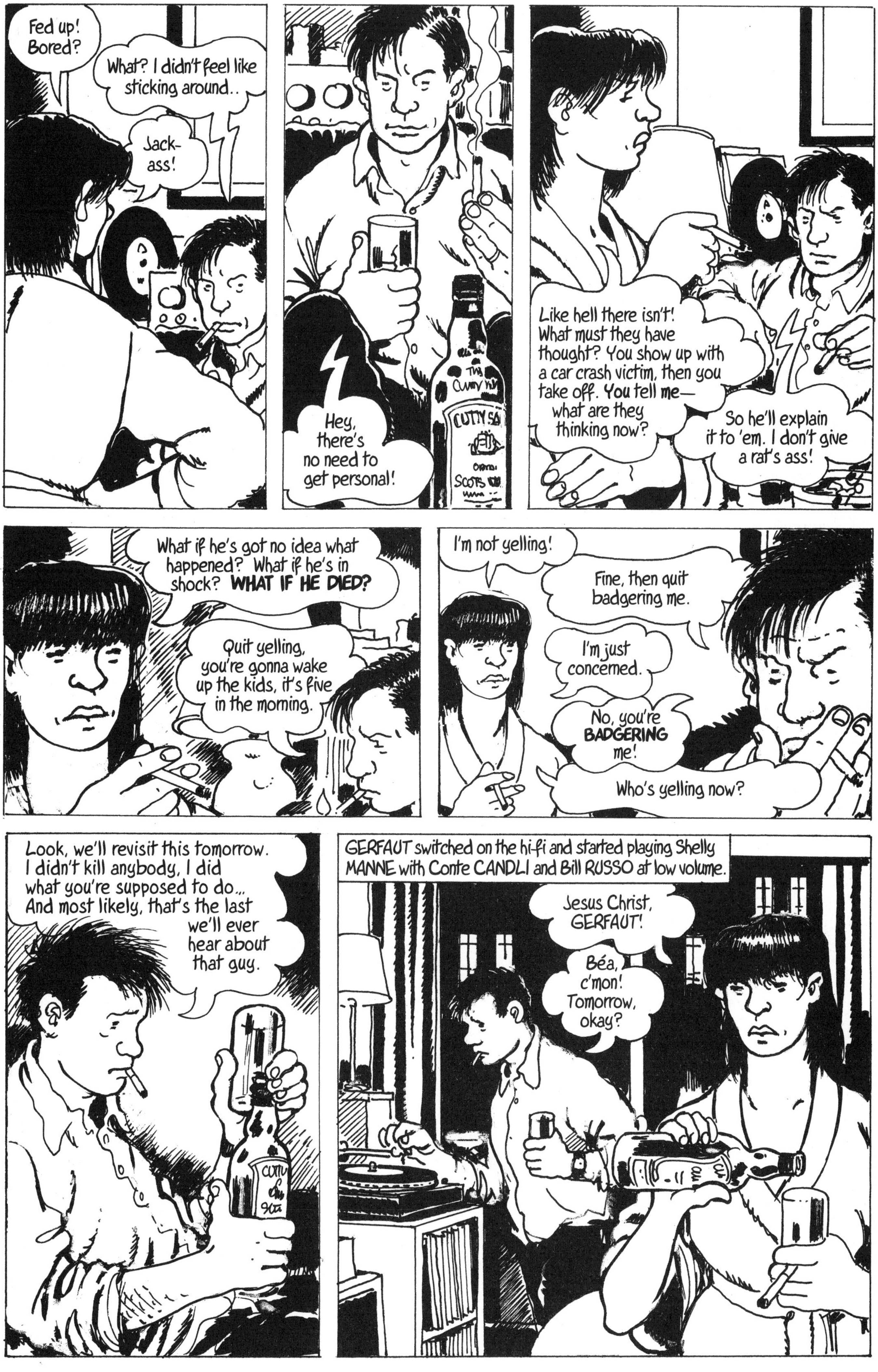

Fed up! Bored?
What? I didn't feel like sticking around..
Jack-ass!
Hey, there's no need to get personal!
Like hell there isn't! What must they have thought? You show up with a car crash victim, then you take off. You tell me— what are they thinking now?
So he'll explain it to 'em. I don't give a rat's ass!
What if he's got no idea what happened? What if he's in shock? **WHAT IF HE DIED?**
Quit yelling, you're gonna wake up the kids, it's five in the morning.
I'm not yelling!
Fine, then quit badgering me.
I'm just concerned.
No, you're **BADGERING** me!
Who's yelling now?
Look, we'll revisit this tomorrow. I didn't kill anybody, I did what you're supposed to do... And most likely, that's the last we'll ever hear about that guy.
GERFAUT switched on the hi-fi and started playing Shelly MANNE with Conte CANDLI and Bill RUSSO at low volume.
Jesus Christ, GERFAUT!
Béa, c'mon! Tomorrow, okay?

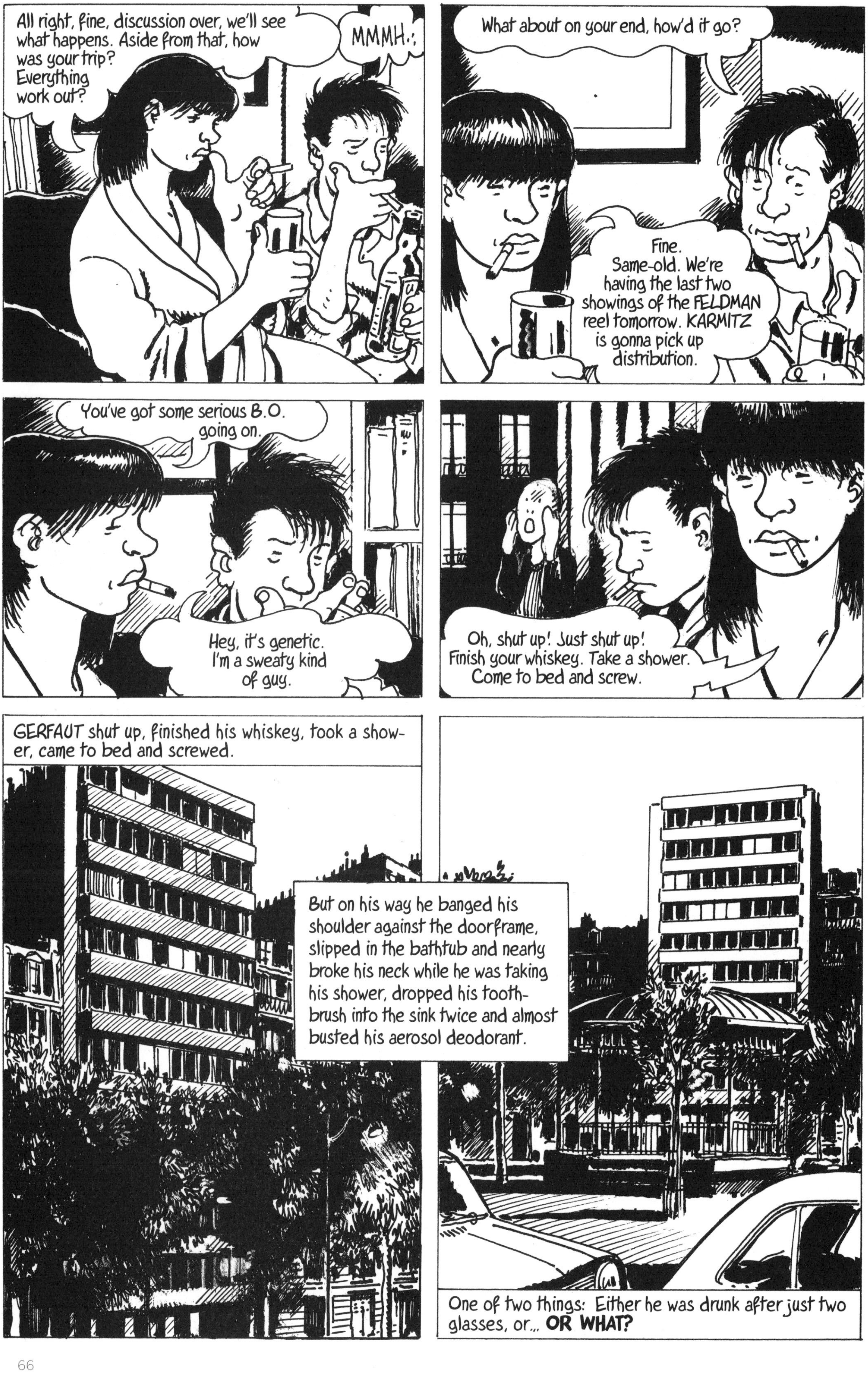
All right, fine, discussion over, we'll see what happens. Aside from that, how was your trip? Everything work out?
MMMH...
What about on your end, how'd it go?
Fine. Same-old. We're having the last two showings of the FELDMAN reel tomorrow. KARMITZ is gonna pick up distribution.
You've got some serious B.O. going on.
Hey, it's genetic. I'm a sweaty kind of guy.
Oh, shut up! Just shut up! Finish your whiskey. Take a shower. Come to bed and screw.
GERFAUT shut up, finished his whiskey, took a shower, came to bed and screwed.
But on his way he banged his shoulder against the doorframe, slipped in the bathtub and nearly broke his neck while he was taking his shower, dropped his toothbrush into the sink twice and almost busted his aerosol deodorant.
One of two things: Either he was drunk after just two glasses, or... OR WHAT?

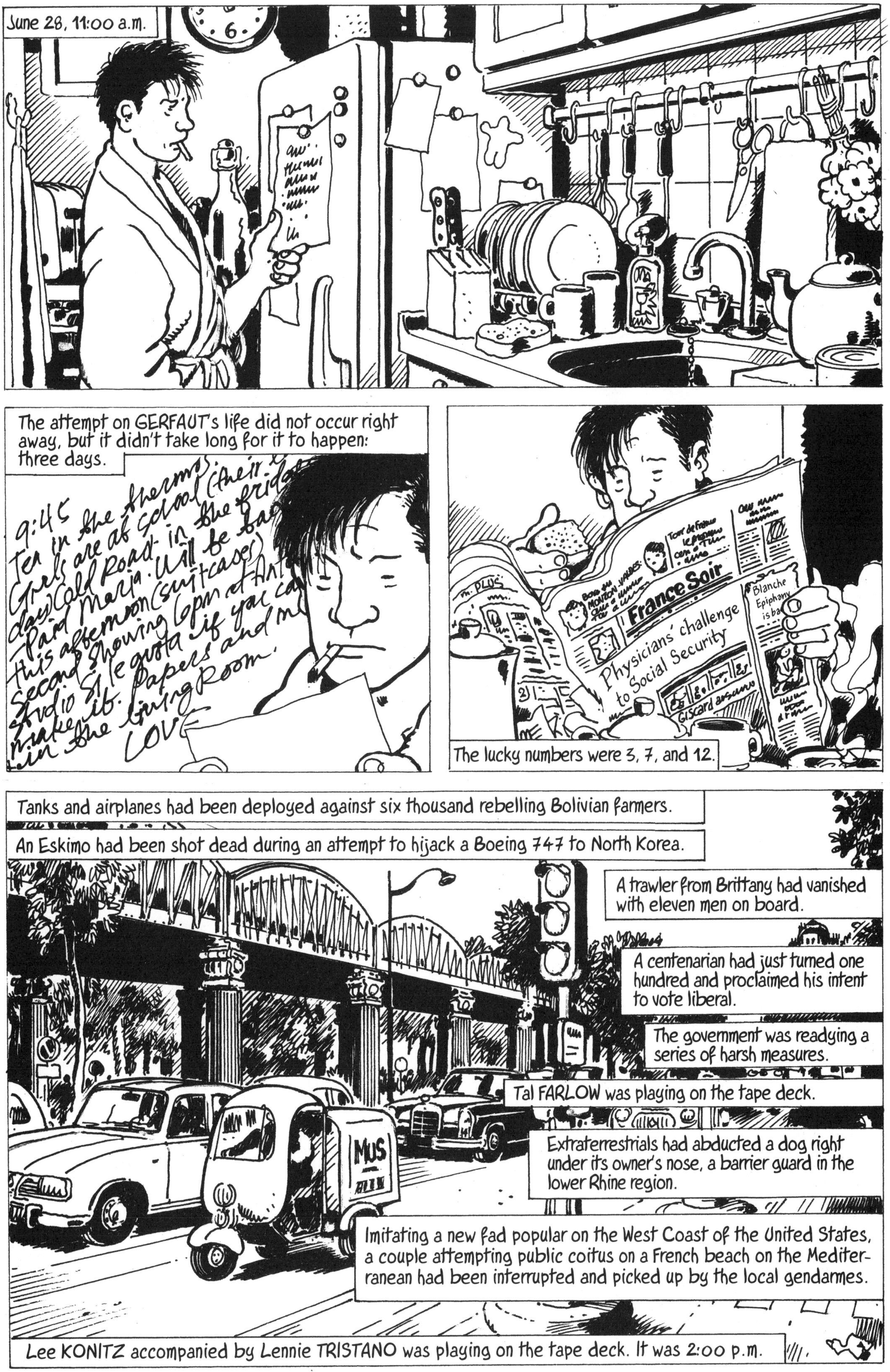
June 28, 11:00 a.m.
The attempt on GERFAUT's life did not occur right away, but it didn't take long for it to happen: three days.
9:45
Tea in the thermos
Girls are at school
day) Cold Roast in the
Paid Maria. Will be
this afternoon (suitcases)
Second showing 6pm at
Studio St. le gusta if you
make it. Papers and
in the living room
LOVE
France Soir
Physicians' challenge to Social Security
Giscard
Blanche Epiphany
The lucky numbers were 3, 7, and 12.
Tanks and airplanes had been deployed against six thousand rebelling Bolivian farmers.
An Eskimo had been shot dead during an attempt to hijack a Boeing 747 to North Korea.
A trawler from Brittany had vanished with eleven men on board.
A centenarian had just turned one hundred and proclaimed his intent to vote liberal.
The government was readying a series of harsh measures.
Tal FARLOW was playing on the tape deck.
Extraterrestrials had abducted a dog right under its owner's nose, a barrier guard in the lower Rhine region.
Imitating a new fad popular on the West Coast of the United States, a couple attempting public coitus on a French beach on the Mediterranean had been interrupted and picked up by the local gendarmes.
Lee KONITZ accompanied by Lennie TRISTANO was playing on the tape deck. It was 2:00 p.m.

The following morning, the family arose at dawn and headed out for the holidays.

They got TV where we're goin'?

What do you need a TV for? You planning on staying informed by watching the news? You expect to learn anything by watching TV?

Television's for selling noodles, that's all it's good for!

Oh, Daddy, you're talkin' bull again!

One of the men who on June 30 would try to kill George GERFAUT was sitting, at 11:50 on June 29, in the parked LANCIA Beta sedan 1800 two hundred feet from the entrance to GERFAUT's apartment building.

The man was poring over a comic-book magazine that related the adventures of CAPTAIN MARVEL, the intrepid DAREDEVIL, SPIDER-MAN, and other super-heroes.

A series of emotions was flickering across his face.

He was totally into the comic.

LE JOURNAL DE SPIDER-MAN EN COMICS
MARVEL
Strange

You smell like grease!

Deep-fry oil! The super was making french fries. He's gone on holiday for a month. I got us the address.

SPIDER-MAN EN COULEURS
MARVEL

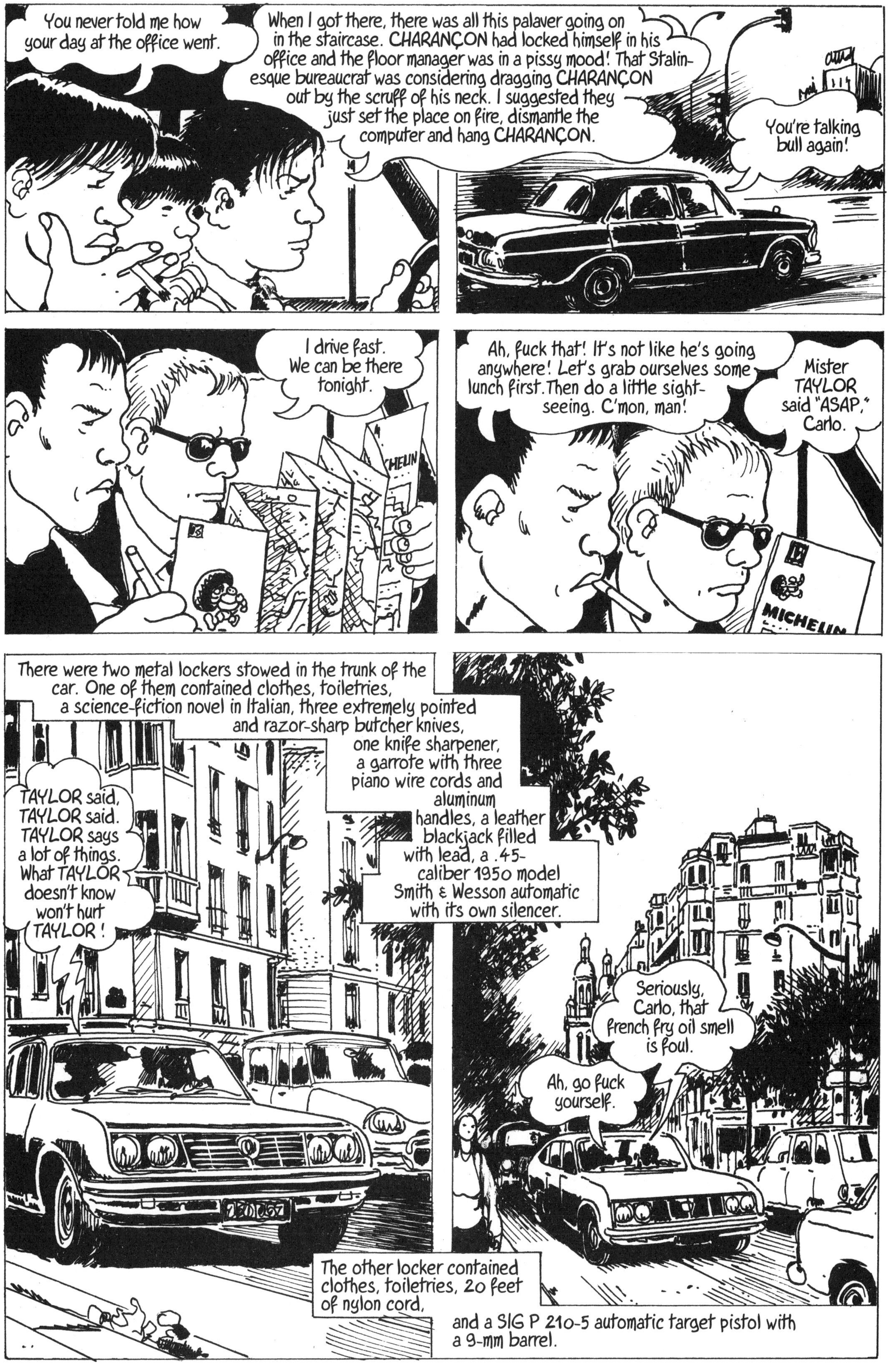
You never told me how your day at the office went.
When I got there, there was all this palaver going on in the staircase. CHARANÇON had locked himself in his office and the floor manager was in a pissy mood! That Stalin-esque bureaucrat was considering dragging CHARANÇON out by the scruff of his neck. I suggested they just set the place on fire, dismantle the computer and hang CHARANÇON.
You're talking bull again!
I drive fast. We can be there tonight.
Ah, fuck that! It's not like he's going anywhere! Let's grab ourselves some lunch first. Then do a little sight-seeing. C'mon, man!
Mister TAYLOR said "ASAP," Carlo.
There were two metal lockers stowed in the trunk of the car. One of them contained clothes, toiletries, a science-fiction novel in Italian, three extremely pointed and razor-sharp butcher knives, one knife sharpener, a garrote with three piano wire cords and aluminum handles, a leather blackjack filled with lead, a .45-caliber 1950 model Smith & Wesson automatic with its own silencer.
TAYLOR said, TAYLOR said. TAYLOR says a lot of things. What TAYLOR doesn't know won't hurt TAYLOR!
Seriously, Carlo, that french fry oil smell is foul.
Ah, go fuck yourself.
The other locker contained clothes, toiletries, 20 feet of nylon cord,
and a SIG P 210-5 automatic target pistol with a 9-mm barrel.

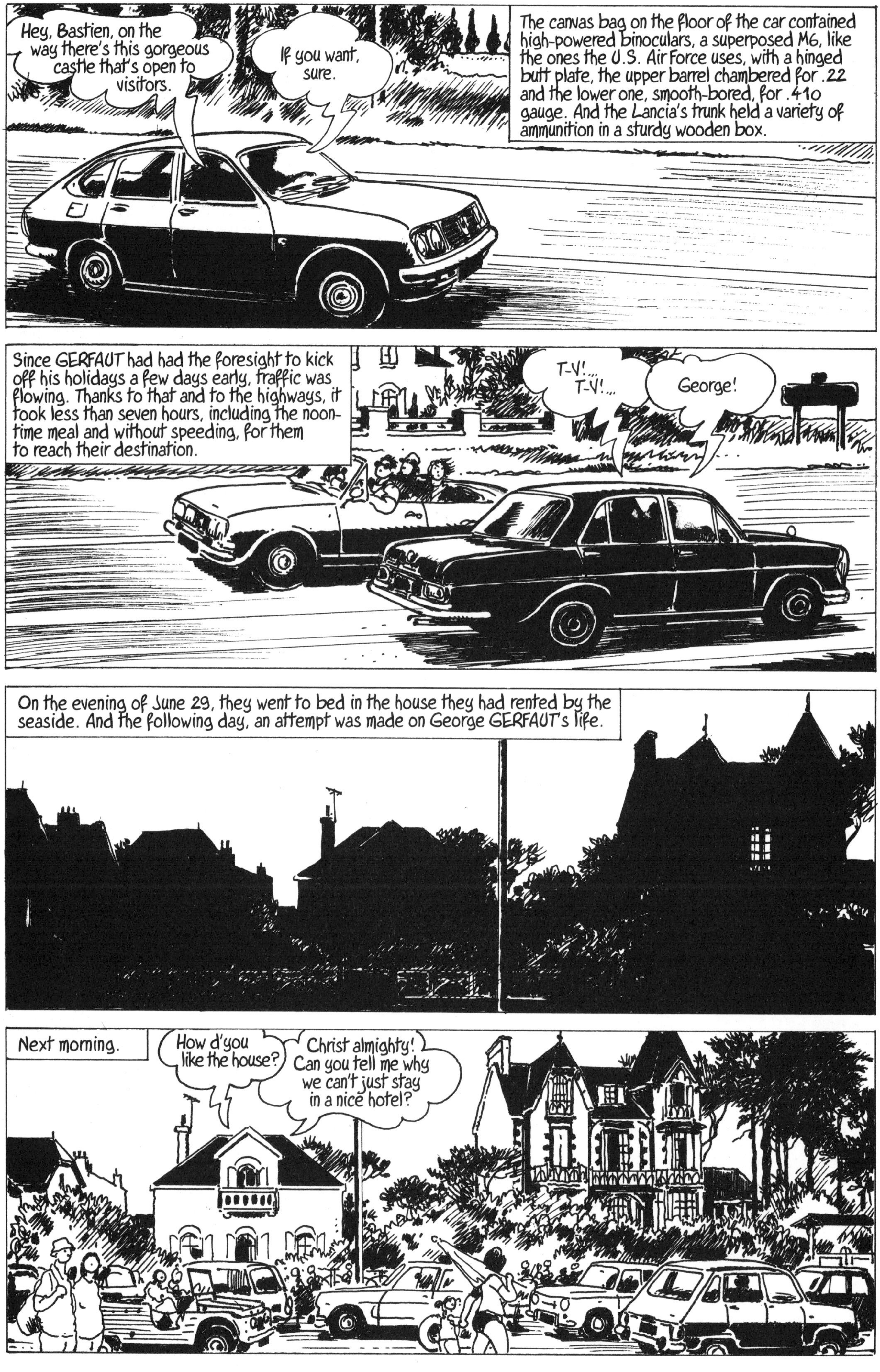
Hey, Bastien, on the way there's this gorgeous castle that's open to visitors.
If you want, sure.
The canvas bag on the floor of the car contained high-powered binoculars, a superposed M6, like the ones the U.S. Air Force uses, with a hinged butt plate, the upper barrel chambered for .22 and the lower one, smooth-bored, for .410 gauge. And the Lancia's trunk held a variety of ammunition in a sturdy wooden box.
Since GERFAUT had had the foresight to kick off his holidays a few days early, traffic was flowing. Thanks to that and to the highways, it took less than seven hours, including the noontime meal and without speeding, for them to reach their destination.
T-V!... T-V!...
George!
On the evening of June 29, they went to bed in the house they had rented by the seaside. And the following day, an attempt was made on George GERFAUT's life.
Next morning.
How d'you like the house?
Christ almighty! Can you tell me why we can't just stay in a nice hotel?

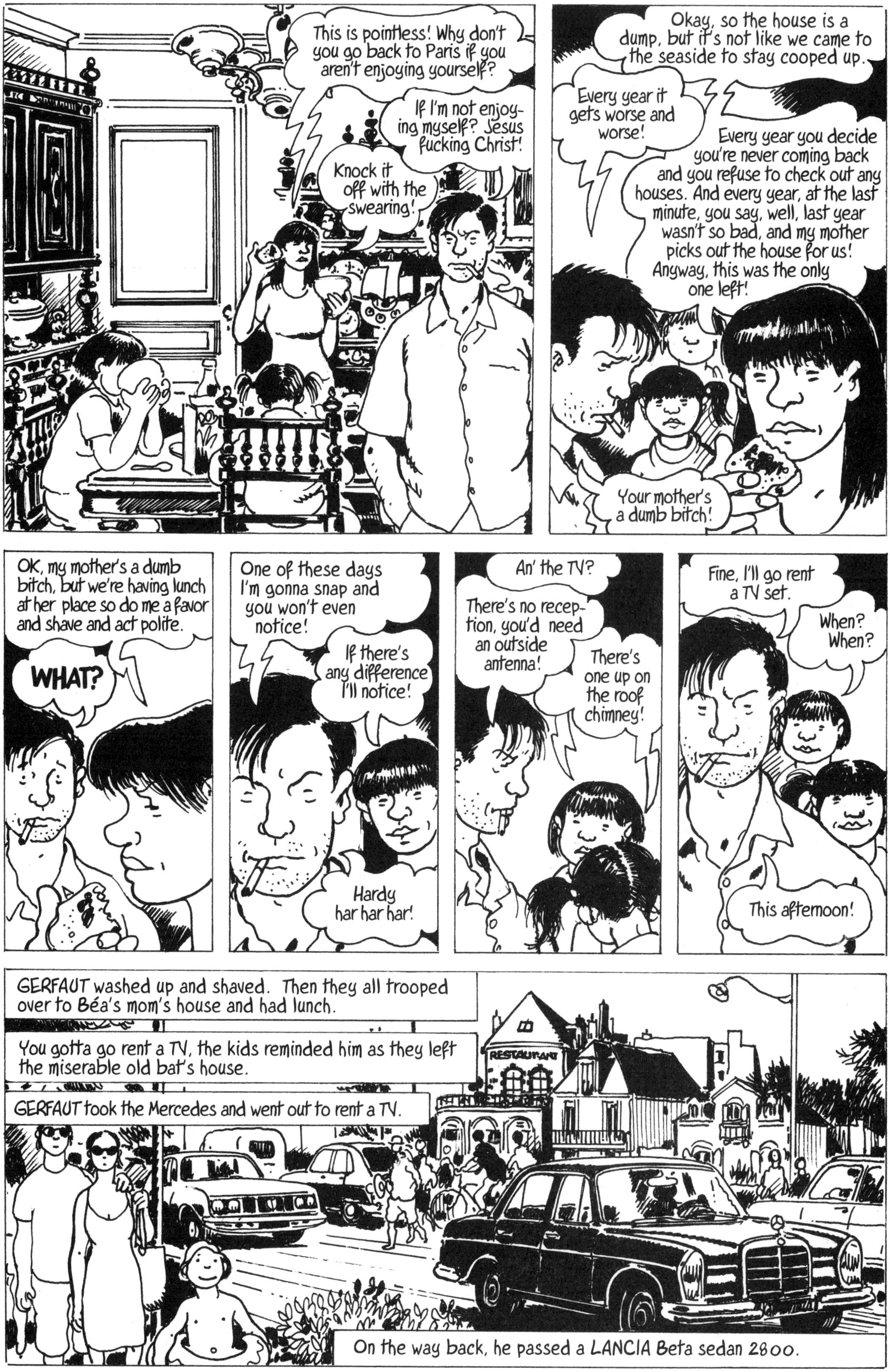
This is pointless! Why don't you go back to Paris if you aren't enjoying yourself?
If I'm not enjoying myself? Jesus fucking Christ!
Knock it off with the swearing!
Okay, so the house is a dump, but it's not like we came to the seaside to stay cooped up.
Every year it gets worse and worse!
Every year you decide you're never coming back and you refuse to check out any houses. And every year, at the last minute, you say, well, last year wasn't so bad, and my mother picks out the house for us! Anyway, this was the only one left!
Your mother's a dumb bitch!
OK, my mother's a dumb bitch, but we're having lunch at her place so do me a favor and shave and act polite.
WHAT?
One of these days I'm gonna snap and you won't even notice!
If there's any difference I'll notice!
Hardy har har har!
An' the TV?
There's no reception, you'd need an outside antenna!
There's one up on the roof chimney!
Fine, I'll go rent a TV set.
When? When?
This afternoon!
GERFAUT washed up and shaved. Then they all trooped over to Béa's mom's house and had lunch.
You gotta go rent a TV, the kids reminded him as they left the miserable old bat's house.
GERFAUT took the Mercedes and went out to rent a TV.
RESTAURANT
On the way back, he passed a LANCIA Beta sedan 2800.

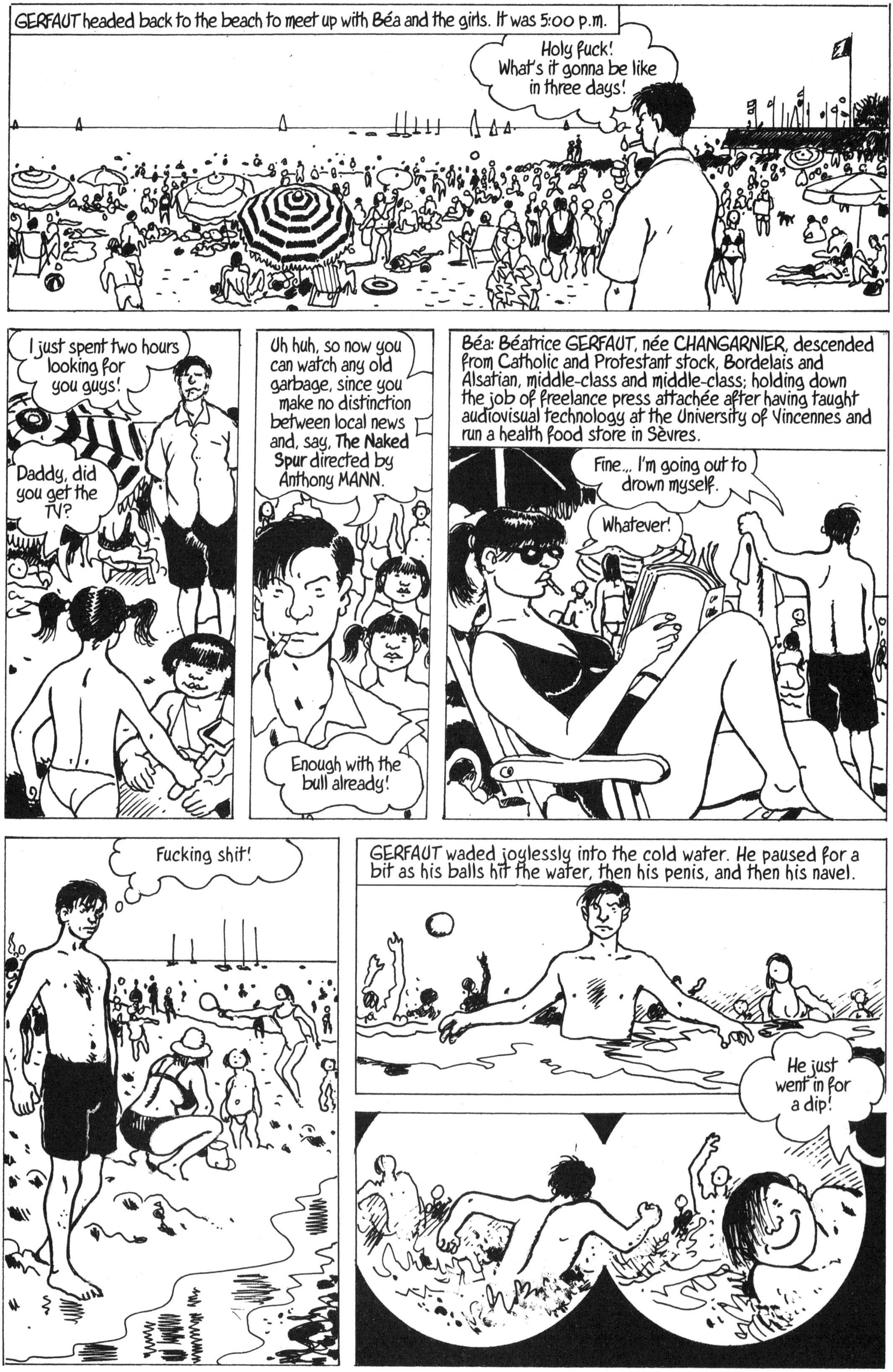
GERFAUT headed back to the beach to meet up with Béa and the girls. It was 5:00 p.m.
Holy fuck! What's it gonna be like in three days!
I just spent two hours looking for you guys!
Daddy, did you get the TV?
Uh huh, so now you can watch any old garbage, since you make no distinction between local news and, say, **The Naked Spur** directed by Anthony MANN.
Enough with the bull already!
Béa: Béatrice GERFAUT, née CHANGARNIER, descended from Catholic and Protestant stock, Bordelais and Alsatian, middle-class and middle-class; holding down the job of freelance press attachée after having taught audiovisual technology at the University of Vincennes and run a health food store in Sèvres.
Fine... I'm going out to drown myself.
Whatever!
Fucking shit!
GERFAUT waded joylessly into the cold water. He paused for a bit as his balls hit the water, then his penis, and then his navel.
He just went in for a dip!

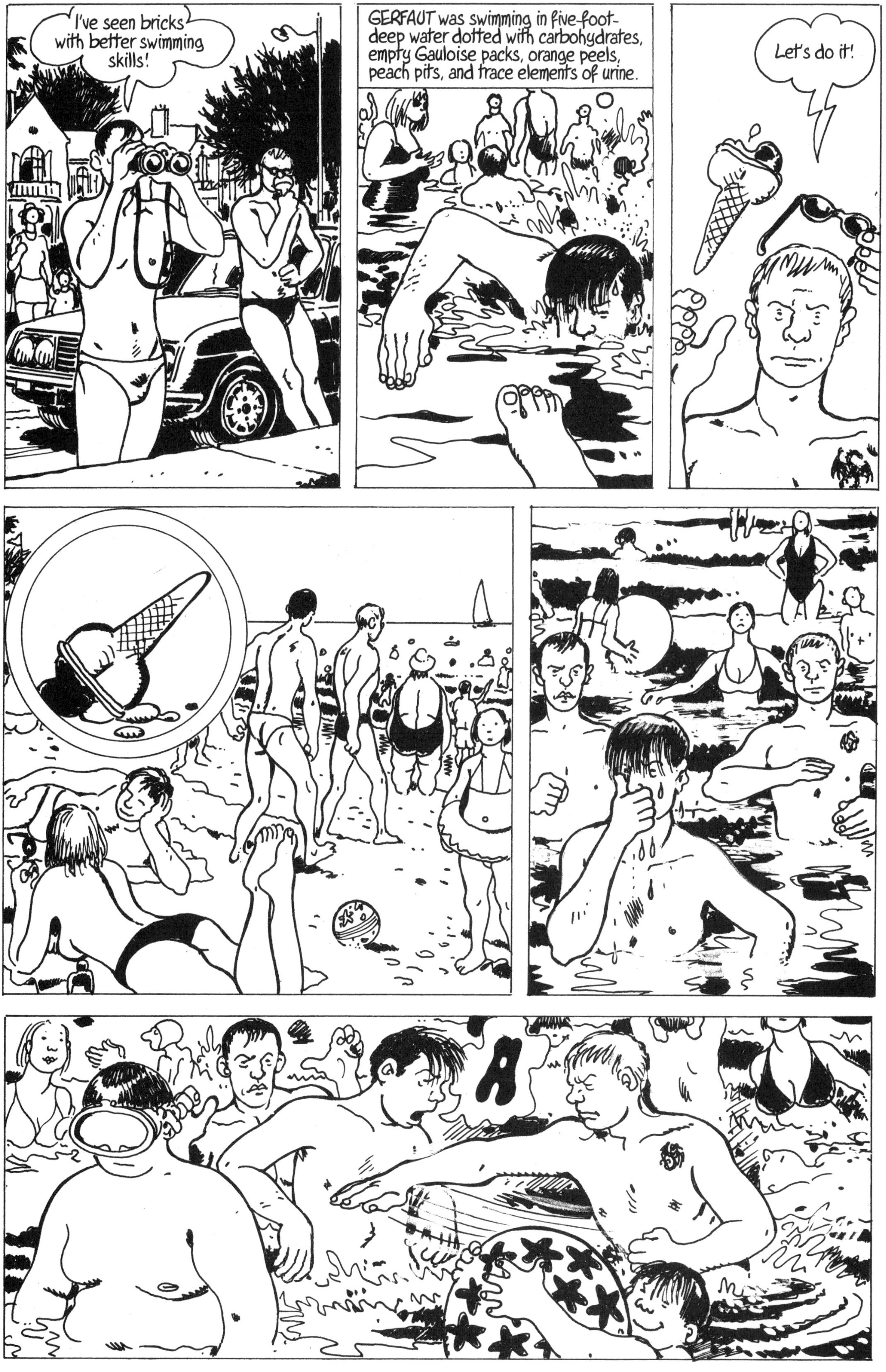
I've seen bricks with better swimming skills!
GERFAUT was swimming in five-foot-deep water dotted with carbohydrates, empty Gauloise packs, orange peels, peach pits, and trace elements of urine.
Let's do it!

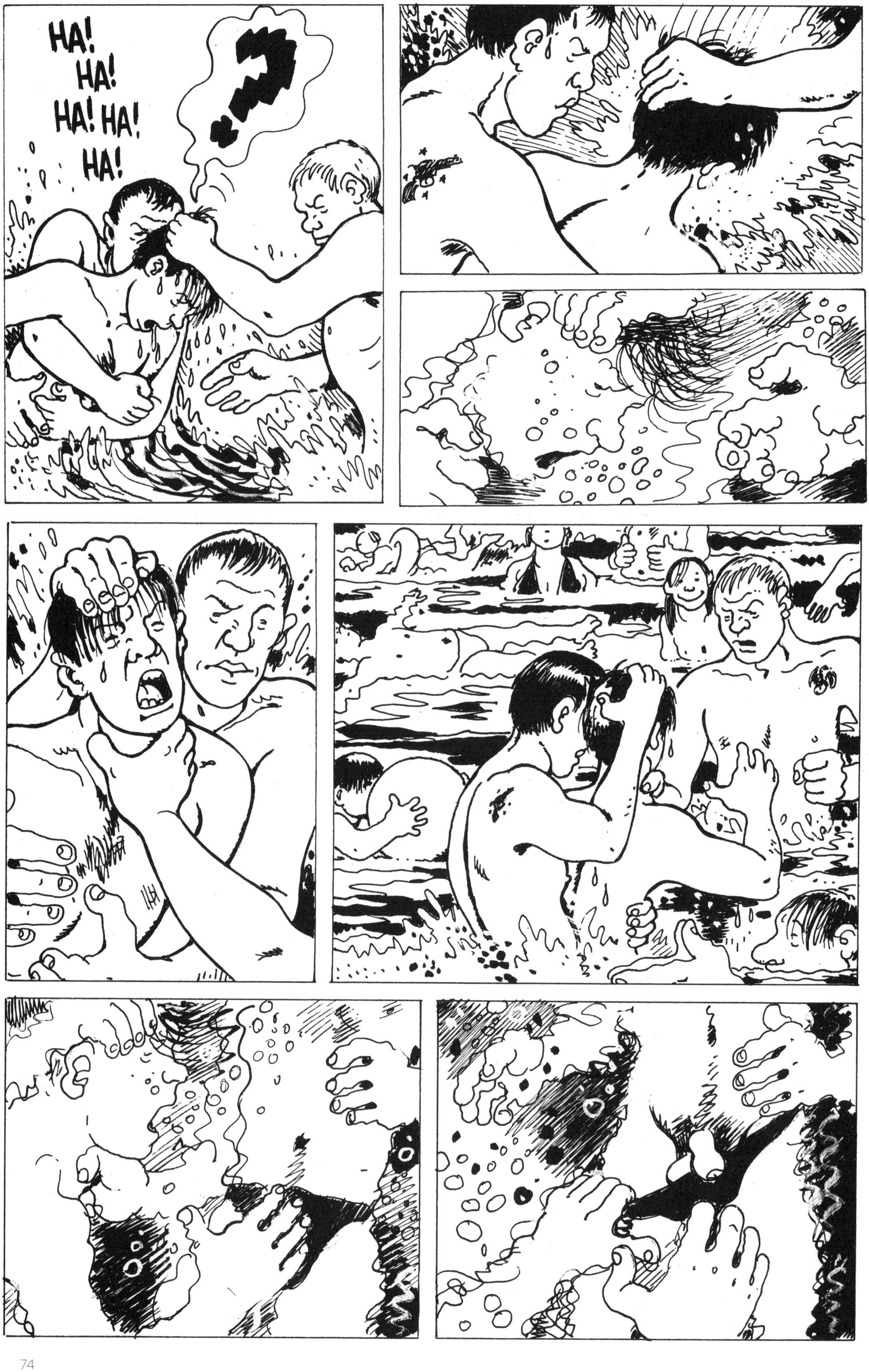
HA! HA! HA! HA! HA!
?

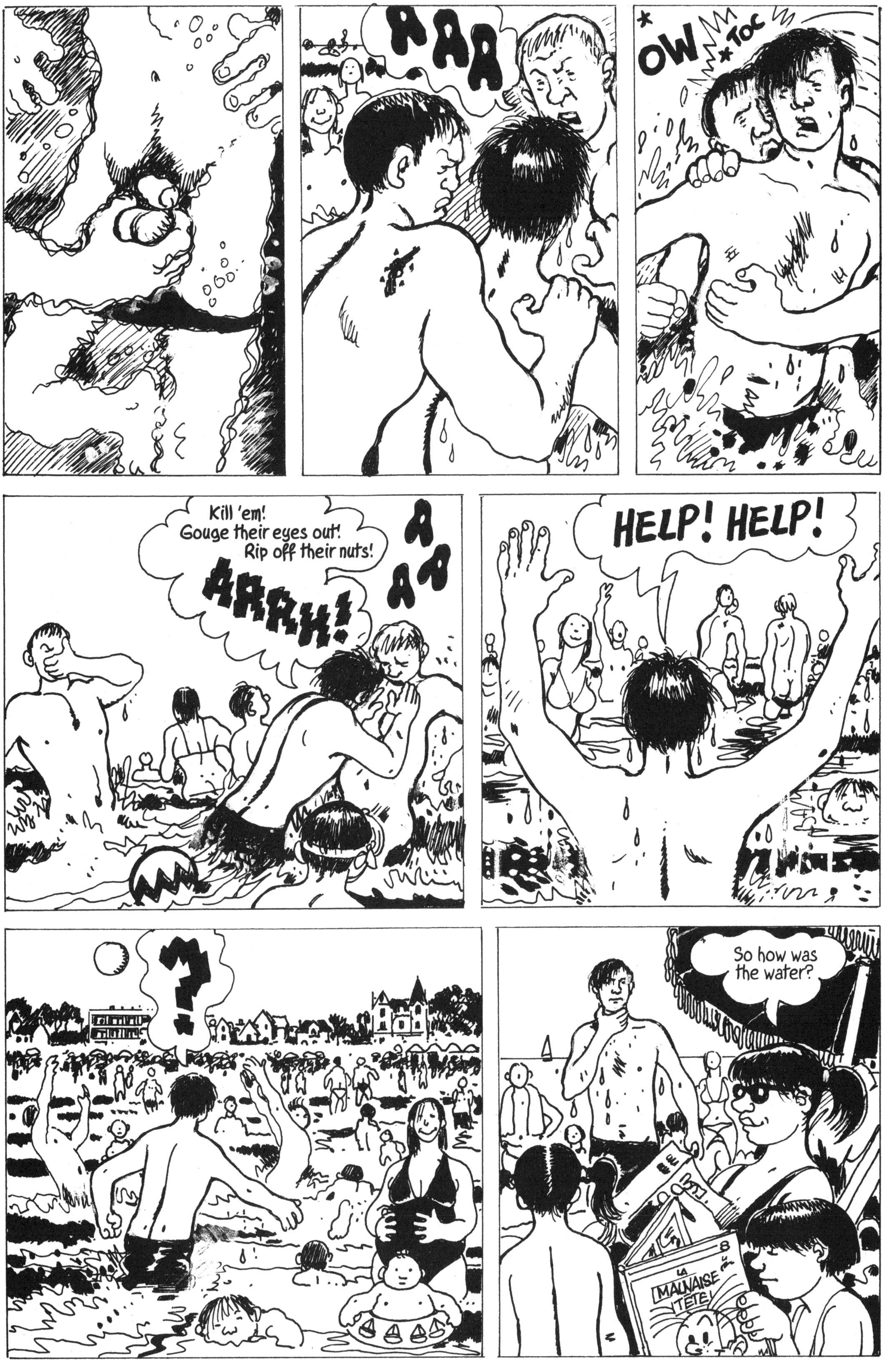

AAA
OW
*TOC
Kill 'em! Gouge their eyes out! Rip off their nuts!
ARRH!
A A A
HELP! HELP!
?
So how was the water?
LA MAUVAISE TÊTE

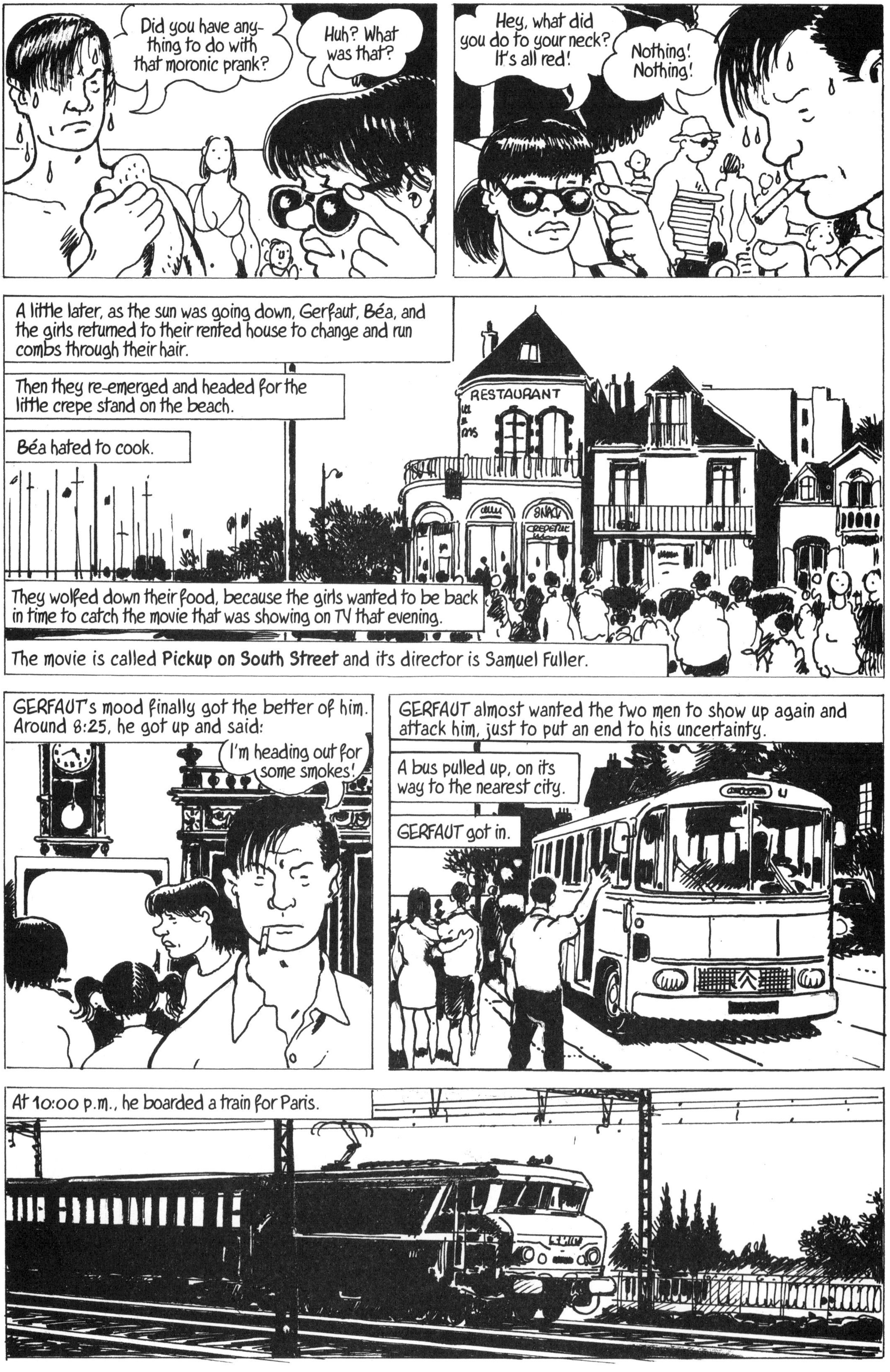
Did you have anything to do with that moronic prank?
Huh? What was that?
Hey, what did you do to your neck? It's all red!
Nothing! Nothing!
A little later, as the sun was going down, Gerfaut, Béa, and the girls returned to their rented house to change and run combs through their hair.
Then they re-emerged and headed for the little crepe stand on the beach.
Béa hated to cook.
RESTAURANT
They wolfed down their food, because the girls wanted to be back in time to catch the movie that was showing on TV that evening.
The movie is called Pickup on South Street and its director is Samuel Fuller.
GERFAUT's mood finally got the better of him. Around 8:25, he got up and said:
I'm heading out for some smokes!
GERFAUT almost wanted the two men to show up again and attack him, just to put an end to his uncertainty.
A bus pulled up, on its way to the nearest city.
GERFAUT got in.
At 10:00 p.m., he boarded a train for Paris.

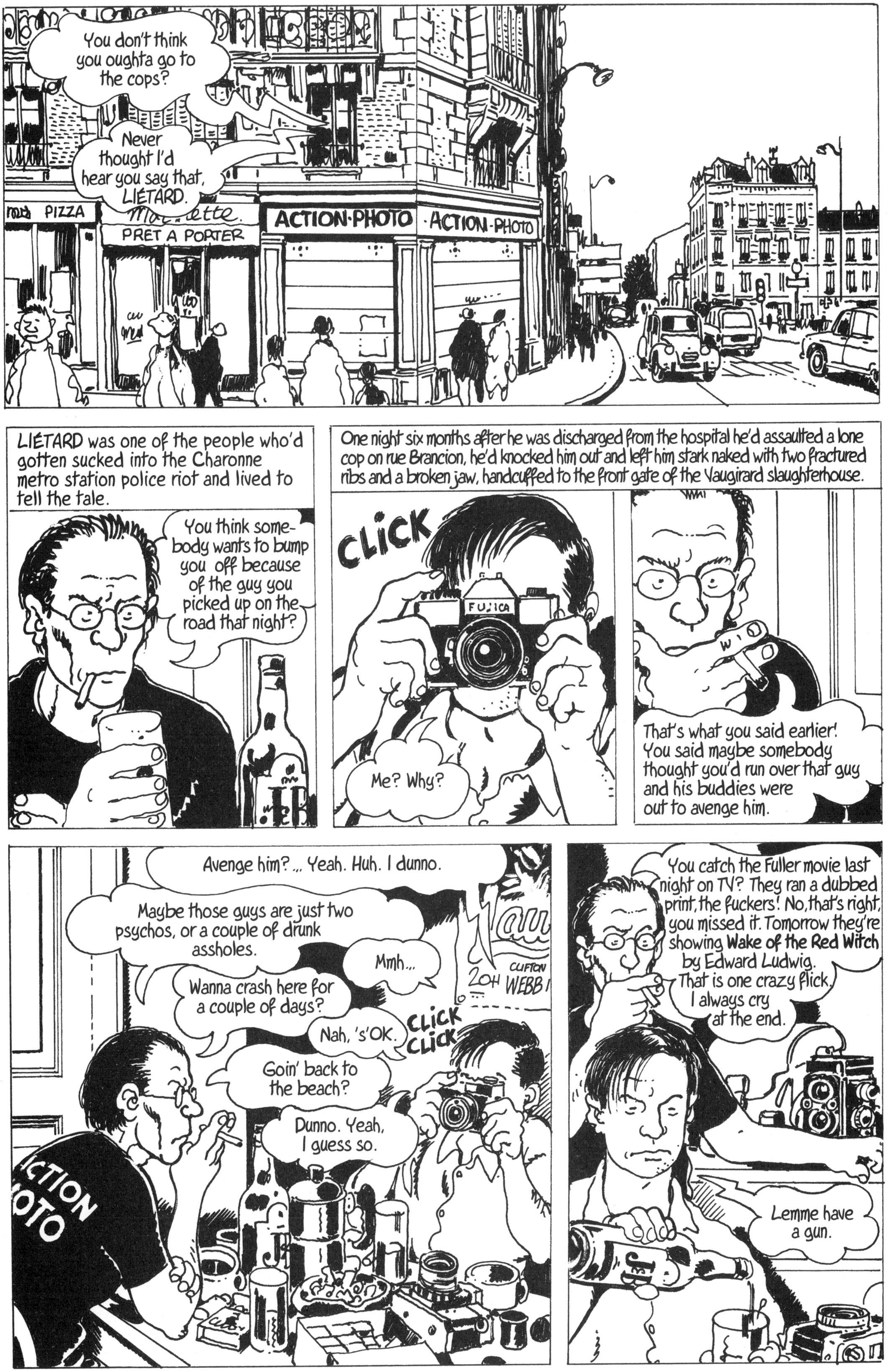

You don't think you oughta go to the cops?
Never thought I'd hear you say that, LIÉTARD.
PIZZA
PRET A PORTER
ACTION·PHOTO
ACTION·PHOTO
LIÉTARD was one of the people who'd gotten sucked into the Charonne metro station police riot and lived to tell the tale.
You think somebody wants to bump you off because of the guy you picked up on the road that night?
One night six months after he was discharged from the hospital he'd assaulted a lone cop on rue Brancion, he'd knocked him out and left him stark naked with two fractured ribs and a broken jaw, handcuffed to the front gate of the Vaugirard slaughterhouse.
CLICK
FUJICA
Me? Why?
That's what you said earlier! You said maybe somebody thought you'd run over that guy and his buddies were out to avenge him.
Avenge him? ... Yeah. Huh. I dunno.
Maybe those guys are just two psychos, or a couple of drunk assholes.
Mmh...
Wanna crash here for a couple of days?
Nah, 's'OK.
CLICK CLICK
Goin' back to the beach?
Dunno. Yeah, I guess so.
CLIFTON WEBB
ACTION PHOTO
You catch the Fuller movie last night on TV? They ran a dubbed print, the fuckers! No, that's right, you missed it. Tomorrow they're showing **Wake of the Red Witch** by Edward Ludwig. That is one crazy flick. I always cry at the end.
Lemme have a gun.

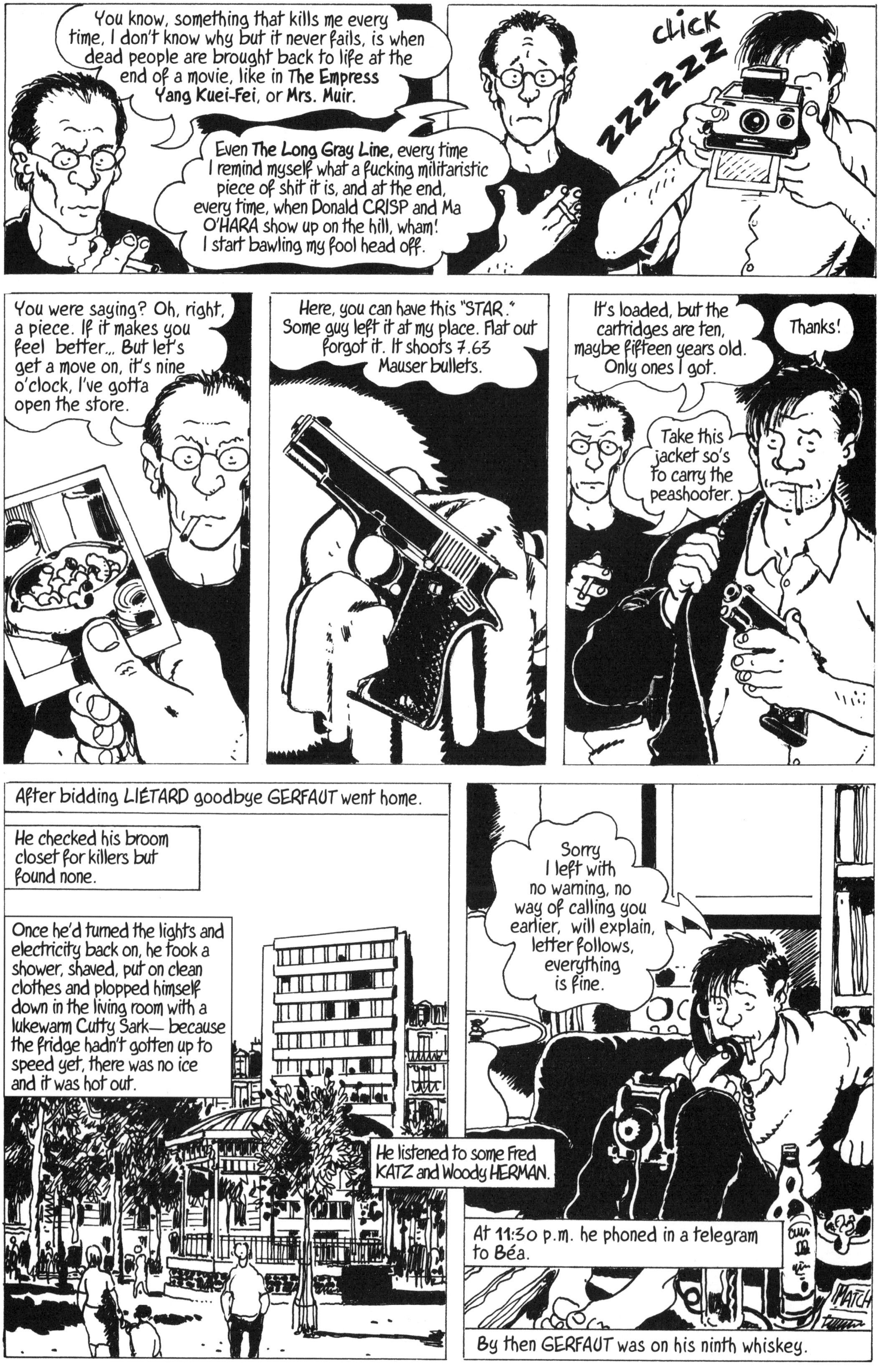

You know, something that kills me every time, I don't know why but it never fails, is when dead people are brought back to life at the end of a movie, like in The Empress Yang Kuei-Fei, or Mrs. Muir.
Even The Long Gray Line, every time I remind myself what a fucking militaristic piece of shit it is, and at the end, every time, when Donald CRISP and Ma O'HARA show up on the hill, wham! I start bawling my fool head off.
CLICK
ZZZZZZ
You were saying? Oh, right, a piece. If it makes you feel better... But let's get a move on, it's nine o'clock, I've gotta open the store.
Here, you can have this "STAR." Some guy left it at my place. Flat out forgot it. It shoots 7.63 Mauser bullets.
It's loaded, but the cartridges are ten, maybe fifteen years old. Only ones I got.
Thanks!
Take this jacket so's to carry the peashooter.
After bidding LIÉTARD goodbye GERFAUT went home.
He checked his broom closet for killers but found none.
Once he'd turned the lights and electricity back on, he took a shower, shaved, put on clean clothes and plopped himself down in the living room with a lukewarm Cutty Sark— because the fridge hadn't gotten up to speed yet, there was no ice and it was hot out.
He listened to some Fred KATZ and Woody HERMAN.
Sorry I left with no warning, no way of calling you earlier, will explain, letter follows, everything is fine.
At 11:30 p.m. he phoned in a telegram to Béa.
By then GERFAUT was on his ninth whiskey.

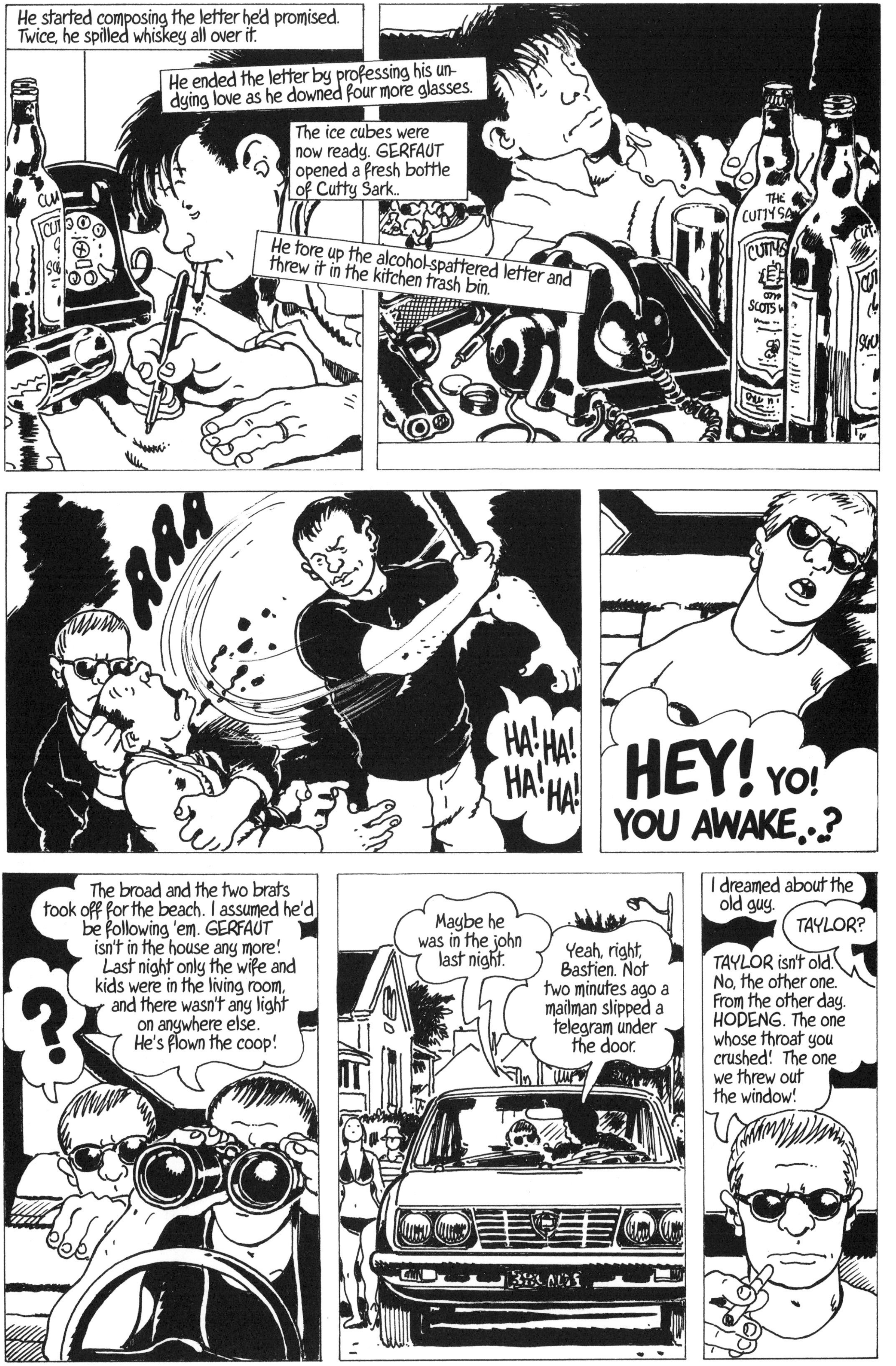
He started composing the letter he'd promised. Twice, he spilled whiskey all over it.
He ended the letter by professing his undying love as he downed four more glasses.
The ice cubes were now ready. GERFAUT opened a fresh bottle of Cutty Sark..
He tore up the alcohol-spattered letter and threw it in the kitchen trash bin.
THE CUTTY SARK
SCOTS
AAA
HA! HA! HA! HA!
HEY! YO! YOU AWAKE..?
The broad and the two brats took off for the beach. I assumed he'd be following 'em. GERFAUT isn't in the house any more! Last night only the wife and kids were in the living room, and there wasn't any light on anywhere else. He's flown the coop!
?
Maybe he was in the john last night.
Yeah, right, Bastien. Not two minutes ago a mailman slipped a telegram under the door.
I dreamed about the old guy.
TAYLOR?
TAYLOR isn't old. No, the other one. From the other day. HODENG. The one whose throat you crushed! The one we threw out the window!

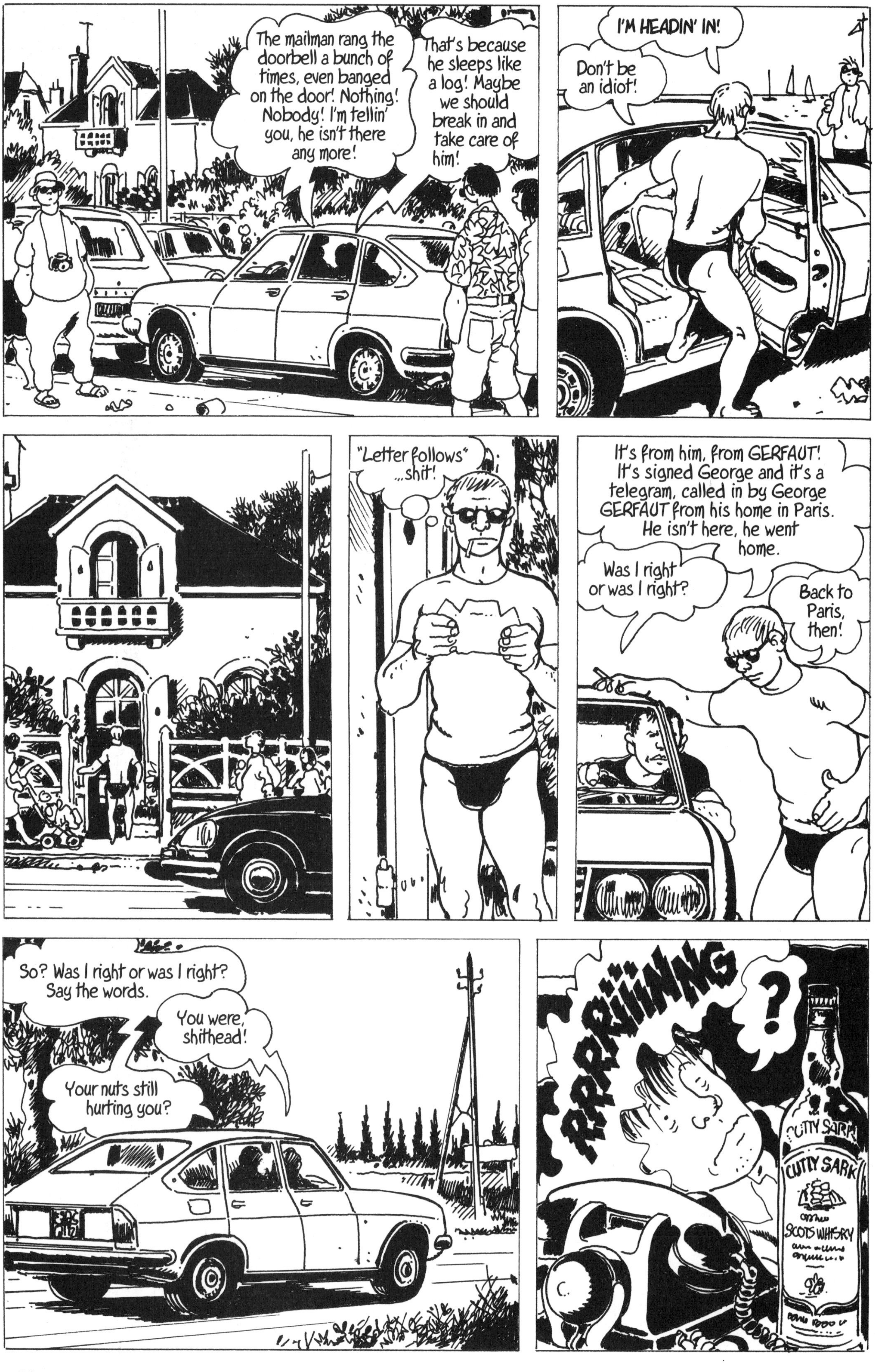
The mailman rang the doorbell a bunch of times, even banged on the door! Nothing! Nobody! I'm tellin' you, he isn't there any more!
That's because he sleeps like a log! Maybe we should break in and take care of him!
I'M HEADIN' IN!
Don't be an idiot!
"Letter follows" ...shit!
It's from him, from GERFAUT! It's signed George and it's a telegram, called in by George GERFAUT from his home in Paris. He isn't here, he went home.
Was I right or was I right?
Back to Paris, then!
So? Was I right or was I right? Say the words.
You were, shithead!
Your nuts still hurting you?
RRRRIIIING
?
CUTTY SARK
CUTTY SARK
SCOTS WHISKY

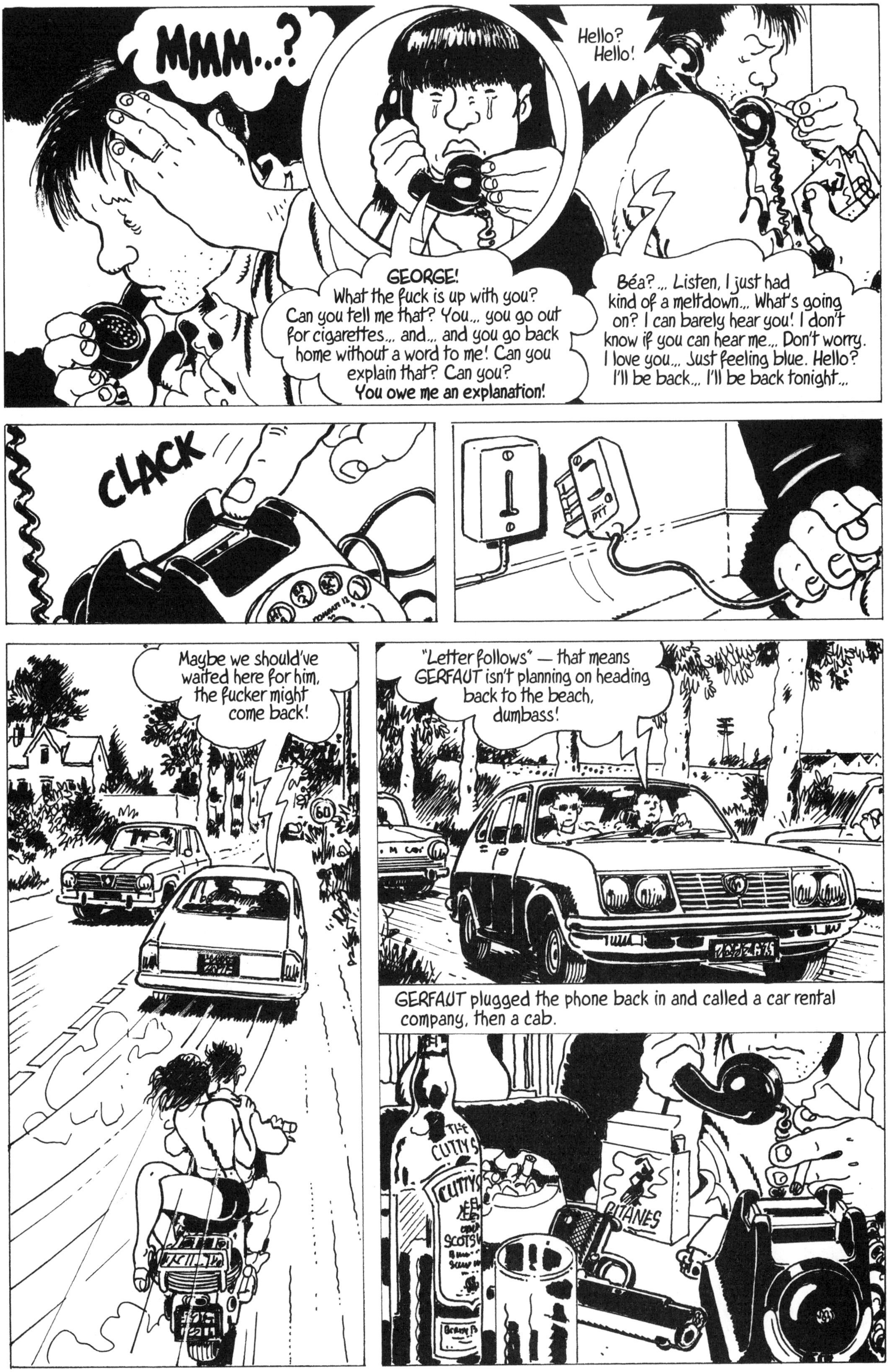
MMM...?
Hello? Hello!
GEORGE! What the fuck is up with you? Can you tell me that? You... you go out for cigarettes... and... and you go back home without a word to me! Can you explain that? Can you? You owe me an explanation!
Béa? ... Listen, I just had kind of a meltdown... What's going on? I can barely hear you! I don't know if you can hear me... Don't worry. I love you... Just feeling blue. Hello? I'll be back... I'll be back tonight...
CLACK
Maybe we should've waited here for him, the fucker might come back!
"Letter follows" — that means GERFAUT isn't planning on heading back to the beach, dumbass!
GERFAUT plugged the phone back in and called a car rental company, then a cab.

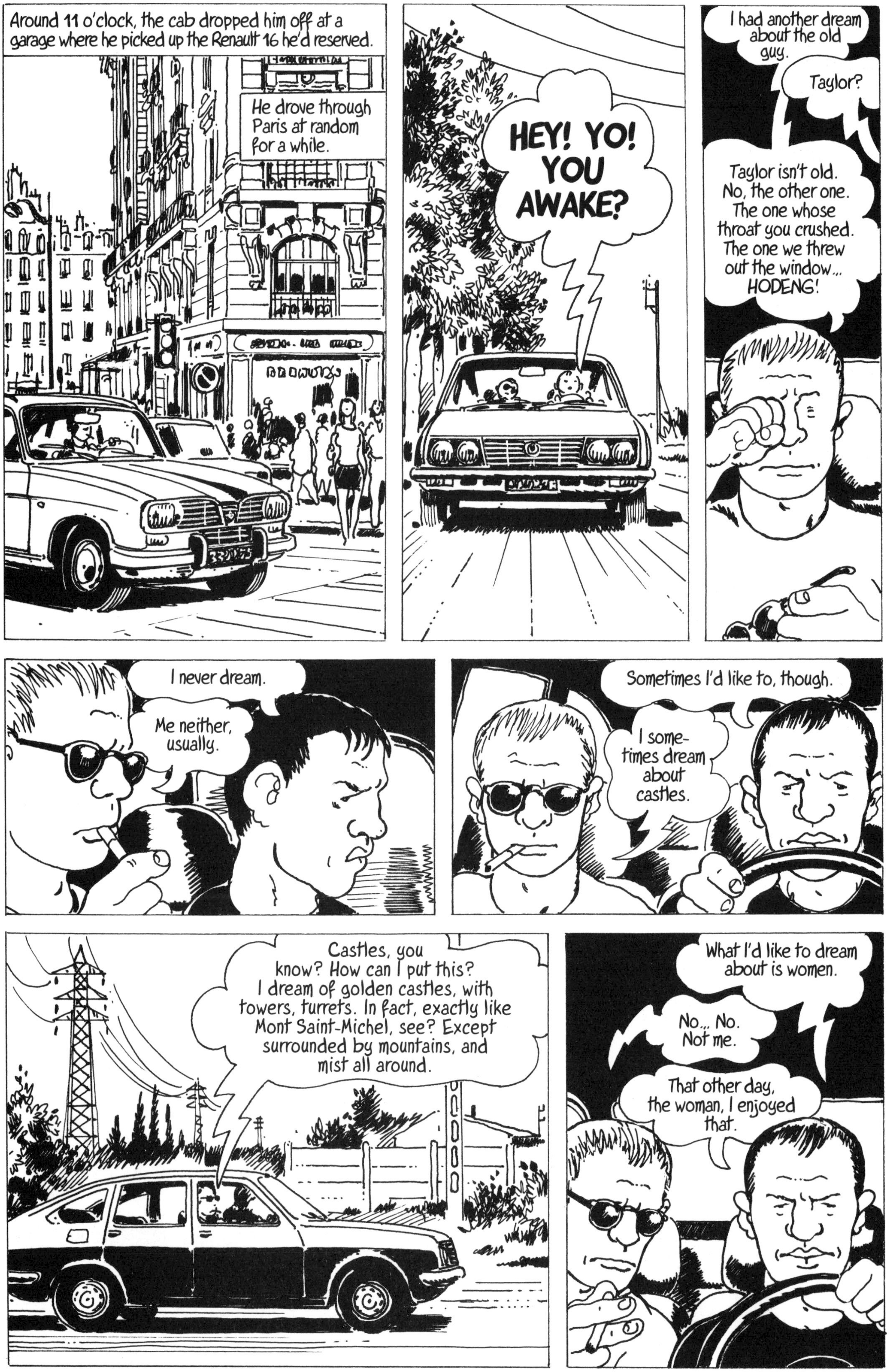

Around 11 o'clock, the cab dropped him off at a garage where he picked up the Renault 16 he'd reserved.
He drove through Paris at random for a while.
HEY! YO! YOU AWAKE?
I had another dream about the old guy.
Taylor?
Taylor isn't old. No, the other one. The one whose throat you crushed. The one we threw out the window... HODENG!
I never dream.
Me neither, usually.
Sometimes I'd like to, though.
I sometimes dream about castles.
Castles, you know? How can I put this? I dream of golden castles, with towers, turrets. In fact, exactly like Mont Saint-Michel, see? Except surrounded by mountains, and mist all around.
What I'd like to dream about is women.
No... No. Not me.
That other day, the woman, I enjoyed that.

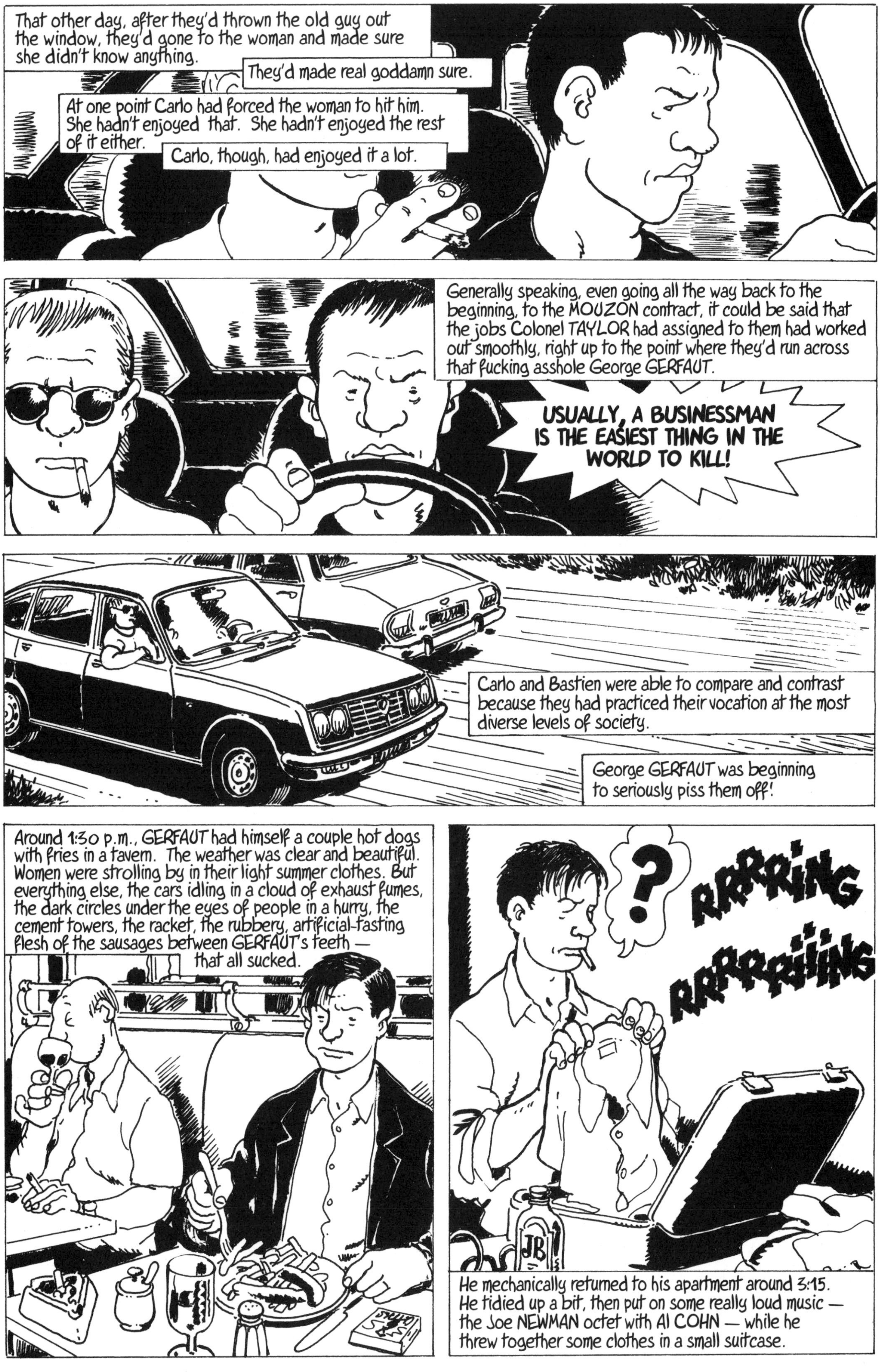
That other day, after they'd thrown the old guy out the window, they'd gone to the woman and made sure she didn't know anything.
They'd made real goddamn sure.
At one point Carlo had forced the woman to hit him. She hadn't enjoyed that. She hadn't enjoyed the rest of it either.
Carlo, though, had enjoyed it a lot.
Generally speaking, even going all the way back to the beginning, to the MOUZON contract, it could be said that the jobs Colonel TAYLOR had assigned to them had worked out smoothly, right up to the point where they'd run across that fucking asshole George GERFAUT.
USUALLY, A BUSINESSMAN IS THE EASIEST THING IN THE WORLD TO KILL!
Carlo and Bastien were able to compare and contrast because they had practiced their vocation at the most diverse levels of society.
George GERFAUT was beginning to seriously piss them off!
Around 1:30 p.m., GERFAUT had himself a couple hot dogs with fries in a tavern. The weather was clear and beautiful. Women were strolling by in their light summer clothes. But everything else, the cars idling in a cloud of exhaust fumes, the dark circles under the eyes of people in a hurry, the cement towers, the racket, the rubbery, artificial-tasting flesh of the sausages between GERFAUT's teeth —
that all sucked.
?
RRRRING
RRRRIIING
JB
He mechanically returned to his apartment around 3:15. He tidied up a bit, then put on some really loud music — the Joe NEWMAN octet with Al COHN — while he threw together some clothes in a small suitcase.

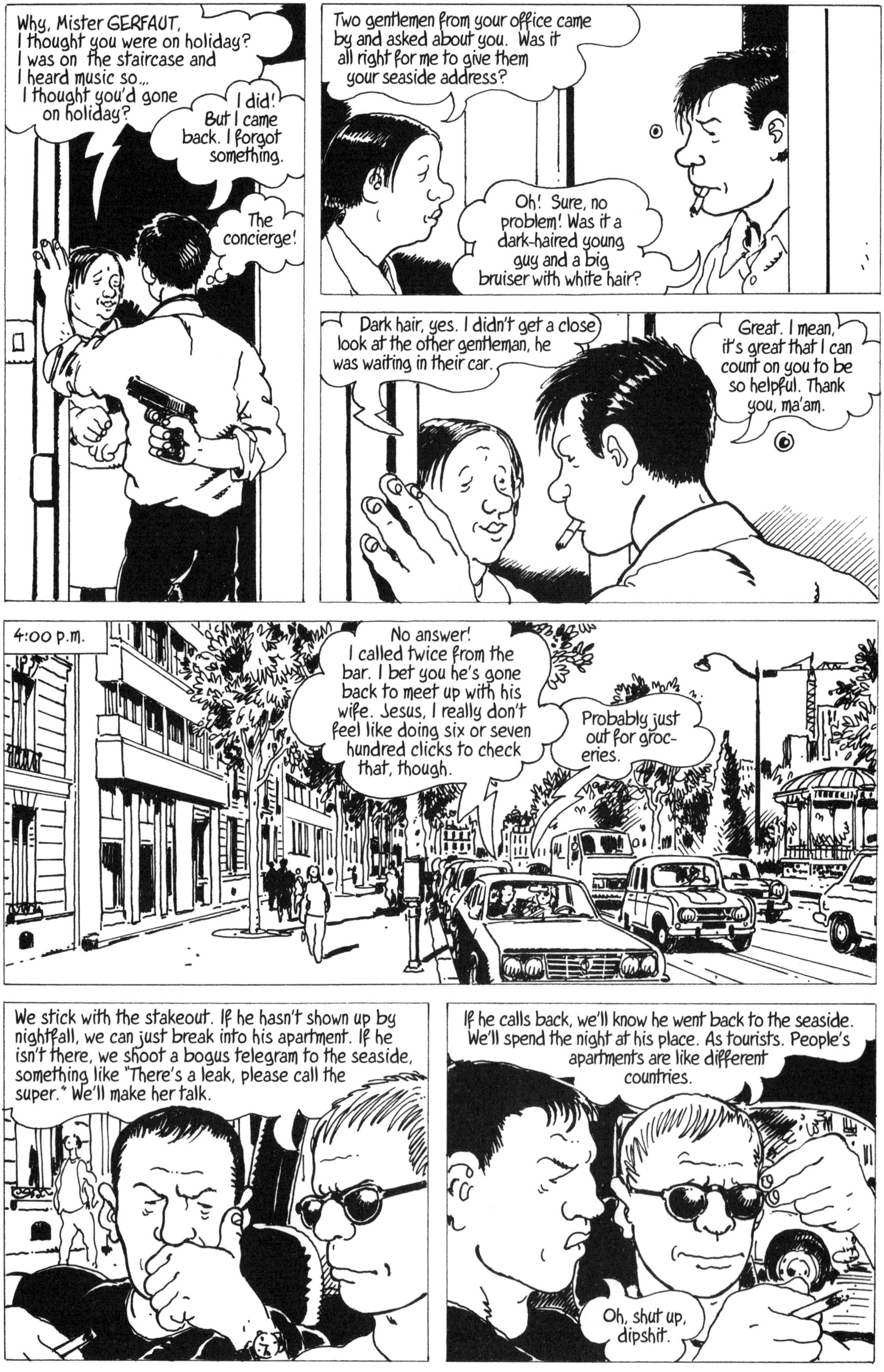
Why, Mister GERFAUT, I thought you were on holiday? I was on the staircase and I heard music so... I thought you'd gone on holiday?
I did! But I came back. I forgot something.
The concierge!
Two gentlemen from your office came by and asked about you. Was it all right for me to give them your seaside address?
Oh! Sure, no problem! Was it a dark-haired young guy and a big bruiser with white hair?
Dark hair, yes. I didn't get a close look at the other gentleman, he was waiting in their car.
Great. I mean, it's great that I can count on you to be so helpful. Thank you, ma'am.
4:00 p.m.
No answer! I called twice from the bar. I bet you he's gone back to meet up with his wife. Jesus, I really don't feel like doing six or seven hundred clicks to check that, though.
Probably just out for groceries.
We stick with the stakeout. If he hasn't shown up by nightfall, we can just break into his apartment. If he isn't there, we shoot a bogus telegram to the seaside, something like "There's a leak, please call the super." We'll make her talk.
If he calls back, we'll know he went back to the seaside. We'll spend the night at his place. As tourists. People's apartments are like different countries.
Oh, shut up, dipshit.

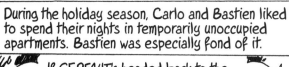

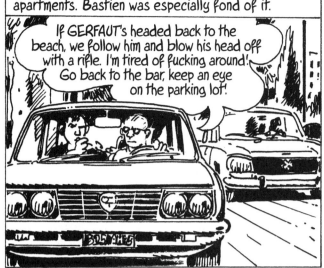

During the holiday season, Carlo and Bastien liked to spend their nights in temporarily unoccupied apartments. Bastien was especially fond of it.
If GERFAUT's headed back to the beach, we follow him and blow his head off with a rifle. I'm tired of fucking around! Go back to the bar, keep an eye on the parking lot!
Bea!... I'm just feeling sort of depressed. I'll get over it, don't worry. I figure I'll get back into town in about three days four on the outside. George
CUTTY SARK
SCOTS WHISKY
BUT SPIDERMAN HAS A SIXTH SENSE THAT ALLOWS HIM TO SENSE THE DANGER... AND HE STOPS SHORT AT THE VERY LAST INSTANT! WHAT TH–? AN ELECTRICAL DISCHARGE! I ONLY ESCAPED BY A MIRACLE!
SPIDERMAN
POSTES
SHIT! GERFAUT!
HE'S GOING INTO HIS APARTMENT!
HE'S HERE, THE FUCKER'S HERE!
POSTES

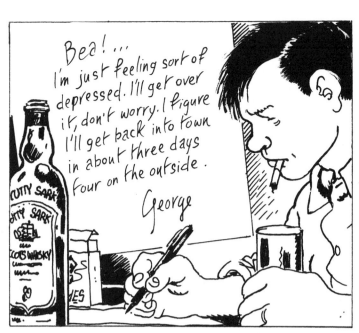

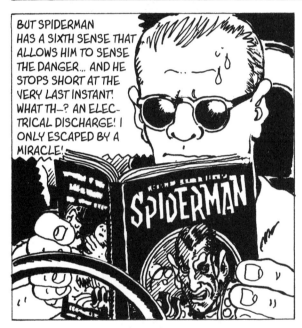

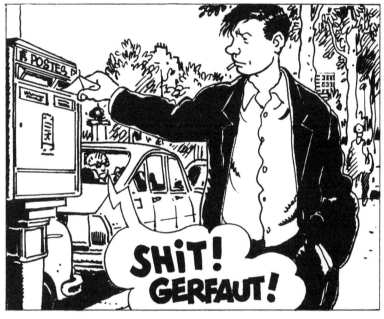

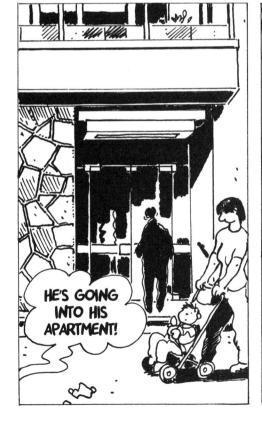

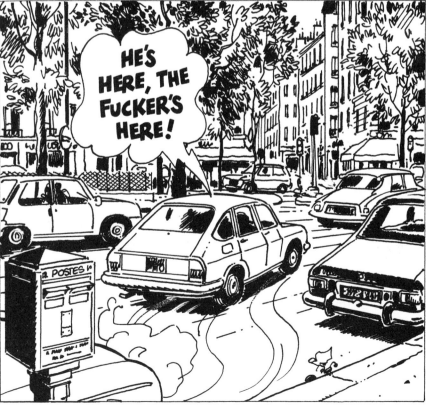

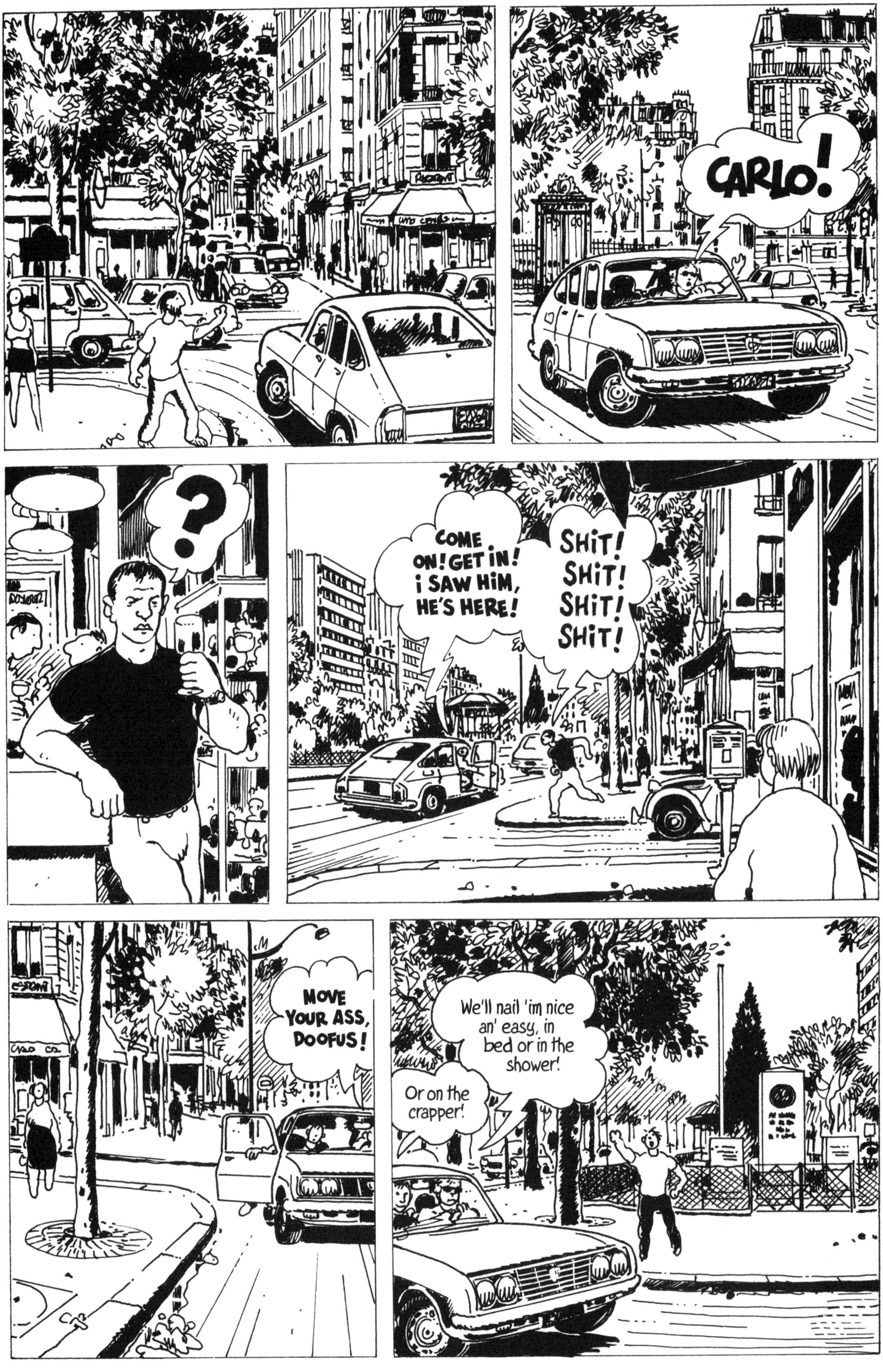
CARLO!
?
COME ON! GET IN! I SAW HIM, HE'S HERE!
SHIT! SHIT! SHIT! SHIT!
MOVE YOUR ASS, DOOFUS!
We'll nail 'im nice an' easy, in bed or in the shower!
Or on the crapper!

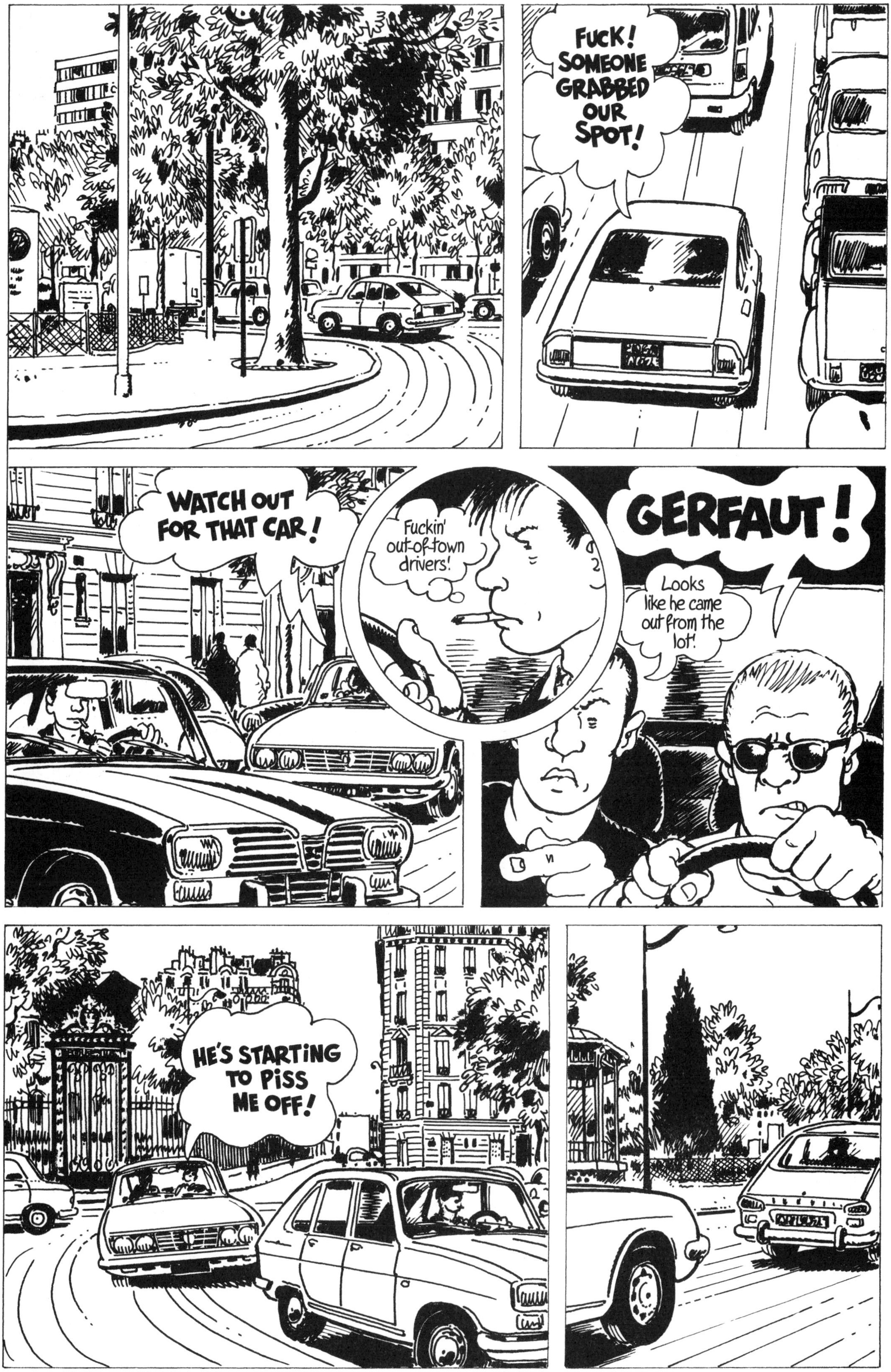
FUCK! SOMEONE GRABBED OUR SPOT!
WATCH OUT FOR THAT CAR!
Fuckin' out-of-town drivers!
GERFAUT!
Looks like he came out from the lot!
HE'S STARTING TO PISS ME OFF!

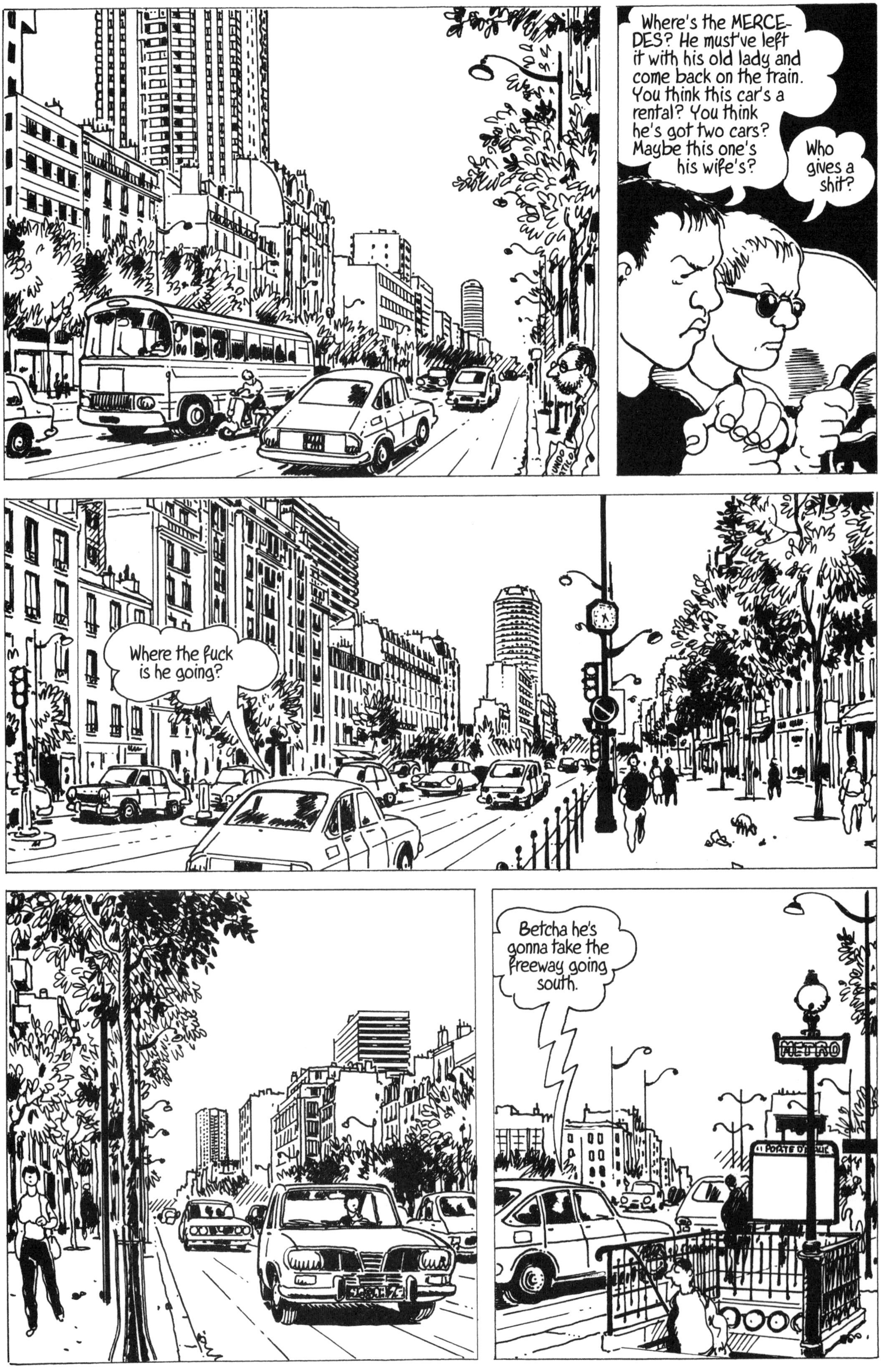
Where's the MERCEDES? He must've left it with his old lady and come back on the train. You think this car's a rental? You think he's got two cars? Maybe this one's his wife's?
Who gives a shit?
Where the fuck is he going?
METRO
PORTE D'ITALIE
Betcha he's gonna take the freeway going south.

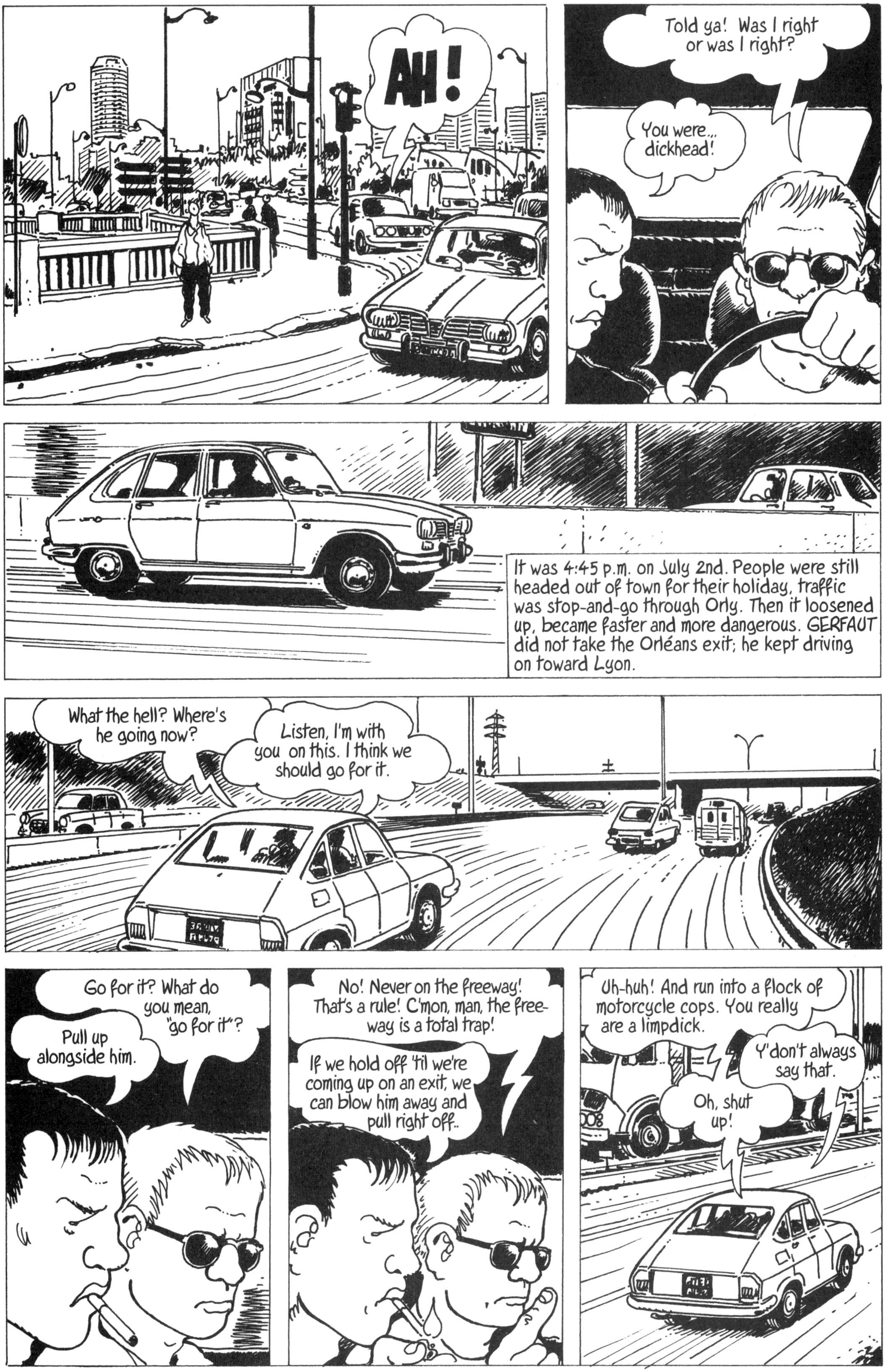
AH!
Told ya! Was I right or was I right?
You were... dickhead!
It was 4:45 p.m. on July 2nd. People were still headed out of town for their holiday, traffic was stop-and-go through Orly. Then it loosened up, became faster and more dangerous. GERFAUT did not take the Orléans exit; he kept driving on toward Lyon.
What the hell? Where's he going now?
Listen, I'm with you on this. I think we should go for it.
Go for it? What do you mean, "go for it"?
Pull up alongside him.
No! Never on the freeway! That's a rule! C'mon, man, the freeway is a total trap!
If we hold off 'til we're coming up on an exit, we can blow him away and pull right off..
Uh-huh! And run into a flock of motorcycle cops. You really are a limpdick.
Y'don't always say that.
Oh, shut up!

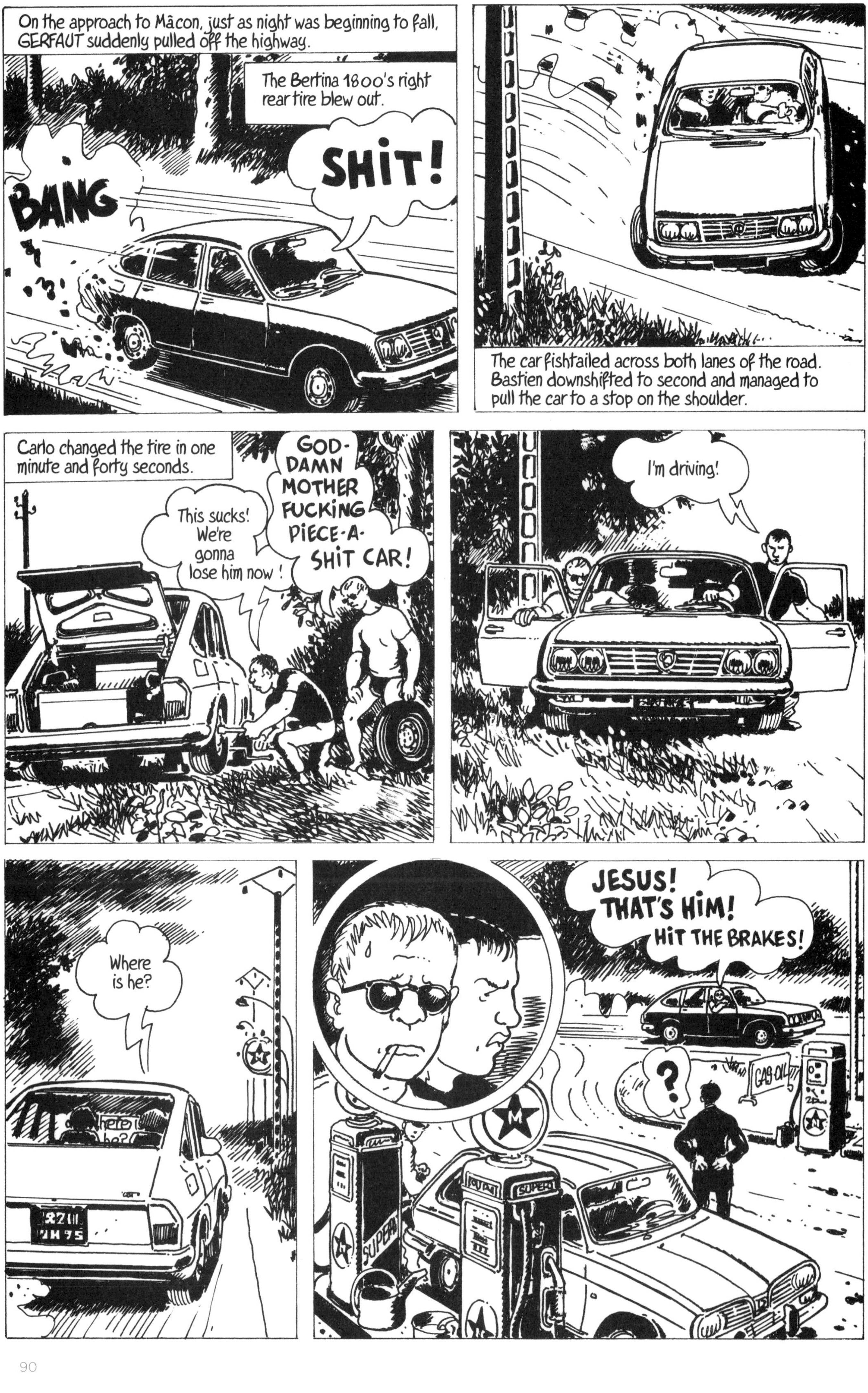
On the approach to Mâcon, just as night was beginning to fall, GERFAUT suddenly pulled off the highway.
The Bertina 1800's right rear tire blew out.
BANG
SHIT!
The car fishtailed across both lanes of the road. Bastien downshifted to second and managed to pull the car to a stop on the shoulder.
Carlo changed the tire in one minute and forty seconds.
This sucks! We're gonna lose him now!
GOD-DAMN MOTHER FUCKING PIECE-A-SHIT CAR!
I'm driving!
Where is he?
JESUS! THAT'S HIM! HIT THE BRAKES!
?
GAS-OIL
SUPER

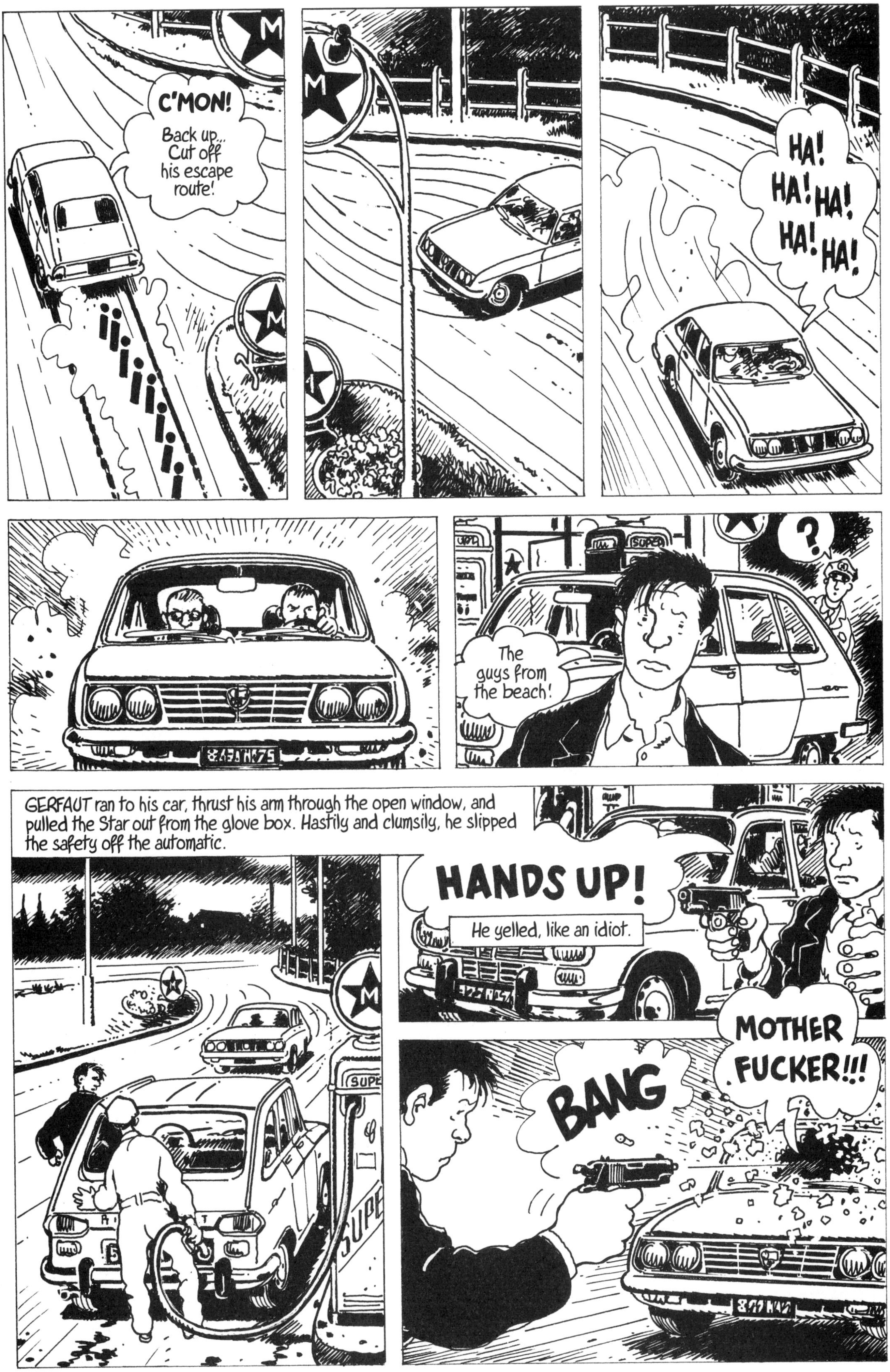
C'MON!
Back up... Cut off his escape route!
HA! HA! HA! HA! HA!
The guys from the beach!
?
GERFAUT ran to his car, thrust his arm through the open window, and pulled the Star out from the glove box. Hastily and clumsily, he slipped the safety off the automatic.
HANDS UP!
He yelled, like an idiot.
BANG
MOTHER FUCKER!!!

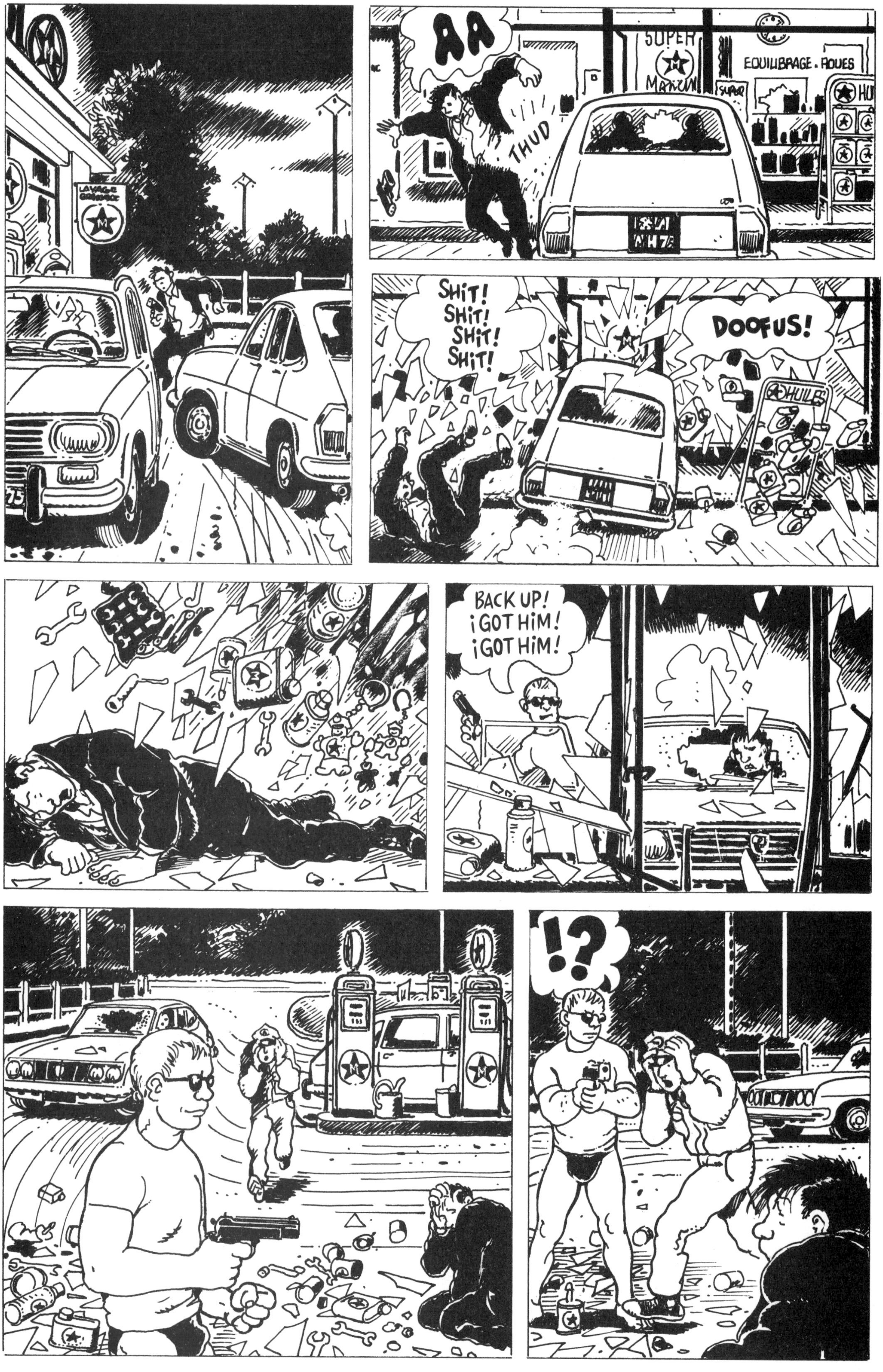
AA
THUD
SUPER
EQUILIBRAGE • ROUES
SHIT! SHIT! SHIT! SHIT!
DOOFUS!
HUILES
BACK UP! ¡GOT HIM! ¡GOT HIM!
!?

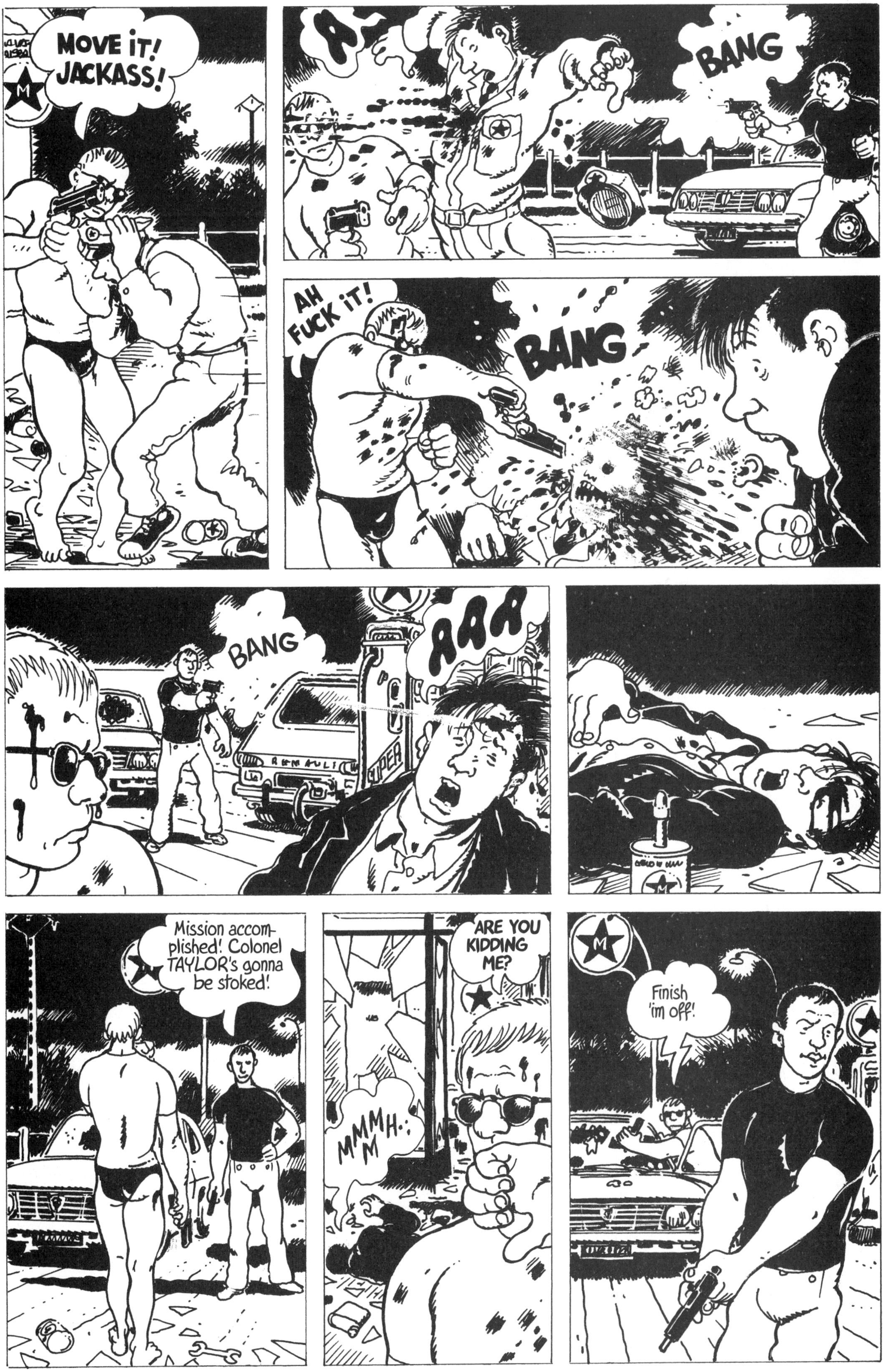
MOVE IT! JACKASS!
A
BANG
AH FUCK IT!
BANG
BANG
AAA
Mission accom-plished! Colonel TAYLOR's gonna be stoked!
ARE YOU KIDDING ME?
MMMH.: M
Finish 'im off!

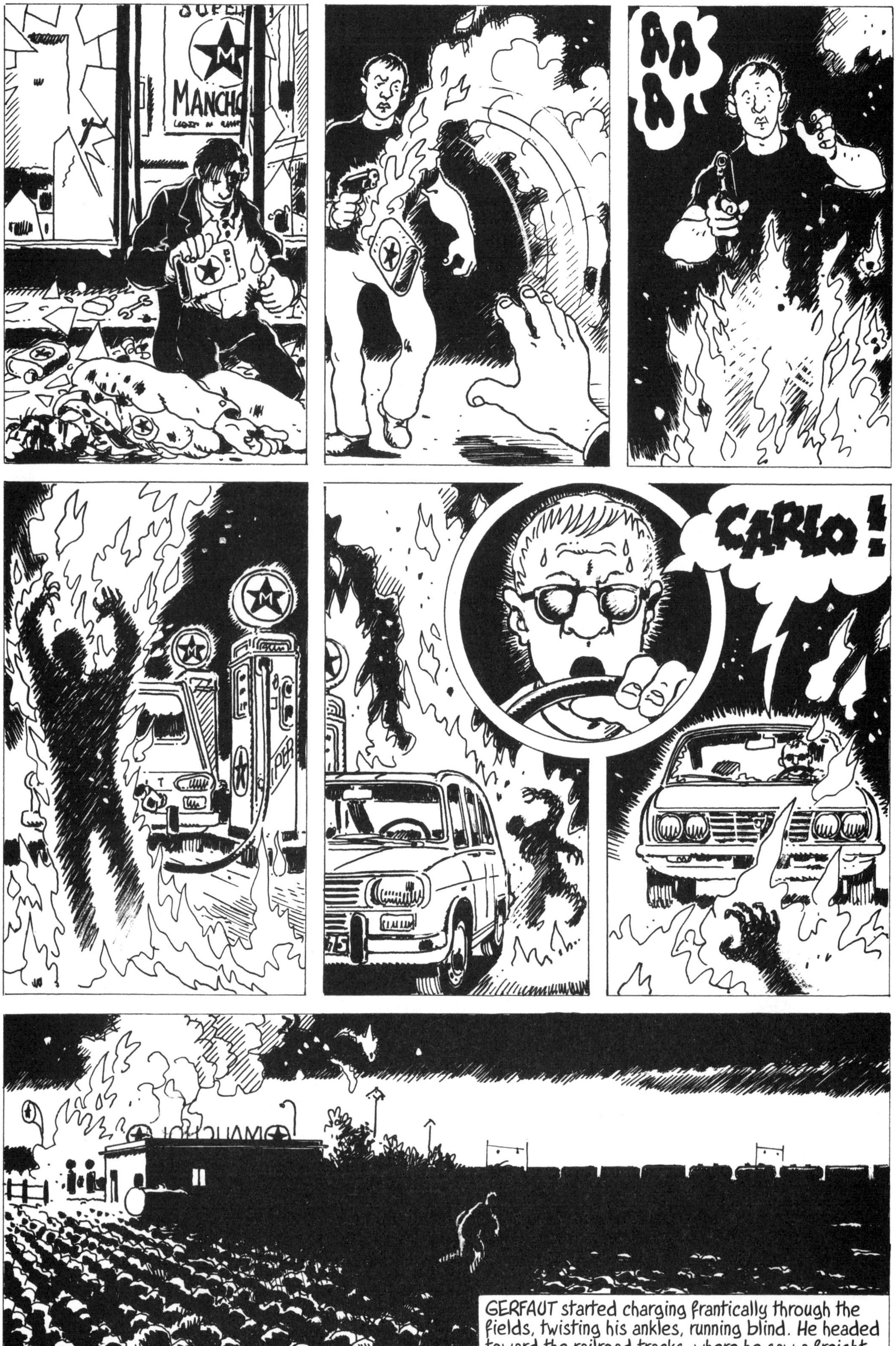
RAAA
CARLO!
GERFAUT started charging frantically through the fields, twisting his ankles, running blind. He headed toward the railroad tracks, where he saw a freight train rolling along at low speed.

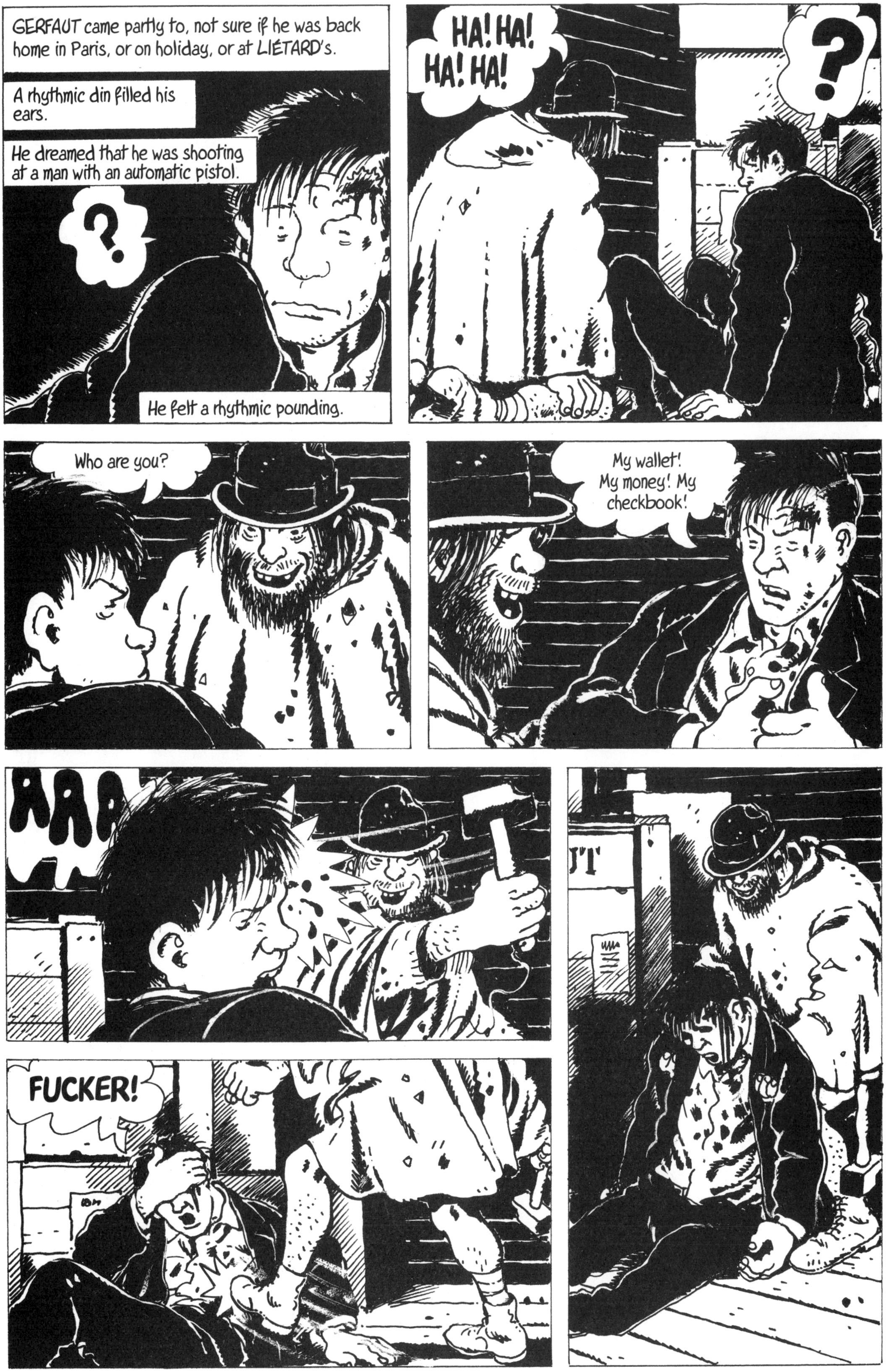

GERFAUT came partly to, not sure if he was back home in Paris, or on holiday, or at LIÉTARD's.
A rhythmic din filled his ears.
He dreamed that he was shooting at a man with an automatic pistol.
?
He felt a rhythmic pounding.
HA! HA! HA! HA!
?
Who are you?
My wallet! My money! My checkbook!
AAA
FUCKER!

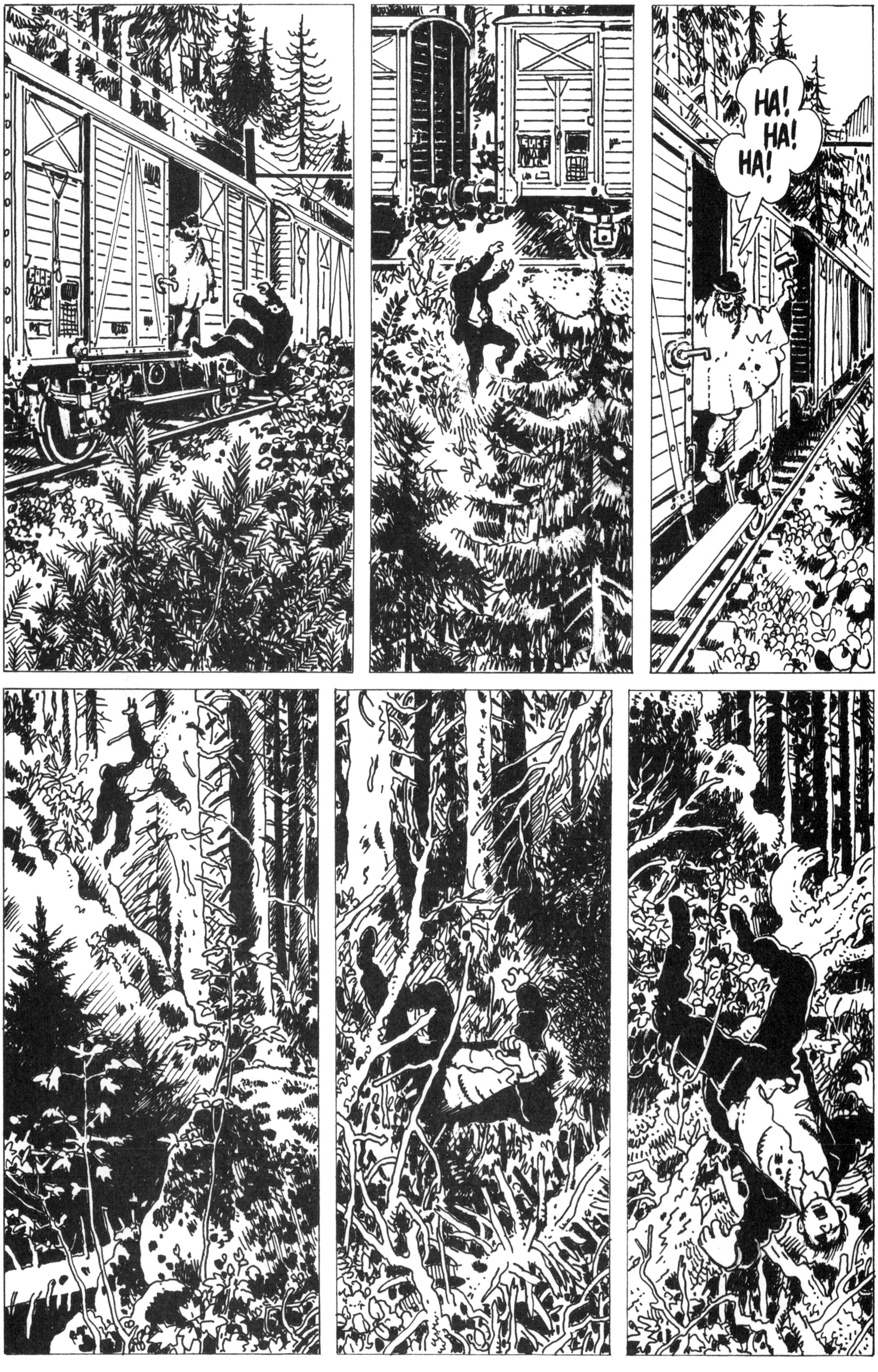
HA! HA! HA!

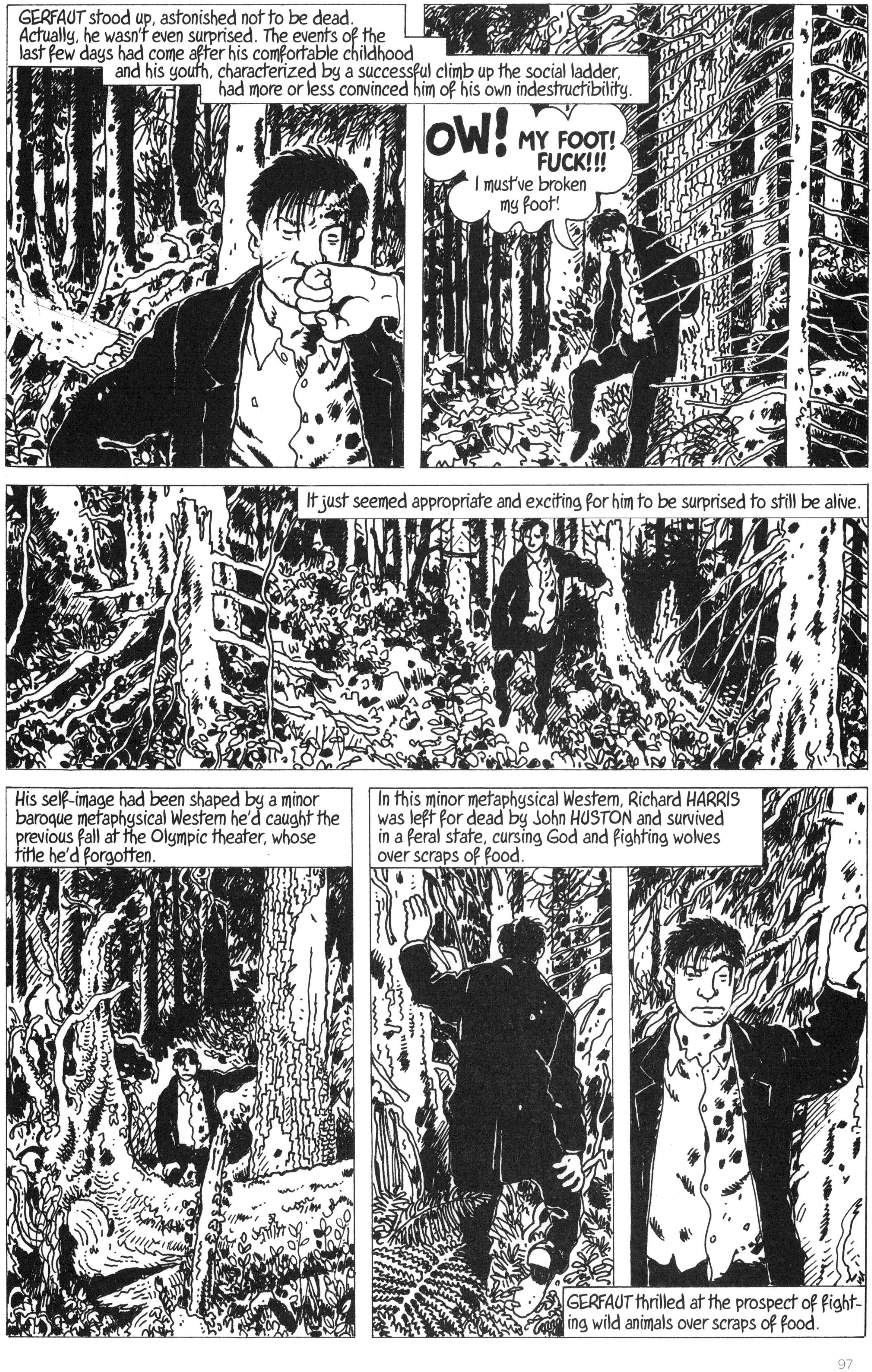
GERFAUT stood up, astonished not to be dead. Actually, he wasn't even surprised. The events of the last few days had come after his comfortable childhood and his youth, characterized by a successful climb up the social ladder, had more or less convinced him of his own indestructibility.
OW! MY FOOT! FUCK!!!
I must've broken my foot!
It just seemed appropriate and exciting for him to be surprised to still be alive.
His self-image had been shaped by a minor baroque metaphysical Western he'd caught the previous fall at the Olympic theater, whose title he'd forgotten.
In this minor metaphysical Western, Richard HARRIS was left for dead by John HUSTON and survived in a feral state, cursing God and fighting wolves over scraps of food.
GERFAUT thrilled at the prospect of fighting wild animals over scraps of food.

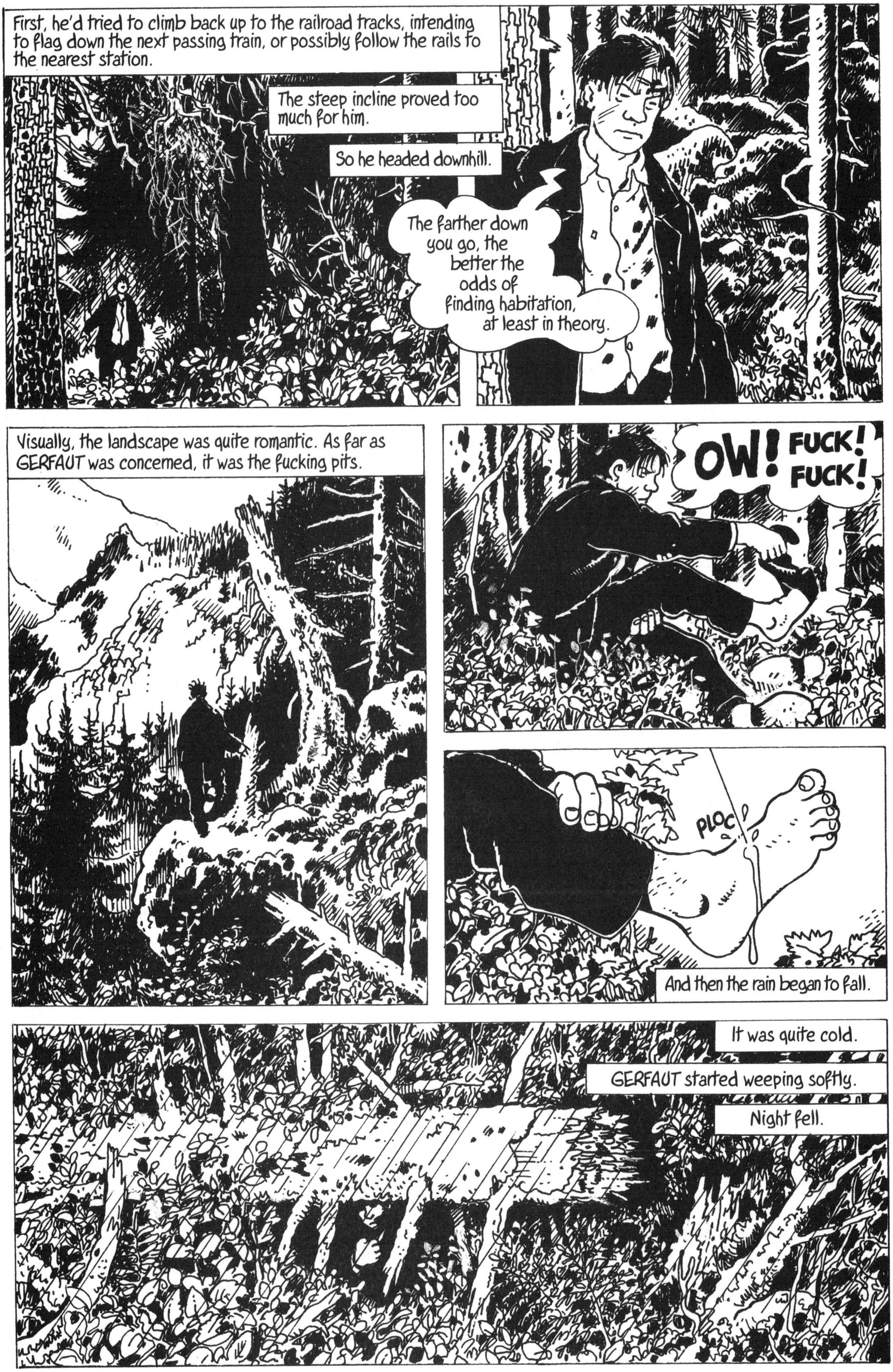
First, he'd tried to climb back up to the railroad tracks, intending to flag down the next passing train, or possibly follow the rails to the nearest station.
The steep incline proved too much for him.
So he headed downhill.
The farther down you go, the better the odds of finding habitation, at least in theory.
Visually, the landscape was quite romantic. As far as GERFAUT was concerned, it was the fucking pits.
OW! FUCK! FUCK!
PLOC
And then the rain began to fall.
It was quite cold.
GERFAUT started weeping softly.
Night fell.

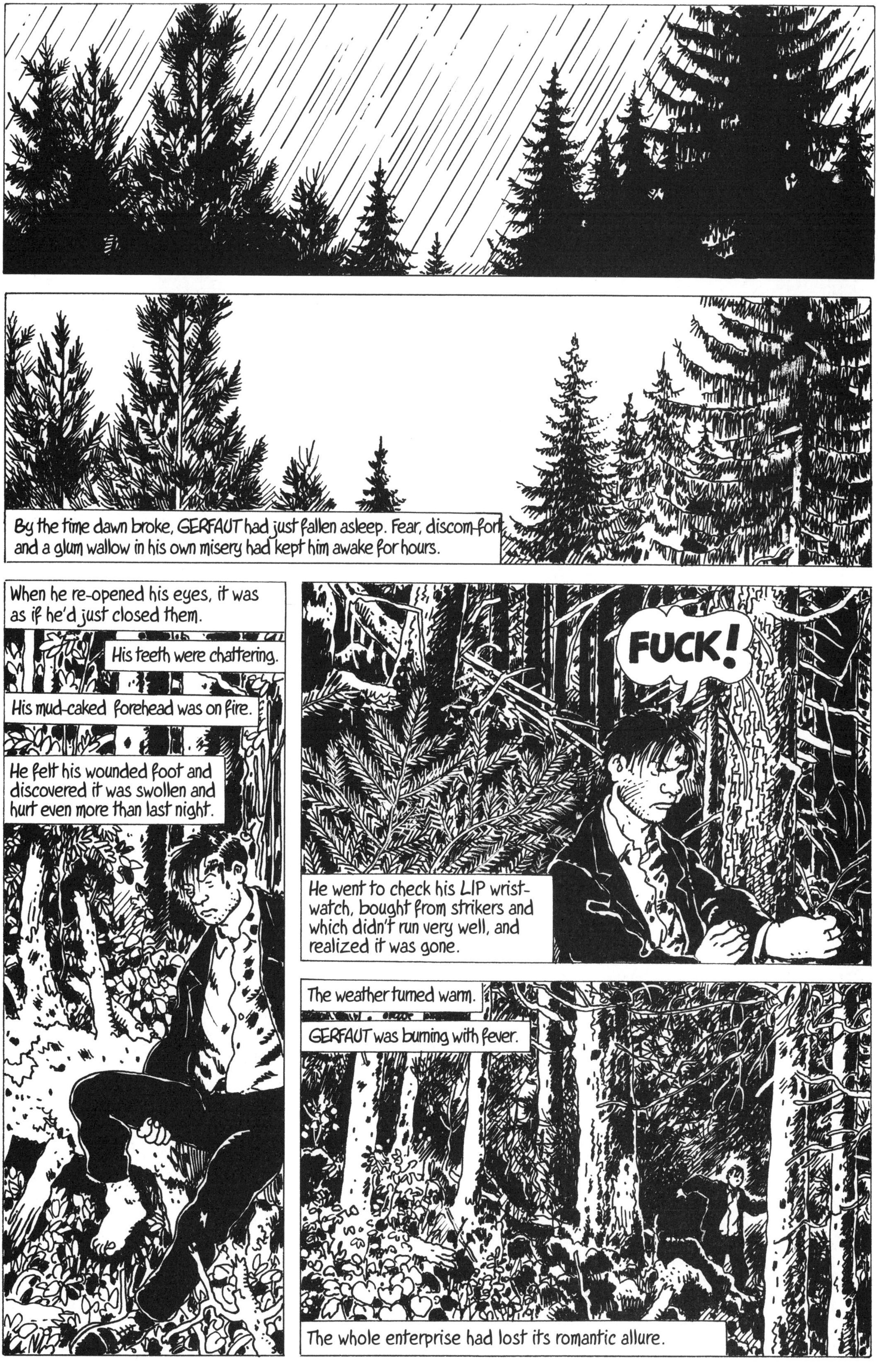

By the time dawn broke, GERFAUT had just fallen asleep. Fear, discom-fort and a glum wallow in his own misery had kept him awake for hours.
When he re-opened his eyes, it was as if he'd just closed them.
His teeth were chattering.
His mud-caked forehead was on fire.
He felt his wounded foot and discovered it was swollen and hurt even more than last night.
FUCK!
He went to check his LIP wrist-watch, bought from strikers and which didn't run very well, and realized it was gone.
The weather turned warm.
GERFAUT was burning with fever.
The whole enterprise had lost its romantic allure.

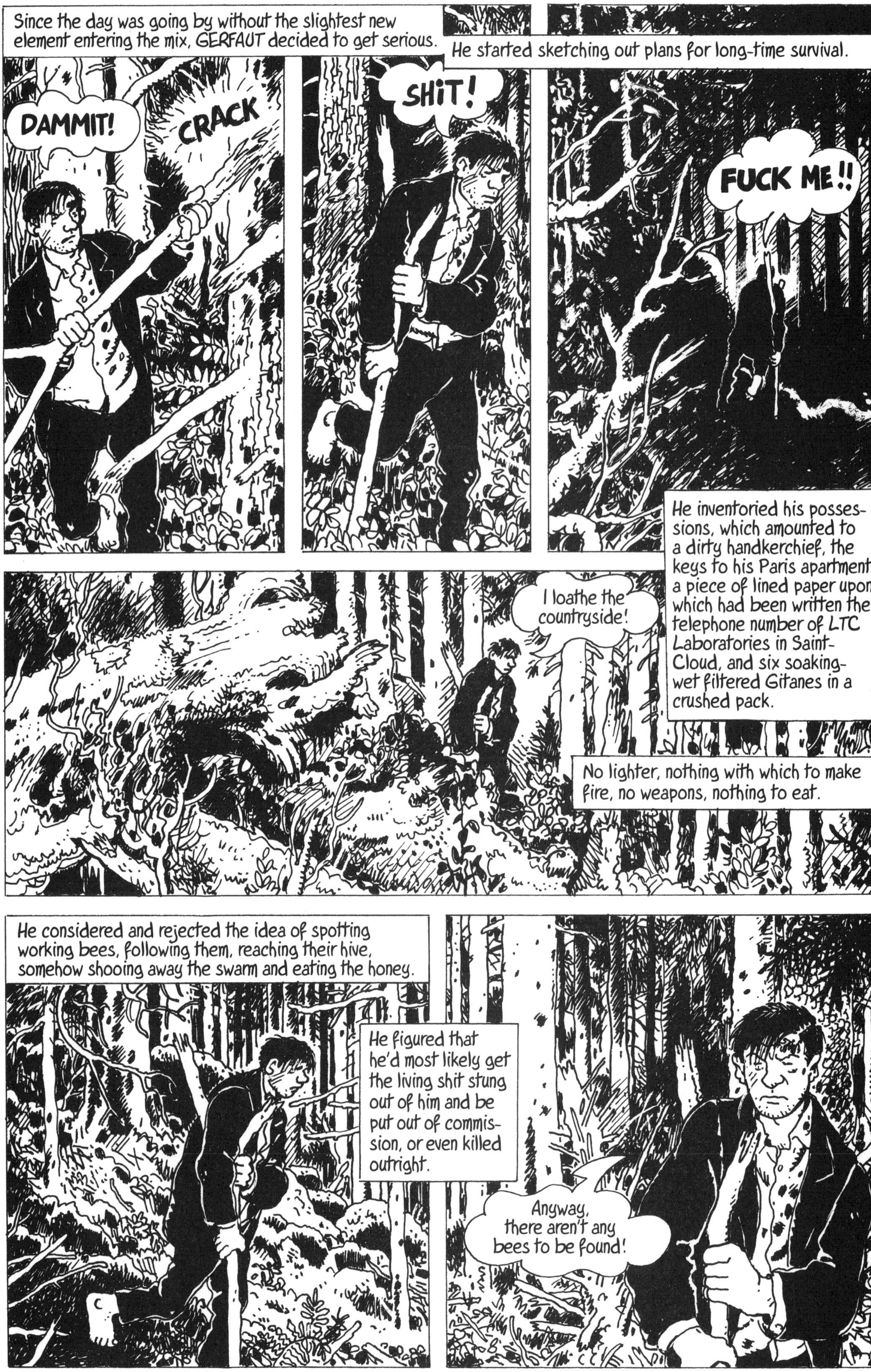

Since the day was going by without the slightest new element entering the mix, GERFAUT decided to get serious.
DAMMIT!
CRACK
He started sketching out plans for long-time survival.
SHIT!
FUCK ME!!
He inventoried his possessions, which amounted to a dirty handkerchief, the keys to his Paris apartment, a piece of lined paper upon which had been written the telephone number of LTC Laboratories in Saint-Cloud, and six soaking-wet filtered Gitanes in a crushed pack.
I loathe the countryside!
No lighter, nothing with which to make fire, no weapons, nothing to eat.
He considered and rejected the idea of spotting working bees, following them, reaching their hive, somehow shooing away the swarm and eating the honey.
He figured that he'd most likely get the living shit stung out of him and be put out of commission, or even killed outright.
Anyway, there aren't any bees to be found!

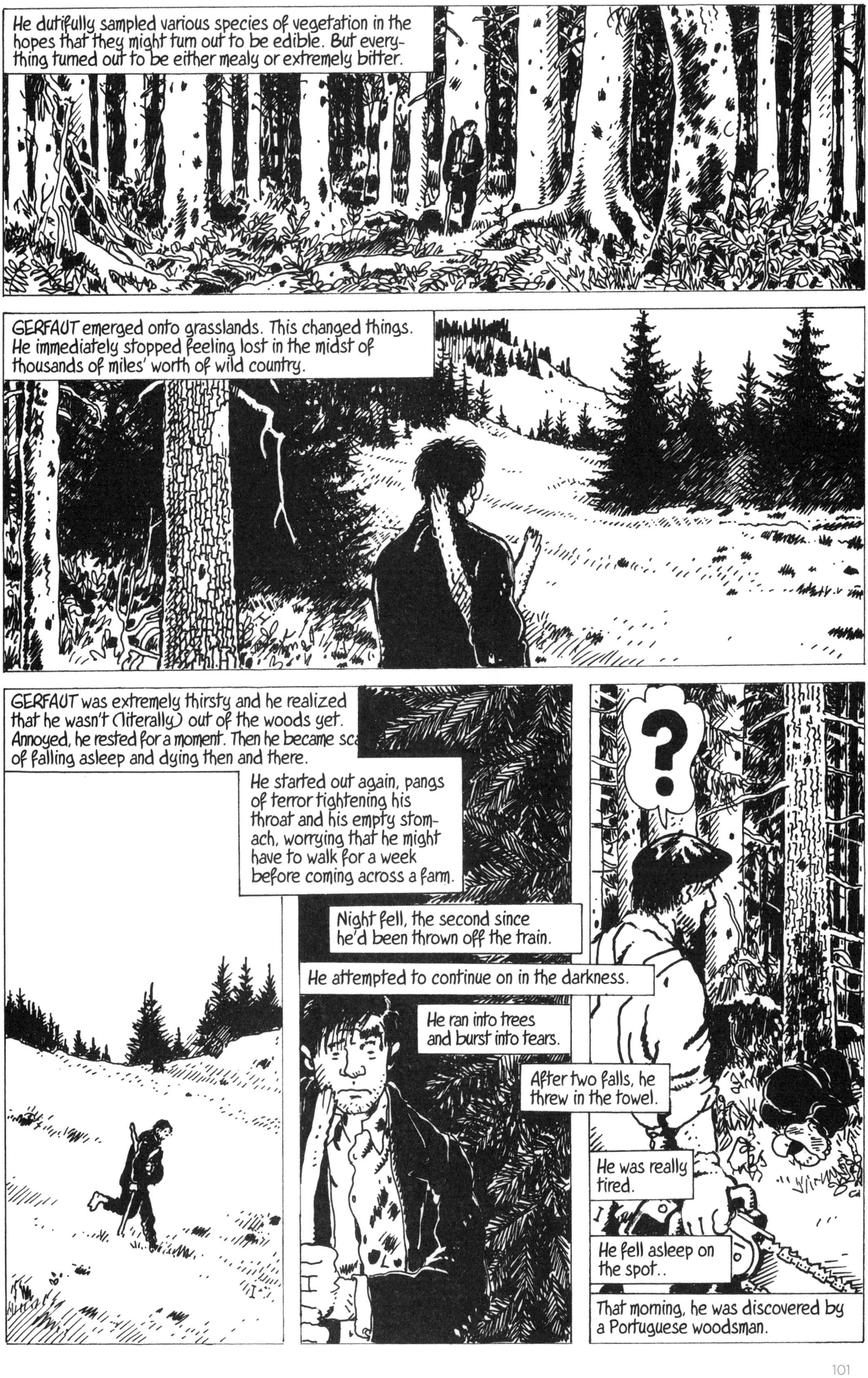
He dutifully sampled various species of vegetation in the hopes that they might turn out to be edible. But everything turned out to be either mealy or extremely bitter.
GERFAUT emerged onto grasslands. This changed things. He immediately stopped feeling lost in the midst of thousands of miles' worth of wild country.
GERFAUT was extremely thirsty and he realized that he wasn't (literally) out of the woods yet. Annoyed, he rested for a moment. Then he became sca of falling asleep and dying then and there.
He started out again, pangs of terror tightening his throat and his empty stomach, worrying that he might have to walk for a week before coming across a farm.
Night fell, the second since he'd been thrown off the train.
He attempted to continue on in the darkness.
He ran into trees and burst into tears.
After two falls, he threw in the towel.
He was really tired.
He fell asleep on the spot..
?
That morning, he was discovered by a Portuguese woodsman.

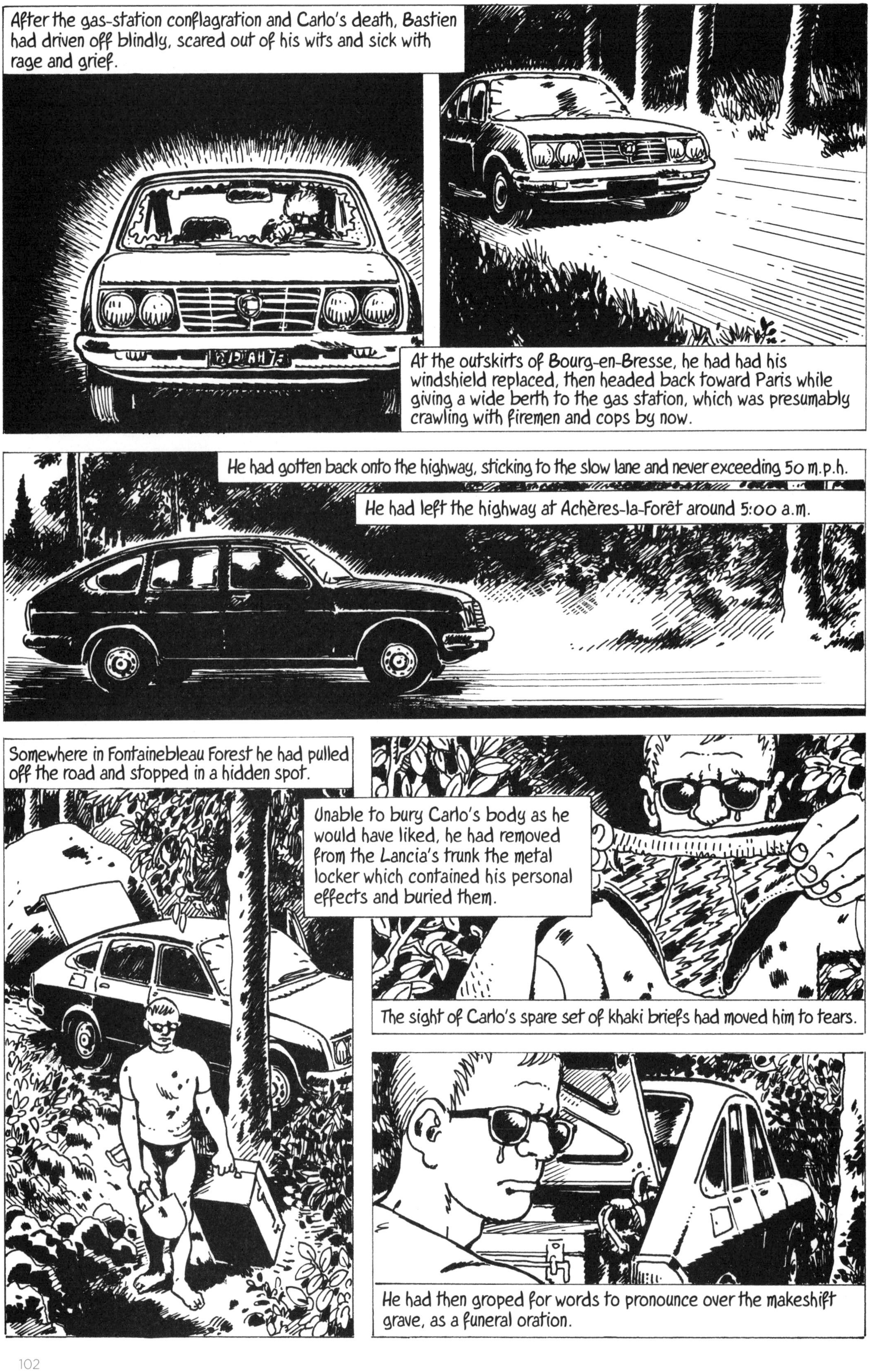
After the gas-station conflagration and Carlo's death, Bastien had driven off blindly, scared out of his wits and sick with rage and grief.
At the outskirts of Bourg-en-Bresse, he had had his windshield replaced, then headed back toward Paris while giving a wide berth to the gas station, which was presumably crawling with firemen and cops by now.
He had gotten back onto the highway, sticking to the slow lane and never exceeding 50 m.p.h.
He had left the highway at Achères-la-Forêt around 5:00 a.m.
Somewhere in Fontainebleau Forest he had pulled off the road and stopped in a hidden spot.
Unable to bury Carlo's body as he would have liked, he had removed from the Lancia's trunk the metal locker which contained his personal effects and buried them.
The sight of Carlo's spare set of khaki briefs had moved him to tears.
He had then groped for words to pronounce over the makeshift grave, as a funeral oration.

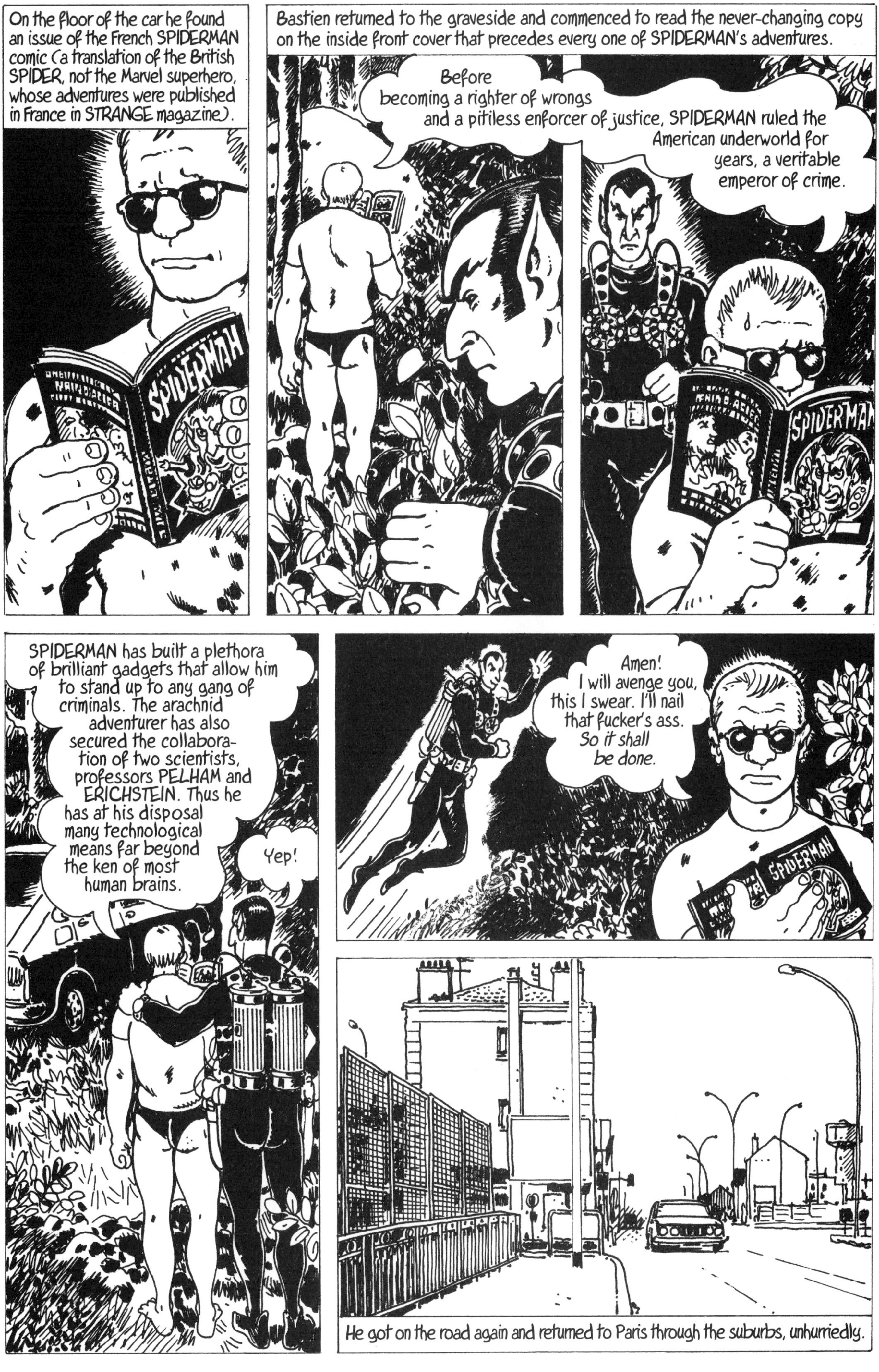
On the floor of the car he found an issue of the French SPIDERMAN comic (a translation of the British SPIDER, not the Marvel superhero, whose adventures were published in France in STRANGE magazine).
SPIDERMAN
Bastien returned to the graveside and commenced to read the never-changing copy on the inside front cover that precedes every one of SPIDERMAN's adventures.
Before becoming a righter of wrongs and a pitiless enforcer of justice, SPIDERMAN ruled the American underworld for years, a veritable emperor of crime.
SPIDERMAN
SPIDERMAN has built a plethora of brilliant gadgets that allow him to stand up to any gang of criminals. The arachnid adventurer has also secured the collaboration of two scientists, professors PELHAM and ERICHSTEIN. Thus he has at his disposal many technological means far beyond the ken of most human brains.
Yep!
Amen! I will avenge you, this I swear. I'll nail that fucker's ass. So it shall be done.
SPIDERMAN
He got on the road again and returned to Paris through the suburbs, unhurriedly.

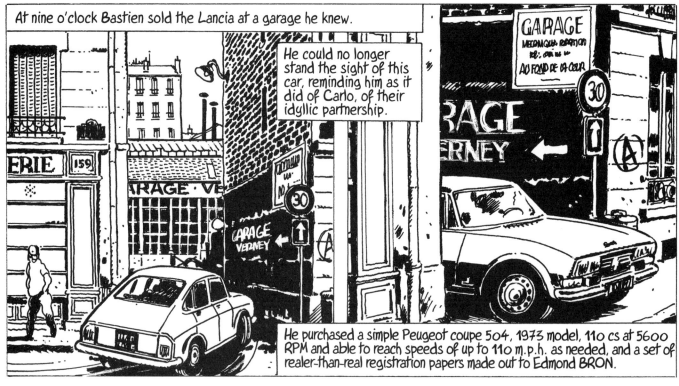

At nine o'clock Bastien sold the Lancia at a garage he knew.
He could no longer stand the sight of this car, reminding him as it did of Carlo, of their idyllic partnership.
GARAGE
AU FOND DE LA COUR
30
RAGE
ERNEY
ERIE
159
ARAGE
GARAGE VERNEY
He purchased a simple Peugeot coupe 504, 1973 model, 110 cs at 5600 RPM and able to reach speeds of up to 110 m.p.h. as needed, and a set of realer-than-real registration papers made out to Edmond BRON.
Then he returned to Paris, unknowingly passing by the photography store LIÉTARD ran near Issy-les-Moulineaux' city hall.
PIZZA
Manchette
PRET A PORTER
ACTION·PHOTO
ACTION·PHOTO
At the exact moment when GERFAUT was thrown out of the railroad car it was announced that the R16 had been identified, that it had been rented, on the same day as the "gas station shootout," by a Parisian salesman who had since vanished.
Listeners were reminded that the gas-station attendant and one other man whose identity remained unknown had perished on that evening of July 2nd.
PLM
The presenter read the remainder of the newsbreak in an uninflected voice, followed by some commercials, then the station identification and a Leonard COHEN song.

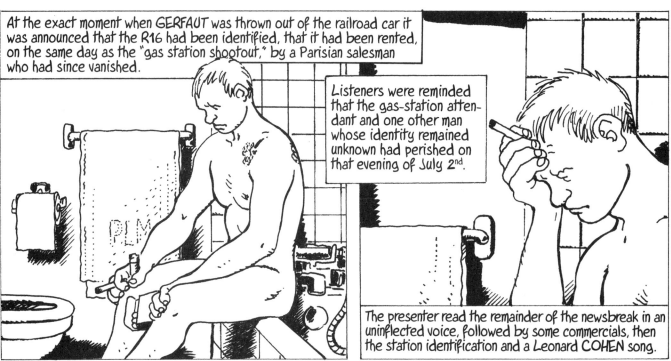

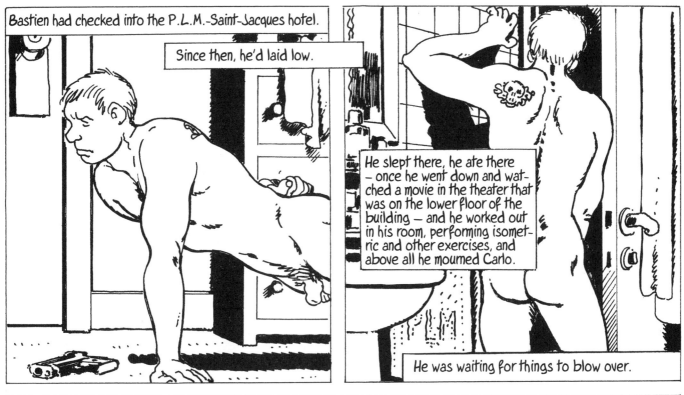

Bastien had checked into the P.L.M.-Saint-Jacques hotel.

Since then, he'd laid low.

He slept there, he ate there – once he went down and watched a movie in the theater that was on the lower floor of the building – and he worked out in his room, performing isometric and other exercises, and above all he mourned Carlo.

He was waiting for things to blow over.

That was some serious sleepin', son!

Where am I? Who are you?

You're in my home and I'm Corporal RAGUSE. Y'shouldn't be farting around on mountains if you aren't good on your feet. Tourist, eh?

The Portuguese came and got me. Brought you back down on my mule. I took care of your foot. I reset the bones and put a cast on it.

You're a bonesetter?

Military physician! What's your name?

George... George SOREL.

So what exactly happened to you?

I fell off a train! I'm homeless. You understand? A hobo, a bindlestiff, whatever you want to call it. A vagabond, basically.

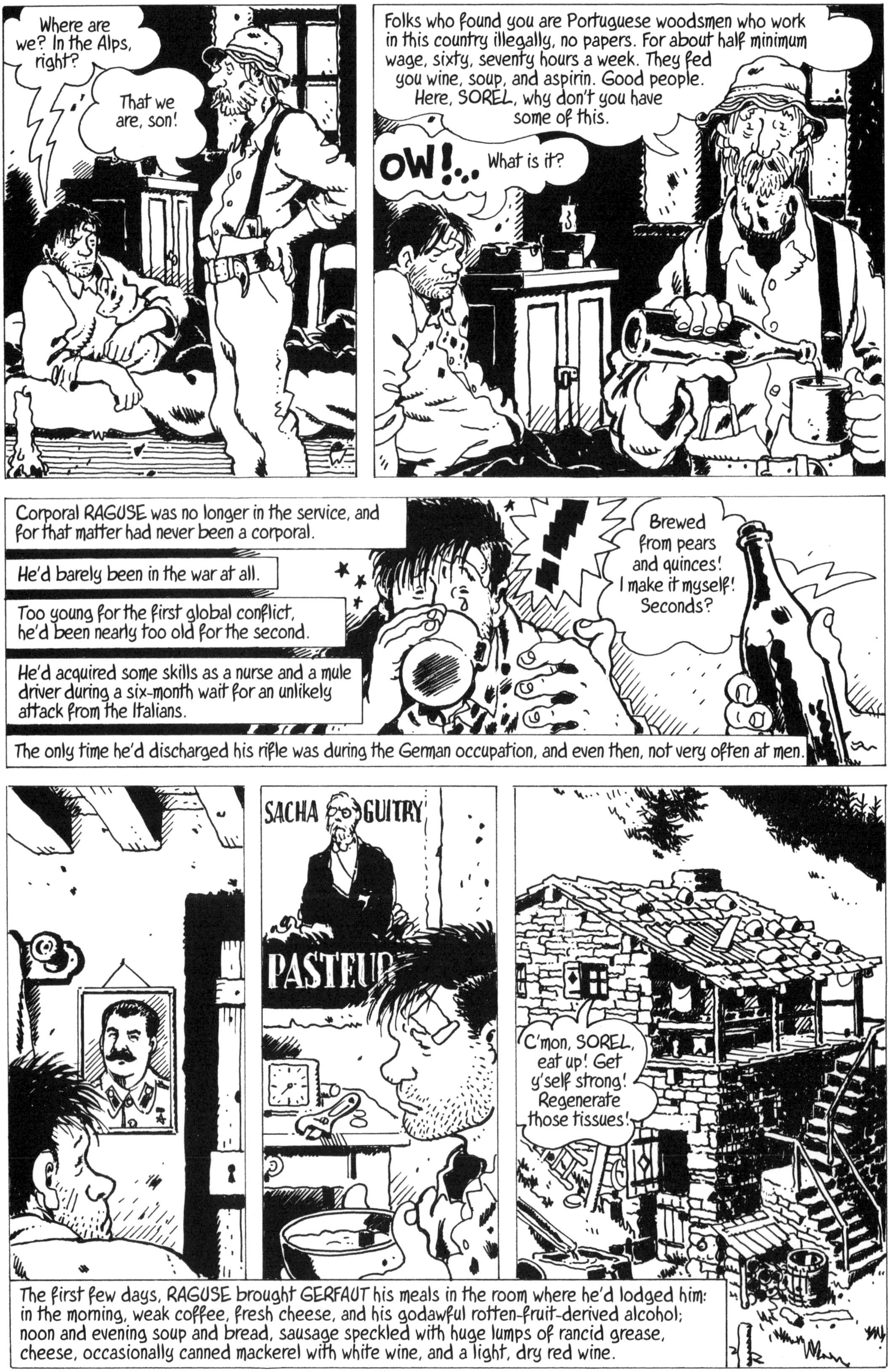
Where are we? In the Alps, right?
That we are, son!
Folks who found you are Portuguese woodsmen who work in this country illegally, no papers. For about half minimum wage, sixty, seventy hours a week. They fed you wine, soup, and aspirin. Good people. Here, SOREL, why don't you have some of this.
OW!...
What is it?
Corporal RAGUSE was no longer in the service, and for that matter had never been a corporal.
He'd barely been in the war at all.
Too young for the first global conflict, he'd been nearly too old for the second.
He'd acquired some skills as a nurse and a mule driver during a six-month wait for an unlikely attack from the Italians.
Brewed from pears and quinces! I make it myself! Seconds?
The only time he'd discharged his rifle was during the German occupation, and even then, not very often at men.
SACHA GUITRY
PASTEU
C'mon, SOREL, eat up! Get y'self strong! Regenerate those tissues!
The first few days, RAGUSE brought GERFAUT his meals in the room where he'd lodged him: in the morning, weak coffee, fresh cheese, and his godawful rotten-fruit-derived alcohol; noon and evening soup and bread, sausage speckled with huge lumps of rancid grease, cheese, occasionally canned mackerel with white wine, and a light, dry red wine.

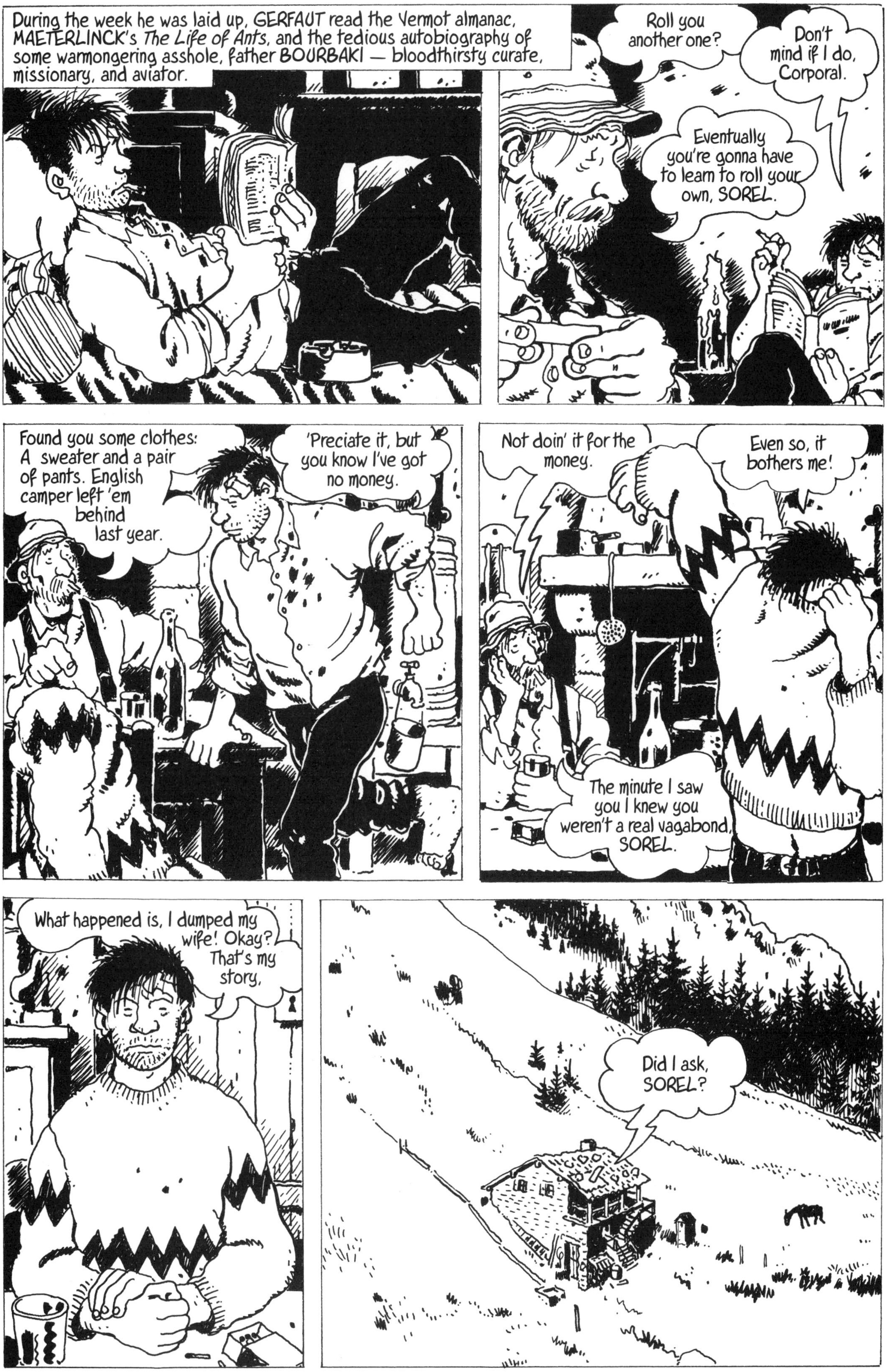

During the week he was laid up, GERFAUT read the Vermot almanac, MAETERLINCK's *The Life of Ants*, and the tedious autobiography of some warmongering asshole, father BOURBAKI — bloodthirsty curate, missionary, and aviator.
Roll you another one?
Don't mind if I do, Corporal.
Eventually you're gonna have to learn to roll your own, SOREL.
Found you some clothes: A sweater and a pair of pants. English camper left 'em behind last year.
'Preciate it, but you know I've got no money.
Not doin' it for the money.
Even so, it bothers me!
The minute I saw you I knew you weren't a real vagabond, SOREL.
What happened is, I dumped my wife! Okay? That's my story,
Did I ask, SOREL?

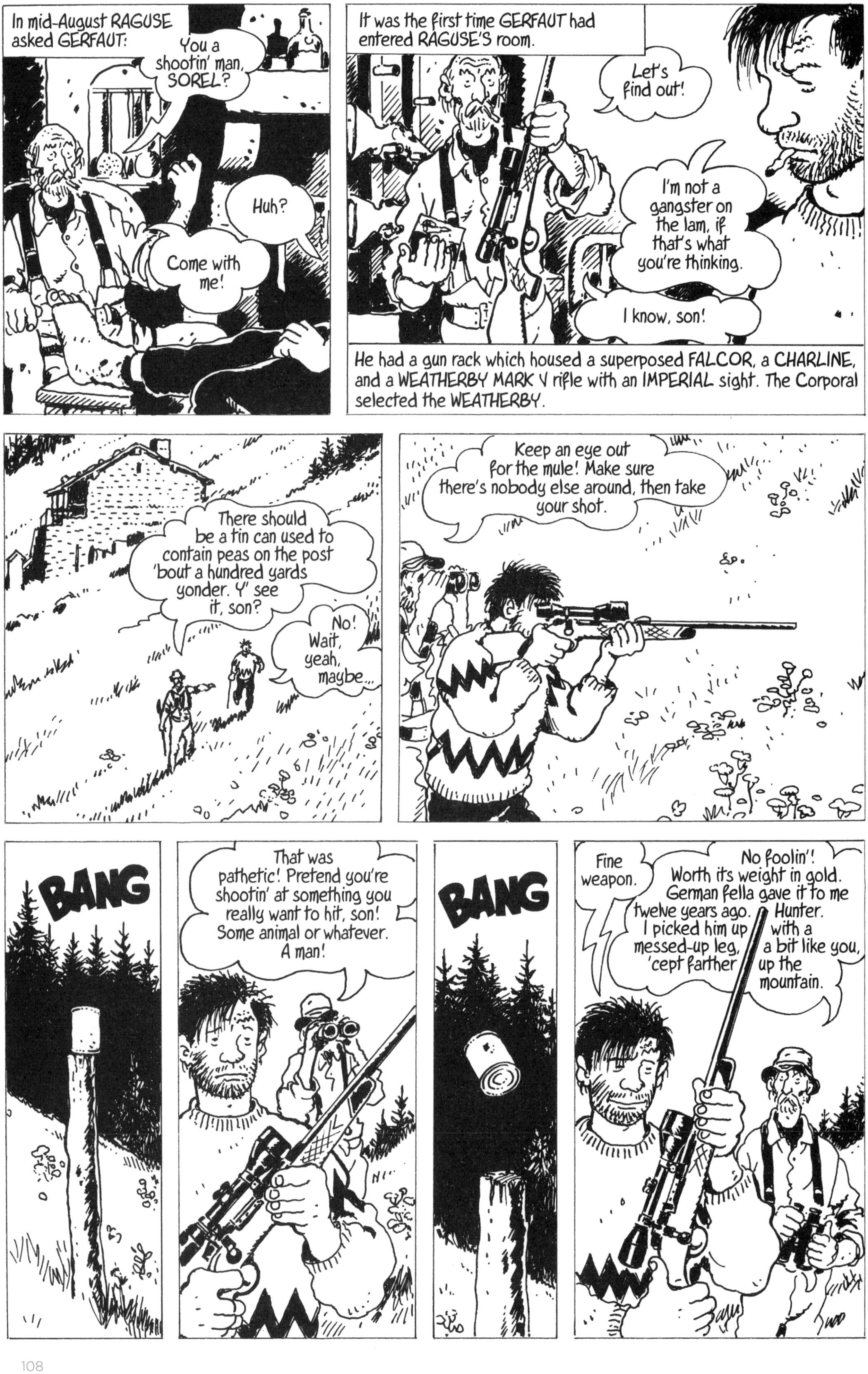
In mid-August RAGUSE asked GERFAUT:
You a shootin' man, SOREL?
Huh?
Come with me!
It was the first time GERFAUT had entered RAGUSE'S room.
Let's find out!
I'm not a gangster on the lam, if that's what you're thinking.
I know, son!
He had a gun rack which housed a superposed FALCOR, a CHARLINE, and a WEATHERBY MARK V rifle with an IMPERIAL sight. The Corporal selected the WEATHERBY.
There should be a tin can used to contain peas on the post 'bout a hundred yards yonder. Y' see it, son?
No! Wait, yeah, maybe...
Keep an eye out for the mule! Make sure there's nobody else around, then take your shot.
BANG
That was pathetic! Pretend you're shootin' at something you really want to hit, son! Some animal or whatever. A man!
BANG
Fine weapon.
No foolin'! Worth its weight in gold. German fella gave it to me twelve years ago. Hunter. I picked him up with a messed-up leg, a bit like you, 'cept farther up the mountain.

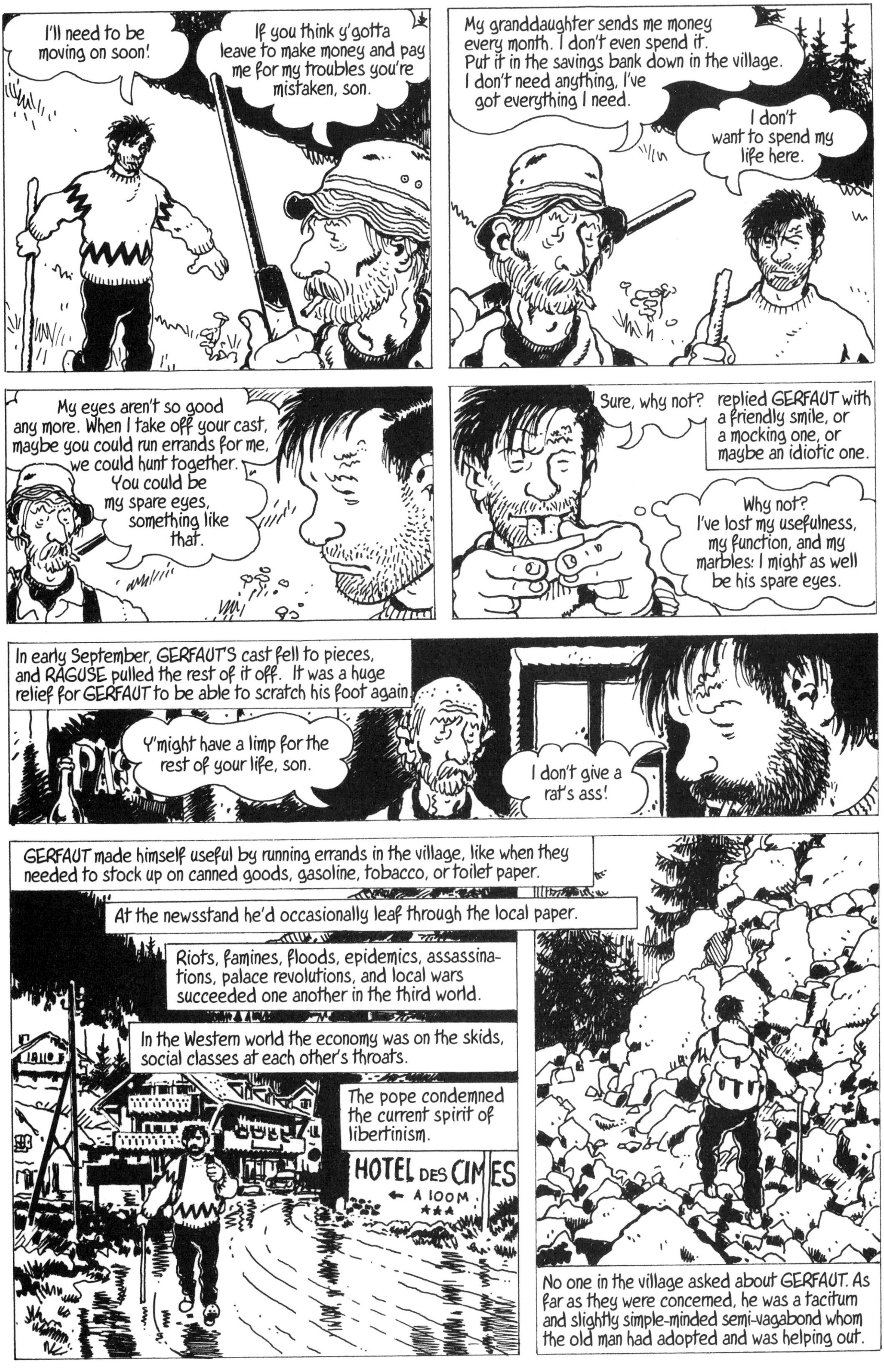
I'll need to be moving on soon!
If you think y'gotta leave to make money and pay me for my troubles you're mistaken, son.
My granddaughter sends me money every month. I don't even spend it. Put it in the savings bank down in the village. I don't need anything, I've got everything I need.
I don't want to spend my life here.
My eyes aren't so good any more. When I take off your cast, maybe you could run errands for me, we could hunt together. You could be my spare eyes, something like that.
Sure, why not?
replied GERFAUT with a friendly smile, or a mocking one, or maybe an idiotic one.
Why not? I've lost my usefulness, my function, and my marbles: I might as well be his spare eyes.
In early September, GERFAUT'S cast fell to pieces, and RAGUSE pulled the rest of it off. It was a huge relief for GERFAUT to be able to scratch his foot again.
Y'might have a limp for the rest of your life, son.
I don't give a rat's ass!
GERFAUT made himself useful by running errands in the village, like when they needed to stock up on canned goods, gasoline, tobacco, or toilet paper.
At the newsstand he'd occasionally leaf through the local paper.
Riots, famines, floods, epidemics, assassinations, palace revolutions, and local wars succeeded one another in the third world.
In the Western world the economy was on the skids, social classes at each other's throats.
The pope condemned the current spirit of libertinism.
HOTEL DES CIMES
← A 100M
No one in the village asked about GERFAUT. As far as they were concerned, he was a taciturn and slightly simple-minded semi-vagabond whom the old man had adopted and was helping out.

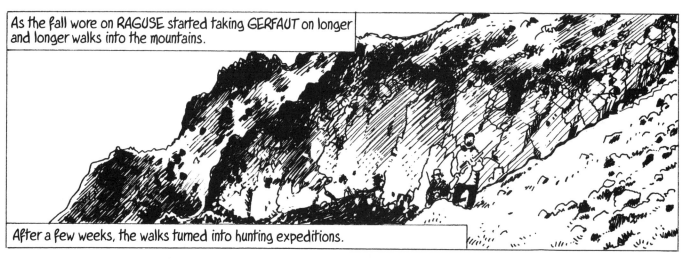

As the fall wore on RAGUSE started taking GERFAUT on longer and longer walks into the mountains.

After a few weeks, the walks turned into hunting expeditions.

Toward the end of October they ascended farther than they ever had. The Corporal, whose eyesight had deteriorated considerably, missed everything he aimed for. Eventually he gave up shooting entirely, leaving it to GERFAUT.

During the month of January, on one of these treks, GERFAUT killed a horned animal — a chamois or mountain goat, he had no idea what it was. It might as well been an antelope or a snail for all he cared.

I can sell the horns to damn fools. To hang in their living room.

Jesus, what am I doing here? I've spent my entire life just fucking around.

Hey, now, SOREL, you can leave anytime you want! You're free to piss off! Totally free!

But it's the same shit everywhere!

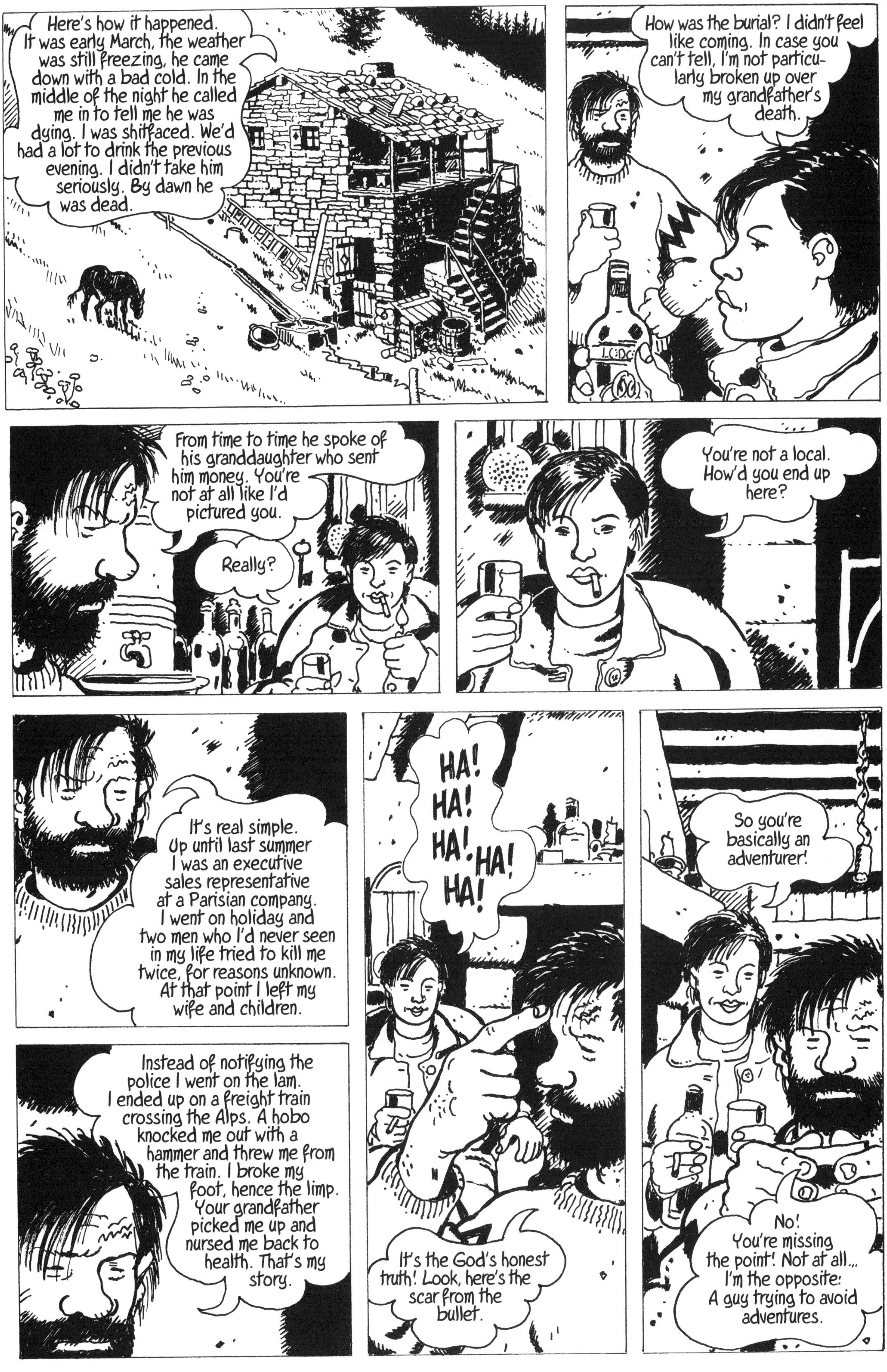
Here's how it happened. It was early March, the weather was still freezing, he came down with a bad cold. In the middle of the night he called me in to tell me he was dying. I was shitfaced. We'd had a lot to drink the previous evening. I didn't take him seriously. By dawn he was dead.
How was the burial? I didn't feel like coming. In case you can't tell, I'm not particularly broken up over my grandfather's death.
From time to time he spoke of his granddaughter who sent him money. You're not at all like I'd pictured you.
Really?
You're not a local. How'd you end up here?
It's real simple. Up until last summer I was an executive sales representative at a Parisian company. I went on holiday and two men who I'd never seen in my life tried to kill me twice, for reasons unknown. At that point I left my wife and children.
Instead of notifying the police I went on the lam. I ended up on a freight train crossing the Alps. A hobo knocked me out with a hammer and threw me from the train. I broke my foot, hence the limp. Your grandfather picked me up and nursed me back to health. That's my story.
HA! HA! HA! HA! HA!
It's the God's honest truth! Look, here's the scar from the bullet.
So you're basically an adventurer!
No! You're missing the point! Not at all... I'm the opposite: A guy trying to avoid adventures.

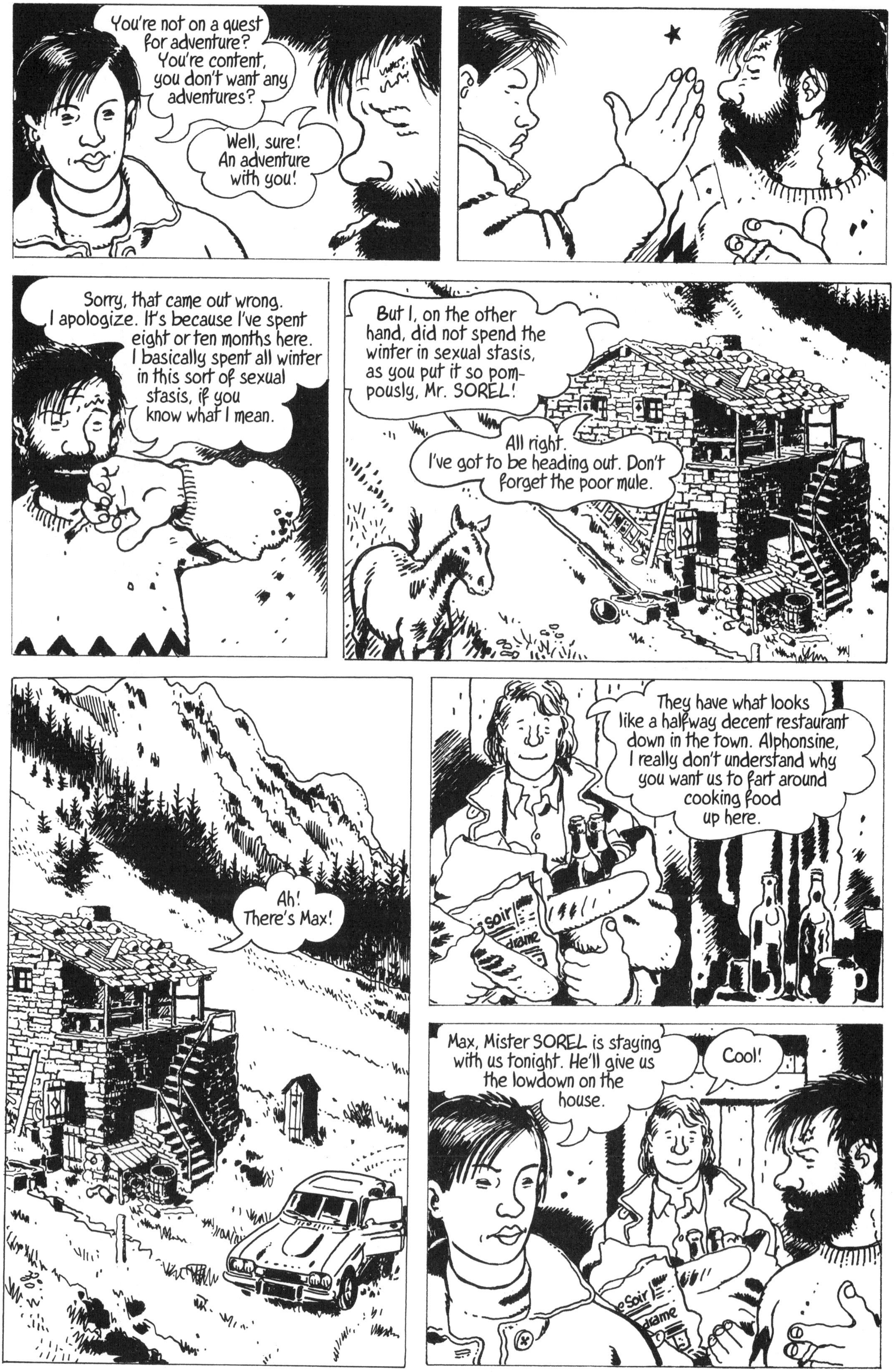
You're not on a quest for adventure? You're content, you don't want any adventures?
Well, sure! An adventure with you!
Sorry, that came out wrong. I apologize. It's because I've spent eight or ten months here. I basically spent all winter in this sort of sexual stasis, if you know what I mean.
But I, on the other hand, did not spend the winter in sexual stasis, as you put it so pompously, Mr. SOREL!
All right. I've got to be heading out. Don't forget the poor mule.
Ah! There's Max!
They have what looks like a halfway decent restaurant down in the town. Alphonsine, I really don't understand why you want us to fart around cooking food up here.
Max, Mister SOREL is staying with us tonight. He'll give us the lowdown on the house.
Cool!

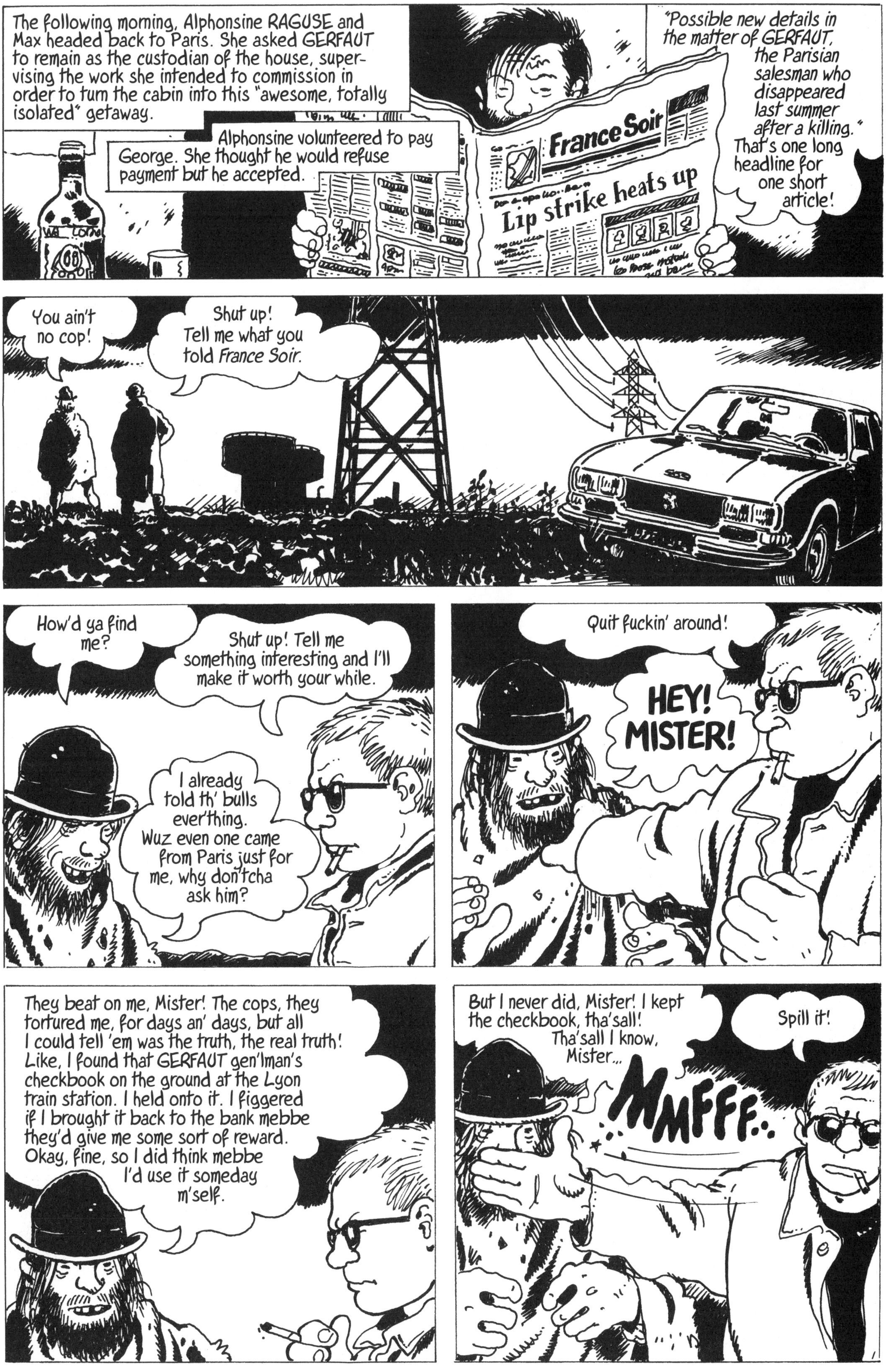

The following morning, Alphonsine RAGUSE and Max headed back to Paris. She asked GERFAUT to remain as the custodian of the house, supervising the work she intended to commission in order to turn the cabin into this "awesome, totally isolated" getaway.
Alphonsine volunteered to pay George. She thought he would refuse payment but he accepted.
France Soir
Lip strike heats up
"Possible new details in the matter of GERFAUT, the Parisian salesman who disappeared last summer after a killing." That's one long headline for one short article!
You ain't no cop!
Shut up! Tell me what you told France Soir.
How'd ya find me?
Shut up! Tell me something interesting and I'll make it worth your while.
I already told th' bulls ever'thing. Wuz even one came from Paris just for me, why don'tcha ask him?
Quit fuckin' around!
HEY! MISTER!
They beat on me, Mister! The cops, they tortured me, for days an' days, but all I could tell 'em was the truth, the real truth! Like, I found that GERFAUT gen'lman's checkbook on the ground at the Lyon train station. I held onto it. I figgered if I brought it back to the bank mebbe they'd give me some sort of reward. Okay, fine, so I did think mebbe I'd use it someday m'self.
But I never did, Mister! I kept the checkbook, tha'sall! Tha'sall I know, Mister...
Spill it!
MMFFF...

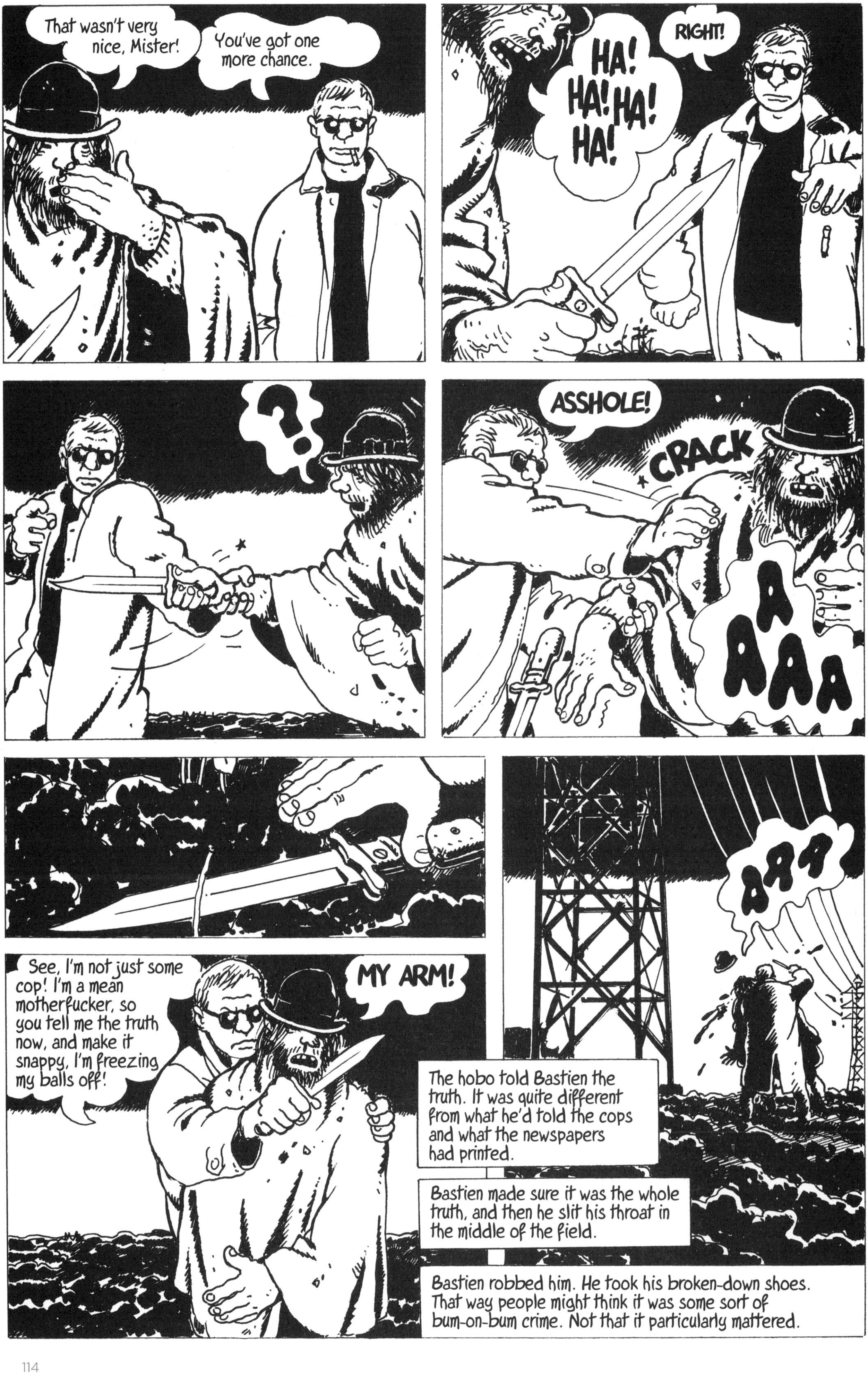
That wasn't very nice, Mister!
You've got one more chance.
HA! HA! HA! HA!
RIGHT!
?
ASSHOLE!
CRACK
AAAA
AAA
See, I'm not just some cop! I'm a mean motherfucker, so you tell me the truth now, and make it snappy, I'm freezing my balls off!
MY ARM!
The hobo told Bastien the truth. It was quite different from what he'd told the cops and what the newspapers had printed.
Bastien made sure it was the whole truth, and then he slit his throat in the middle of the field.
Bastien robbed him. He took his broken-down shoes. That way people might think it was some sort of bum-on-bum crime. Not that it particularly mattered.

Alphonsine RAGUSE returned well before summer.

Jesus, check out the fucking fog.

I kicked that loser Max to the curb. I knew I'd be coming back but I didn't want to rush things. How come you shaved off your beard? You had kind of a cool Captain Haddock look going.

It was May 1st, one of the shittiest May 1sts of the decade, rain over three quarters of France, a storm over the Atlantic, lots of wind, roofs being blown off as far away as Paris.

Alsonso EMERICH y EMERICH was fretting over the wind.

He hadn't heard from the two killers for months, ever since the GERFAUT clusterfuck.

Since Carlo's death, Bastien had executed several contracts. He'd gotten used to working solo and had no plans to take on another partner.

Still intent on avenging Carlo, Bastien had studied the timetables and routes of transalpine freight trains.

He'd drawn up a list of villages near the areas where Gerfaut might have ended up after his fall. The hobo hadn't been very specific.

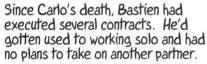

Fucking fog.

HOTEL DES CIMES
← 4100 M
★★★

Alphonsine and GERFAUT had hit it off. They were delighted to have acquired carnal knowledge of one another and intended to deepen this knowledge every chance they got.

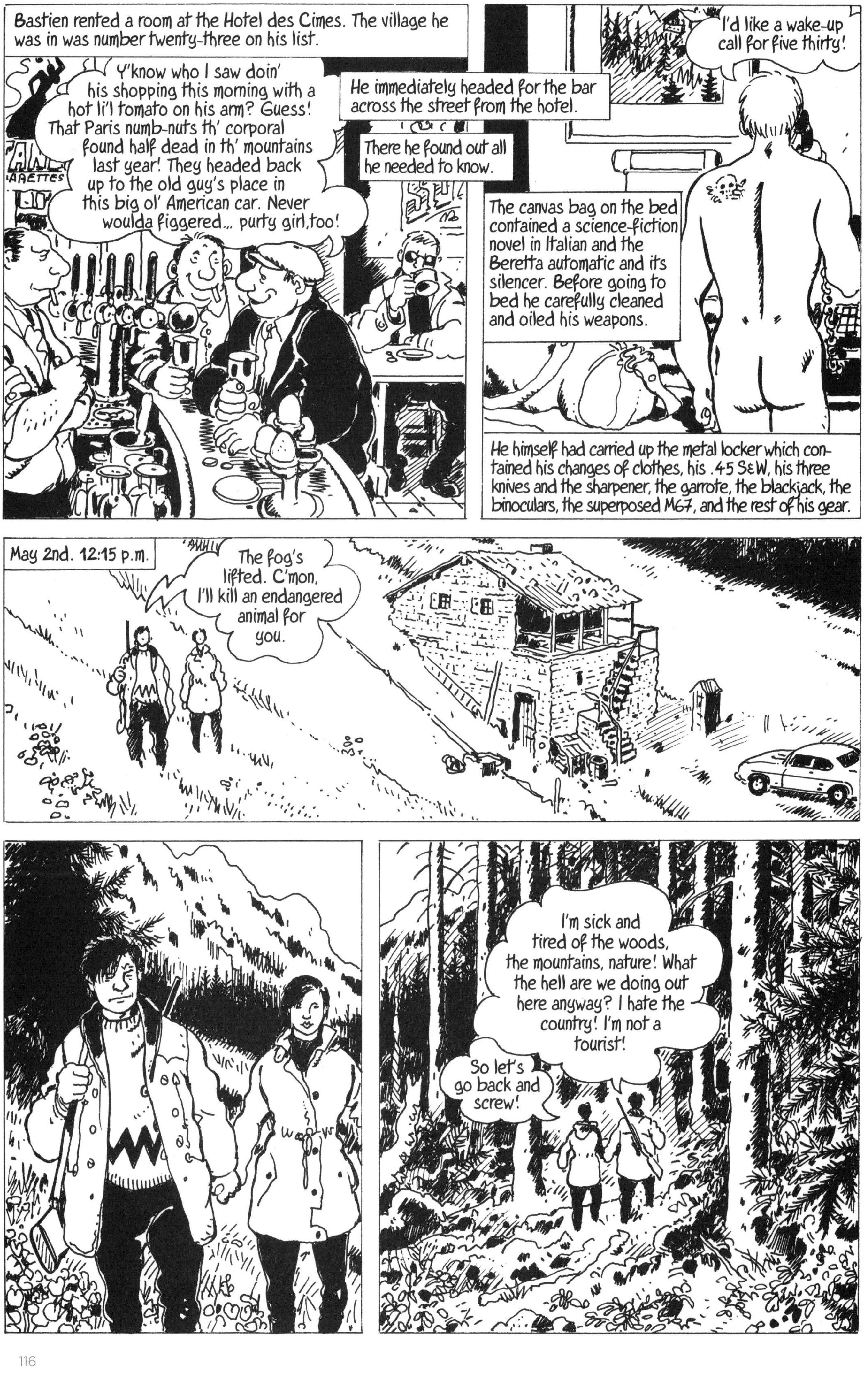
Bastien rented a room at the Hotel des Cimes. The village he was in was number twenty-three on his list.
Y'know who I saw doin' his shopping this morning with a hot li'l tomato on his arm? Guess! That Paris numb-nuts th' corporal found half dead in th' mountains last year! They headed back up to the old guy's place in this big ol' American car. Never woulda figgered... purty girl, too!
He immediately headed for the bar across the street from the hotel.
There he found out all he needed to know.
I'd like a wake-up call for five thirty!
The canvas bag on the bed contained a science-fiction novel in Italian and the Beretta automatic and its silencer. Before going to bed he carefully cleaned and oiled his weapons.
He himself had carried up the metal locker which contained his changes of clothes, his .45 S&W, his three knives and the sharpener, the garrote, the blackjack, the binoculars, the superposed M67, and the rest of his gear.
May 2nd. 12:15 p.m.
The fog's lifted. C'mon, I'll kill an endangered animal for you.
I'm sick and tired of the woods, the mountains, nature! What the hell are we doing out here anyway? I hate the country! I'm not a tourist!
So let's go back and screw!

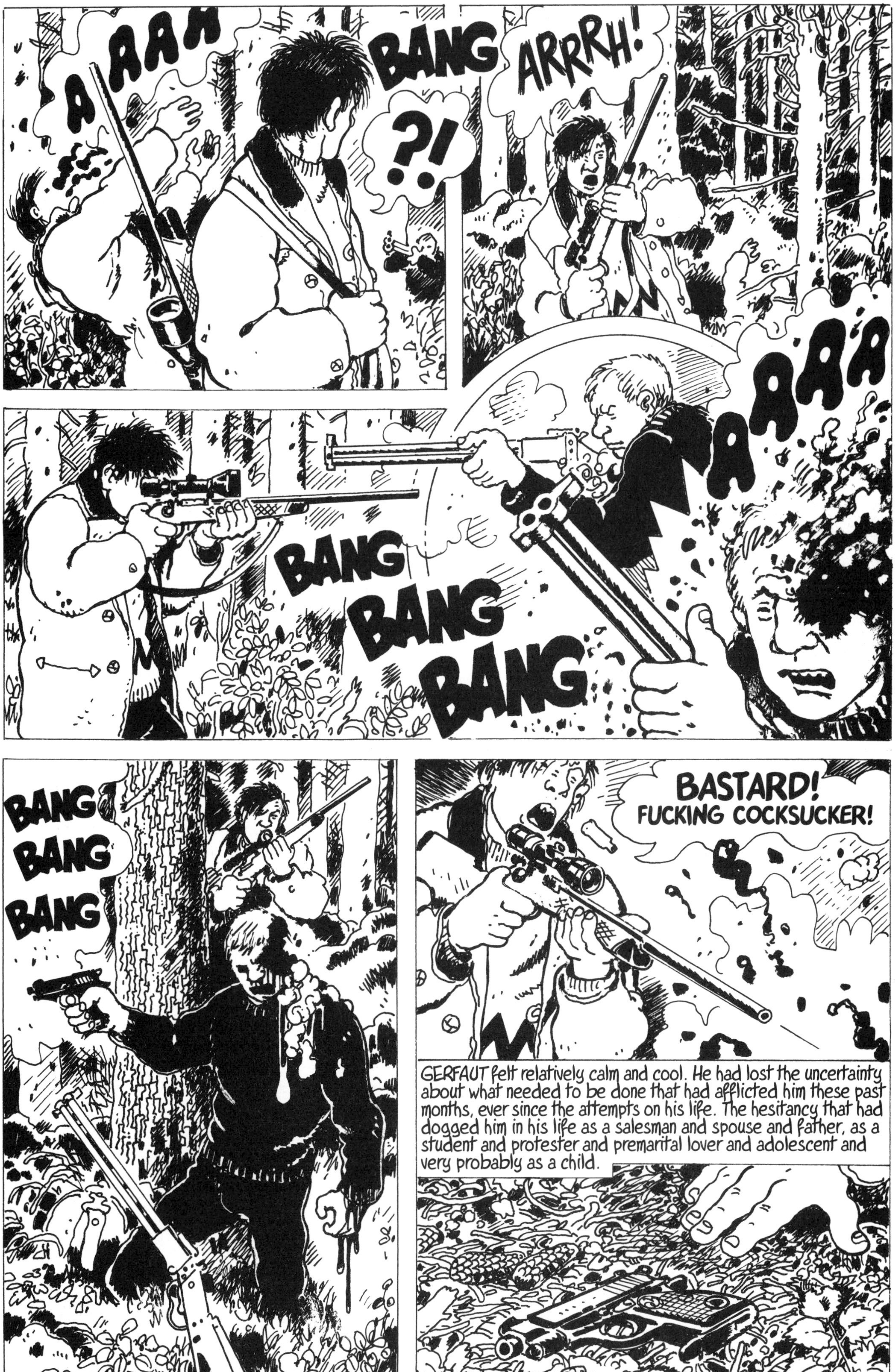

AAAA
BANG
?!
ARRRH!
AAAAA
BANG
BANG
BANG
BANG
BANG
BANG
BASTARD!
FUCKING COCKSUCKER!
GERFAUT felt relatively calm and cool. He had lost the uncertainty about what needed to be done that had afflicted him these past months, ever since the attempts on his life. The hesitancy that had dogged him in his life as a salesman and spouse and father, as a student and protester and premarital lover and adolescent and very probably as a child.

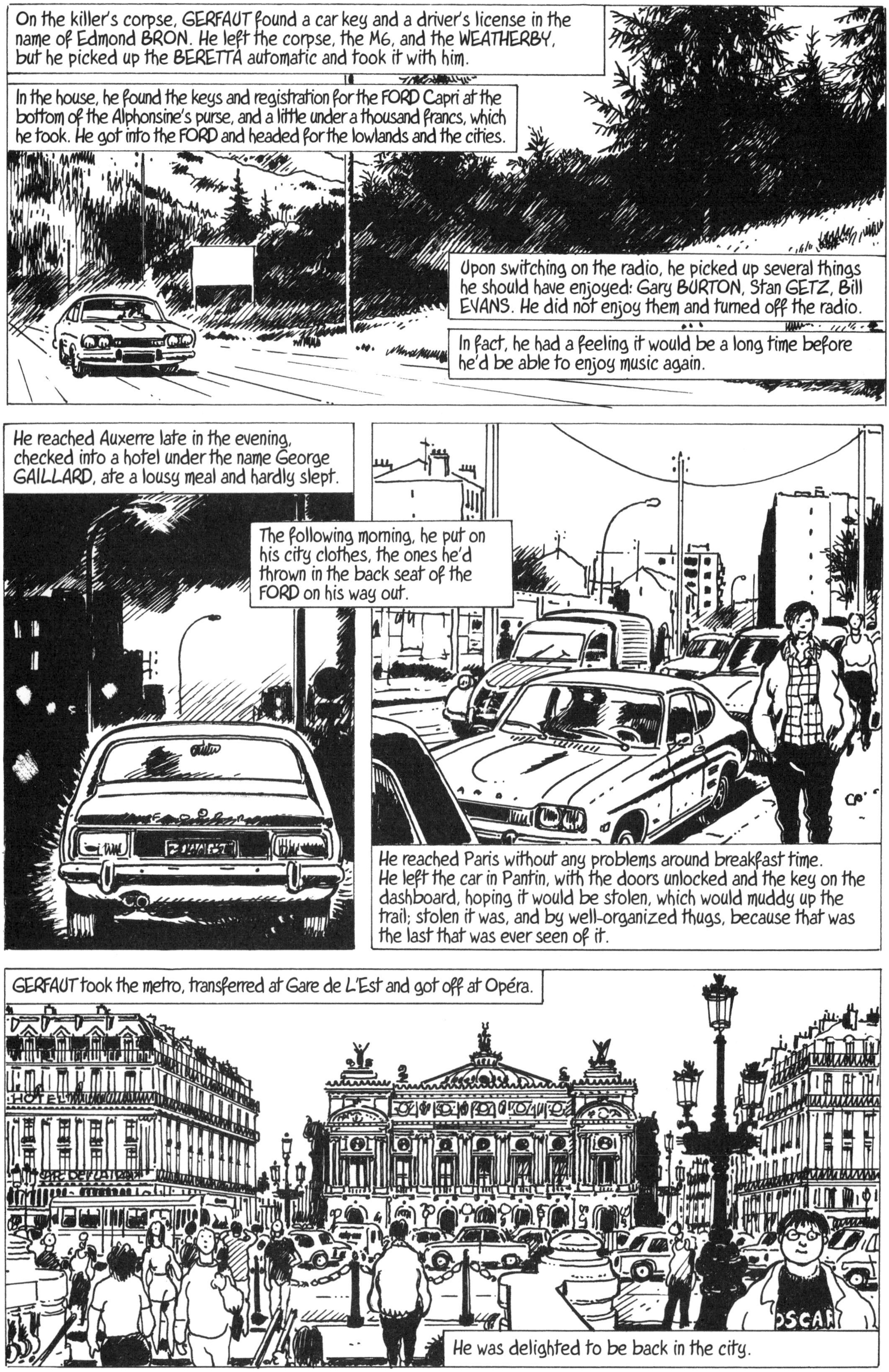
On the killer's corpse, GERFAUT found a car key and a driver's license in the name of Edmond BRON. He left the corpse, the M6, and the WEATHERBY, but he picked up the BERETTA automatic and took it with him.
In the house, he found the keys and registration for the FORD Capri at the bottom of the Alphonsine's purse, and a little under a thousand francs, which he took. He got into the FORD and headed for the lowlands and the cities.
Upon switching on the radio, he picked up several things he should have enjoyed: Gary BURTON, Stan GETZ, Bill EVANS. He did not enjoy them and turned off the radio.
In fact, he had a feeling it would be a long time before he'd be able to enjoy music again.
He reached Auxerre late in the evening, checked into a hotel under the name George GAILLARD, ate a lousy meal and hardly slept.
The following morning, he put on his city clothes, the ones he'd thrown in the back seat of the FORD on his way out.
He reached Paris without any problems around breakfast time. He left the car in Pantin, with the doors unlocked and the key on the dashboard, hoping it would be stolen, which would muddy up the trail; stolen it was, and by well-organized thugs, because that was the last that was ever seen of it.
GERFAUT took the metro, transferred at Gare de L'Est and got off at Opéra.
He was delighted to be back in the city.

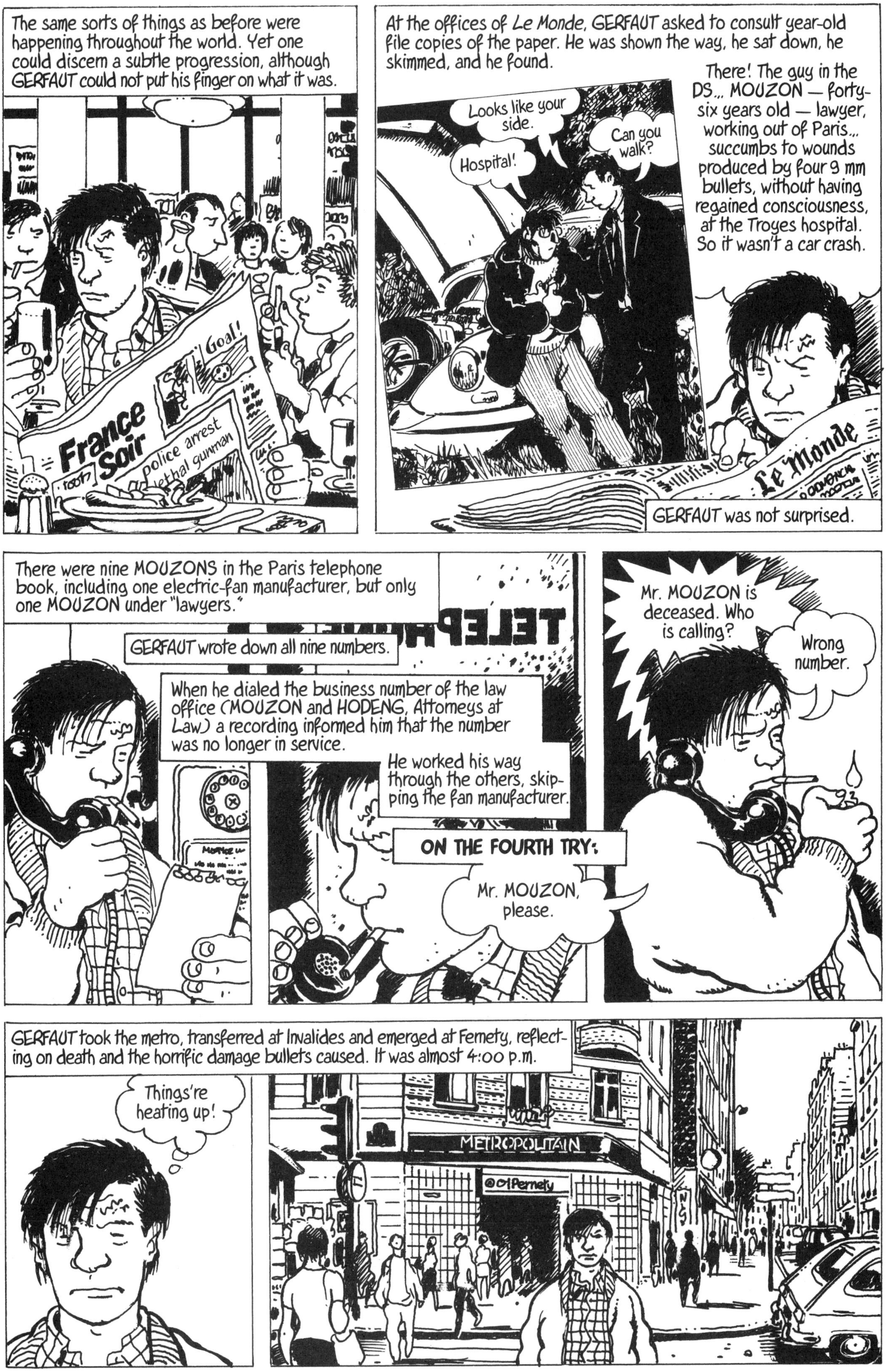

The same sorts of things as before were happening throughout the world. Yet one could discern a subtle progression, although GERFAUT could not put his finger on what it was.
France Soir
Goal!
police arrest lethal gunman
At the offices of Le Monde, GERFAUT asked to consult year-old file copies of the paper. He was shown the way, he sat down, he skimmed, and he found.
Looks like your side.
Hospital!
Can you walk?
There! The guy in the DS... MOUZON — forty-six years old — lawyer, working out of Paris... succumbs to wounds produced by four 9 mm bullets, without having regained consciousness, at the Troyes hospital. So it wasn't a car crash.
Le Monde
GERFAUT was not surprised.
There were nine MOUZONS in the Paris telephone book, including one electric-fan manufacturer, but only one MOUZON under "lawyers."
GERFAUT wrote down all nine numbers.
When he dialed the business number of the law office (MOUZON and HODENG, Attorneys at Law) a recording informed him that the number was no longer in service.
He worked his way through the others, skipping the fan manufacturer.
ON THE FOURTH TRY:
Mr. MOUZON, please.
Mr. MOUZON is deceased. Who is calling?
Wrong number.
GERFAUT took the metro, transferred at Invalides and emerged at Fernety, reflecting on death and the horrific damage bullets caused. It was almost 4:00 p.m.
Things're heating up!
METROPOLITAIN
Pernety

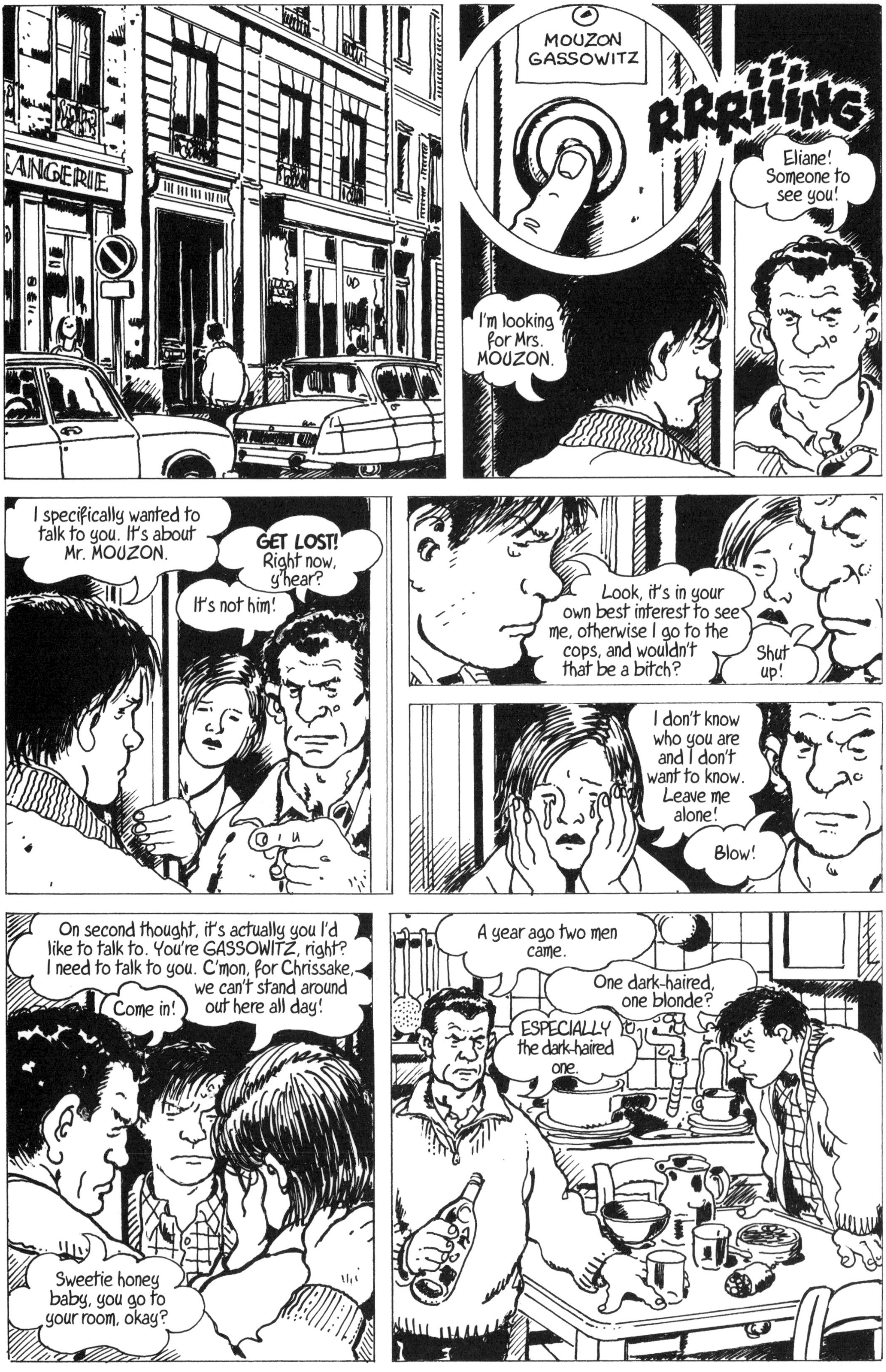

ANGERIE
MOUZON
GASSOWITZ
RRRIIING
Eliane! Someone to see you!
I'm looking for Mrs. MOUZON.
I specifically wanted to talk to you. It's about Mr. MOUZON.
It's not him!
GET LOST! Right now, y'hear?
Look, it's in your own best interest to see me, otherwise I go to the cops, and wouldn't that be a bitch?
Shut up!
I don't know who you are and I don't want to know. Leave me alone!
Blow!
On second thought, it's actually you I'd like to talk to. You're GASSOWITZ, right? I need to talk to you. C'mon, for Chrissake, we can't stand around out here all day!
Come in!
Sweetie honey baby, you go to your room, okay?
A year ago two men came.
One dark-haired, one blonde?
ESPECIALLY the dark-haired one.

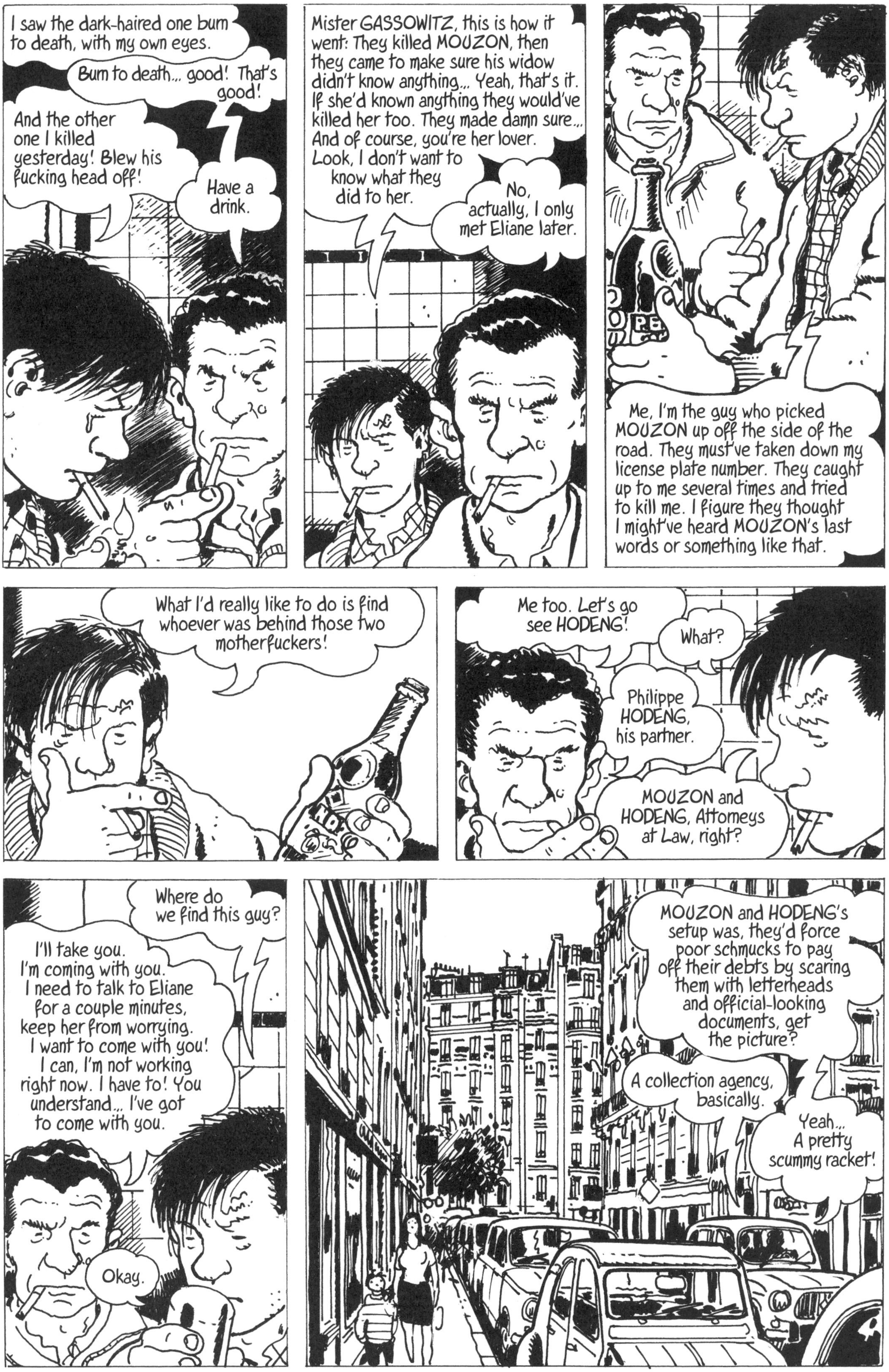
I saw the dark-haired one burn to death, with my own eyes.
Burn to death... good! That's good!
And the other one I killed yesterday! Blew his fucking head off!
Have a drink.
Mister GASSOWITZ, this is how it went: They killed MOUZON, then they came to make sure his widow didn't know anything... Yeah, that's it. If she'd known anything they would've killed her too. They made damn sure... And of course, you're her lover. Look, I don't want to know what they did to her.
No, actually, I only met Eliane later.
Me, I'm the guy who picked MOUZON up off the side of the road. They must've taken down my license plate number. They caught up to me several times and tried to kill me. I figure they thought I might've heard MOUZON's last words or something like that.
What I'd really like to do is find whoever was behind those two motherfuckers!
Me too. Let's go see HODENG!
What?
Philippe HODENG, his partner.
MOUZON and HODENG, Attorneys at Law, right?
Where do we find this guy?
I'll take you. I'm coming with you. I need to talk to Eliane for a couple minutes, keep her from worrying. I want to come with you! I can, I'm not working right now. I have to! You understand... I've got to come with you.
Okay.
MOUZON and HODENG's setup was, they'd force poor schmucks to pay off their debts by scaring them with letterheads and official-looking documents, get the picture?
A collection agency, basically.
Yeah... A pretty scummy racket!

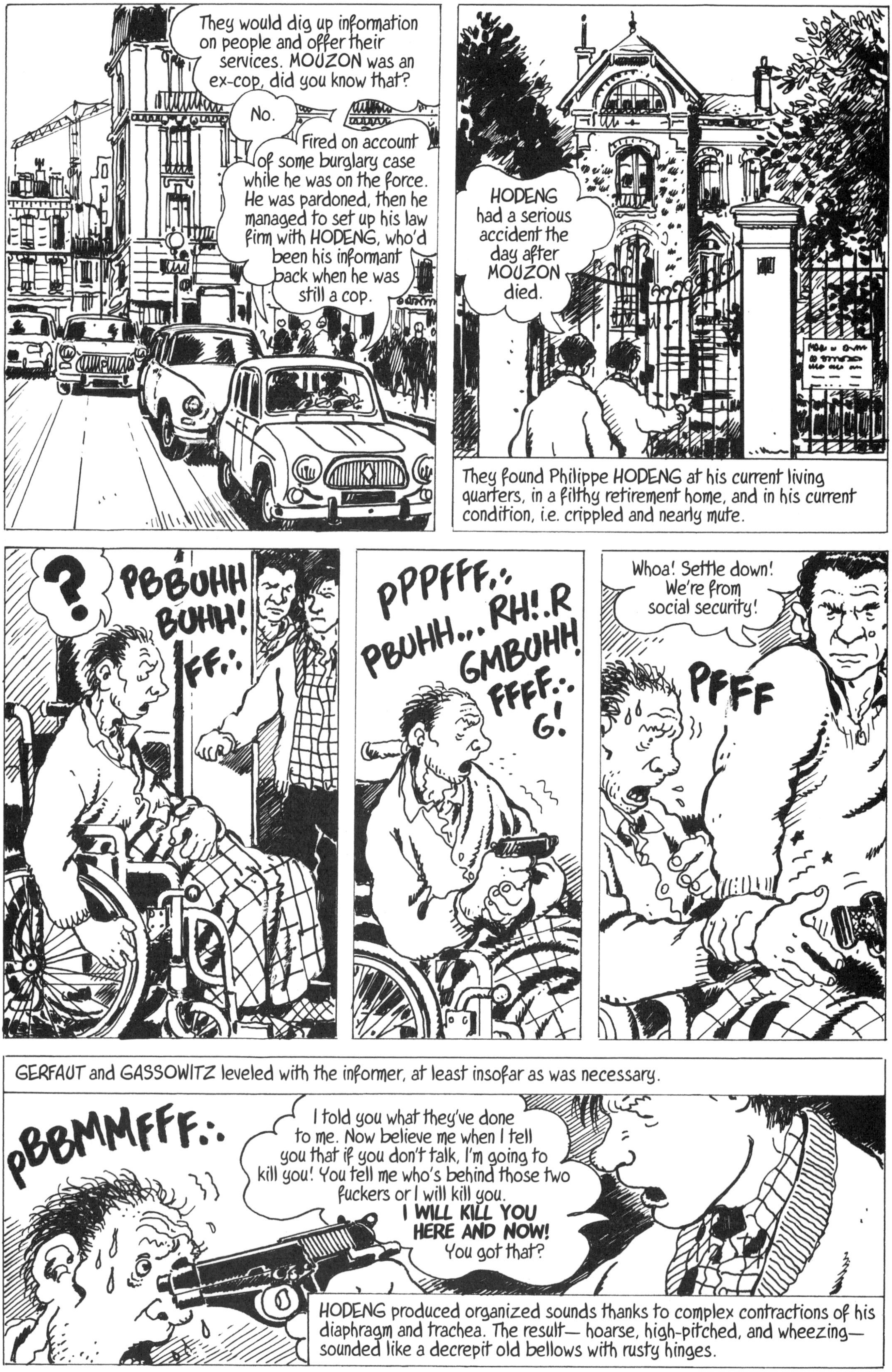

They would dig up information on people and offer their services. MOUZON was an ex-cop, did you know that?
No.
Fired on account of some burglary case while he was on the force. He was pardoned, then he managed to set up his law firm with HODENG, who'd been his informant back when he was still a cop.
HODENG had a serious accident the day after MOUZON died.
They found Philippe HODENG at his current living quarters, in a filthy retirement home, and in his current condition, i.e. crippled and nearly mute.
?
PBBUHH BUHH! FF.:.
PPPFFF.:. PBUHH... RH!.R GMBUHH! FFFF.:. G!
Whoa! Settle down! We're from social security!
PFFF
GERFAUT and GASSOWITZ leveled with the informer, at least insofar as was necessary.
pBBMMFFF.:.
I told you what they've done to me. Now believe me when I tell you that if you don't talk, I'm going to kill you! You tell me who's behind those two fuckers or I will kill you. I WILL KILL YOU HERE AND NOW! You got that?
HODENG produced organized sounds thanks to complex contractions of his diaphragm and trachea. The result— hoarse, high-pitched, and wheezing— sounded like a decrepit old bellows with rusty hinges.

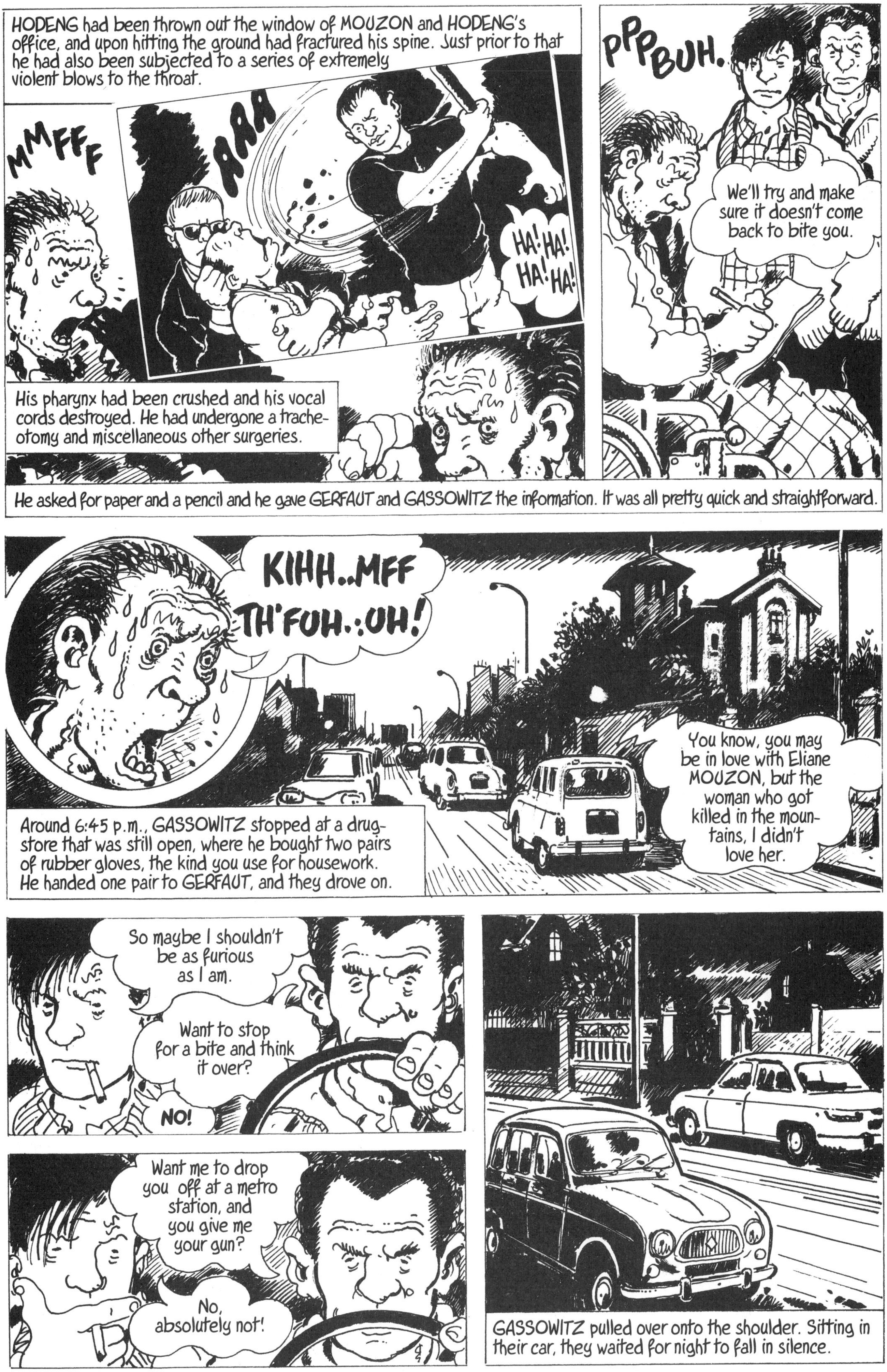
HODENG had been thrown out the window of MOUZON and HODENG's office, and upon hitting the ground had fractured his spine. Just prior to that he had also been subjected to a series of extremely violent blows to the throat.
MMFFF
AAA
HA! HA! HA! HA!
His pharynx had been crushed and his vocal cords destroyed. He had undergone a tracheotomy and miscellaneous other surgeries.
PPPBUH.
We'll try and make sure it doesn't come back to bite you.
He asked for paper and a pencil and he gave GERFAUT and GASSOWITZ the information. It was all pretty quick and straightforward.
KIHH..MFF TH'FUH.:UH!
Around 6:45 p.m., GASSOWITZ stopped at a drugstore that was still open, where he bought two pairs of rubber gloves, the kind you use for housework. He handed one pair to GERFAUT, and they drove on.
You know, you may be in love with Eliane MOUZON, but the woman who got killed in the mountains, I didn't love her.
So maybe I shouldn't be as furious as I am.
Want to stop for a bite and think it over?
NO!
Want me to drop you off at a metro station, and you give me your gun?
No, absolutely not!
GASSOWITZ pulled over onto the shoulder. Sitting in their car, they waited for night to fall in silence.

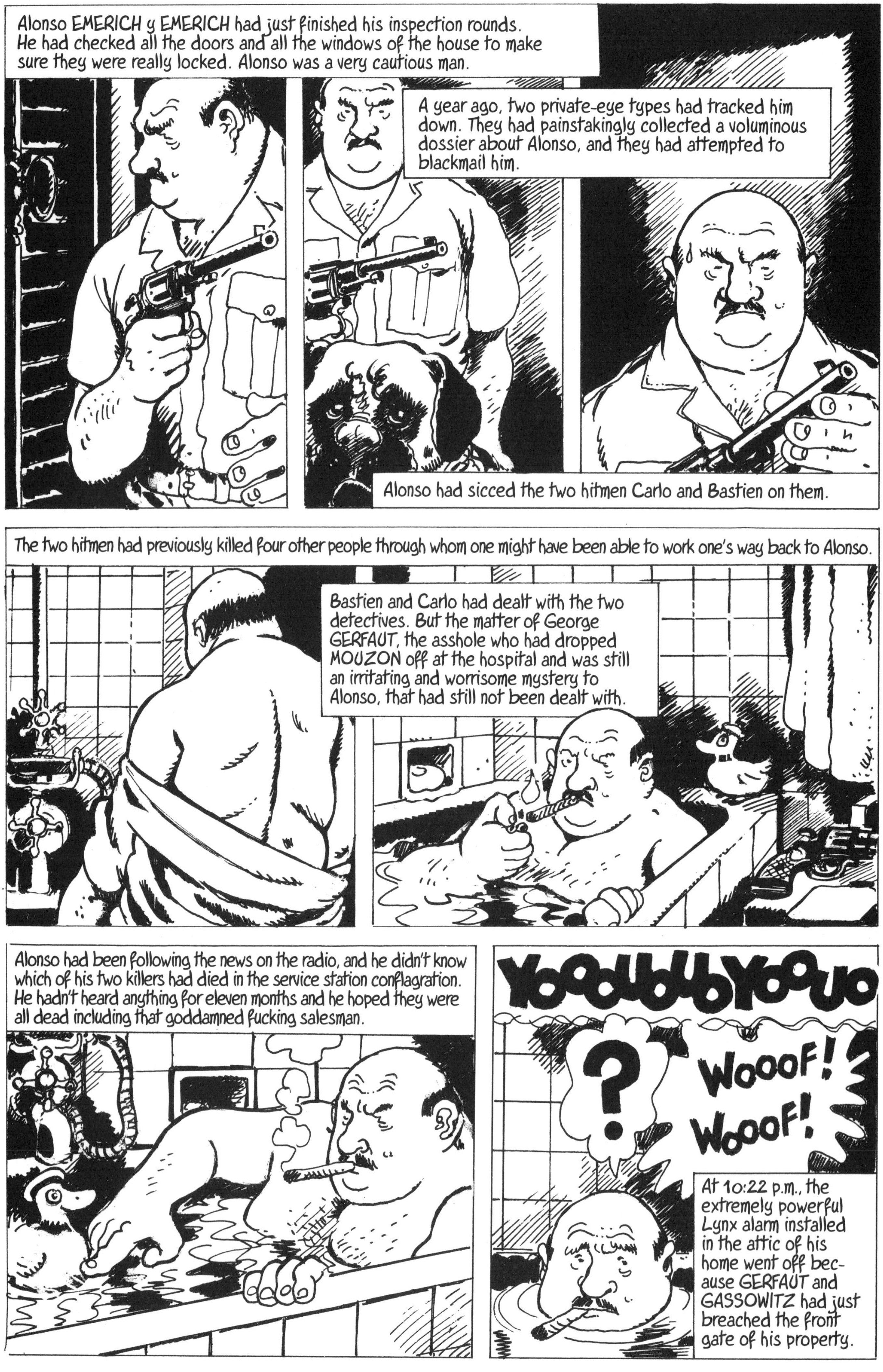
Alonso EMERICH y EMERICH had just finished his inspection rounds. He had checked all the doors and all the windows of the house to make sure they were really locked. Alonso was a very cautious man.
A year ago, two private-eye types had tracked him down. They had painstakingly collected a voluminous dossier about Alonso, and they had attempted to blackmail him.
Alonso had sicced the two hitmen Carlo and Bastien on them.
The two hitmen had previously killed four other people through whom one might have been able to work one's way back to Alonso.
Bastien and Carlo had dealt with the two detectives. But the matter of George GERFAUT, the asshole who had dropped MOUZON off at the hospital and was still an irritating and worrisome mystery to Alonso, that had still not been dealt with.
Alonso had been following the news on the radio, and he didn't know which of his two killers had died in the service station conflagration. He hadn't heard anything for eleven months and he hoped they were all dead including that goddamned fucking salesman.
YOOOUOUOYOOUO
?
WOOOF! WOOOF!
At 10:22 p.m., the extremely powerful Lynx alarm installed in the attic of his home went off because GERFAUT and GASSOWITZ had just breached the front gate of his property.

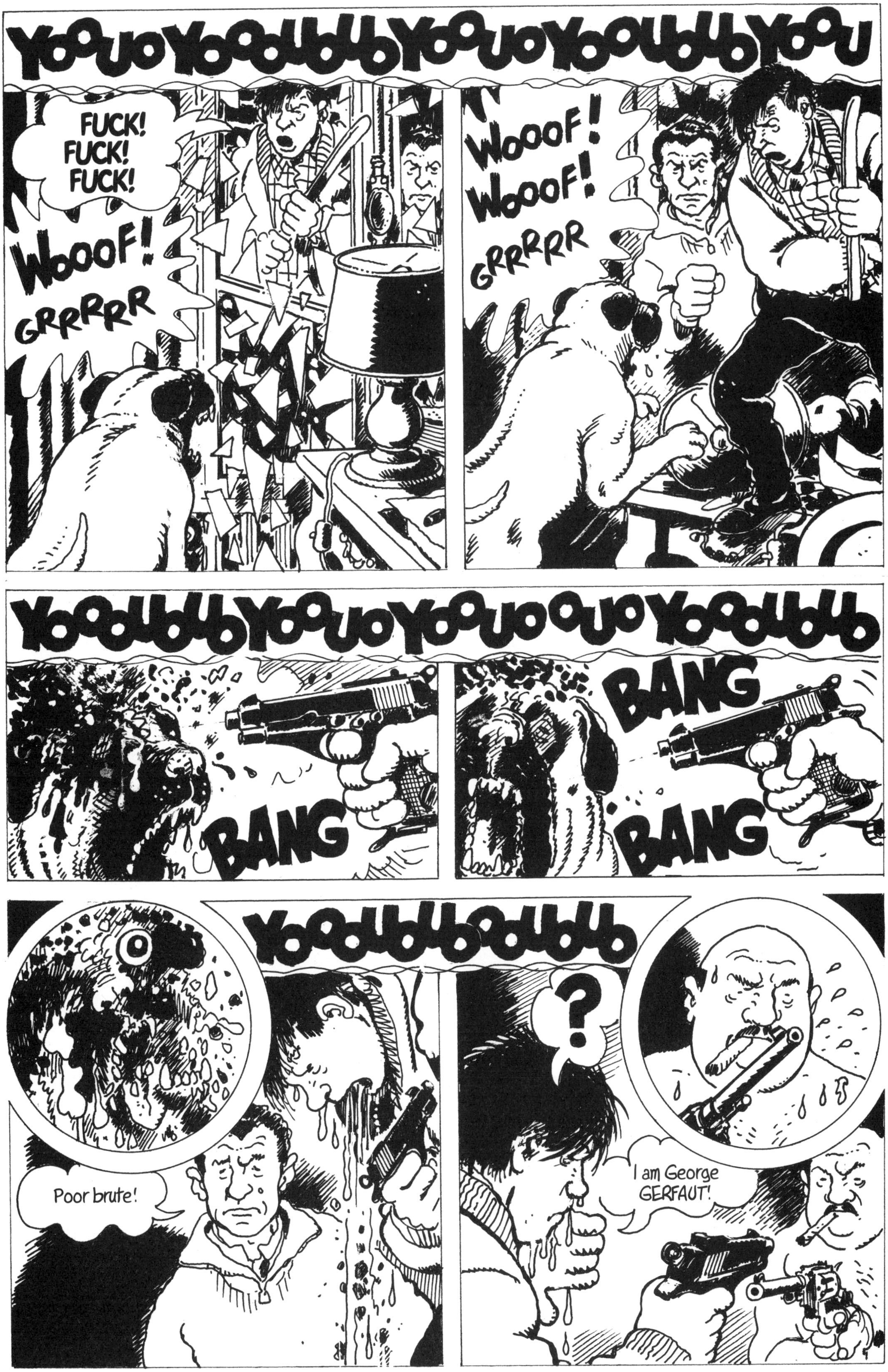
YOOUOYOOOUUUUYOOUOYOOOUUUUYOOU
FUCK! FUCK! FUCK!
WOOOF!
GRRRRR
WOOOF! WOOOF!
GRRRRR
BANG
BANG
BANG
?
Poor brute!
I am George GERFAUT!

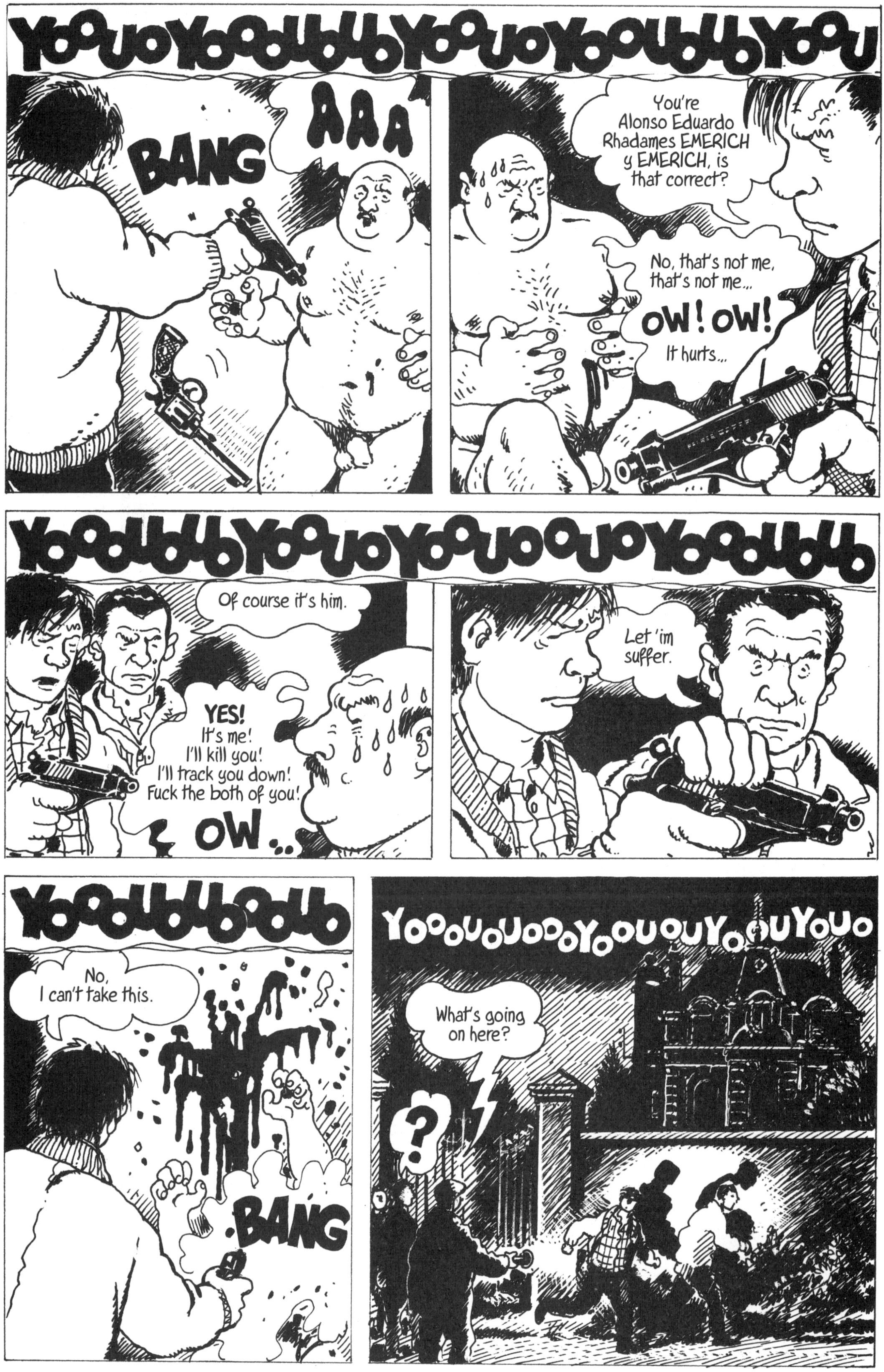
BANG
AAA
You're Alonso Eduardo Rhadames EMERICH y EMERICH, is that correct?
No, that's not me, that's not me...
OW! OW!
It hurts...
Of course it's him.
YES! It's me! I'll kill you! I'll track you down! Fuck the both of you!
OW..
Let 'im suffer.
No, I can't take this.
BANG
What's going on here?
?

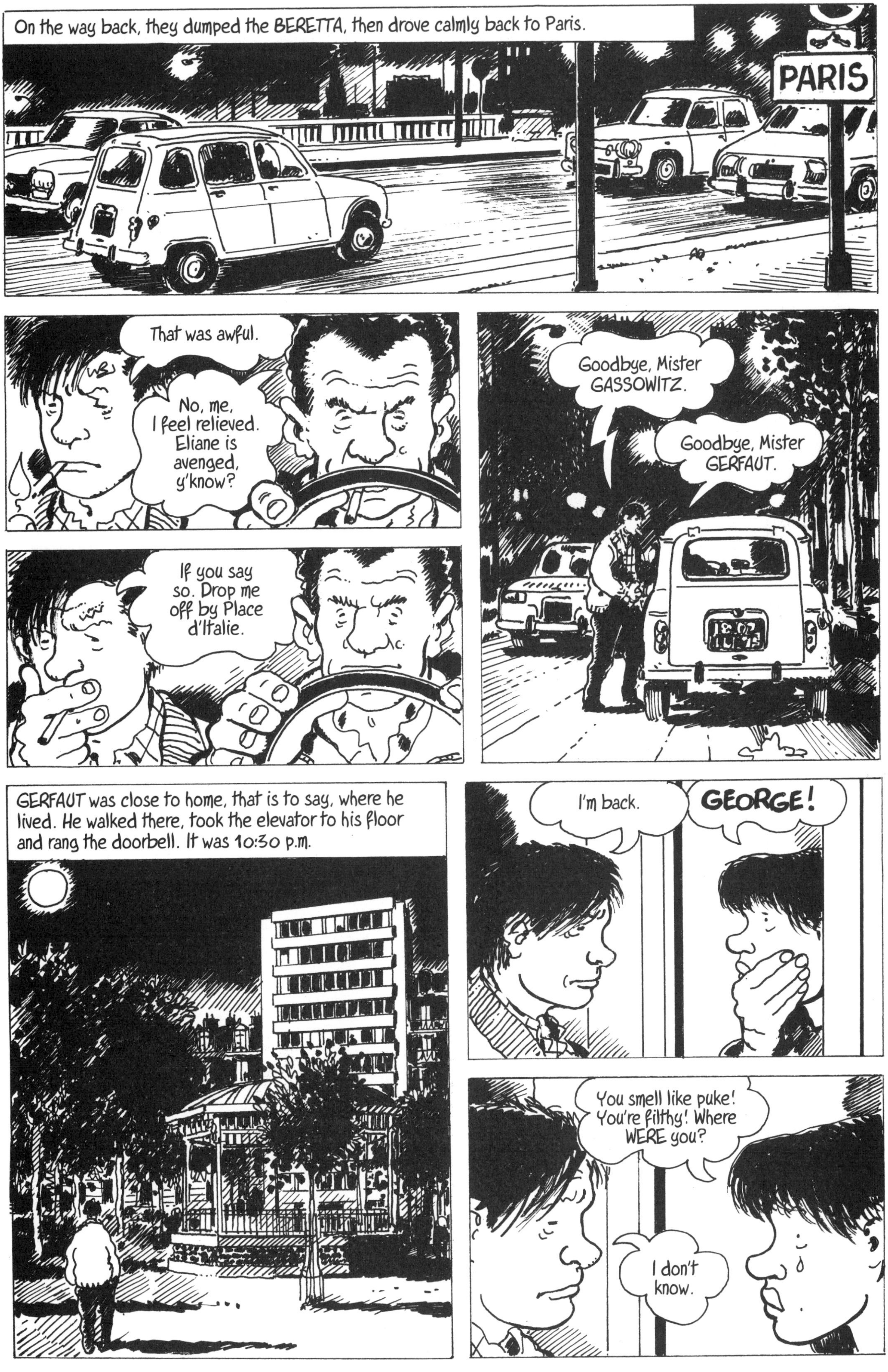
On the way back, they dumped the BERETTA, then drove calmly back to Paris.
PARIS
That was awful.
No, me, I feel relieved. Eliane is avenged, y'know?
If you say so. Drop me off by Place d'Italie.
Goodbye, Mister GASSOWITZ.
Goodbye, Mister GERFAUT.
GERFAUT was close to home, that is to say, where he lived. He walked there, took the elevator to his floor and rang the doorbell. It was 10:30 p.m.
I'm back.
GEORGE!
You smell like puke! You're filthy! Where WERE you?
I don't know.

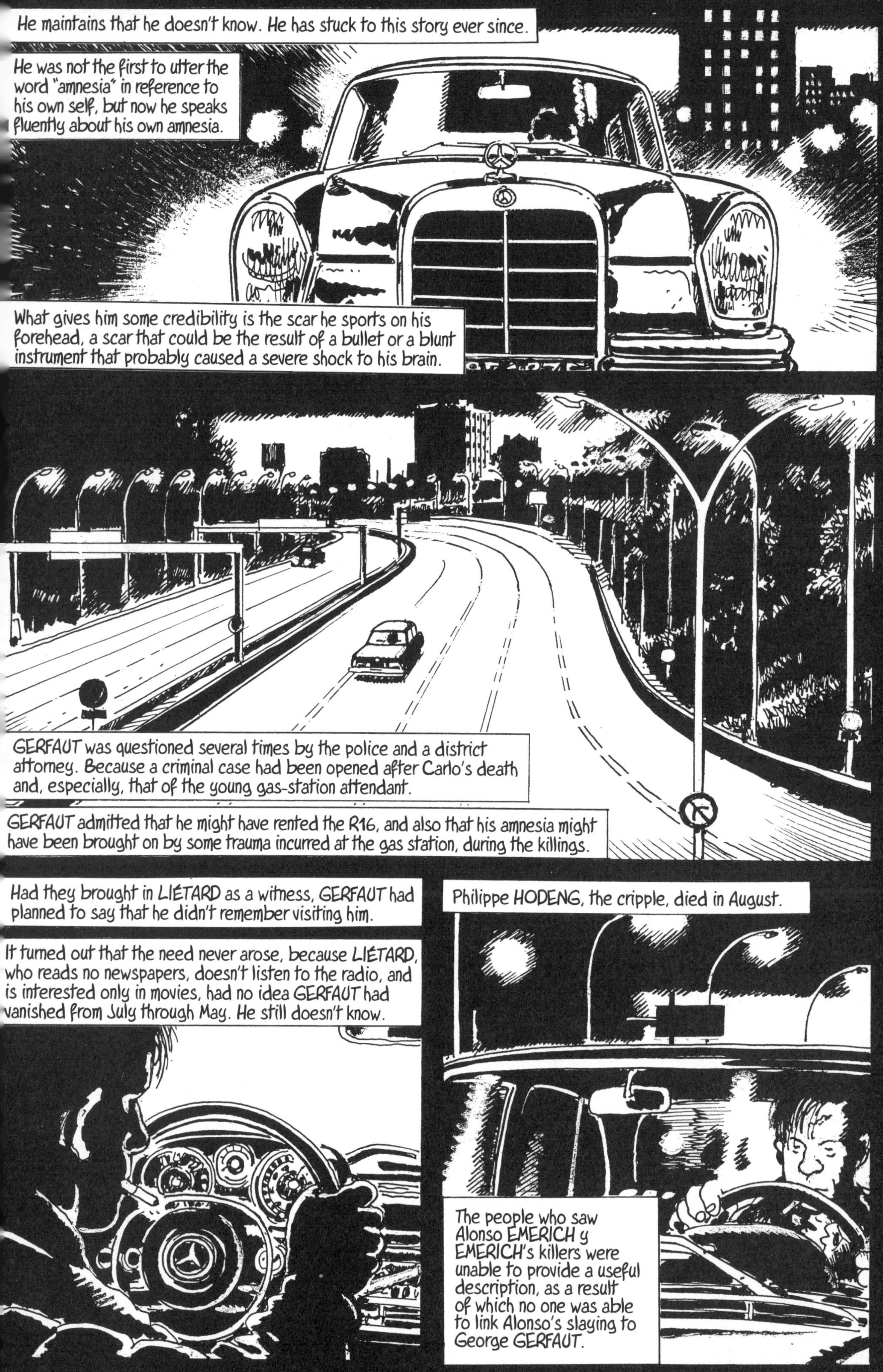
He maintains that he doesn't know. He has stuck to this story ever since.
He was not the first to utter the word "amnesia" in reference to his own self, but now he speaks fluently about his own amnesia.
What gives him some credibility is the scar he sports on his forehead, a scar that could be the result of a bullet or a blunt instrument that probably caused a severe shock to his brain.
GERFAUT was questioned several times by the police and a district attorney. Because a criminal case had been opened after Carlo's death and, especially, that of the young gas-station attendant.
GERFAUT admitted that he might have rented the R16, and also that his amnesia might have been brought on by some trauma incurred at the gas station, during the killings.
Had they brought in LIÉTARD as a witness, GERFAUT had planned to say that he didn't remember visiting him.
It turned out that the need never arose, because LIÉTARD, who reads no newspapers, doesn't listen to the radio, and is interested only in movies, had no idea GERFAUT had vanished from July through May. He still doesn't know.
Philippe HODENG, the cripple, died in August.
The people who saw Alonso EMERICH y EMERICH's killers were unable to provide a useful description, as a result of which no one was able to link Alonso's slaying to George GERFAUT.

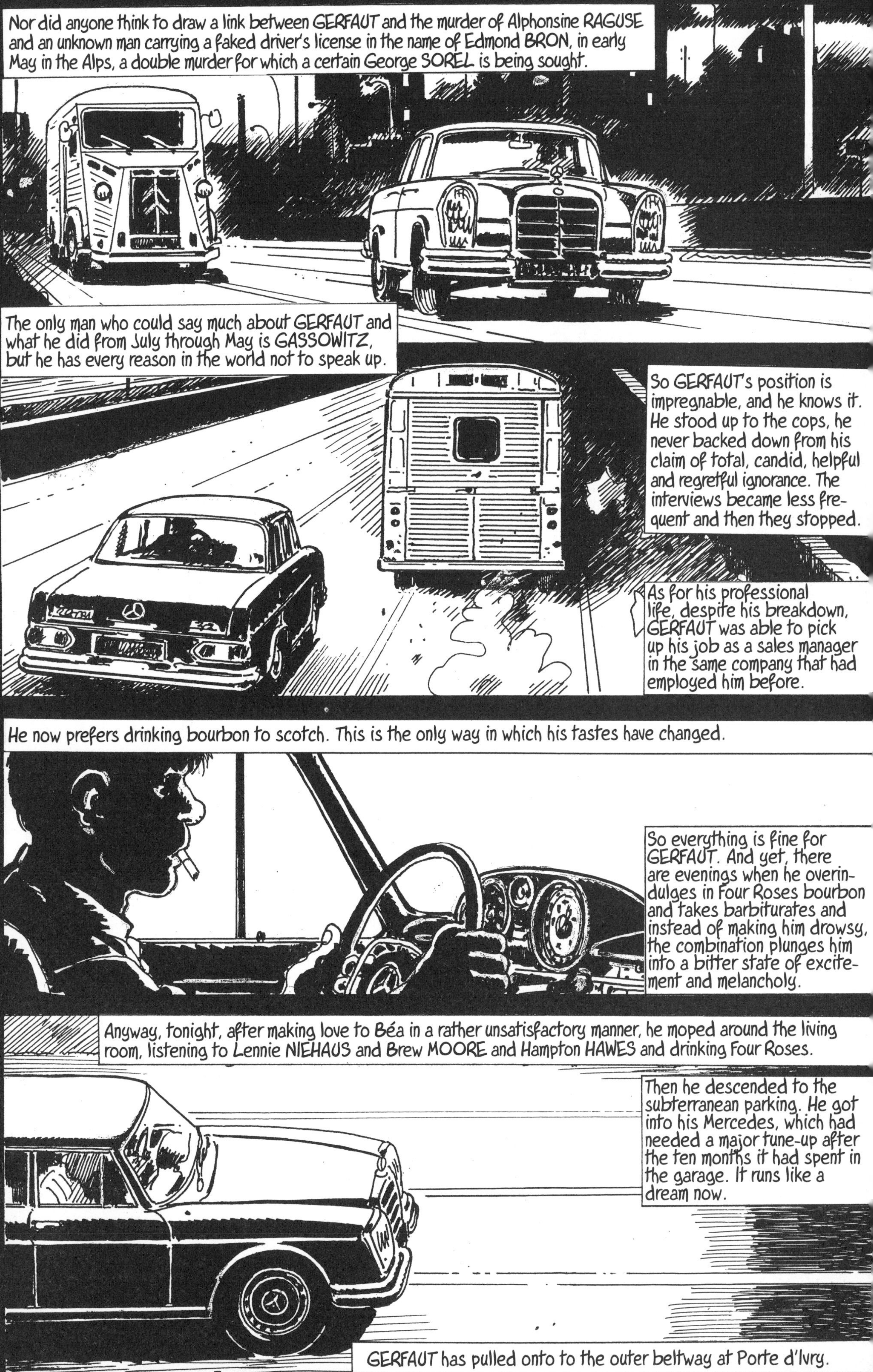
Nor did anyone think to draw a link between GERFAUT and the murder of Alphonsine RAGUSE and an unknown man carrying a faked driver's license in the name of Edmond BRON, in early May in the Alps, a double murder for which a certain George SOREL is being sought.
The only man who could say much about GERFAUT and what he did from July through May is GASSOWITZ, but he has every reason in the world not to speak up.
So GERFAUT's position is impregnable, and he knows it. He stood up to the cops, he never backed down from his claim of total, candid, helpful and regretful ignorance. The interviews became less frequent and then they stopped.
As for his professional life, despite his breakdown, GERFAUT was able to pick up his job as a sales manager in the same company that had employed him before.
He now prefers drinking bourbon to scotch. This is the only way in which his tastes have changed.
So everything is fine for GERFAUT. And yet, there are evenings when he overindulges in Four Roses bourbon and takes barbiturates and instead of making him drowsy, the combination plunges him into a bitter state of excitement and melancholy.
Anyway, tonight, after making love to Béa in a rather unsatisfactory manner, he moped around the living room, listening to Lennie NIEHAUS and Brew MOORE and Hampton HAWES and drinking Four Roses.
Then he descended to the subterranean parking. He got into his Mercedes, which had needed a major tune-up after the ten months it had spent in the garage. It runs like a dream now.
GERFAUT has pulled onto to the outer beltway at Porte d'Ivry.

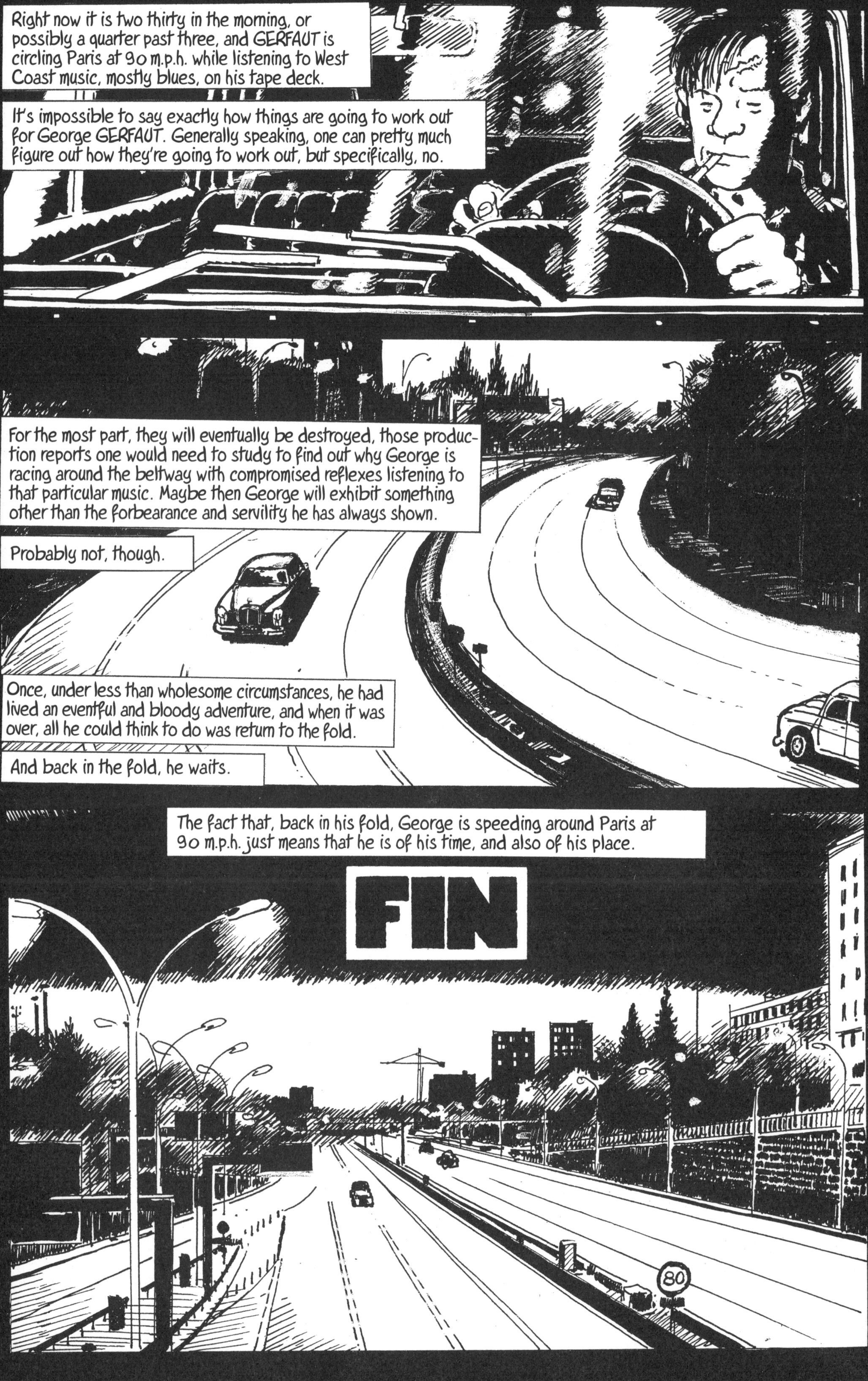

Right now it is two thirty in the morning, or possibly a quarter past three, and GERFAUT is circling Paris at 90 m.p.h. while listening to West Coast music, mostly blues, on his tape deck.
It's impossible to say exactly how things are going to work out for George GERFAUT. Generally speaking, one can pretty much figure out how they're going to work out, but specifically, no.
For the most part, they will eventually be destroyed, those production reports one would need to study to find out why George is racing around the beltway with compromised reflexes listening to that particular music. Maybe then George will exhibit something other than the forbearance and servility he has always shown.
Probably not, though.
Once, under less than wholesome circumstances, he had lived an eventful and bloody adventure, and when it was over, all he could think to do was return to the fold.
And back in the fold, he waits.
The fact that, back in his fold, George is speeding around Paris at 90 m.p.h. just means that he is of his time, and also of his place.
FIN
80

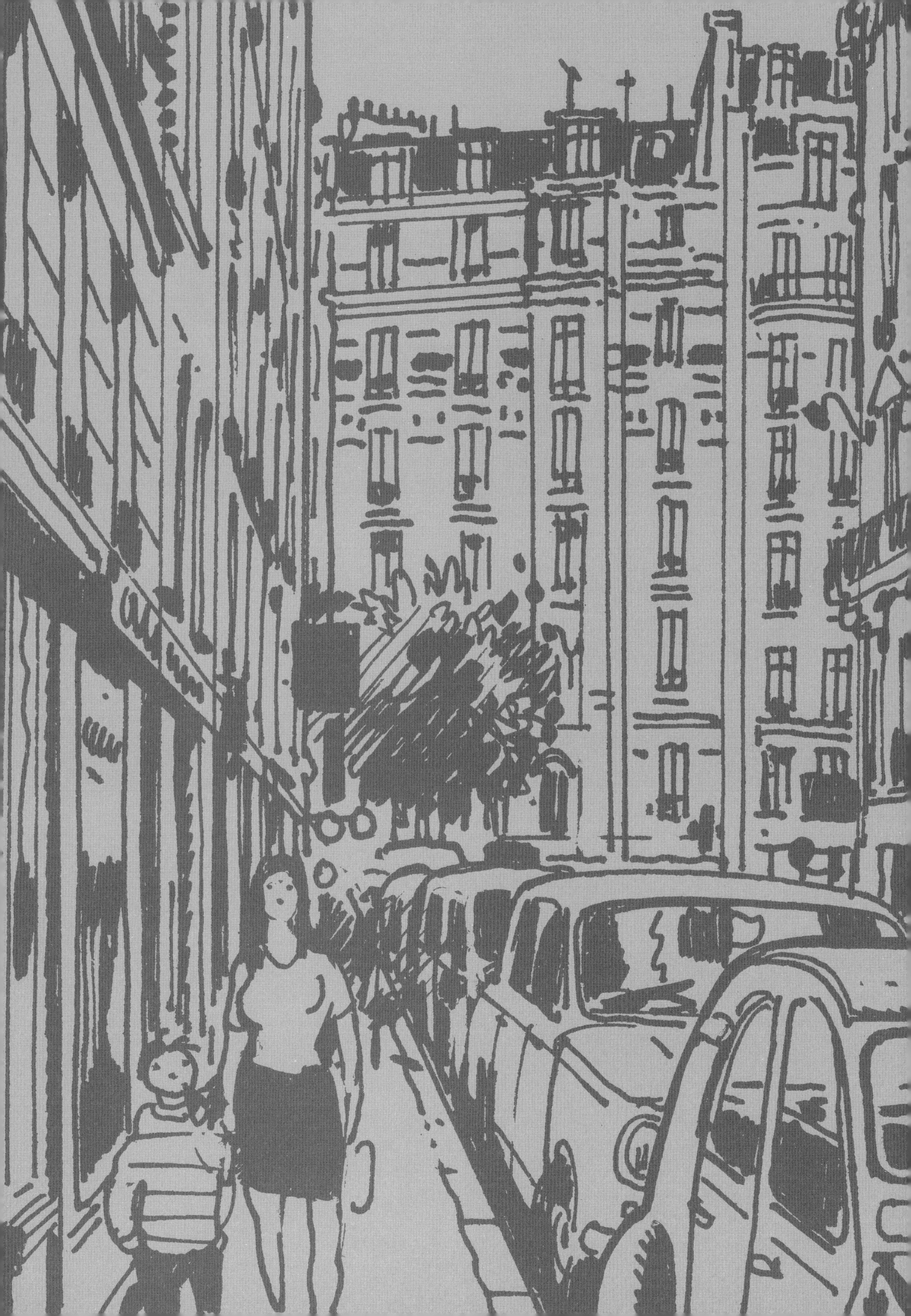

UNFINISHED STORIES

To Manchette, the noir novel was a form of popular literature that — under the guise of entertainment — allowed him to slip in a few subtle themes that, with a bit of luck, would make the reader think. I totally see myself in this approach to comics.

— TARDI

I discovered Manchette from his earliest works, which he had written with Jean-Pierre Bastid, but particularly *Run Like Crazy, Run Like Hell* and *The N'Gustro Affair*. I was immediately blown away by the writing, the solid plots, and, most of all, the visuals that made me want to draw them. We were coming from the detective novels, notably the old French crime novels such as Leo Malet's. Manchette's novels were in direct contact with the zeitgeist, the political climate of the time, which I saw in the streets in front of my home.

I met Manchette through Jean-Pierre Dionnet (editor at Humanoïdes Associés and the comics anthology *Métal Hurlant*) with the idea of working with him. At the time, Manchette was finishing a novel, *Fatale*. He was on the last chapters and suggested that we worked in tandem on a comics adaptation of his novel, because he didn't want to start on a new script.

We started working on the adaptation. We found ourselves in a bistro, working face-to-face. He would tell me the story, and I would do the layout, and then very quickly, the conversation would turn to something else, mostly cinema. Manchette was enough of a film buff that he could name the director of photography of a film, all over half-pints of German beer. He started writing the dialogue for the first two pages of my layouts. At that time, as Manchette described the scenes to me, I hadn't read his manuscript. I didn't actually read the novel until after it was published!

We worked on that project for Jean-Pierre Dionnet, but not for *Métal Hurlant*, the new magazine that he was planning to launch. We didn't have a contract. We didn't get a cent for that story! Then we had the chance to work for *BD*, the new weekly published by Éditions du Square — Wolinski was the editor-in-chief. [Tragically, Georges Wolinski was one of the cartoonists murdered in the terrorist attack on the *Charlie Hebdo* offices in Paris on January 7, 2015.] We forgot *Fatale* and charged ahead with *Griffu*. We had no safety net since we only had three weeks before its debut.

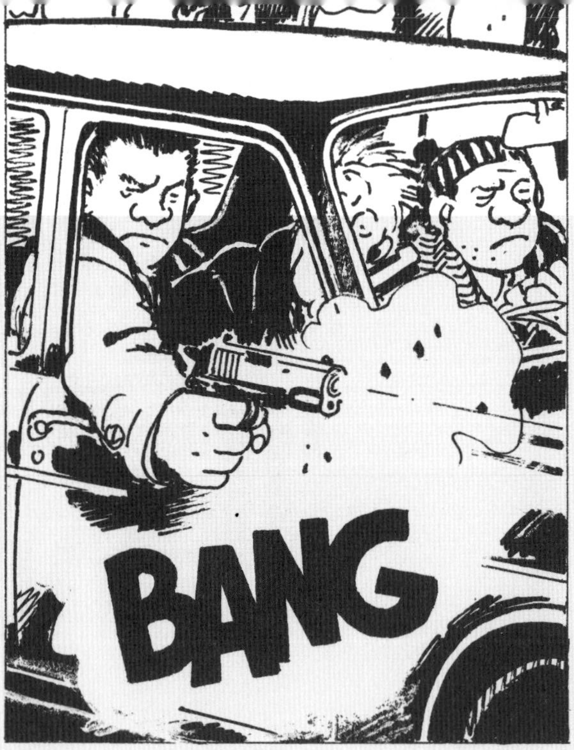
BANG

The basic concept of *Griffu* came from Manchette. A guy, a legal adviser and amateur investigator, that's Griffu. We started with the real estate scandals surrounding the Les Halles market in Paris, the evictions, which were the inspiration for our tale that took place during the [French President Georges] Pompidou years, the same time period in which we were creating it. It was a very intense time for me, because I was also concurrently finishing *Adèle Blanc-Sec*, and I had just begun *You Are There* with Jean-Claude Forest (again, without a publisher — *À Suivre* magazine didn't exist yet).

Weekly magazines like *Pilote* were disappearing. Only the monthlies remained. Yet I thought that comics were made for the weeklies or dailies. The launch of *BD* was a chance not to be missed!

In the beginning, we continued to work as we had done on *Fatale* — we met at a bistro, he narrated the scene, and I made the layout on the spot, always surrounded by an impressive number of beers!

But eventually, Manchette began sending me the scenes bit by bit, and I did the layouts by myself. He wrote the dialogue on the pages like a serial novelist at the rate of two pages a week. I didn't know how it would end. Manchette must have known. Anyway, I don't remember knowing it before finishing the last pages.

It was an intense time, but I have good memories of it. Then, at Éditions du Square, I met the protest singer Dominique Grange, who became my wife. After two years, the magazine ended its run. Manchette went back to his novels (*Like a Sniper Lining Up His Shot*), and I to my stories. I don't remember why we didn't go back to *Fatale*. However, we did go to Dieppe, to locations from the novel, to scout some locations, but after that, we didn't see each other again. We had our separate projects.

After Manchette's death, I wanted to return to the world of his novels. *Griffu* had been created under the pressures of serialization, and I wanted to take my time in adapting one of his stories. That led to *West Coast Blues*.

When I adapt Manchette, I don't change a thing. I have the utmost respect for the text. Manchette's writing describes a character's habits and environment. All these bits of information tell us about the character, to genuinely feel them. Manchette's characters have their own internal logic.

Most of his works have been adapted to film, and sometimes I'm surprised by them — *West Coast Blues* featured Alain Delon, and I have never understood why the director or producer bought the rights to the book. In the novel, Gerfaut, the hero, is a middle manager uncomfortable with his wife, his family, and his job. In the film, he turns into a poker player who spends his nights gambling in dives! It's not even the same character!

Manchette set the crime novel free of all its conventions. In Manchette's stories, there's no investigation. We follow unconventional characters, often isolated, who escape morality, but who live in their time, within society. Terrier, in *Like a Sniper Lining Up His Shot*, is a guy who became a killer and started living on the fringes. He wants to rejoin society, but he can't manage to do it. He wants to get back to a girl, marry her, and live a normal life with her.

With Manchette, it's a contemporary world. The adaptations of his novels are some of the very few contemporary comics I've done. My interest lies in stepping outside the serialized novels that I'm fond of, like *Fantômas* or *Arsène Lupin*. Manchette gives me the opportunity to explore the current world that I've always been hesitant to draw. I don't like to draw cars — the everyday things I see around me don't inspire me. I have zero interest in drawing a computer. Visually, I need to cling to richer forms, like those of the 19th century, for example.

I love to reconstruct, gather materials, buy old newspapers, to try to bring the past back to life, like with Nestor Burma or Adele Blanc-Sec.

That said, these days, Manchette's novels become interesting in that sense. We see the 1970s now like we used to see the 1950s. I collected materials in the same way while creating *Like a Sniper Lining Up His Shot* as I did years ago when I was drawing *Fog Over Tolbiac Bridge*, even though I'm very familiar with the 1970s!

What I enjoy about Manchette's characters is that, most of the time, they aren't in control of the situation. They hop aboard a story, in spite of themselves, a story that overtakes them. That's the case with Terrier but also Gerfaut, in *West Coast Blues*.

I have the feeling that at the end of the 1970s and the 1980s, there were a lot of authors who took Manchette's place but didn't quite replace him. There are authors who started off publishing under crime imprints with hopes of publishing under literary imprints, as if crime imprints were less rewarding, something Manchette rejected. To him, crime novels weren't airport novels, they were airplane novels — books that were enjoyable to read, but with a few elements to perturb the reader for the length of a flight, and so it must be necessarily short. A popular literature, which — under the guise of entertainment — allowed him to slip in a few important issues that, with a bit of luck, would make the reader think. This is exactly my approach to comics.

— TARDI

FATALE

Fatale
STORY – Jean-Patrick Manchette
ART – Tardi
TRANSLATION – Jenna Allen

The 21 pages of *Fatale* (out of the 60 or so originally planned) were published in Thierry Groensteen's book dedicated to Tardi, published by Magic Strip in 1980.

The pages have remained unedited since.

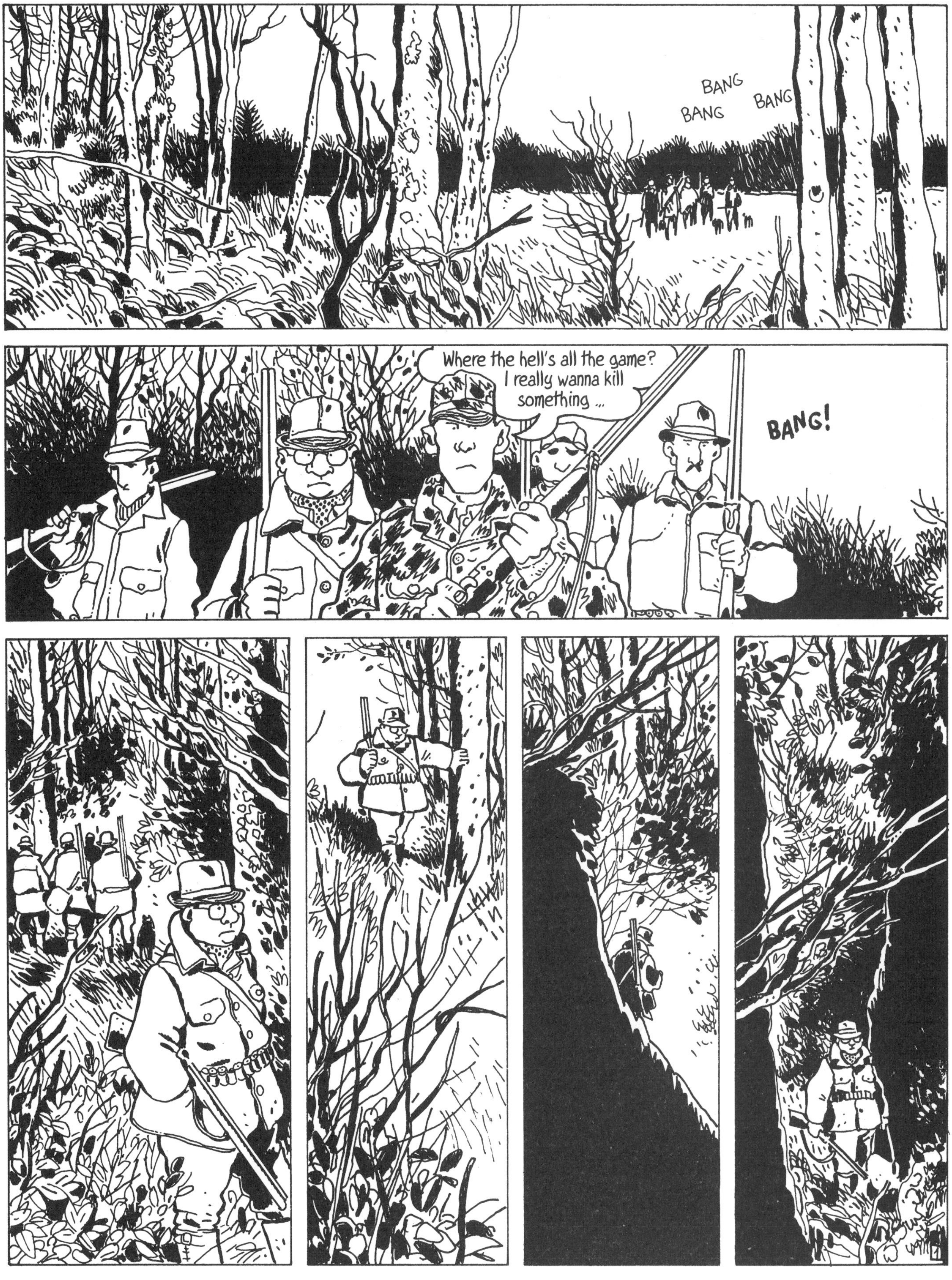
BANG
BANG
BANG
Where the hell's all the game? I really wanna kill something ...
BANG!

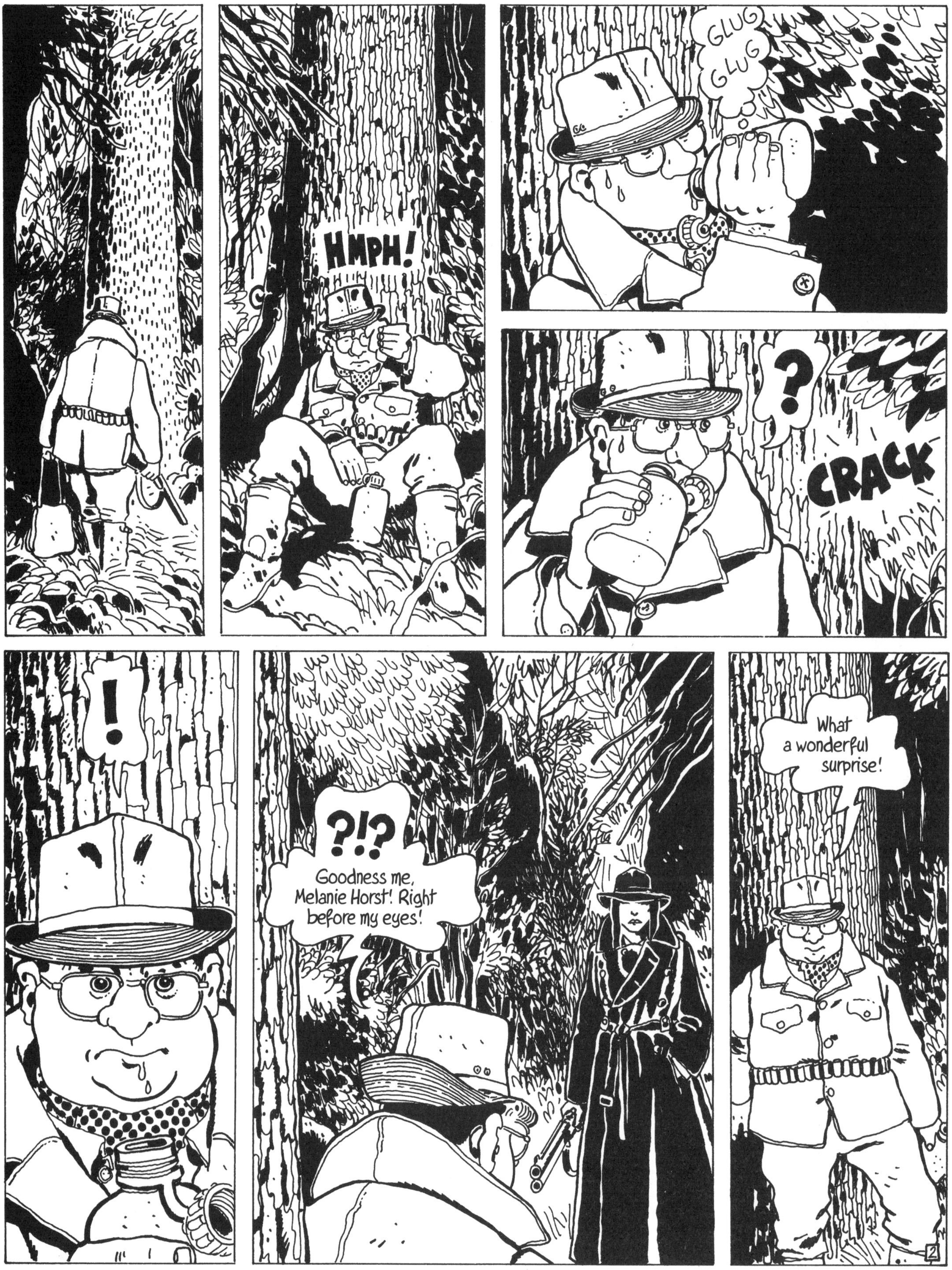
HMPH!
GLUG GLUG
?
CRACK
!
?!?
Goodness me, Melanie Horst! Right before my eyes!
What a wonderful surprise!
2

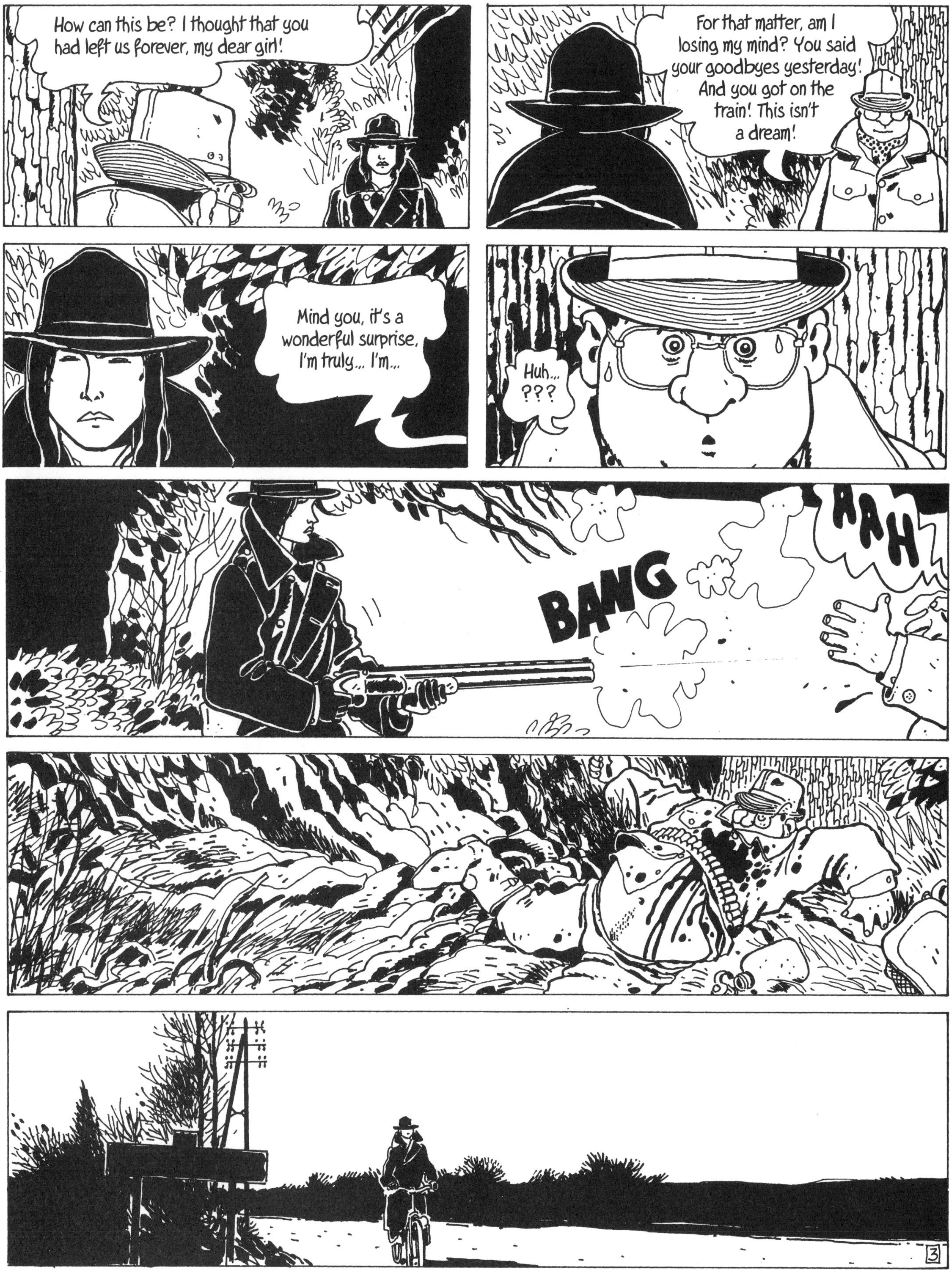
How can this be? I thought that you had left us forever, my dear girl!
For that matter, am I losing my mind? You said your goodbyes yesterday! And you got on the train! This isn't a dream!
Mind you, it's a wonderful surprise, I'm truly... I'm...
Huh... ???
BANG
AAAH
3

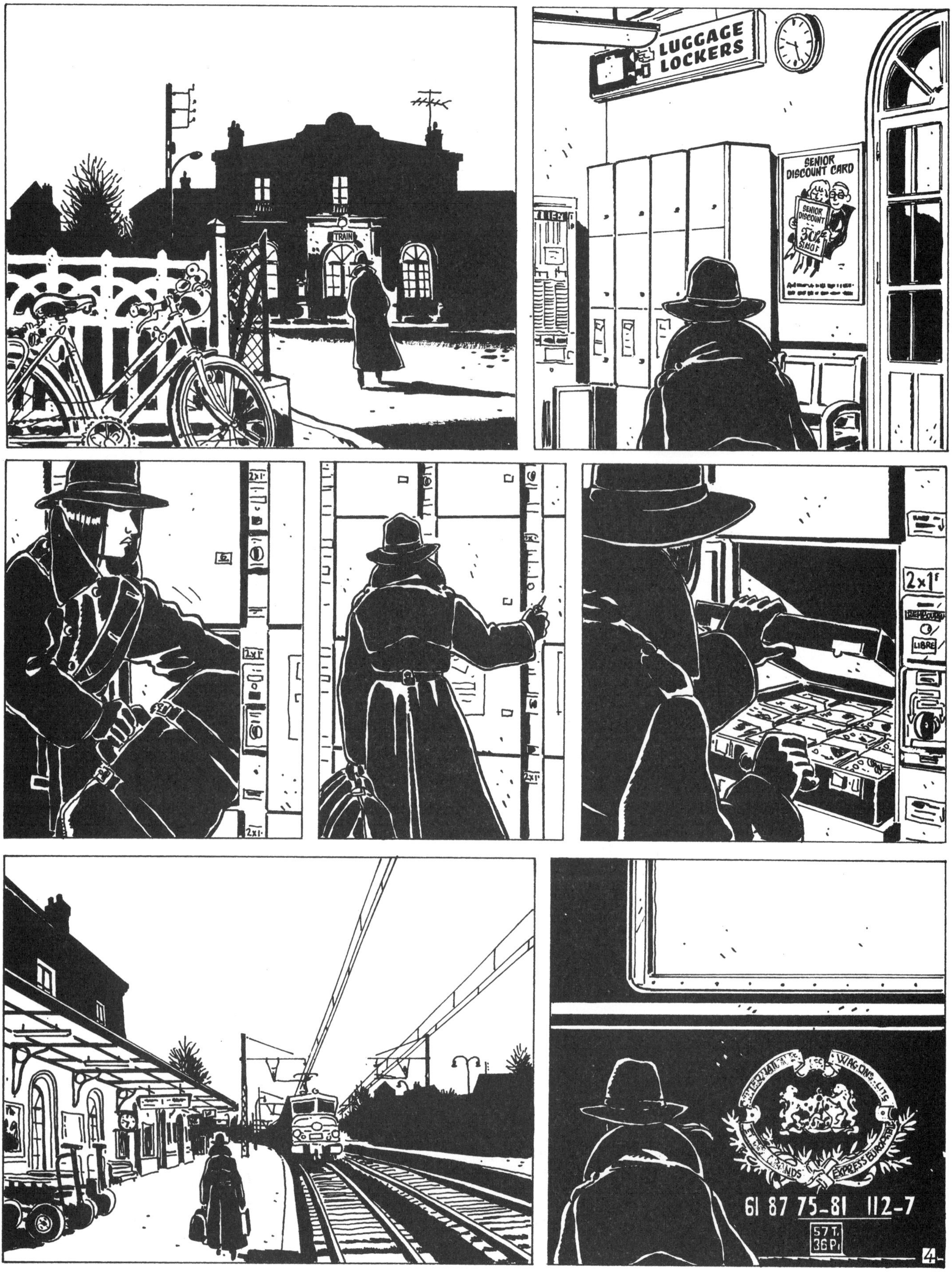
TRAIN
LUGGAGE LOCKERS
SENIOR DISCOUNT CARD
SENIOR DISCOUNT
2x1F
LIBRE
61 87 75-81 112-7
4

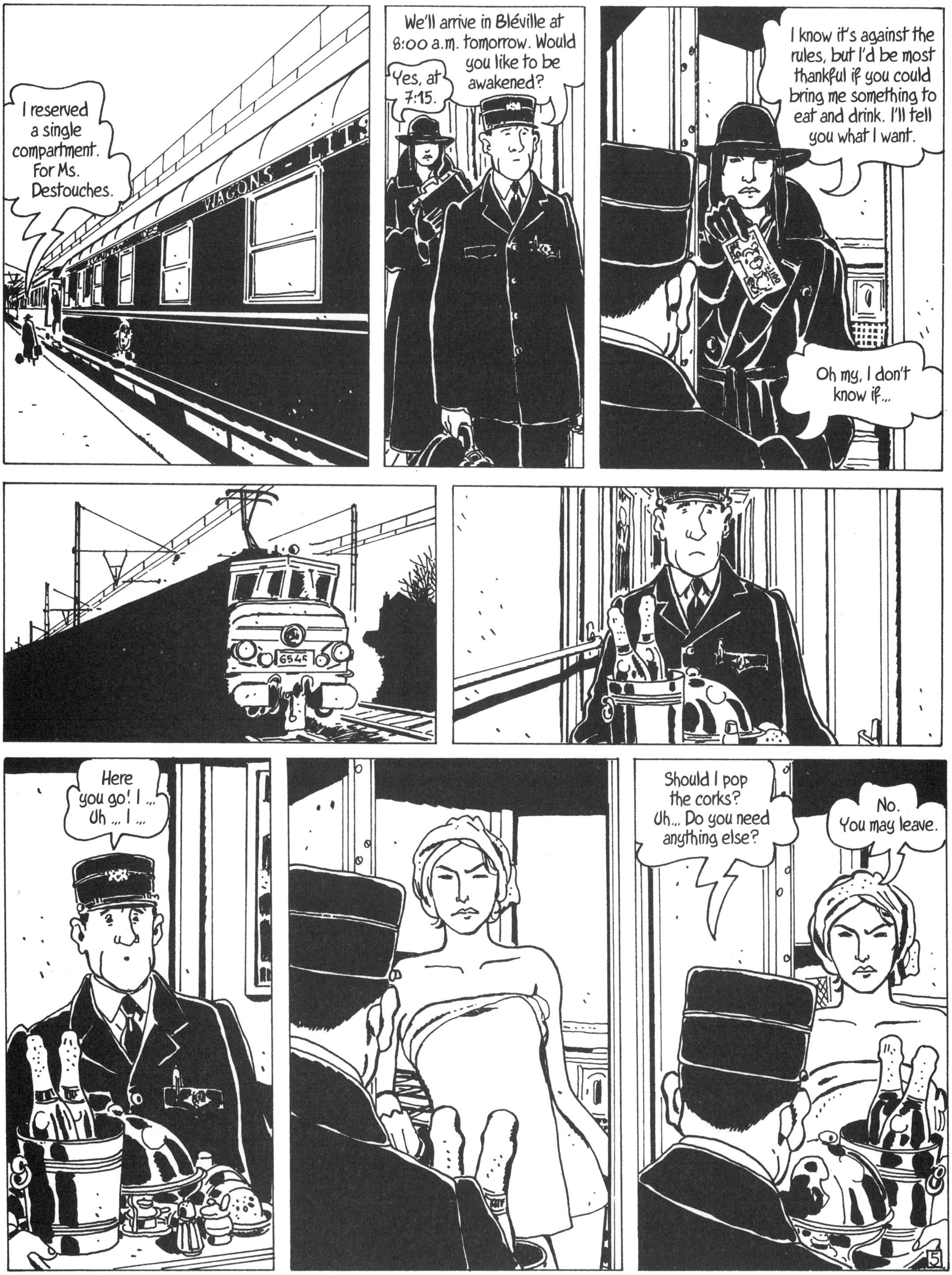
I reserved a single compartment. For Ms. Destouches.
We'll arrive in Bléville at 8:00 a.m. tomorrow. Would you like to be awakened?
Yes, at 7:15.
I know it's against the rules, but I'd be most thankful if you could bring me something to eat and drink. I'll tell you what I want.
Oh my, I don't know if...
Here you go! I ... Uh ... I ...
Should I pop the corks? Uh... Do you need anything else?
No. You may leave.
5

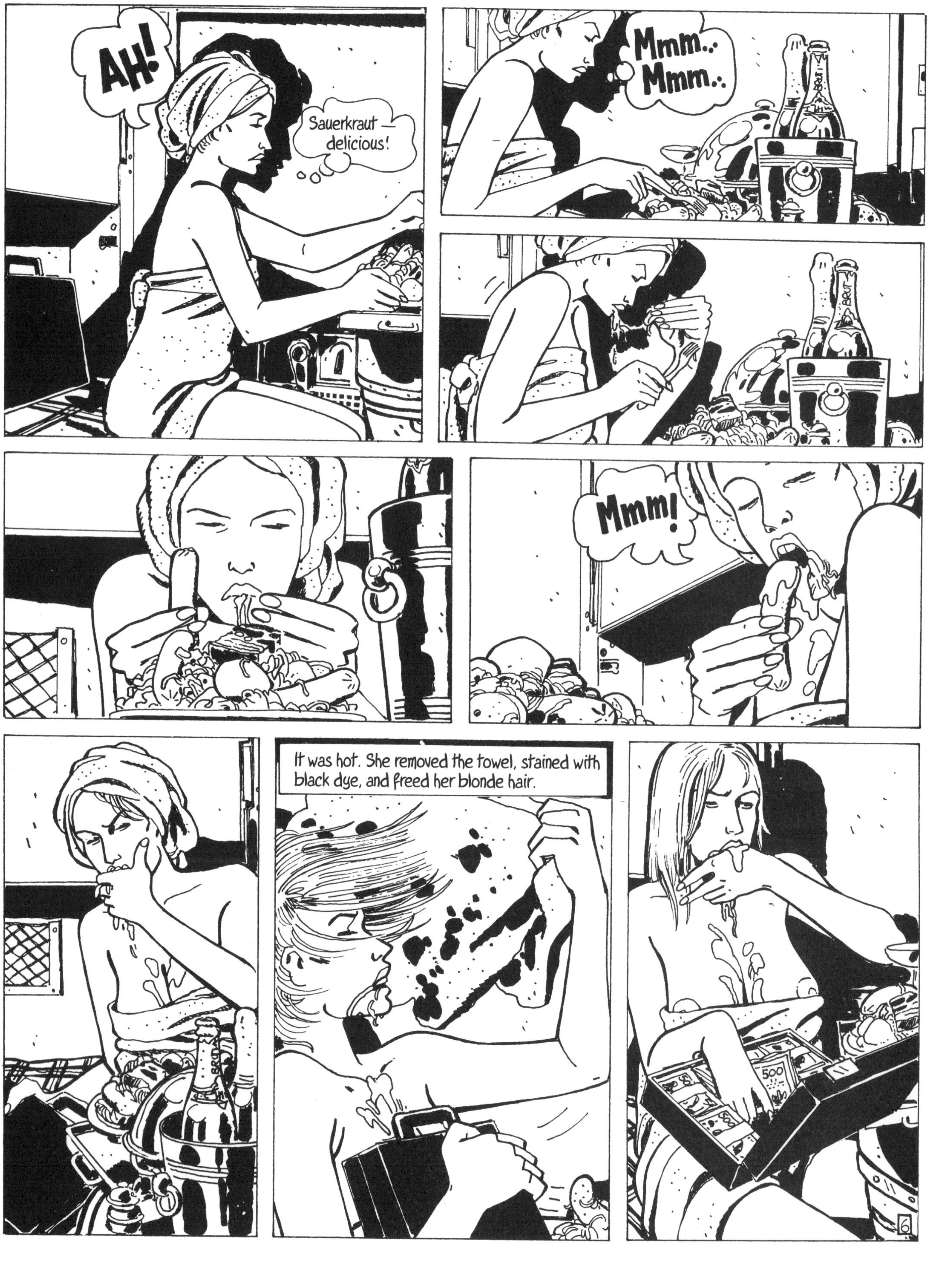
AH!
Sauerkraut — delicious!
Mmm... Mmm...
Mmm!
It was hot. She removed the towel, stained with black dye, and freed her blonde hair.
500

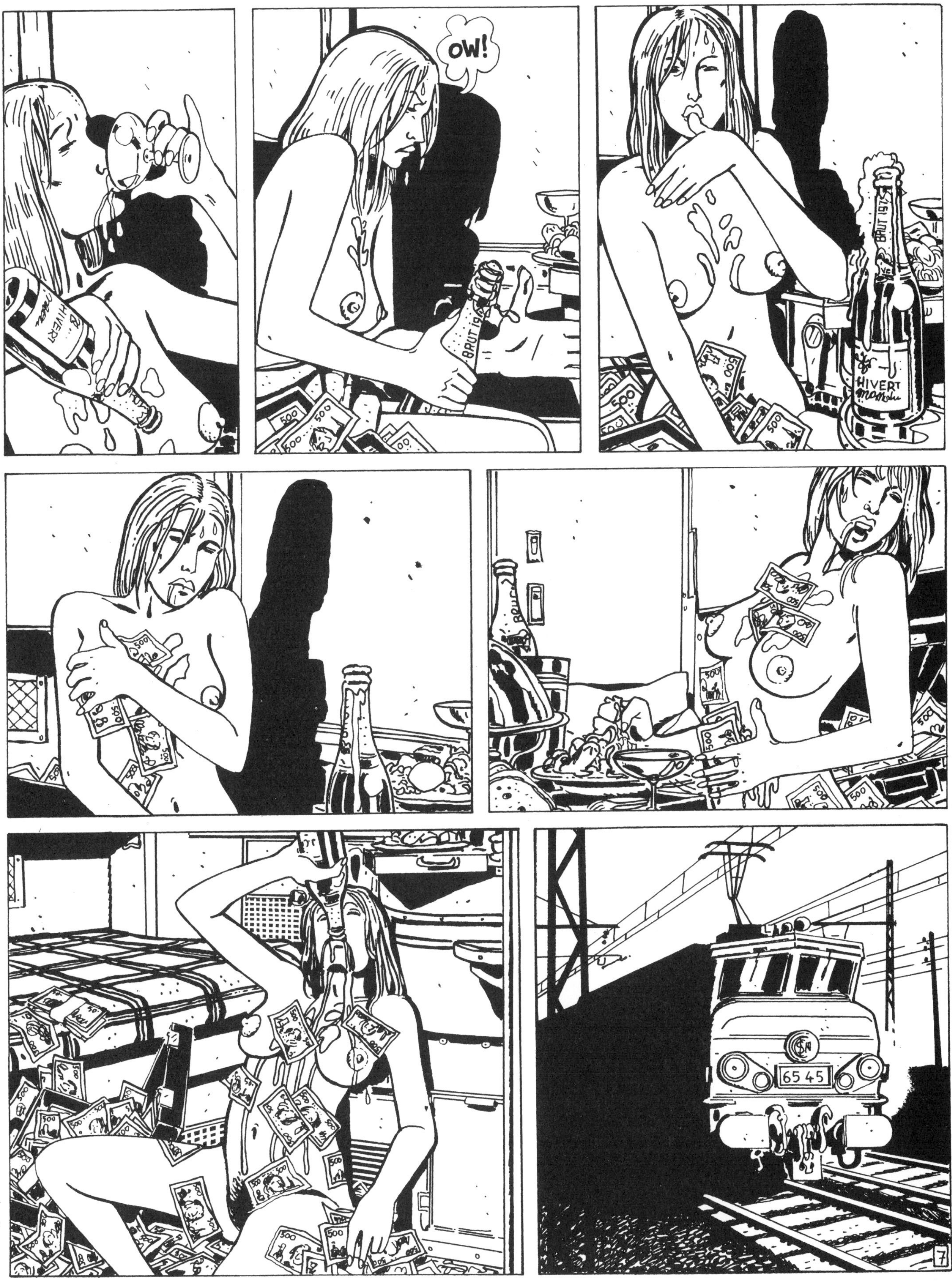
OW!
HIVERT
65 45

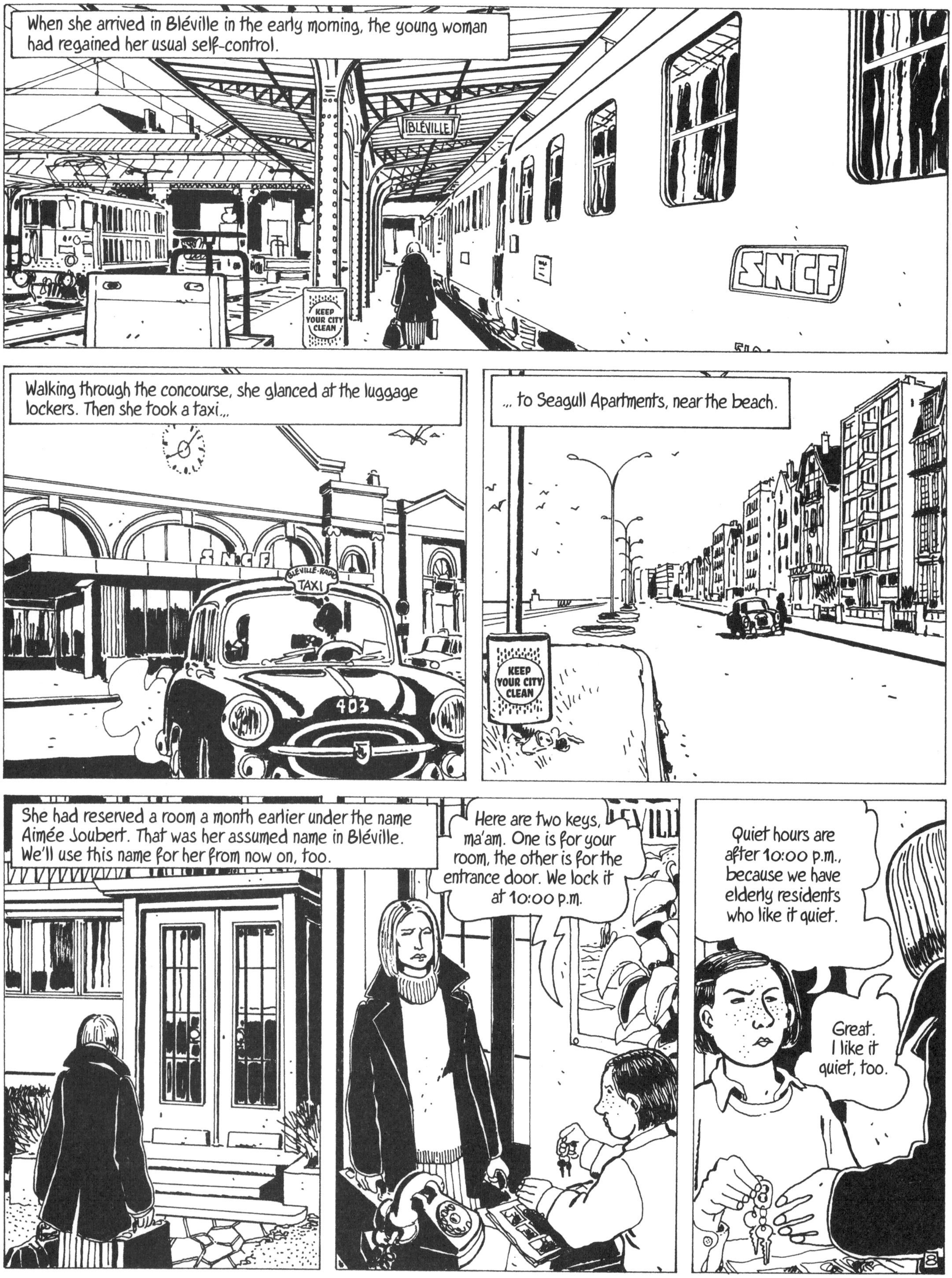
When she arrived in Bléville in the early morning, the young woman had regained her usual self-control.
BLÉVILLE
KEEP YOUR CITY CLEAN
SNCF
Walking through the concourse, she glanced at the luggage lockers. Then she took a taxi...
TAXI
403
... to Seagull Apartments, near the beach.
KEEP YOUR CITY CLEAN
She had reserved a room a month earlier under the name Aimée Joubert. That was her assumed name in Bléville. We'll use this name for her from now on, too.
Here are two keys, ma'am. One is for your room, the other is for the entrance door. We lock it at 10:00 p.m.
Quiet hours are after 10:00 p.m., because we have elderly residents who like it quiet.
Great. I like it quiet, too.

Ugh,
it could be
worse!

When she finished settling in, it was time for her daily training.

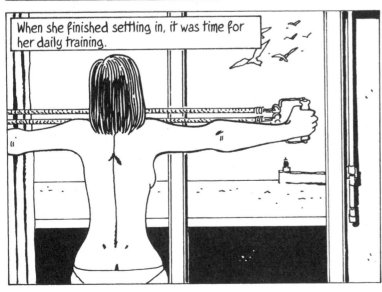

HA!

THUNK

to the Millenarians as a
world.
Partially destroyed by King Philip II, the city was reconstructed at the dawn of the 13th century. A sturdy castle and ramparts were erected from which you can still view the ruins. But it was with the rise of long-distance sailing that the city's riches were permanently established. Bléville residents achieved renown against the English, then the Portuguese, and reached as far as the shores of Canada and the islands of southeast Asia. Under King Louis XIV, commerce and commerce raiding were the mother's milk of Bléville's prosperity. After the decline in port activity in the 19th century, Bléville waited until the 1960s for another economic boom. Chemical and food factories were established in the valley, and the suburban workers saw rapid expansion. Today, Bléville can
Fig. 12
THE BLÉVILLE AREA
Just before 2:00, informed and refreshed, Aimée left her studio and walked briskly toward the heart of the city.
BLÉVILLE DISPATCH
LE FIGARO
France Soir
First, she bought all the newspapers with prominent human-interest stories, but she didn't find what she was looking for.
APERS
Evening News
She immediately threw them all in the trash, including the two local papers — one with a pro-capitalist slant and the other an anti-capitalist slant.
KEEP YOUR CITY CLEAN
BLÉVILLE NEWS
Next, she bought a touring bicycle — a good brand, expensive and reliable — for the trip she had to take.
Grand Café de l'Anglais
10

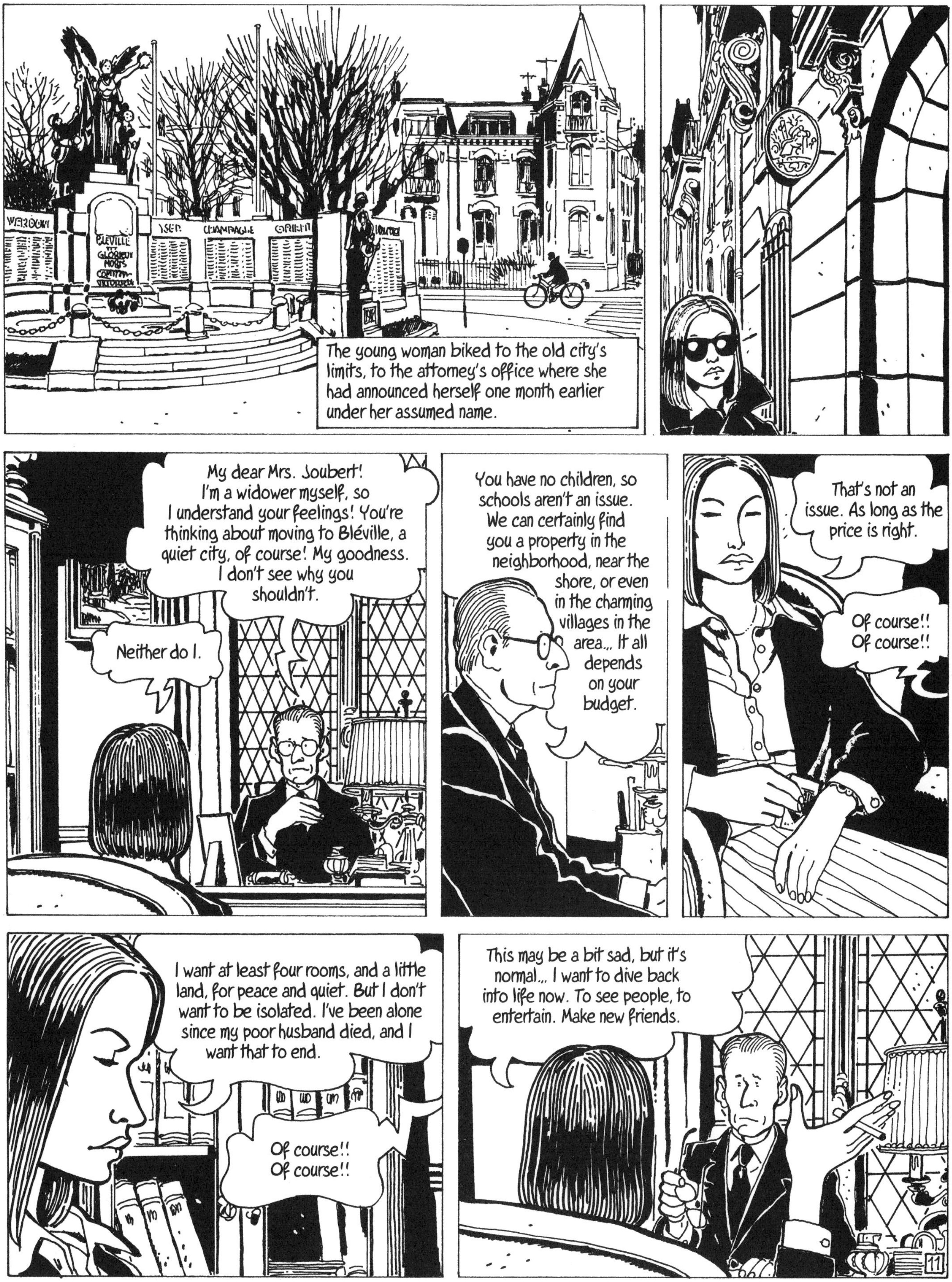
The young woman biked to the old city's limits, to the attorney's office where she had announced herself one month earlier under her assumed name.
My dear Mrs. Joubert! I'm a widower myself, so I understand your feelings! You're thinking about moving to Bléville, a quiet city, of course! My goodness. I don't see why you shouldn't.
Neither do I.
You have no children, so schools aren't an issue. We can certainly find you a property in the neighborhood, near the shore, or even in the charming villages in the area... It all depends on your budget.
That's not an issue. As long as the price is right.
Of course!! Of course!!
I want at least four rooms, and a little land, for peace and quiet. But I don't want to be isolated. I've been alone since my poor husband died, and I want that to end.
Of course!! Of course!!
This may be a bit sad, but it's normal... I want to dive back into life now. To see people, to entertain. Make new friends.
11

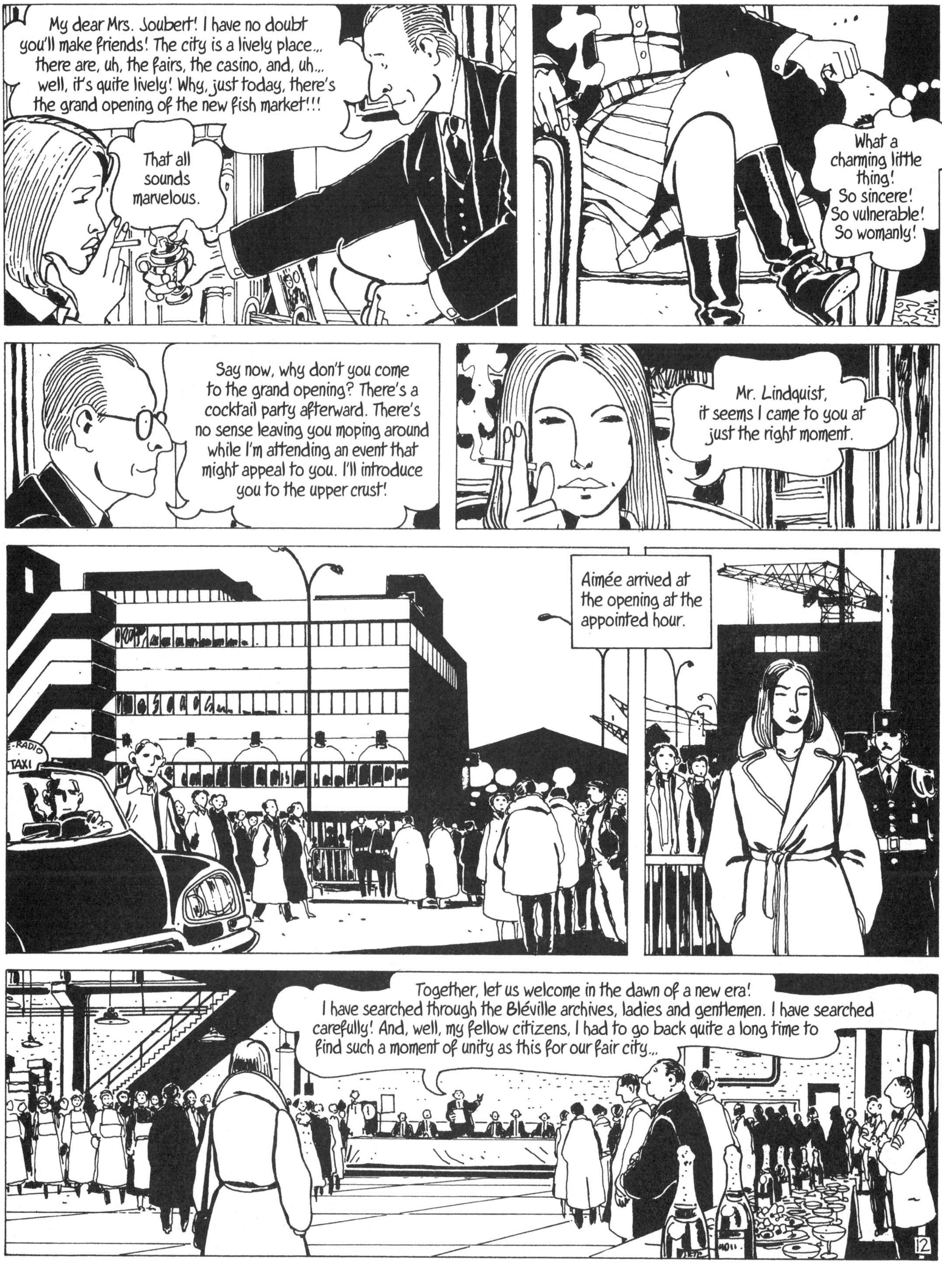
My dear Mrs. Joubert! I have no doubt you'll make friends! The city is a lively place... there are, uh, the fairs, the casino, and, uh... well, it's quite lively! Why, just today, there's the grand opening of the new fish market!!!
That all sounds marvelous.
...
What a charming little thing! So sincere! So vulnerable! So womanly!
Say now, why don't you come to the grand opening? There's a cocktail party afterward. There's no sense leaving you moping around while I'm attending an event that might appeal to you. I'll introduce you to the upper crust!
Mr. Lindquist, it seems I came to you at just the right moment.
TAXI
Aimée arrived at the opening at the appointed hour.
Together, let us welcome in the dawn of a new era! I have searched through the Bléville archives, ladies and gentlemen. I have searched carefully! And, well, my fellow citizens, I had to go back quite a long time to find such a moment of unity as this for our fair city...
12

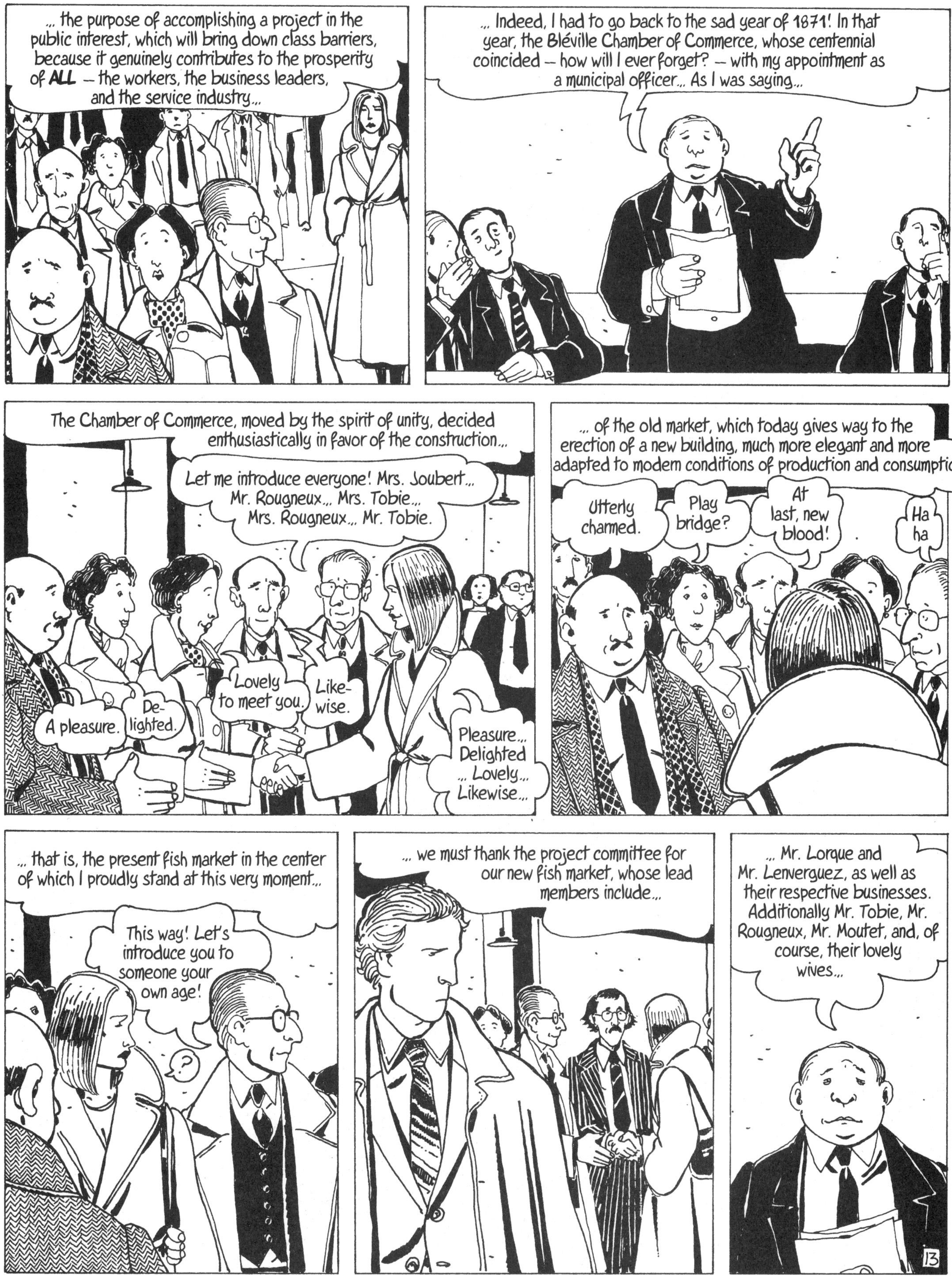
... the purpose of accomplishing a project in the public interest, which will bring down class barriers, because it genuinely contributes to the prosperity of ALL — the workers, the business leaders, and the service industry...
... Indeed, I had to go back to the sad year of 1871! In that year, the Bléville Chamber of Commerce, whose centennial coincided — how will I ever forget? — with my appointment as a municipal officer... As I was saying...
The Chamber of Commerce, moved by the spirit of unity, decided enthusiastically in favor of the construction...
Let me introduce everyone! Mrs. Joubert... Mr. Rougneux... Mrs. Tobie... Mrs. Rougneux... Mr. Tobie.
A pleasure.
De-lighted.
Lovely to meet you.
Like-wise.
Pleasure... Delighted ... Lovely... Likewise...
... of the old market, which today gives way to the erection of a new building, much more elegant and more adapted to modern conditions of production and consumption.
Utterly charmed.
Play bridge?
At last, new blood!
Ha ha
... that is, the present fish market in the center of which I proudly stand at this very moment...
This way! Let's introduce you to someone your own age!
?
... we must thank the project committee for our new fish market, whose lead members include...
... Mr. Lorque and Mr. Lenverguez, as well as their respective businesses. Additionally Mr. Tobie, Mr. Rougneux, Mr. Moutet, and, of course, their lovely wives...
13

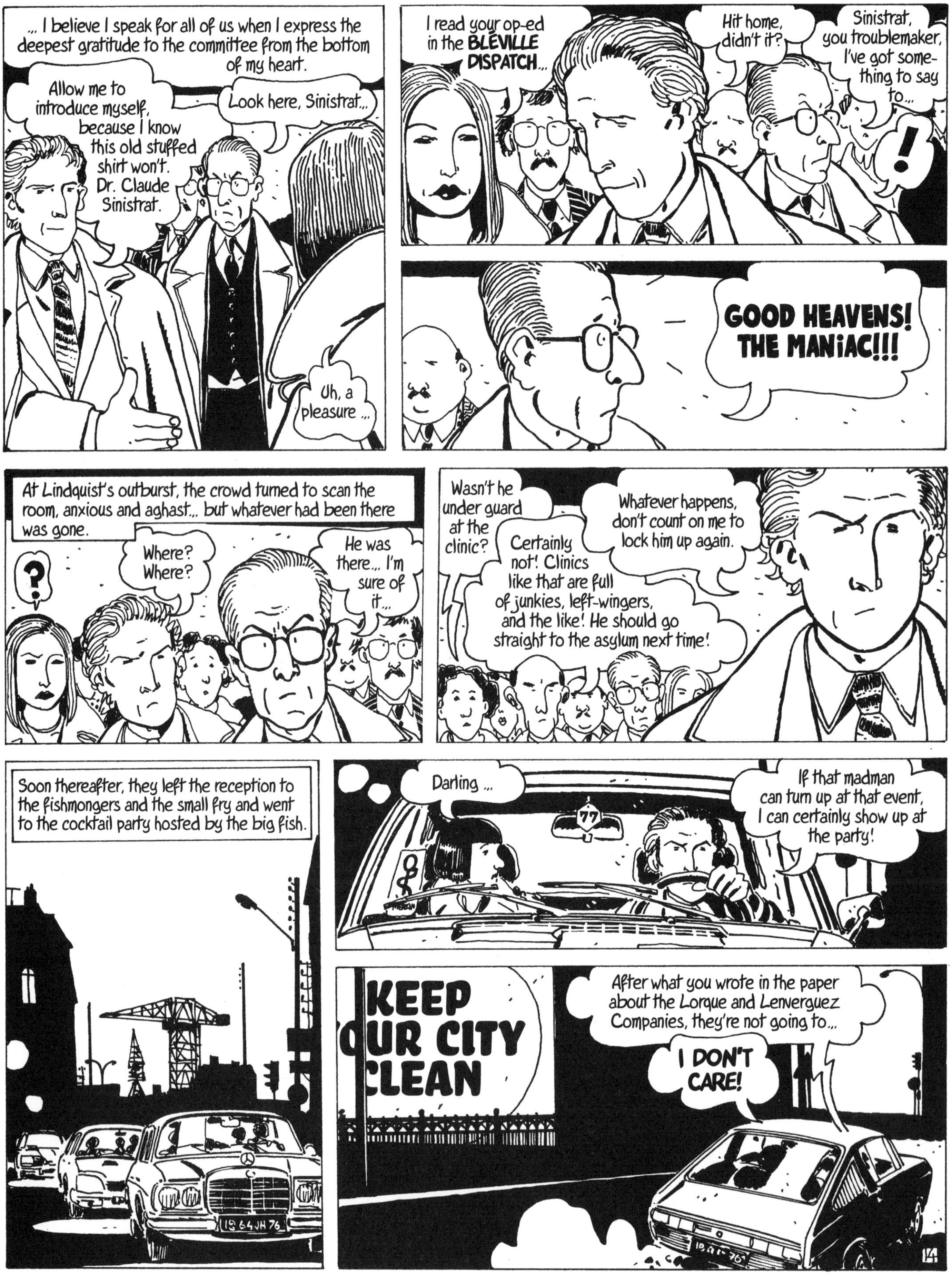
... I believe I speak for all of us when I express the deepest gratitude to the committee from the bottom of my heart.
Allow me to introduce myself, because I know this old stuffed shirt won't. Dr. Claude Sinistrat.
Look here, Sinistrat...
Uh, a pleasure ...
I read your op-ed in the BLÉVILLE DISPATCH...
Hit home, didn't it?
Sinistrat, you troublemaker, I've got something to say to...
!
GOOD HEAVENS! THE MANIAC!!!
At Lindquist's outburst, the crowd turned to scan the room, anxious and aghast... but whatever had been there was gone.
?
Where? Where?
He was there... I'm sure of it...
Wasn't he under guard at the clinic?
Certainly not! Clinics like that are full of junkies, left-wingers, and the like! He should go straight to the asylum next time!
Whatever happens, don't count on me to lock him up again.
Soon thereafter, they left the reception to the fishmongers and the small fry and went to the cocktail party hosted by the big fish.
Darling ...
If that madman can turn up at that event, I can certainly show up at the party!
KEEP OUR CITY CLEAN
After what you wrote in the paper about the Lorque and Lenverguez Companies, they're not going to...
I DON'T CARE!
14

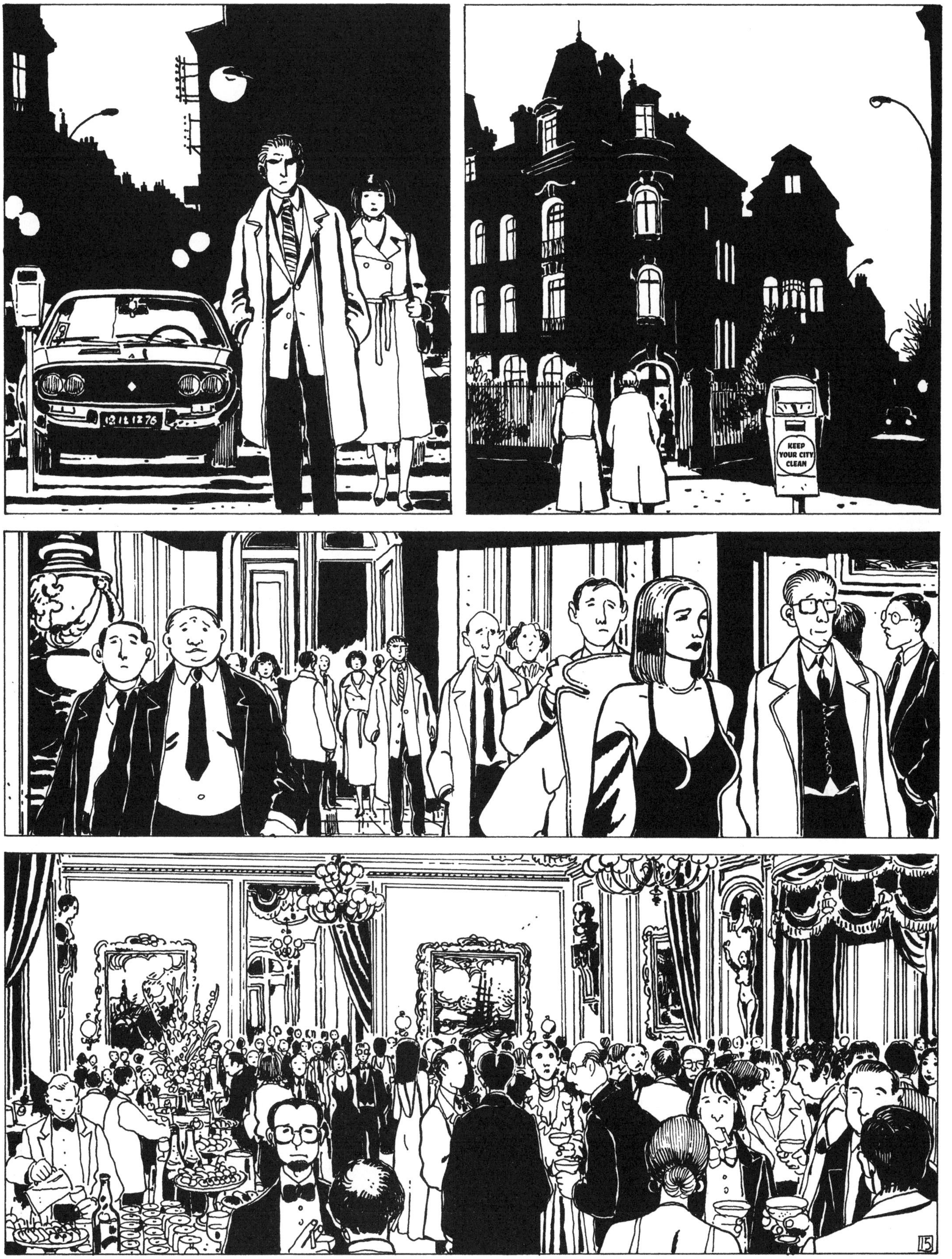
KEEP YOUR CITY CLEAN

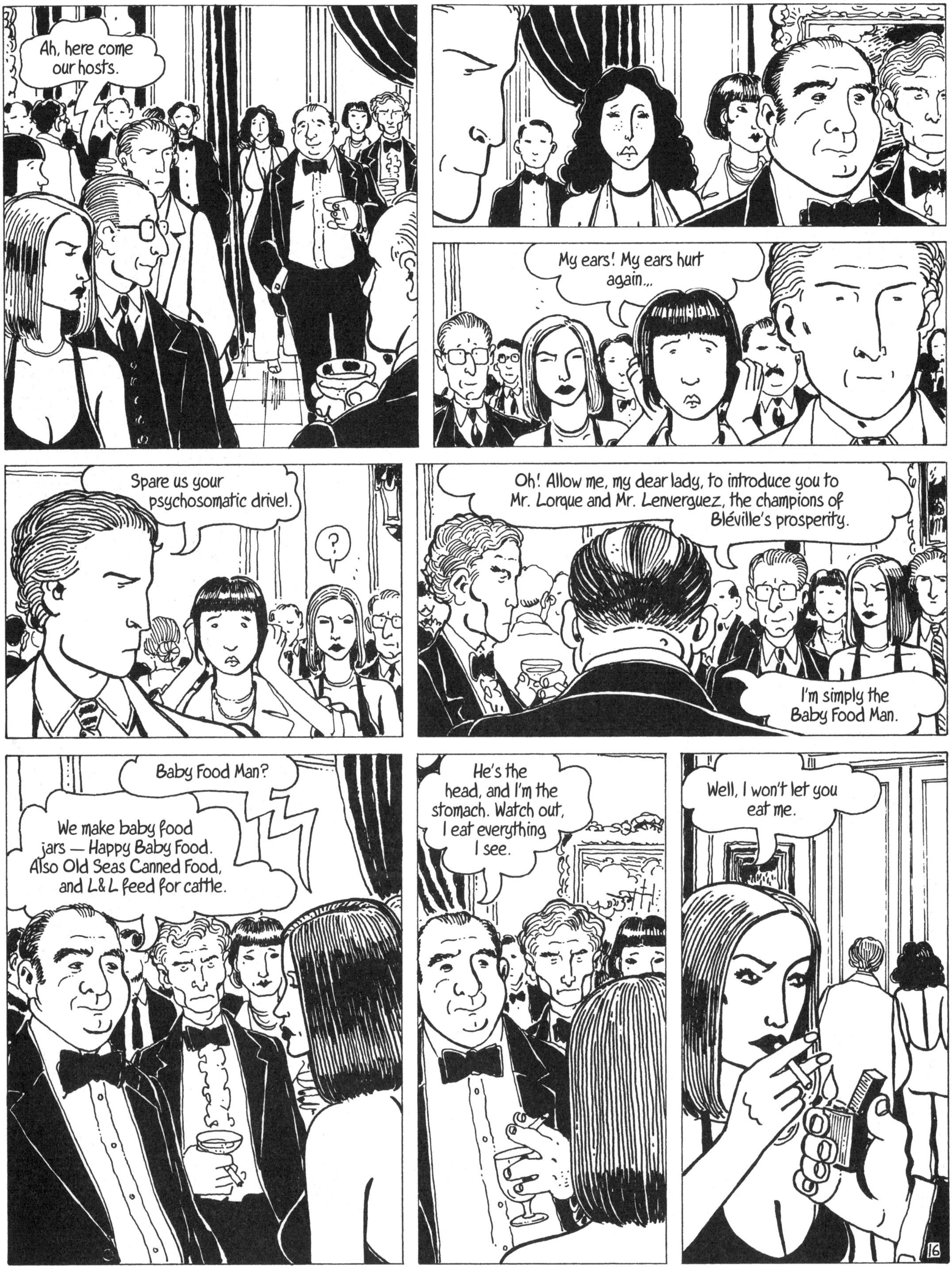
Ah, here come our hosts.
My ears! My ears hurt again...
Spare us your psychosomatic drivel.
?
Oh! Allow me, my dear lady, to introduce you to Mr. Lorque and Mr. Lenverguez, the champions of Bléville's prosperity.
I'm simply the Baby Food Man.
Baby Food Man?
We make baby food jars — Happy Baby Food. Also Old Seas Canned Food, and L&L feed for cattle.
He's the head, and I'm the stomach. Watch out, I eat everything I see.
Well, I won't let you eat me.
16

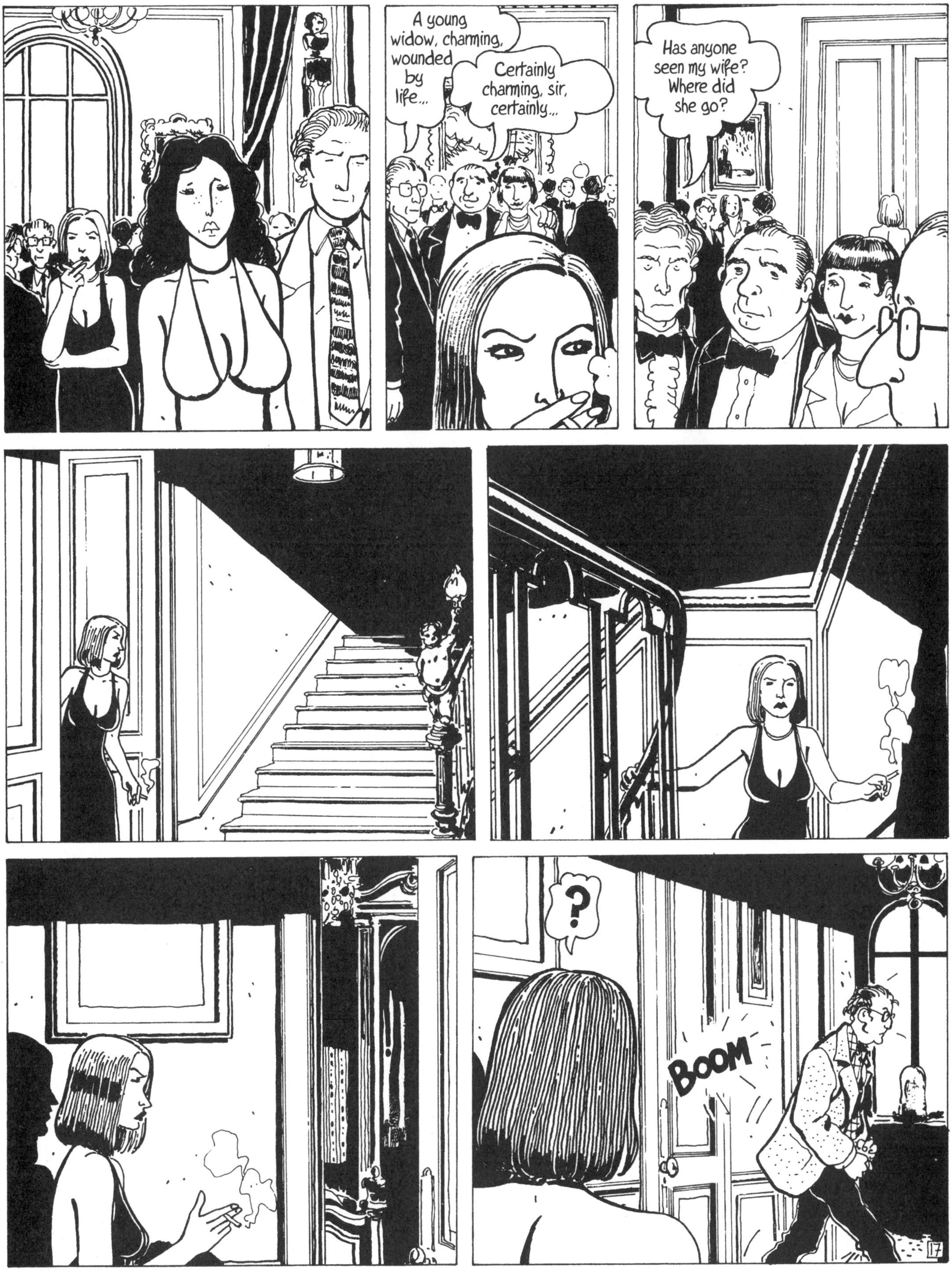
A young widow, charming, wounded by life...
Certainly charming, sir, certainly...
Has anyone seen my wife? Where did she go?
?
BOOM
17

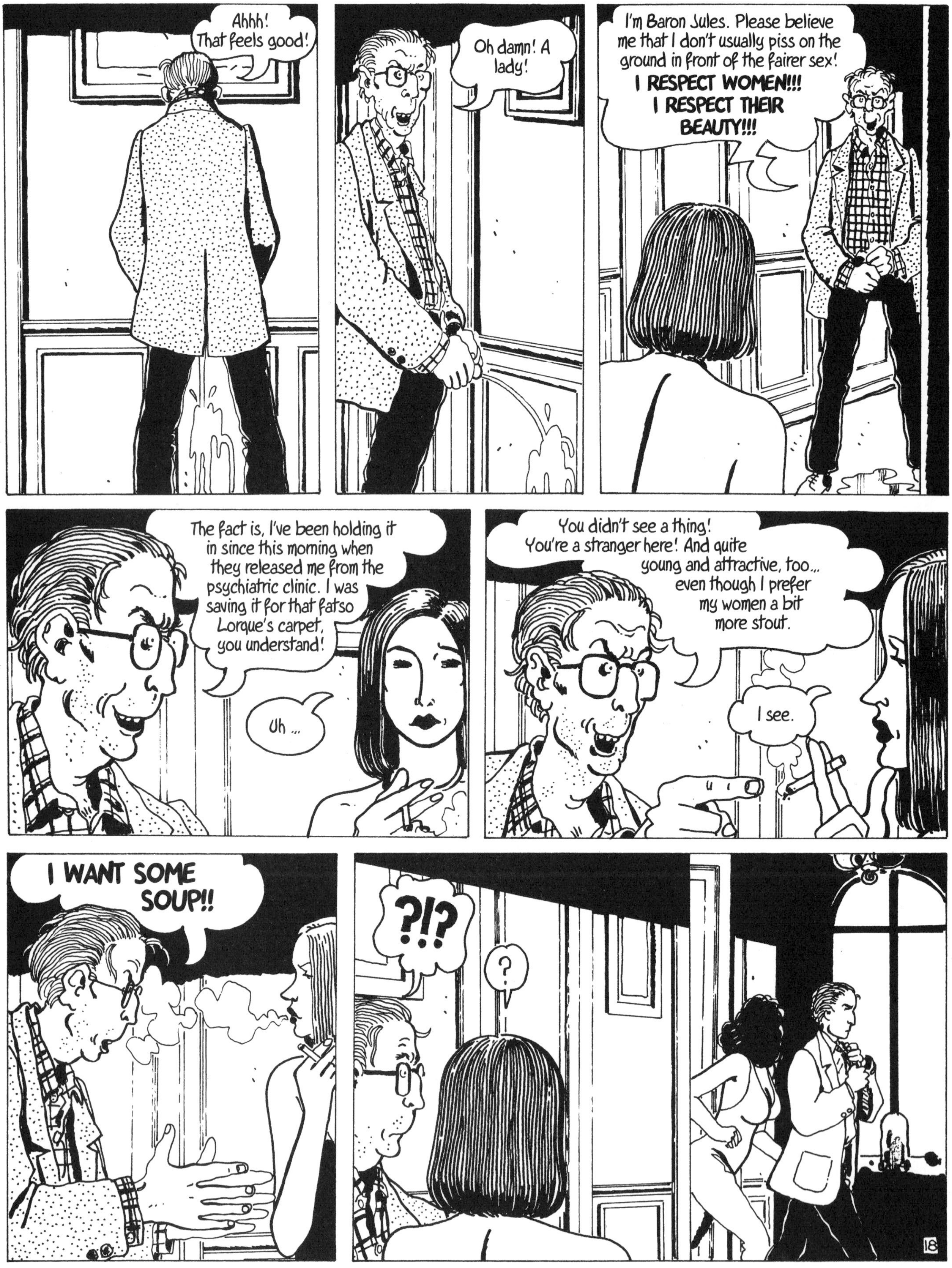
Ahhh! That feels good!
Oh damn! A lady!
I'm Baron Jules. Please believe me that I don't usually piss on the ground in front of the fairer sex!
I RESPECT WOMEN!!! I RESPECT THEIR BEAUTY!!!
The fact is, I've been holding it in since this morning when they released me from the psychiatric clinic. I was saving it for that fatso Lorque's carpet, you understand!
Uh ...
You didn't see a thing! You're a stranger here! And quite young and attractive, too... even though I prefer my women a bit more stout.
I see.
I WANT SOME SOUP!!
?!?
?
18

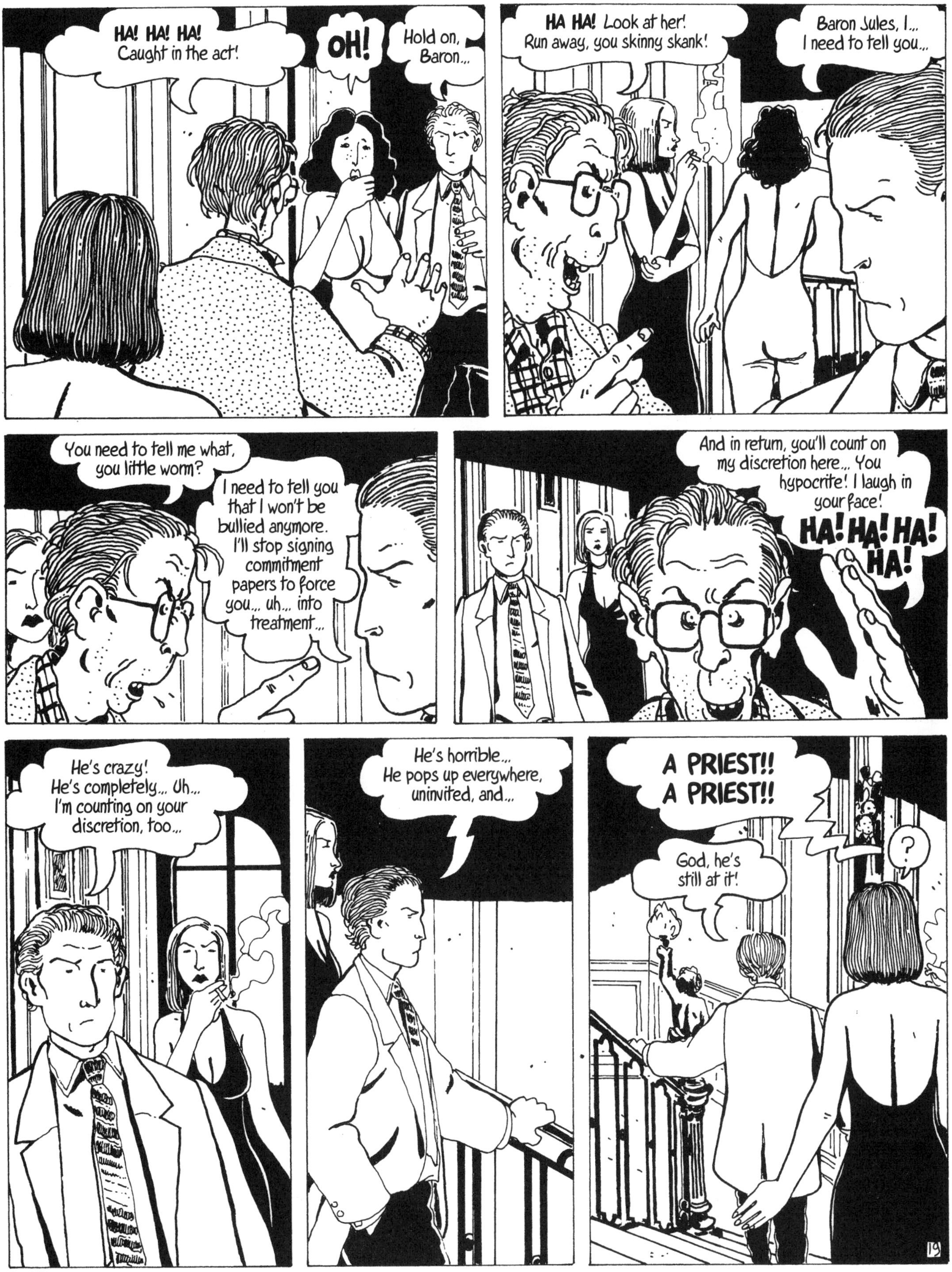
HA! HA! HA! Caught in the act!
OH!
Hold on, Baron...
HA HA! Look at her! Run away, you skinny skank!
Baron Jules, I... I need to tell you...
You need to tell me what, you little worm?
I need to tell you that I won't be bullied anymore. I'll stop signing commitment papers to force you... uh... into treatment...
And in return, you'll count on my discretion here... You hypocrite! I laugh in your face!
HA! HA! HA! HA!
He's crazy! He's completely... Uh... I'm counting on your discretion, too...
He's horrible... He pops up everywhere, uninvited, and...
A PRIEST!! A PRIEST!!
?
God, he's still at it!
19

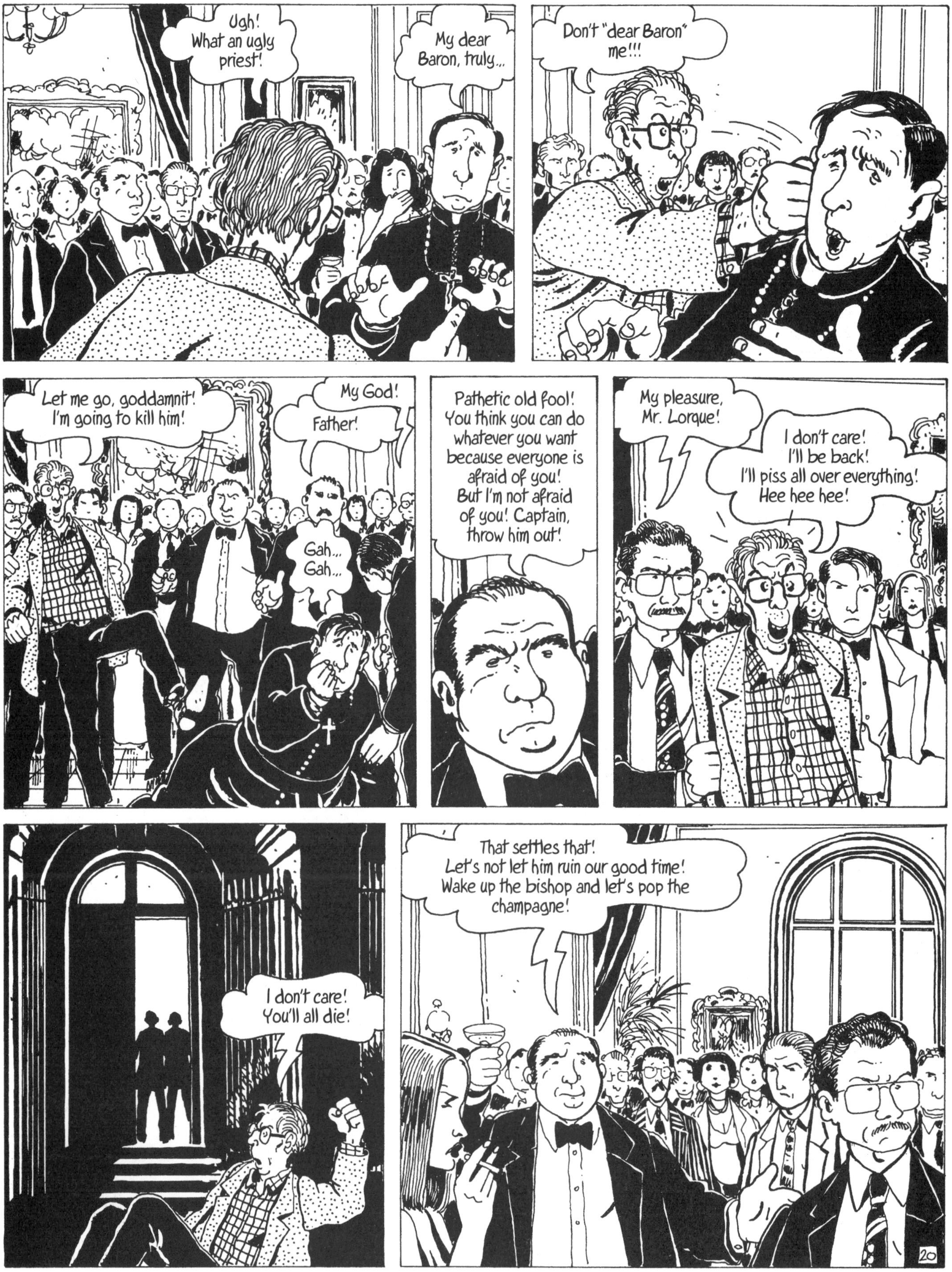
Ugh! What an ugly priest!
My dear Baron, truly...
Don't "dear Baron" me!!!
Let me go, goddamnit! I'm going to kill him!
My God!
Father!
Gah... Gah...
Pathetic old fool! You think you can do whatever you want because everyone is afraid of you! But I'm not afraid of you! Captain, throw him out!
My pleasure, Mr. Lorque!
I don't care! I'll be back! I'll piss all over everything! Hee hee hee!
I don't care! You'll all die!
That settles that! Let's not let him ruin our good time! Wake up the bishop and let's pop the champagne!
20

In the following three weeks, Aimée visited quite a few properties accompanied by Mr. Lindquist. Each time, she showed herself to be indecisive, yet charming.

I'll have to think about it.

Of course! Take all the time you need!

FOR SALE
Lindquist & Co.

She drank tea in the morning, ate something grilled for lunch, and had eggs or soup for dinner. It would be a long time before she would want to eat sauerkraut again.

We're counting on you at Christiane's on Tuesday!

She mingled with high society and bonded with them. Twice a week, she went riding...

... Three times a week, she played tennis. She golfed, and Friday evenings she spent at the casino, though she rarely gambled.

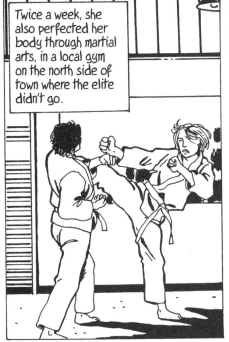

Twice a week, she also perfected her body through martial arts, in a local gym on the north side of town where the elite didn't go.

She was invited to elegant homes for tea or to play bridge. She became familiar with the wealthy of Bléville, and they with her.

What did I ever do to God to get a hand like this!

Shut up and play!

She observed their ways and habits, and particularly — attentively, tirelessly, patiently — their tensions...

21

NADA

Nada
STORY - Jean-Patrick Manchette
ART - Tardi
TRANSLATION - Jenna Allen

After *West Coast Blues*, I decided to adapt Manchette's novel *Nada*, the story of a group of young anarchists who decide to kidnap the American ambassador from a Parisian brothel.

The book, published in 1972, was written before the attacks by the terrorist group Action Directe in the 1980s. The young anarchists' motivations in the story were not very well developed, and it seemed to me that I had to shore them up and not ignore recent events. But alas, I had strayed from the tone of the book.

After completing one page and some notes, I turned my attention to another novel, *Like a Sniper Lining Up His Shot*.

— TARDI

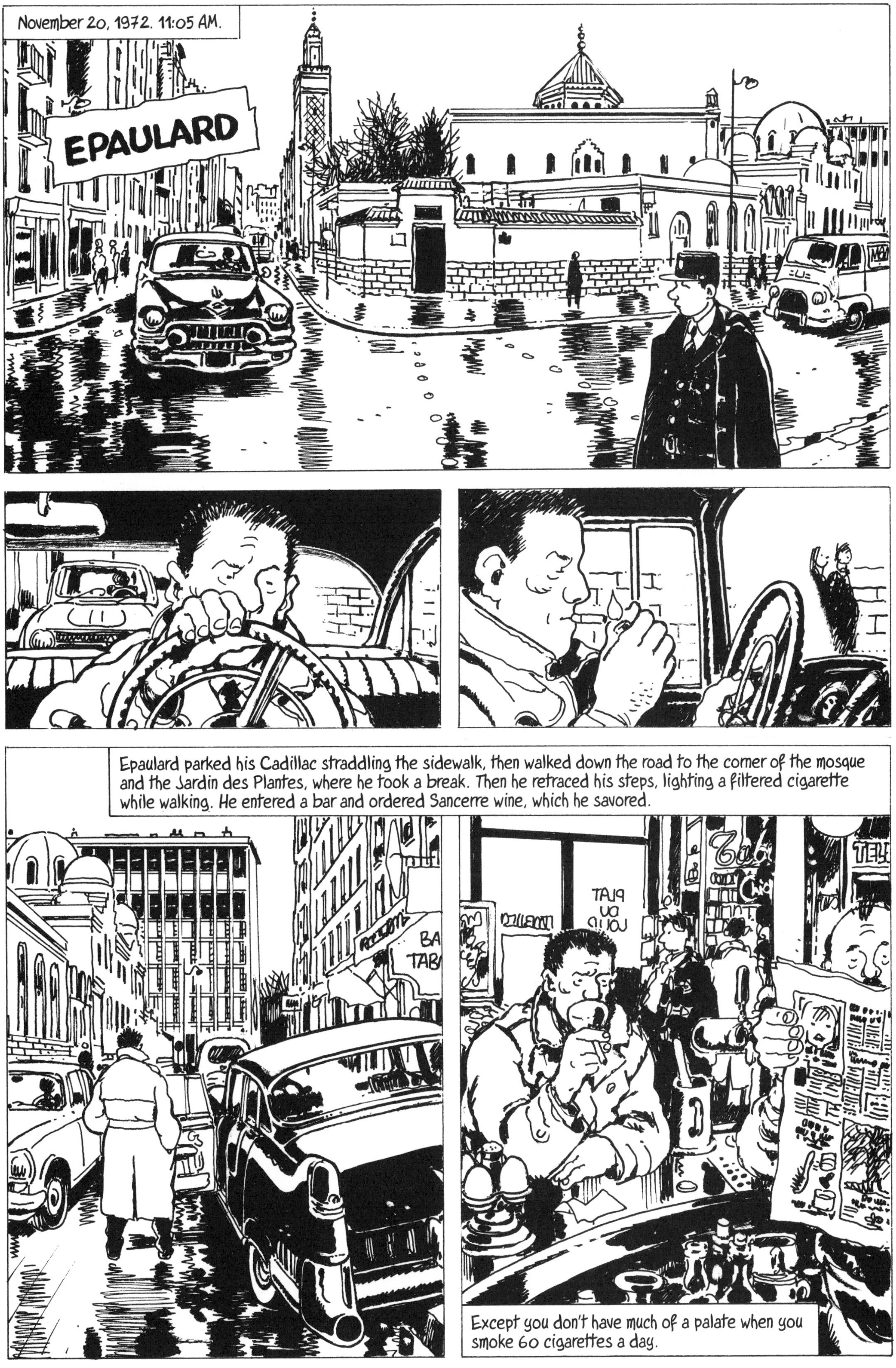
November 20, 1972. 11:05 AM.
EPAULARD
Epaulard parked his Cadillac straddling the sidewalk, then walked down the road to the corner of the mosque and the Jardin des Plantes, where he took a break. Then he retraced his steps, lighting a filtered cigarette while walking. He entered a bar and ordered Sancerre wine, which he savored.
Except you don't have much of a palate when you smoke 60 cigarettes a day.

THE FANTAGRAPHICS

TARDI LIBRARY

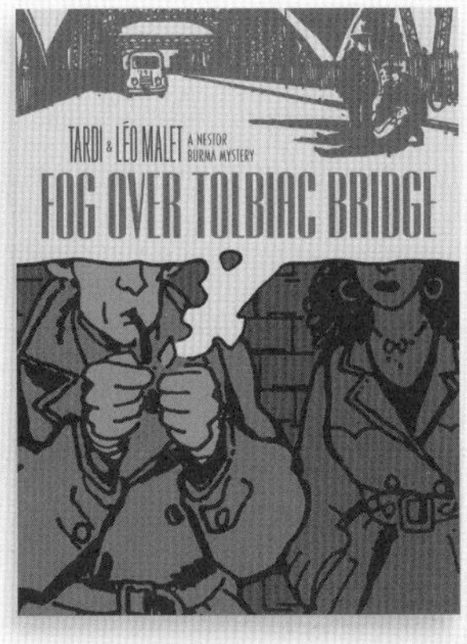
TARDI & LÉO MALET
A NESTOR BURMA MYSTERY
FOG OVER TOLBIAC BRIDGE

Fog Over Tolbiac Bridge:
A Nestor Burma Mystery

BY TARDI AND LÉO MALET

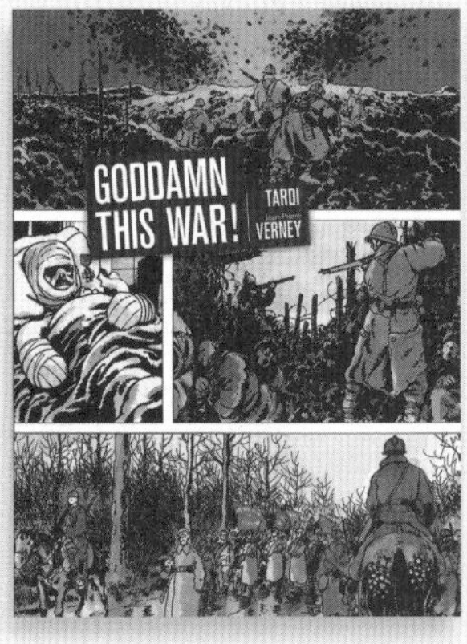
GODDAMN THIS WAR!
TARDI
VERNEY

Goddamn This War!

BY TARDI

With historical material
by Jean-Pierre Verney

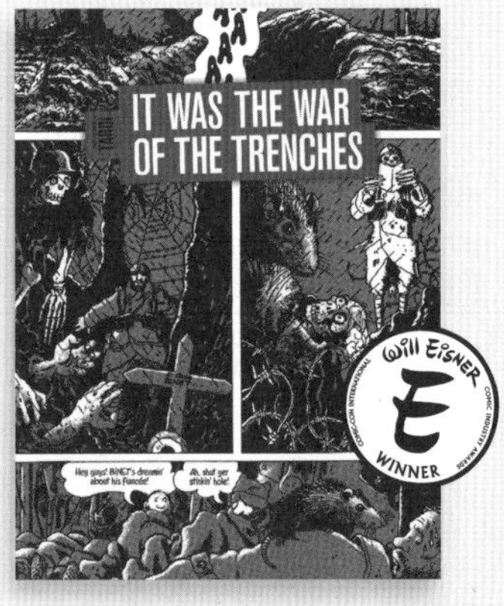
TARDI
IT WAS THE WAR OF THE TRENCHES
WILL EISNER
WINNER

It Was the War
of the Trenches

BY TARDI

Eisner Award Winner

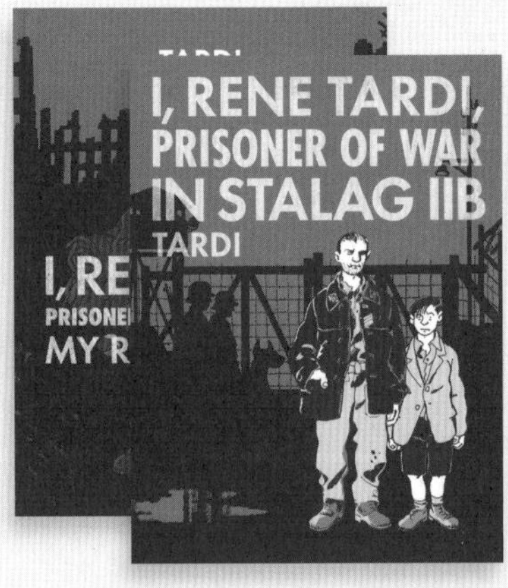
I, RENE TARDI, PRISONER OF WAR IN STALAG IIB
TARDI

I, René Tardi, Prisoner of War
in Stalag IIB Vol. 1

I, Rene Tardi, Prisoner of War in Stalag
IIB Vol. 2: My Return Home

BY TARDI

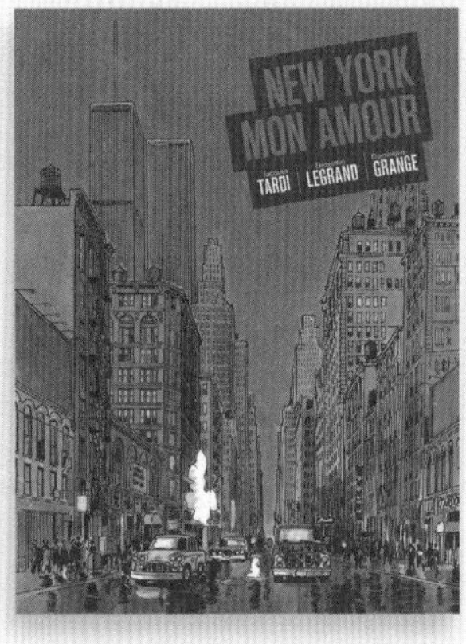
NEW YORK MON AMOUR
TARDI LEGRAND GRANGE

New York Mon Amour

BY TARDI
WITH BENJAMIN LEGRAND
AND DOMINIQUE GRANGE

Eisner and Harvey Award Nominee

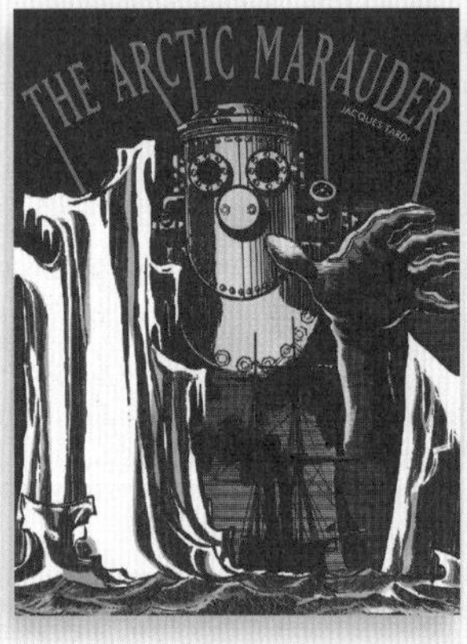
THE ARCTIC MARAUDER
JACQUES TARDI

The Arctic Marauder

BY TARDI

One of Library Journal's Best Books 2011

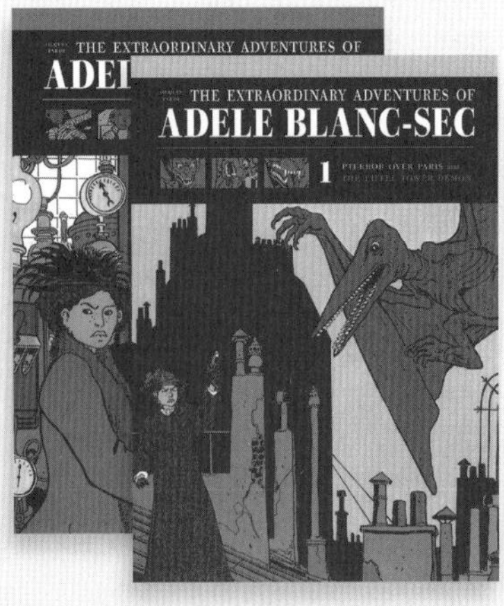
THE EXTRAORDINARY ADVENTURES OF
ADELE BLANC-SEC
1

The Extraordinary Adventures of Adèle Blanc-Sec
Vol. 1: Pterror Over Paris & The Eiffel Tower Demon

The Extraordinary Adventures of Adèle Blanc-Sec
Vol. 2: The Mad Scientist & Mummies on Parade

BY TARDI

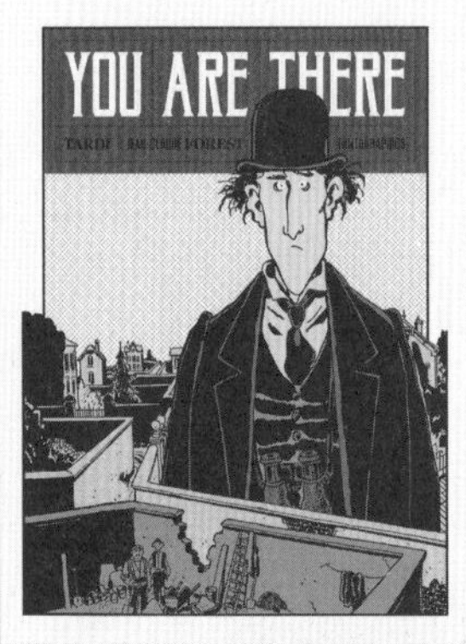
YOU ARE THERE

You Are There

BY TARDI
AND JEAN-CLAUDE FOREST

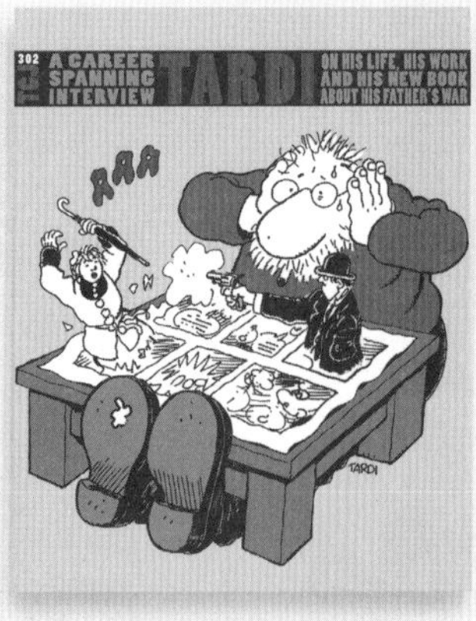
302
A CAREER SPANNING INTERVIEW
TARDI
ON HIS LIFE, HIS WORK AND HIS NEW BOOK ABOUT HIS FATHER'S WAR
RAA

The Comics Journal #302
featuring an interview with
Tardi by Kim Thompson

FANTAGRAPHICS.COM/TARDI

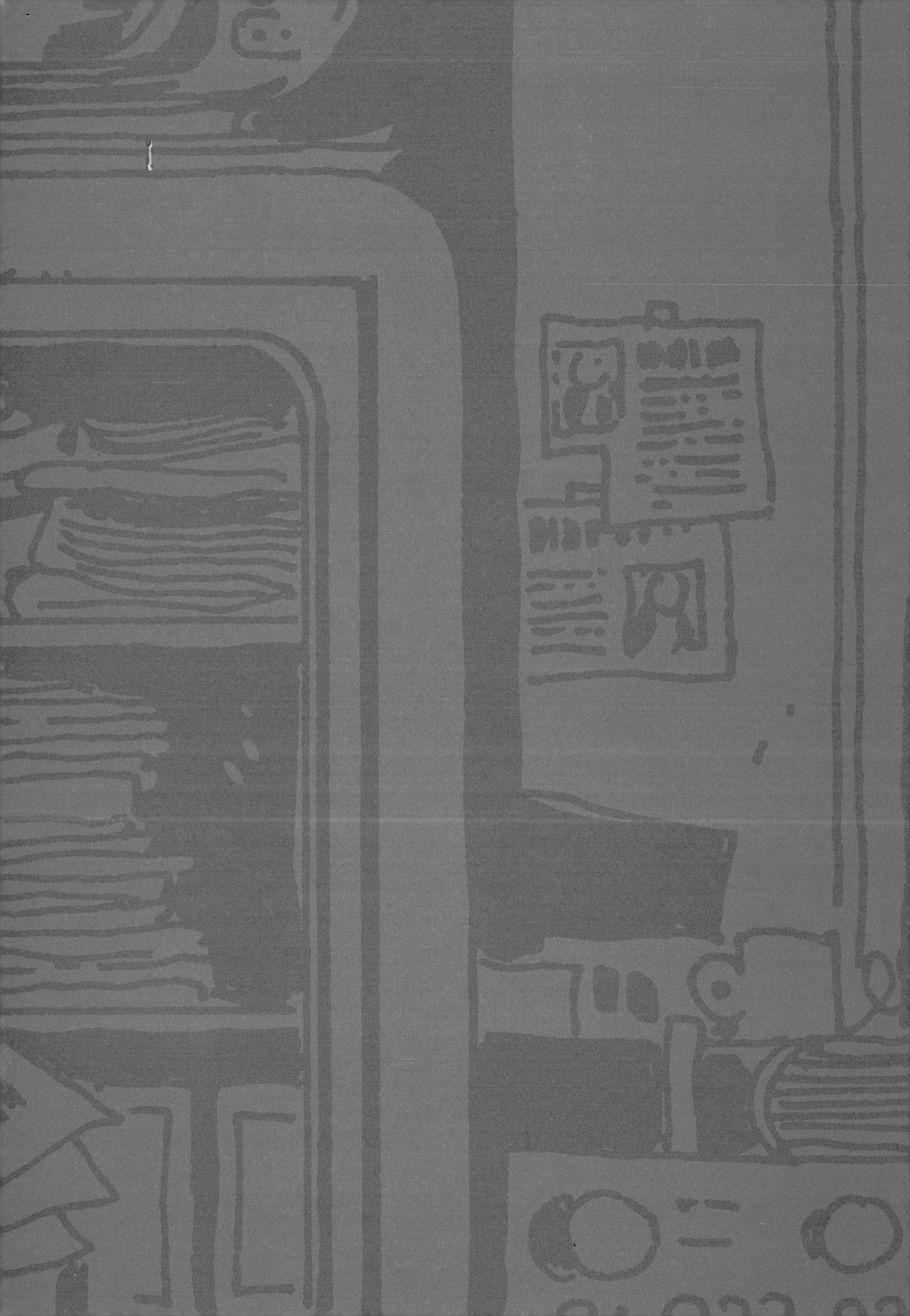